Sally Worboyes

Lipstick & Powder
Handbags & Gladrags

Sally Worboyes was born and grew up in Stepney with four brothers and a sister. She now lives in Norfolk with her family. The author of seventeen previous novels, she has also written plays for TV and radio, and adapted her own play and novel *Wild Hops* as a musical, *The Hop-Pickers*.

By Sally Worboyes

NOVELS

Wild Hops
Docker's Daughter
The Dinner Lady
Red Sequins
Keep on Dancing
Down Stepney Way
Over Bethnal Green
Whitechapel Mary
At the Mile End Gate
Banished from Bow
Girl from Brick Lane
Down by Tobacco Dock
Where Sparrows Nest
Time Will Tell
Jamaica Street
Room for a Lodger
Lipstick and Powder
Handbags & Gladrags

MEMOIR

East End Girl

Sally Worboyes

Lipstick & Powder
Handbags & Gladrags

Lipstick & Powder
First published in Great Britain by Orion in 2007

Handbags & Gladrags
First published in Great Britain by Orion in 2008

This omnibus edition published in 2011
by Orion Books Ltd
Orion House, 5 Upper St Martin's Lane
London WC2H 9EA

An Hachette UK Company

A CIP catalogue record for this book is available
from the British Library.

ISBN 9781407234212

Printed and bound in Great Britain by Clays Ltd, St Ives plc

www.orionbooks.co.uk

Lipstick & Powder

This book is dedicated to my lovely niece, Sarah Brody,
and my youngest nephew, Billy Lipka.

My thanks to the team at Orion for the lovely welcome
into the group that I received, especially from
Kate Mills and Jon Wood.

Chapter One

After what had been a run-of-the-mill June day, Anna Watson, who was approaching her twenty-sixth birthday, yawned and stretched as she got up from her comfortable dark red and gold sofa – the sofa that her once caring husband, Frank, had bought her at an antique shop in Portobello Road when she was pregnant with their twins. This chaise-longue type of a couch was something that he knew she had always hankered after because, for one thing, it reminded her of her late gran's little two-up-two-down, a few turnings away from where she was now living.

Anna had spent a lot of time with her maternal grandmother as a child, when the quietly spoken woman had looked after her before she was old enough to go to school. And this evening, for no reason in particular, she had been thinking of those early days when her own mother, Ivy, worked full time at the local umbrella factory in Cambridge Heath Road. This work, which had afforded her a decent take-home pay at the time, had been Ivy's saving grace, because not only had she worked every God-given day but she had also to take care of her family of three daughters.

Apart from this, the woman had also to endure the stigma of her husband having left her for another. But all this of course was now considered part of a former life, the ghost buried, and Anna, just like her two elder sisters, was looking out for their mother without too much fuss being shown. Back in the early days Ivy had been fiercely independent but now, in the comfort years of retirement, she was content to let her adult offspring feather her nest as and when they felt like it. She had her memories of good times as well as bad. Over Bank Holidays she had taken her daughters to Margate by train to picnic on the beach, enjoy a little nap in a deckchair, and traipse back home again in the late afternoon. Those had been lovely days out for Anna and her sisters.

In her sitting room, her little comfort zone, Anna had been looking through an Avon catalogue in between thinking about her life and her marriage, and all to the low sound of *Coronation Street* in the background. This evening had been quite relaxed because her six-month-old twins had been – and still were – happy to lie in their playpen enjoying each other's company as well as their attached colourful mobile toy. Their tall and handsome dad, Frank, would be working late as usual, and no doubt coming home after midnight with the smell of drink on his breath and perfume on his shirt.

Glancing at herself in her old wax-polished pine mirror above the Victorian fireplace, Anna ruffled her shoulder-length dark blonde hair and then twisted it into a pleat at the back, wondering if it was time for a new cut and style and maybe a colour tint. 'I suppose you could try being a redhead for a change . . .' she quietly told herself. 'That should go all right with those green eyes of yours.' Then, her smile fading, her confidence on the wane, her shoulders slumped and she sighed loudly as she stared at her reflection and let her hair tumble down. She wondered if it might be time to take her sisters' advice and get out of the house now and then to meet up with old friends. Most of her mates, like herself, were married now, but from the few telephone calls that she had had before they gave up on her it had been clear that, even though they were no longer single, they were keeping in touch with each other. One or two had joined a fitness club and another, who had attended pottery classes one evening a week, was now selling handmade and hand-painted pots from a stall in Hackney market. One of her very best friends during her schooldays had broken a barrier and was working as a part-time driving instructor and was one of the first women to do so.

She glanced across to the small bureau in the corner of the room on which stood a lovely framed photograph of her and Frank on their wedding day, when they had been deeply in love and gloriously happy. Shaking off the memory of that day, she contemplated the idea of fetching her address book out of the dark and phoning some friends to see what kind of a response she might get after her long spell of silence. It was nobody's fault but her own that the phone had stopped ringing, because she had all but cut her mates dead. When she and Frank were first married Anna had drawn a circle around what had been her wonderful little oasis and, not too long after this, there had been the exciting house-hunting episode which had taken up most of her spare time. Then came her all-consuming

3

desire to have babies – which hadn't been as easy as she thought it would be.

Taking the bull by the horns she collected her address book and a biro and went into the passage to sit on the padded stall next to the little shelf on which the black telephone perched. Flicking through the pages, she couldn't decide who to call first so started at the beginning. Beryl Andrews was the first name and this brought a smile to her face. Amongst other girls, she and Beryl had each at one time been captain of the netball team at both the junior and senior school and, since Beryl had been a bit of a daredevil flirt, it had come as no surprise that she was the first to marry at the age of seventeen having got herself pregnant by a favourite boyfriend.

A touch eager now, Anna dialled her old chum's number and felt a rush of euphoria as she waited for her to pick up the phone. But it wasn't Beryl who answered. It was an older voice. Momentarily silenced, Anna quickly collected herself and said, 'I'm sorry to have troubled you but I think I might have dialled the wrong number. I was hoping to reach an old friend of mine called Beryl.'

'Well, the only way you can do that sweetheart is to go to your local church. My Beryl died from breast cancer three months ago,' said the voice on the end of the line.

Stunned by this news all Anna managed to say was, 'I'm so sorry . . . I didn't know she had cancer.'

'Well, that's probably because people won't mention the word, will they? Anyone would think it was some kind of punishment from God for being a devil worshipper. You'd be surprised just how rampant cancer is, and still it's hushed up. I've moved in to look after her little family though, so the kids will be fine.'

Shocked by this news Anna could hardly speak. When she finally found her voice all she could say was, 'I'm really sorry.'

'You and me both, darling. The good Lord is looking after her now. Take care sweetheart.' And that was it. Anna heard a click and then the dialling tone. She had only just recognised the woman's voice from the few times she had been in her house as a schoolgirl, spending time in her friend's bedroom listening to her records and talking about boys and sex. Pushing this horrible news from her mind, she collected herself and turned the pages to call another of her old school friends but there was no answer. She tried another but all she heard was the unobtainable tone. Deflated by her failures she drifted back into the sitting room, sat down on the sofa and shed a few tears. She had never felt as alone as she did right then.

Anna had had a lot of fun with her friend Beryl in particular because in the old days they had been like two peas in a pod. She smiled sadly as she remembered how, when just thirteen, they had wished for each other's eyes and joked about exchanging them via surgery. Beryl's eyes had been big and round and a lovely warm tone of brown but she had longed for them to be like Anna's, wide and sloping and a soft shade of green.

She snapped herself out of this worsening dark mood that seemed to have been dragged into the house, possibly because of the old romance that she had been watching on TV that afternoon while feeding one twin after the other. The film apart, though, worries over her failing marriage had clouded her mind as she remembered a time when her and Frank's world was filled with laughter and socialising, parties and music. A time when she always wore lipstick and powder whether she was going out or not. Slowly shaking her head, she spoke softly to herself. 'You've got to get out more, Anna. You're behaving like your own jailer – shutting yourself away. Life is too short and the proof of that is Beryl. She shouldn't have suffered and she shouldn't have died so young. She was full of life.'

The gentle sound of her babies gurgling in their playpen brought a faint smile to her lips. She looked around the room and brought to mind the time when she and Frank had first purchased this house. They had been so in love, content to spend hours together talking about the way they might decorate their nest. They had agonised over things that now seemed trivial, such as choosing between the Heal's modern Seventies look or keeping the mid-Victorian feel with appropriate replica wallpaper which they had seen when browsing in the Sanderson's gallery off Oxford Street.

Anna had no idea why something so frivolous, compared to what she had just heard about an old friend, should have floated to the surface other than the fact that she didn't want to think about the tragedy. In the early days, furnishing their home had been the most important thing in her and Frank's life and the centre of their little love world. They had enjoyed every minute of window-shopping and delivery once this house, which they had renovated together, was ready. They had stripped dark varnish away from the solid pine floorboards before giving it a coat of wax polish and a good buff so as to match the carved pine fire surround. They had decorated the ceiling and walls a brilliant white and thrown down red and black Afghan rugs, bought cheaply at a warehouse in Aldgate East.

The jewel in the crown for Anna was the brass Georgian companion set and matching fender that contrasted beautifully with the colourful patterned Victorian fireplace tiles. The fender, purchased from a second-hand stall in Whitechapel market, had been black with age before Anna cleaned and polished it until it shone like gold. All of this had, of course, taken place earlier on in their marriage when the inseparable couple loved to curl up by the small coal fire and watch the reflection of the flames on the small burnished copper scuttle while listening to love songs playing on the stereo. One of the best things to have come out of the so-called Swinging Sixties, as far as Anna was concerned, was the trend of mixing new styles with old and, especially, stripped pine furniture.

Wrapping her arms around herself, she looked about the room where she had always felt comfortable and snug and wished that she wasn't spending so much time in it by herself. Pulling herself out of this low mood she turned her attention to the outside world and a heartening smile spread across her face as she glanced through the glass panes of the door that led onto her walled garden. She could just see the head and shoulders of Rachel, her old Jewish neighbour next door, tending to her plants in the soft glow of the light shining out from the woman's back door, and recalled how neighbourly she had been on the day she and Frank moved into the turning. She smiled again as she remembered Rachel saying, 'These houses might be old fashioned but they are a lot safer than what they build nowadays. Look at what happened to Ronan Point. What a disaster.' The woman had been referring to a brand new high-rise block of flats that had partly collapsed while people were living inside. And during other little chats over the garden fence with her neighbour, Rachel had criticised the government for dismantling London Bridge for dispatch to a tourist park in Arizona and praised Bernadette Devlin who, at the age of twenty-two and the youngest MP, had demonstrated against government trying to remodel union law. Anna was always amazed at how the old woman kept up with everything that was going on in the world.

When Frank and Anna had purchased this late Victorian two-up-two-down terraced house from a private landlord some three years ago, being a local girl meant that Anna's family was not far away. Her grandparents had lived close by to this quiet and scantily tree-lined back street before they passed away and this in itself had been a reason why she wanted to be in this little corner of East London. She felt so much at home here. There had always been a relaxed neighbourly atmosphere, another reason why she and Frank felt that they could not have wished for a better place to bring up children. And as for Rachel ... she was like an old-fashioned adopted grandmother who

8

upheld an old-fashioned wartime spirit of *one for all and all for one.*

Soon after they were married Anna had wanted to start a family and had often sat huddled up with Frank on the sofa, talking about their future and what it would be like to be parents. As it turned out, she hadn't found it quite so easy to conceive as she first thought and after trying for two years and failing she had been advised by a gynaecologist to take a fertility drug. This had proved successful for hundreds of women with problems similar to her own and eventually resulted in Anna getting pregnant with not one baby but two. Twin boys. Oliver and James.

Frank had been over the moon at the news of her pregnancy and, protective where his wife and their unborn were concerned, put caution before passion when in bed for fear of anything going wrong. So, for most of the nine months while she was carrying, Anna did little more in the bedroom than kiss and hug her young husband and satisfy his desires in her own sweet way. She had hardly been able to believe it when, towards the end of her term, every now and then she thought that she could smell a hint of someone else's perfume on Frank's shirts when she was putting them into the washing machine. Why all of this was filling her mind now was no mystery. She knew why she had been thinking about better times and doing her best to force away the dark stomach-churning worries inside. Little cameos of better and worse times had been floating in and out of her mind all afternoon, even though she had tried to lose herself in her favourite serial, *Crossroads.*

And now, in the silence broken only by the chimes

of the distant clock tower striking seven, she instinctively glanced at her wristwatch to confirm that it was time for her babies to be fed. She drew the curtains and then smiled down at the twins as they vied for attention, gurgling and kicking their legs excitedly. At least they were happy and content in their unhurried safe little world. Looking from one to the other she felt as though her heart was melting.

'I'll never be able to thank the Lord Jesus enough for you two, will I?' she murmured as she wiped her eyes with the back of her hand. Then, lifting her face, she closed her eyes and whispered, 'Please, God, if I am left to look after the twins by myself, help me to be strong.'

As much as Anna loved her twins there were times when she felt as if she could scream with frustration. Times when one or the other or both would cry non-stop even though they had been fed, changed and cuddled. But at least they were there, and one-sided conversations were better than having nobody to talk to. Much better. And now it was time for her to feed and get them ready to go down for the night. She needed a little break from them so that she could think seriously about what she could do to improve her lonely world. She had her future to think about as well as theirs. A future which was looking a touch bleak and one that she didn't think anyone else knew about. She was going through a private hell and had been for quite a while. But it helped to know that there were others in the same boat, others who were possibly listening to or watching the same programmes and who would understand what it was like to move around in silence or have only the radio and television for company.

Earlier that afternoon she had read an article in a magazine about unmarried mothers and how they not only had to cope alone but also live with the stigma of not having a husband.

Anna had been caring for her twins almost single-handed but at least she was married. She had been keeping up the appearance of everything being all right while she went about doing the housework and taking care of the laundry. She glanced across to the Moses basket next to the garden doors and felt anxiety sweep through her for not having done the task she liked least – the ironing. The basket was full to almost overflowing with the white shirts that Frank wore to work, as well as other dry laundry that was ready for a steam press.

Shrugging off her sense of guilt at having watched television for most of the afternoon, she decided to leave the ironing until the next day. In any case she could see that the twins were brewing up for a crying session to let her know they were hungry. Her saving grace this evening was that her neighbours' seventeen-year-old daughter, the lovely Jackie, had promised to call in with her Summer Avon products catalogue and this she was looking forward to. Jackie had said that she would spend time with Anna, enjoying a glass of wine while she chose and placed an order for scented products in pretty pots and jars. Such little interludes as this were important contacts with the outside world because, while Anna had her catalogue, she felt that she was one of a club of hundreds of other housewives who were turning and admiring the same pages and choosing the same products.

Asking herself if perhaps the time had come for her

to enjoy more than just motherhood and wondering if she should reinvent herself by going on a little shopping therapy trip, she went into the kitchen to warm the twins' bottles which had been made up earlier and kept in the fridge. She thought about Jackie, the young redhead who was so full of aspirations and dreams as well as a determination to work every hour that God sent so as to save enough money to travel on economy through Europe. Jackie's dream was to go from one country to the other working in bars, restaurants, or on the land picking fruit crops for a living. This wasn't so out of the ordinary because some young folk had, since the late Fifties, been catching the ferry to France then traipsing around the Continent. It had all been part of a new and growing fad. This ambition of Jackie's was something that had brought her and Anna a little closer than they might have been if all they had in common was the Avon products. Anna had toyed with the idea of travelling herself at the age of sixteen once she had left school but, as with most girls, hadn't done anything about it. The only difference that she could see between the pair of them apart from their age was that, whereas her husband Frank had been her first love, Jackie was enjoying more than one relationship and had said that she had no intention of tying the knot until she was thirty.

In her late teens and already independent the girl didn't seem to give a toss if she was labelled 'spinster' and the irony of this made Anna smile. The word 'spinster' was such an old-fashioned expression for a Seventies girl to use. The differences between Anna and Jackie was that Anna had always been a home-girl, with the maternal instinct from as far back as the days when she played with her dolls. But during the Sixties, once she had started to earn a living, she had saved a little each week so as to be able to enjoy one or two annual cheap package holidays on the Costa Brava. This had been more than enough to satisfy any lust for travel. The dream of working during long summers picking grapes in Spain or grafting as a chambermaid in hotels had not been on her agenda. She had loved London all through the Sixties when she was working as a telephonist for an insurance company in Covent Garden. That was when she had really got into fashion and the general swing of all that was going on around her, right through to when Biba in High Street, Kensington in the late 1960s copied the fashion of the Twenties and the Thirties when girls had worn floppy hats and flowers in their hair.

With memories of these times floating through her mind, Anna bottle-fed one baby after the other, enjoying the recall of her teens when she had been as free as a bird to do as she pleased. And now, on the surface, she had little to complain about because she had her adorable babies and her standard of living was all right. She and Frank enjoyed a good income from Prima Pasta, the restaurant that they had started up four years earlier, and she didn't have to worry about money. Her own mother, Ivy, one of the closest people to her, had not been able to enjoy the small luxuries earlier in her life that Anna and her sisters were now almost taking for granted.

In this somewhat prosperous time though, her mother was enjoying a bit of the affluence that seemed buoyant in comparison with the way it was before, during and after the Second World War. Ivy was more than happy with this bubbling new era – and happier still with a little of her other two daughters' ill-gotten gains coming her way every now and then. Hazel and Linda, Anna's sisters, enjoyed a vibrant lifestyle while running their exclusive brothel in old Bethnal Green.

After the twins had been fed, bathed and were sleepy, Anna thought that she would have little trouble in settling them down for the night but she was wrong. Once in their matching cots in their small shared bedroom, decorated in pale blue and primrose, Oliver, the less contented of the two, began to grizzle, which in turn started James off. Leaving the room, Anna slowly pulled the door shut behind her and went downstairs, intending to pour herself a glass of red wine to take into the sitting room, but one of her babies was not letting her off that easily. Oliver, who was a little more prone to stress than James, was now crying loudly. Doing her best to sit it out and not fall into the trap of spoiling either of them, she pulled her favourite LP from the rack on a shelf and placed it on the turntable.

She wanted to listen to the Beatles and her favourite song from the early Sixties, 'Please Please Me'. This reminded her of the time when she had seen the group at a concert in North London before she had met Frank. A time when she and a friend had tried to pose as staff so as to slip in through the back door and up to their dressing rooms. Of course they were thrown out along with other fans that had had the same idea.

With this and other past events floating in and out of her mind, and with the setting sun casting a warm glow into the sitting room, Anna did her best to try and block out the sound of her babies crying above. Cursing under her breath for having to look after them all by herself all of the time, she made herself busy by folding their playpen and carrying it into the front of the house to the dining room, which hardly got used now. 'You're a selfish man, Frank,' she murmured. 'You should be here with me taking care of your sons.' She only just stopped herself from throwing the playpen across the room. 'They're your babies as well as mine! You should be here with me!' Drawing a long and trembling breath she then shook her head, saying, 'I'm not going to do this. I'm not going to let you push me to the edge. I *can* take care of the twins. We don't need *you*.' She then slowly dropped to her knees and cried into her hands in the room with the delicate black and white William Morris patterned wallpaper and the red fitted carpet that she and Frank had chosen together. The room where they had once enjoyed so many dinner parties with their friends. She could almost hear the laughter in the now silent unlived-in room.

Their friends who had once been an important part of their lives had gradually fallen away because of Frank having been too busy at work during the week and too tired to entertain or socialise at weekends. And as so often was the case, this evening the house seemed too quiet and empty, her only company her babies howling above.

Tired though she was, she went back upstairs, supporting herself on the old polished pine handrail as she went. Once in the twins' bedroom she picked up Oliver, who really seemed unusually distressed as tears

15

trickled down his face and into the collar of his pale blue Babygro. Pacing the floor with him and patting his back, she smiled down at James who had quietened since she had come into the room. Patting one and soothing the other with a gentle voice she gradually quietened the pair of them and before too long Oliver was asleep, his head resting on her shoulder. To the sound of an occasional sob she gently lowered him back into his cot, which was a touch premature because he woke up straightaway and began crying again. She tucked him in and gently patted his back in case he had trapped wind and this seemed to do the trick. She sat on the chair next to the cots and quietly sang the same lullaby that she could remember her mum singing to her many years ago. Eventually both babies drifted into a contented sleep until she was left sitting there wondering why she felt so empty when she had them to love.

Glancing from one baby to the other she realised that James was awake again and, in his own sweet way, about to make it clear that it was now his turn. Leaning over his cot, a dull ache now in her back, she turned him onto his side, tucked him in and gently shushed him back to sleep. This done, she crept out of the room and went downstairs only to hear one of them start up again. She told herself to be strong and not go back upstairs and so left him to it, and this as it turned out was the right thing to do. After a few minutes there was silence.

She poured herself a small glass of sherry and went back into the sitting room to put her feet up and relax properly now that she felt sure that they were settled for the night. With the sound turned down low she switched on her old record player – her first record player – one that she had been given as a present when she was fourteen and which she had refused to get rid of. Her taste in music had changed along the way but she loved to listen to her old favourites.

When Frank had brought home his much treasured and brand new Bang & Olufsen a few weeks before, he had wanted Anna to pack hers away but she had resisted. Frank's music centre was his prized possession and lately, when he *was* at home, he was often stretched out on the sofa, his head sunk into a big feather cushion, his personal bulky black earphones on. In one hand would be a glass of malt whisky and in the other a small cigar. Here he would listen to favourite tracks from his favourite LPs. He had wanted to shut out all other noises and sounds but Anna felt that his earphones were also a way of excluding her from his private little world of love songs.

Settled in an armchair by the fireplace where no fire burned tonight, she tried to think of where she had gone wrong: why it was that Frank didn't seem to love her any more and how she might win back his affections. She thought about a new wardrobe and whether this would be the answer. Perhaps some new and sexy underwear? A different hairstyle or a new shade of lipstick? Too upset by the cause of having to think like a single person again she glanced at her wristwatch and saw that it was almost eight o'clock. She could hardly believe how quickly the time had passed and presumed that Jackie had changed her mind about calling in. But then, just as she was resigned to another evening alone, she heard the lovely welcoming chime of her doorbell.

For no particular reason she glanced at herself in the mirror over the Victorian mantelshelf and pushed her dark blonde hair into place as she checked that without make-up she didn't look too washed out. All that was called for was a visit to the hairdresser for that new cut and style which she had been wondering about. The soft chimes of her doorbell went again and she went to let in Jackie, anticipating her smart blue and black Avon case filled with samples. She smiled inwardly as she left the room because this visit was not only going to mean a bit of company for her but a chance to choose whatever she wanted from the new catalogue.

When she opened the front door though, there was no Jackie, but a familiar red Jaguar sports car parked outside, and on her doorstep were Hazel and Linda, her beautiful classy sisters, who shared their stylish converted house in old Bethnal Green from which they ran their upmarket team of attractive and fun-loving prostitutes. When she could, Anna enjoyed herself at their home, sipping champagne with the girls in the gaudy gilt-furnished plush sitting room, listening to their illicit talk about the fun side of the business and the clients.

This evening, looking as stunning as ever in their up-to-the-minute designer clothes, the girls were armed with a Chinese takeaway and a bottle of best port, the favourite drink of all three of them. They breezed past Anna, smiling broadly as she gazed back at them, a touch bemused. They looked in the mood for a celebration and were intending to have one by the look of things because, apart from the bottle of port Hazel was carrying, there were two bottles of red wine in an off-licence carrier bag. Too taken aback to think of anything to say, Anna smiled when they joked about the shocked expression on her face. 'We'll 'ave to do this more often,' said Linda with the long wavy brown hair, who was just two years older than Anna.

'Or better still find a reliable babysitter so that we can drag Madam out and about town,' added Hazel, who was the eldest of the three girls at thirty, and had beautiful long black hair.

Following them through to the sitting room Anna wondered why they had come round to see her. She knew her sisters like the back of her hand and to her this buoyant mood was a veneer and they were covering the real reason for this visit. But after just a few minutes of asking no questions and from the expressions on their faces she decided that they were simply in high spirits and that was all. She assumed that this was because they had notched up another name to add to the client list of their small and lucrative business – the Call A Girl Company. The highly successful so-called dating agency situated on the border of old Bethnal Green and Shoreditch, in what had once been a small Victorian boot and shoe factory, was now a beautiful home from which business and pleasure were conducted.

'So ... what's brought about this little surprise visit then?' said Anna as she collected three wine glasses off the shelf of her pine Welsh dresser. 'Gonna name-drop, are you? Someone famous under your wing, is there? Who is it this time, a rock star or a notorious villain?'

19

'This is purely a social call, babe. A night in with good food and wine. We're here to sister-sit.' Hazel smiled. 'Nothing wrong with that is there? You spend too much time on your own, Anna. And besides, we want to see our godsons more often – it's our right. I'm going to go up and look at them in a minute. Might even cough a little so as to wake 'em up for a cuddle.'

'Oh really,' said Anna teasing her sister. 'Do I detect a hint of maternal longing, Hazel? Or have you already gone and got yourself pregnant by one of your millionaire clients?'

'Pregnant? Me? No chance, sweetheart. We leave that kind of domestic wonderland stuff for you to wallow in. Keep on churning them out, babe.'

'I don't think so.' Anna went quiet and then said, 'I'm happy with what I've got. I don't need any more.'

'Famous last words!' called Linda from the adjoining kitchen as she opened the cartons of takeaway Chinese. 'I'll put this little lot on the kitchen tray and we'll eat it while it's hot so we won't 'ave to warm the plates up!'

In the sitting room, Anna handed Hazel a corkscrew for the bottle of wine and looked directly into her sister's face. 'So what's this all about then? This impromptu visit with no phone call first to say you were coming?'

'God – you're a worrier,' said Hazel, shaking her head. 'We fancied having a girls' night in. That's all. Lighten up, babe.'

'Fair enough.' Anna smiled. 'I'm not complaining. I'm glad you're here. I was feeling a bit low as it happens . . .'

'Oh? And why's that?'

Regretting the little slip of the tongue, Anna covered her tracks and showed a smiling face. She didn't want anyone to know what she was going through. 'Time of the month probably,' she said, shrugging it off.

'Oh, right . . . but you weren't hoping to be pregnant again were you, sweetheart?' Hazel asked, with a touch of concern in her voice. 'Because that would be daft and far too soon after our twins.'

'No. No, I don't want any more babies, Hazel. One of you two can deliver Mum with granddaughters that she can hug. I'm more than satisfied with my boys. And let's face it – it wasn't easy for me to fall as it turned out, was it.'

'Will be now though,' said Linda coming back into the room. 'All you have to do is take the fertility drug again and Bob's your uncle. There shouldn't be any stopping you now. If you wanted a bigger family, that is. Or, more to the point if Frank wants another baby – a little girl perhaps?' For reasons of her own, Linda had deliberately brought Frank into the conversation. 'You know what men are like with daughters.'

'Never mind what Frank wants or doesn't want. I might try for a little girl in a few years' time. I'm hardly old and I might even be married to someone else later on. Someone who *wants* to spend time with his offspring.'

'Oh dear . . . Frank been neglecting you, 'as he?' said Linda, outwardly smiling but sick inside at the thought of her brother-in-law.

Anna lowered her eyes. 'I suppose he has been neglecting me a bit, yes. But I don't mind. I'm lucky to

21

have my twins; they're as much as any mother could wish for.'

'They're our little miracle babies,' said Hazel, cutting in with a smile and a wink. 'And you deserve them. Let's hope they don't grow up too much like their daddy.'

Anna looked from one sister to the other and after a short pause, said, 'What's that supposed to mean?'

'Well, I s'pose he's no different from all men in that they can't keep their dick from rising when a tease comes along. And that waitress you both took on is a bit of a tease, babe.'

'Is she? I wouldn't know.' Anna wanted to change the subject. 'Anyway, who gives a toss? And getting back to my boys – you're right, they are our little miracle.' She smiled at Hazel as she recollected the many months when she had been disappointed at not having conceived. The day when she found out that she had still had a wonderful magical ring to it. This was when Anna had left the small room of her private gynaecologist in a cul-de-sac just off Harley Street, and had to do her best not to walk along grinning like a Cheshire cat. She had been going to the London Hospital as an outpatient for two years before her GP asked if she could afford to go private. Having said yes without hesitation, whether it meant she would have had to take out a loan or not, she was referred to a specialist, one of the top men in his field who was tall, slim and handsome and turned out to be Anna's knight in shining armour.

'I reckon you deserved a medal the way you just kept

on picking yourself up after every disappointment. You were a star then, babe, and you still are.'

'If you say so. I don't think I could go through all of that again though.' Anna slowly shook her head as she remembered the disappointments every month for over two years, before she fell pregnant with the twins. 'I was ecstatic when I got that positive result, wasn't I,' she said. 'I don't think I've experienced anything like that before or since. I walked away from Harley Street as if I was on some weird and wonderful planet and was happier than I ever imagined I could be.'

'We know that, babe. You came and told us that same evening, if you remember. You were miles of smiles that night.'

'I know. It was incredible,' she said, helping herself to a spring roll. 'You should have seen me when I came out of that little clinic. I had to stop myself from telling complete strangers about it. And before I knew what I was doing, I was pushing open one of the huge glass doors of John Lewis's and heading for the nearest counter. And when the girl offered me a free squirt of the perfume she was pitching that week, I was so stupidly bowled over that I said, "I didn't come in for perfume. I came in to tell you that I'm gonna have a baby."'

'As if she would 'ave been interested,' said Hazel, quietly laughing at her sister.

'I know, but … well … on that day I have no idea how many strangers I told.' She slowly shook her head as she remembered it all. Then, her smile dissolving, she murmured, 'I was *so* happy.' Shrugging, she let out a little sigh and looked from one sister to the other. 'I've

23

got something to tell the pair of you that you're not going to like.'

'Fire away,' said Hazel as she piled hot food onto her plate. 'It can't be the insurance man you're having a fling with because they don't come door to door to perk up bored housewives any more, do they?'

'No,' said Anna, 'they don't. If they did and a handsome salesman knocked on my door I might just drag him in for company though.'

Hazel leaned back in her chair and studied her sister's face, then said, 'That's not like you, Anna. We two old scrubbers might come out with something like that but not you. What's the matter, babe?'

'You're not scrubbers. Don't use that word.' Anna pushed a hand through her hair and drew a trembling breath. She didn't want to break down in tears but there was no denying that they were welling up behind her eyes. She smiled sadly at one sister and then the other. 'I love the twins more than I thought possible and I was fantastically happy when my gynaecologist broke the news to me that they were in there. The two women in John Lewis seemed really pleased for me when I told them.' Then snapping out of the past, she said, 'Frank wasn't as thrilled with the news as I thought he would be though.'

'He looked as proud as Punch to me,' said Hazel.

'I know. And I think he was once it really sank in. But I can't forget the response I got when I phoned him from a telephone kiosk in Oxford Street to give him the news. He was short and offhand and this, if I'm honest, knocked me sideways.' Her eyes glazed over a little and she went quiet again before saying, 'Do

24

you know what he said to me when I phoned him after I had got those results . . . when he was serving behind the bar in our restaurant?'

'No, but you're gonna tell us,' said Hazel.

'I whispered to him – because it felt like our private bit of news of the century – "I'm pregnant, Frank. I'm actually pregnant." And he said, "Great. Fantastic. I'll talk to you later. Gotta go darling. Busy." Then he hung up. He didn't even make the effort to come home from the restaurant earlier that night. One of his brothers would have stood in for him, he's given them a helping hand at Tower Hill enough times. Still does.'

'So Frank didn't come rushing home? No surprises there then.' Hazel drew breath and forced herself to stay on track. She had to get a message across to Anna who she still saw as her baby sister. 'What else did you expect, Anna? Frank lives for that place, for the work, the kudos, and the women he loves to flirt with. Flirting for the sake of the business is no bad thing, I suppose.'

'He doesn't flirt, Hazel. He keeps the customers happy and that's what brings them back. They're just as bad as he is and it's all a bit of fun. It's ginger-nut Bridget that's the problem. *She* flirts with *him* and in front of customers. Sometimes in front of me for that matter. She hangs over my husband like a dangling scarf. I wish her husband, Trevor, would make her pregnant and cart her back to the country village where she came from.'

Hazel glanced at Linda and gave her a sly knowing wink before topping up Anna's glass. They had got Anna talking much sooner than they had hoped. And getting her to open up about her marriage was the very

25

reason they had breezed in out of the blue. 'She's a good little worker though, babe, isn't she? And that's always good for business surely?'

'Yes, she is a good worker, Hazel, but I don't know about her being good for business. Other women who are in for a night out don't want a bloody flirt swanning around the place and teasing their men. It makes my stomach turn over every time I see her up to her tricks on the rare occasions that I do go in these days.'

'The trouble is – with girls like her – you have to watch they don't go too far,' said Linda. 'Before you know it that little tease might well start to lure Frank up into the flat above the restaurant for a cuddle. And men being men, who would blame him if he did follow that pert little wiggling arse of hers up the staircase to heaven.' Linda already knew that the waitress at Prima was familiar with the flat above the restaurant. She was simply drawing Anna in to see just how aware she was of what was going on. 'At least she keeps the punters happy ... not to mention Frank.'

'Oh?' said Anna as she leaned back in her chair and stared into Linda's face. 'And you'd go along with that, would you? You'd make allowances if Frank was at it with her in what used to be our little flat when we were first married?'

'Men will be men, sweetheart. But then I doubt that she would do something like that while either of us two is in the restaurant. But there's no telling. I'm just letting you know what I think she's like, that's all. I wouldn't give Frank too much free rein if I were you – that's all I'm saying. Remind him that he's a family man now and then – while *she's* in earshot.'

'Or better still expand your family,' said Hazel. 'Try for a baby girl. You know what men are like with daughters.'

Uncomfortable at the way her sisters were throwing advice at her, which she hadn't asked for, Anna said, 'I'm quite content with my twins thanks. I don't need any more babies. You kick into action, Hazel, or persuade Linda to.'

'You and Frank were over the moon once you'd hit the target, you know that you were.' Linda poured more wine into the three glasses and said, 'Get that down you and don't look so serious.'

'I'm a responsible mother of twins don't forget,' said Anna, still wondering why they had made this impromptu visit. 'I have to take things seriously. It's all right for you two – footloose and fancy free. She sipped her drink and waited. She wasn't daft; there was something on both of their minds and by the look of it, something else was on the tip of Hazel's tongue.

'You know what?' said Hazel, as predictable as ever. 'I don't think I've ever seen a happier face than Frank's after you'd told him you had two babies growing and not one. He walked differently after that. Shoulders back, chest out, proud as punch. That soon wore off though, didn't it?' She looked from one sister to the other and sipped her drink.

A touch miffed by this reminder of how happy she and her Frank used to be, Anna felt herself go cold as her stomach churned. Even though she was angry with him she was just as much in love as she had ever been, but from the way her sisters were talking she could detect a tone of warning. She wondered if both girls

27

knew more than she did. On the surface everything looked rose-tinted and reasonably good when it came to her marriage. She and Frank were seen as the young handsome couple who were able to live a comparatively comfortable lifestyle in the East End. They had their lovely refurbished terraced cottage in a corner of London where they had been born and bred, which was now being promoted as the next best link to the City in years to come. It was also being seen by medical students attached to the London Hospital as an interesting historic place to lodge and this, in turn, was bringing other students attached to various colleges to lodge in the surrounding area.

For others, with ready cash and an eye for a bargain, the area was now reputed to be the place for developers to snap up cheap run-down properties that would soar in price in years to come. With its wealth of history, museums, the Whitechapel art gallery and the vibrant markets, tourists from abroad were also coming into the area, if only to see where the likes of the Kray twins had lived. Similar in a way to 1888, when people from all walks of life poured in after Jack the Ripper hit the headlines.

The pubs down by the river in and around Wapping had long since been the haunt of the young middle- and upper-class students swigging beer and belting out naughty ballads. But the old East Enders were still thick on the ground and this was why Anna loved living so close to where she was born, in Stepney Green. But now, with this particular impromptu visit from her sisters, she felt that her little world was about to be blown apart.

Bringing herself back to the here and now she spoke quietly, saying, 'I have a feeling that we all know that Frank's not interested in us having any more children ... don't we?'

'You tell us,' said Hazel, giving nothing away as she topped us Anna's glass of wine.

'You do sound a bit heavy, sweetheart,' said Linda, knowing full well what was wrong. 'What's the matter, babe?'

Anna shrugged as she splayed both hands. 'I'm just being a misery. Take no notice, I won't slit my wrists.'

'Now stop that. That's not what I meant. We just don't think you're all that happy, that's all. And maybe it's time for you to start going out again? In the evenings? With us, or get in contact with some of your old friends.'

'No thanks. I'm all right as I am. Yes, I will admit that I do sometimes feel a bit low, but it's nothing to get depressed over. I've got my lovely neighbour next door to talk to whenever I want. Rachel's smiling lined face has brought me out of the gloom more than once. Then there's Jackie the Avon girl coming and going with her catalogue ...'

Her sisters hid their feelings well. Of course they were gutted by Anna's pathetic attempt to make light of what was clearly appearing to be a lonely world that she moved around in. Neither of the girls felt comfortable in the silence that now hung in the air after Anna's back-handed confession. Glancing at each other, they couldn't be sure what was coming next or whether or not Anna knew that her husband was having an affair with his assistant manager, Bridget, the girl with the soulless dark brown eyes who dressed to kill. Taking the bull by the horns, Hazel spoke in a quiet voice, saying, 'We weren't sure what to do about the way things were going, babe. Or whether we were reading things wrongly.'

'With Bridget and Frank, you mean?'

'Well, that's not what I was gonna say—'

'Yes you were. So something is going on then?'

'A bit more than flirting, that's all . . . but it might be the time to nip it in the bud. We don't think it's too serious, babe, and we don't think that it's anything for you to worry *too* much over.'

'It's all right, Hazel.' Anna offered a knowing smile. 'You needn't look so worried. Nor you, Linda. I've known for a while what that pair were up to. Well, not *known* exactly, just suspicious – which is worse in a way. But I didn't think that you'd cottoned on to anything going on between them. I would have thought that you would have swung her around by that long curly ginger hair of hers if you had spotted her brushing up close to Frank. Or are you gonna tell me that it's all my husband's doing and that Bridget's just a simple innocent creature that's been lured in by his come-and-get-me eyes?'

'Like hell we are,' said Linda, taking a cigarette from her slim gold case. 'She's lucky I've not scratched her face beyond recognition. And trust me I would have liked to have done. But that's not the way to go about things is it? We don't want her crying on Frank's shoulder, do we?'

Anna suddenly felt sick. This was all sounding too serious for words, as if a proper affair was going on and not just a bit of flirting. 'So what is it you're trying to tell me?'

Hazel looked from Anna to Linda with no words needed. They had come here tonight to warn their younger sister to watch her step where Bridget, the sometimes coy and sometimes brazen flirt, was concerned. 'We're not trying to tell you anything, Anna. We just wanted to make sure that you knew what she's like around men. And Frank in particular.'

'Well, now that you do know that I know, we can drink a toast to it, can't we. I'm glad that you know but at the end of the day it's my problem not yours.' Fighting to control the tears welling behind her eyes, she said, with forced gaiety, 'So ... let's keep the wine flowing and eat, shall we? And while we do, you can fill me in as to what you've picked up in Prima. Is it for instance a bit of flirting and no more than that? Do they have a secret kiss and hug now and then?'

Hazel reached across the table. She squeezed Anna's trembling hand and smiled weakly at her. 'There's nothing we can tell you that is *fact*, babe. But come on, you're obviously ill at ease with this conversation. It's us you're talking to. Your big sisters. You don't have to cover your feelings.'

'Fair enough. Well go on then. Lay it on the line. But don't tell me half of it because that would be worse than you not saying anything.'

Hazel drew breath and leaned back in her chair. She knew that there was no going back now and she hadn't thought for one minute that they would have got this far this quickly. It was actually going better than she had thought it would. So, with both girls' attention on her she quietly laid the cards on the table. She admitted that she and Linda had seen what had gone on and was still going on between Frank and Bridget. She told of the private little innuendos between them and the knowing looks they gave each other which gave them away. They spoke of the little asides that they shared in between serving the customers and the irritating little-girl laughter from the silly cow when the pair of them were behind the bar enjoying a drink or two together. And before they had even got round to dropping the bombshell that they slipped upstairs to the flat now and then, Anna gestured to indicate that she had heard enough.

Unable to take any more, she pursed her lips and covered her face with her hands, still trying her best not to break into tears. Then, taking a deep breath, she managed to say, 'I think I realised, if I'm honest with myself, that by keeping his distance Frank's been hiding his guilt for a long time.' She looked from one sister to the other before breaking into a feeble smile as the tears escaped.

'Even though the bastard's got the looks of a handsome movie star,' she said, as she dabbed her face dry with a tissue, 'he can't act to save his life. Guilt's written all over him.'

'I don't know about a movie star, babe,' murmured Linda, gutted to see her sister this broken. 'But I agree with you about the guilt. He blushes deep red every now and then whenever me and Hazel and the boys are in the restaurant. Especially lately.'

'And what about Bridget? Does she blush or just flash her silk knickers?'

'She flashes those all of the time at all the men, sweetheart.' Linda smiled. 'It's that Trevor Plumb, her husband, that I feel sorry for. It's painful to watch sometimes. There he sits in a corner of the restaurant when he's come in to give her a lift home, trying his best not to let on that he sees what she's up to. She only flirts with the attractive customers and hardly gives the plain and ugly ones a glance. I can't imagine what must go through Trevor's mind at times. Poor sod.'

'I couldn't agree more,' said Hazel. 'He seems a really nice guy. And he's got an honest face. I've seen him in there quite a few times when he's turned up to give that cow a lift home in his second-hand Anglia. He's a tall and handsome feller but obviously can't satisfy her lust for excitement. I love that sandy hair and those freckles. He's better looking than your Frank – in a way.'

Anna didn't need them to tell her who Bridget was married to because she already knew. She also knew that Trevor was a lovely guy, a swimming instructor who taught children locally in and around the East End as well as the disabled in the Stratford East swimming baths. She had found this out during conversations with him when he had dropped into the restaurant when she had been there.

'We don't have much to say to Bridget when we're in Prima,' said Hazel, offhandedly. 'She's makes herself busy coming and going from the kitchen to the tables and the bar when we're in. She's good at what she does when she is in working mode – I'll give her that.'

'I agree,' said Linda. 'But then she would keep busy and out of the way just to keep up appearances. Prima is our sister's restaurant as well as Frank's let's not forget.'

'Exactly,' said Anna. 'She knows when to act as if butter wouldn't melt in her mouth. But all of this apart I'm still jealous of the way Frank pays her more attention than he does me. And I'm frightened that she's stealing him away.' Covering her face and trying not to break down she shook her head. 'I don't want to lose him. I've never loved anyone else. And I never in a million years thought that he would be taken from me by someone else. Especially not her.'

'Us neither,' said Hazel. 'You were the ideal couple. But don't give up on yourself, babe. After all, what's to say you wouldn't meet someone else and fall in love? You'd have to prise yourself out of this house though and start to socialise a bit. Have some fun perhaps? You never go out in the evenings and you're on duty with the twins practically twenty-four hours a day. Mum would baby-sit, you know she would. You're only twenty-six for Christ's sake.'

'It never occurs to me to go out. I'm a married woman with two babies. I didn't even consider it to be an option.'

'Well, maybe it's time you did start getting back to your old self. Once upon a time there was no keeping you down. Remember that cold day in February in Hyde Park three or so years ago when thousands of postal workers came out on strike in favour of a pay claim for telegraphists? There you were giving support even though you were a telephonist and not a telegraphist. Nothing or nobody could have stopped you from shouting the odds against unfairness once your back was up.'

'*Nearly* twenty-six,' said Anna.

'All right, nearly. And you being *nearly* twenty-six is why we're here. We want to arrange a night out doing a pub crawl or going up West to a nightclub. Us three and our wayward girls as Mum calls them, and your old friends. We want you to pick up the phone and ring round.'

Anna raised an eyebrow. 'Your wayward girls are prostitutes. What would any of my old friends make of that? In any case that's exactly what I did earlier on. I phoned Beryl. You remember her?'

'Of course we do. She was your best mate when you were at school, wasn't she?'

'Yes. And for a little while afterwards.'

'That's right. So what about her?'

'She's dead. Her mum answered the phone. She's there looking after the little ones.'

'Good God,' murmured Hazel. 'I can't believe that.'

'Me neither, babe,' said Linda. 'What happened? Was there an accident?'

'No. She had cancer.'

'Jesus wept.' Linda slowly shook her head. 'Cancer at her age?'

'Yep.'

'Phew ... that must 'ave knocked you for six, sweetheart, cos it's kicked me in the guts and she wasn't my best friend.'

'I know. Anyway ...' Anna shrugged and sighed. 'A night out would be great but I don't know about including my old mates.'

'Because of our girls?' said Hazel. 'You don't have to say what they do for a living, babe. And anyway, each and every one is an attractive up-market hostess who sometimes entertains their clients in the classy rooms at the top of our house. They're not common prostitutes. And you know they're a lot of fun to be with.'

'Give me time to think about it. My birthday's not for weeks. Anything could happen in the meantime. I might have kicked Frank out by then or sent Bridget packing so that me and my *husband* can pick up where we left off before *she* came along.'

'Fair enough,' said Linda. 'You've got three weeks to think about where you'd like to go on your birthday.'

'Never mind my birthday. I want my life back. And I want Bridget out of my marriage. I *am* jealous of her – I am. I'm jealous and I hate the feeling. It eats and eats away at you. It takes you over. Wakes you in the night and stops you from thinking about much else during the day.'

'But you've got nothing to be envious of, sweetheart,' murmured Hazel. She was upset to hear her baby sister talking like this. 'You're much better looking than she is. And no one's taken in by that phoney innocent expression of hers. She's a calculating little cow who's not only interested in getting your husband into bed but most likely had her sights set on owning your half share of the restaurant.'

'She's welcome to it.'

'No she's not. And don't you say that again or it might just happen. You fight for every single penny that's rightfully yours ... if it should come to that. I've seen women who've been so fucked up by this kind of thing that they've taken a packed suitcase to walk away and end up with nothing. Why do you think that some girls turn to prostitution? Because they decided when they were innocent little children that this is what they wanted to be when they grew up? A good majority of young women have been left high and dry by their husbands who've gone off with someone else.'

'Don't exaggerate,' said Anna.

'Exaggerate? No, sweetheart. It's real. Respect and faded love goes right down the drain when it's balanced against money. So don't even think of talking like that again or it just might end up happening to you as well. You've got our twins to think of if not yourself.'

Anna went quiet and leaned back in her chair, looking from one to the other of her sisters. When she eventually spoke it was in a more sensible and calm tone. 'All right. You've made your point and it's a good one. Enough said. I know what the pair of you are trying to do. And I *will* pick myself up. I *will* get the old Anna spirit back. And if necessary I'll fight for Frank with both fists and my feet because I want my husband back. I want us to be the way we were.'

Downing her wine in one, Anna reached for the bottle to top it up again. 'I suppose I've been partly to blame for the flirting that's been going on. Frank's been lying through his back teeth as to why he's late home every night and deep down I think I knew why but I didn't want to believe it, never mind face up to it. I was too scared to ask what was going on between him and her if you want the truth. Too scared to ask because I was dreading the answer. Because, after all, what could I have done if he openly admitted it? If he said that he wanted to be with her and not me? I can't nail 'is feet to the floor, can I?'

A silence filled the room until Hazel quietly said, 'I know what you mean, babe. This is more or less what we were worried about. We've seen the chemistry that's developed between the pair of them. And thinking about it, ginger-nut might well have *wanted* us to see it.'

'You could be right there, Hazel.' Linda leaned both elbows on the table and cupped her face as she looked into Anna's. 'She might well have been hoping for this. Hoping to push Frank into telling you. Which, after all's said and done, was not all that bright, was it? But never mind, at least we're ahead of the game now. All three of us. She won't have a leg to stand on if she carries on the way she's going. A broken knee cap can be very painful.'

'Oh stop it,' said Anna, 'stop talking like that. I don't like it. But I have taken on board all that you've said. Now I just need to sit and think about things quietly. I can look at it in a different light now that we've talked. I don't feel as if I'm on my own now. I'll do what I think is best for me and the twins.'

Hazel gave Linda a look to let her know that enough had been said and they had achieved what they had set out to do. She then helped herself to a prawn cracker and shrugged. 'It's the same old story every time. And who is it that gets the blame? The wives at home, getting on with all the drudgery and all the while they haven't got a clue what their old man's getting up to.'

'Tell me about it,' said Anna. 'Tell me about it.'

Chapter Two

Just before the girls left, Hazel suggested that Anna might want to pay a little visit to the restaurant the next day for a coffee while Ivy took care of the twins. But she needn't have worried because this was exactly what Anna intended to do in any case. The girls had made their parting brief, leaving their sister at the table with the half-empty containers of Chinese food and enough wine to send her off to sleep for the night. They wouldn't have been too surprised to learn that once she heard the street door close behind them, Anna wept. While her sisters were there, she had held on tightly to her emotions even when she had felt queasy deep down inside. But now that she knew for certain that Bridget hadn't managed to pull the wool over their eyes, relief balanced the suffering that she had been going through night after night after night.

Soon after midnight Anna, having patiently waited in the silence for Frank to come home so that they could have a little chat, had done her very best to give him the benefit of the doubt and had told herself over and over agan that this affair must be just a flash in the pan – that he had succumbed to a professional tease who could be sacked and sent packing. But she was so tired that she could hardly keep her eyes open and decided to go to bed; perhaps she could talk to him once he was home and in bed, but just before she switched off the lights she heard a black taxi pulling up and its engine running. Her heart felt as if it would leap out of her chest it was pounding so much and she had to ask herself why she was allowing herself to get into this state. Frank was back from Prima, that was all. And if he wasn't too drunk to have a sensible conversation then they would have one. It was that simple. So why then was her heart thumping?

The stumbling footsteps she heard in the passage told her she would get little out of him tonight. He came into the room and stood peering at her as he swayed on his feet and tried to say something, but his speech was so slurred that it was incomprehensible. Anna looked at her husband, wondering why she had not complained before when he had come home in this state. Or why she hadn't got angry over it. Bracing herself, she spoke quietly, saying, 'Why don't you come and sit down. I've opened a nice bottle of red wine.'

'Have you?' he said, still swaying. 'That's nice.'

'Do you want me to pour you a glass?'

'Why not? That would be lovely.'

'Are you hungry? Would you like a sandwich?'

'No. A glass of wine will be enough.' He slumped down onto the sofa and kicked off his shoes. 'Bloody busy at the restaurant, Anna. Fuck me, it was busy. Rushed off our feet. But never mind – it's putting money into our coffers, darling.'

'And that can't be a bad thing,' she said, as she went to the sideboard to pour his drink.

'No. That's not a bad thing. A little house in the countryside, Anna. That's what it's all about. We'll put all our money by and get us a second home. People with a bit of spare cash are doing that now you know. I hear things in that restaurant.'

Anna handed him his glass of wine and sat beside him on the sofa. 'Do you know what I think,' she said. 'I think it's time we had a family holiday. In the country perhaps. Devon or Cornwall for a week. The fresh air would do our babies the world of good.'

'I'm sure it would, darling, but I won't be able to take time off this year.' He put an arm around her shoulders and looked into her face but the smell of drink on his breath made her want to pull away. He had been drinking gin and tonics – probably large ones.

'But you could go away with our boys,' he said. 'You could go with your mum to Butlins for a fortnight. You'd like that wouldn't you?'

'No, not really.' She laughed quietly at him. 'I don't think you would suggest it if you were sober.'

'Wouldn't I?'

'No.'

'Oh. Sorry. Shall we have a cuddle on the sofa instead of talking about holidays then?'

'Like we used to you mean?'

'Yeah. Like we used to.' He slumped back, closed his eyes and quietly giggled. 'We were like fucking rabbits weren't we?'

'Not lately though, Frank. Not lately. Why do you reckon that is?'

'Tired ain't I. Exhausted from running that fucking restaurant. Anyway, it'll all work out. Always does.' He heaved himself up and stumbled out of the room saying, 'Going to bed.'

And that was it. That was all he had to offer her. She could hardly believe just how much he had changed over the past nine months or so. They had been the idyllic couple. Always laughing, always making love, always cracking jokes. Until Bridget came along. She found herself wondering if deep down Frank had always been selfish, always put what he wanted before anything else. She decided not to go there, to resist weighing up the pros and cons, the good and the bad points. The trouble was he hadn't lost his attractive looks, which made her want to be held close by the bastard. His dark blue eyes, tanned complexion and black hair still had her longing to fall into his arms, even though he had gone from a fun-loving guy to someone who seemed like a stranger. This was still what she wanted.

Tired though she was, Anna was not in the right mood to sleep and didn't feel in the least bit like lying next to Frank in bed as if everything was normal. And neither did she want to give vent to her feelings and tell him that the girls had been round and that they knew about Bridget. Her mind switched from one thing to another as she remembered little innuendos that she had heard from her regulars whenever she had been in Prima. She realised now that they had, in their own gentle way, been giving her subtle messages about the affair. So many other little incidents involving the sneaky pair were floating in and out of her mind now, almost as if they were re-runs of an old film. It was all so obvious: Frank and Bridget had been at it from as far back as when she had stopped working at Prima, when she was four months pregnant and Bridget had been promoted from head waitress to assistant manager.

For her own reasons, Anna decided not to let on to Frank that Hazel and Linda had been round that evening. Before he had staggered in she had made sure there were no traces left of their visit. She had dropped all of the takeaway containers and leftover food into a black bin bag and dumped the lot into their dustbin at the back of the garden, knowing that the bin men would be collecting the next day. She had then opened all of the downstairs windows and sprayed the entire ground floor of the house as well as the staircase with fresh air spray to get rid of the lingering smell of the Chinese food. She wanted to keep him totally in the dark as to what she knew for certain and what she wasn't quite sure about.

In her soft, pink and blue checked pyjamas and matching housecoat, as she sat in an armchair close to the fire where no fire burned, she tried to think of what to do for the best. She despised Frank for the damage he had done to their marriage, but at the same time she loved him for all of the good times they had shared together. She wanted to strangle him one minute and hold him close the next as all kinds of conflicting emotions swept through her. Frank had, as usual, made a display of being too exhausted to do much else other than utter those few words before he climbed the stairs to the bedroom with no thoughts of justifying another of his late nights. She knew that there would have been no point in her trying to have a proper conversation with him because he would have dismissed whatever she had to say as boring and gone to bed in any case.

She recalled his expression a week or so earlier when she asked why he was so tired all of the time. His only response was to wipe his forehead and look at her with an expression of apathy before strolling out of the room shaking his head. Tonight, though, she had managed to smile sweetly at him when she had said, 'I'm sure you must have had a hard time at the restaurant, Frank.' And then called him a two-timing bastard under her breath. By keeping her mouth shut and her temper in its place she had proved that she did have the strength of mind to know when to hold her tongue. The only thing that she wasn't comfortable about was that she was going to have to get into the bed next to him and carry on the charade of there being nothing wrong. She didn't want him in her space, never mind their bodies possibly touching when he turned over in the night because, since he hadn't taken a shower, she knew that the scent of Bridget would be on him.

Feeling that she should brave it out, she drew comfort from the fact that when she looked into his face he could have no idea that she knew what he had been getting up to. She realised that this feeble sense of triumph was a sad replacement for feeling loved, but at least it was better than nothing. Much better.

Topping up her glass of wine she quietly spoke to herself, saying, 'It's *her* fault that your heart feels as if it's being gripped and squeezed, but it's your own fault, Anna, for being a coward and not facing up to the truth that has been staring you right in the face.'

She sipped her drink and slowly shook her head. 'You knew all along what you were doing, Bridget. You even had me believe that you were my friend. *My* friend and not Frank's. Well … I might be a little bit drunk now but I won't be tomorrow when I walk into Prima and sack you.' She smiled at the thought of it and then raised her glass, saying, 'Good riddance to bad rubbish. At least horrible suspicion's no longer eating away at me. Hazel and Linda are girls who tell it as it is without frills or exaggeration. So I have no reason to doubt what they told me about you. They're right as a rule about most things and their timing tonight was spot on. I should have known my sisters wouldn't allow someone to pull the wool over my eyes. I should have known they would have seen through all of your phoney sweetness and light.'

Too tired to think anymore, Anna let the tears come. 'You were the only one of my boyfriends that I loved, Frank, the only one I gave myself to – and you've let that cow ruin it all.'

Swallowing against the lump in her throat, Anna wiped away her tears with the back of her hand then gazed at her wedding ring. She felt completely alone in the house even though she was not the only one there. A touch giddy from all the wine, she again whispered to herself. 'This isn't you, Frank … this isn't my Frank who was always so caring before she came along. You *did* love me – I know you did.' She dabbed her face with the hem of her soft blue dressing gown and told herself that she had to be strong, had to look forward and not backward.

Her head now gently throbbing from trying to work things out, she tried to imagine a gentle hand sweeping all of the questions and worry away and a soft voice

45

telling her that it wasn't her fault. That she mustn't blame herself for having been snared in this battlefield of changing emotions. And that she wasn't the only injured party. Bridget's unassuming young husband, Trevor, was also in the ring and now Anna wondered if he knew what was going on. In fact, since it had been so blatantly obvious to others, she wondered how he could possibly have missed it. But none of this mattered in any case because the ball was now in her court and the match was only just beginning.

Ready for her pillow at last, she switched off the lamp and left the comfort of the snug for the bedroom. Once in bed though, with Frank sound asleep, she gazed at his handsome strong face and his broad, naked olive-skinned shoulders and felt her anger rise as vivid images of him in bed with Bridget filled her mind. As she turned over so as to have her back to him she caught a faint, now familiar, whiff of perfume – not one that she ever wore. Pulling herself up again she switched on the bedside lamp and tipped the shade so that the light would shine onto Frank's face. She stared at him as he lay on his side, and had to use every bit of will power to stop herself from grabbing and tugging at his thick dark hair or pressing her pillow over his face.

Moaning contentedly in his sleep Frank, however, was clearly on cloud nine within the dream where she imagined him to be playing the role of the handsome hero screwing the leading actress in a B movie. 'You rotten, stinking, lousy two-timing bastard,' she murmured. 'I hate your guts and I don't want to sleep in the same bed as you.'

Too drunk, and possibly too wrapped up in his own

little world of wet dreams for her animosity to have any chance of filtering through, Frank turned over onto his front without waking up. Now she had a full view of his beautiful strong back which had once been a major attraction. She still couldn't believe that he had changed from a great hunk of a guy to a sneak-around, mendacious bastard. He had had a lot to drink by the time he had arrived home, and had worked a long shift, so perhaps he could be forgiven for hardly having said a word, but he hadn't given their sleeping babies his usual fatherly stroke either.

Staring out at nothing and in no mood to read her book, Anna could hear the echoing sound of her neighbour Rachel bolting her back door. Her ageing friend, who always seemed to have long soft wisps of grey hair escaping from the French pleat at the back of her head, was in her eighties and going to bed later than Anna was. Rachel, whose lined face spoke volumes about her having had a hard life, was energetic enough to plant out her seedlings at night in her walled garden. At least this brought Anna a faint smile because the old girl had said more than once, 'The moon is just as important to bring on seedlings as it is to light the way in the dark when a man can't find his way home.' Anna wondered if she had been alluding to Frank's late-night homecomings. She also wondered what her neighbour, who was full of Jewish jokes and clever sayings, would think if she saw this little scene of a young handsome couple in bed. She glanced at her spouse again and felt nothing but contempt. Here she was, nearly twenty-six years old, and in bed with a book while her husband dreamed of his lover.

*

Rachel had lived by herself for quite a while in her old fashioned two-up-two-down rented house next door. She had been kind on the day that Anna and Frank got the keys to this house, and had remained kind ever since. She sometimes gave Anna homemade soup in a Tupperware container. And occasionally, when Anna had been reclining on her sun-bed in her small walled garden with a broken section between their houses, Rachel would give her a buttered bagel and a glass of orange juice. She was a shining example of an East Ender who had come through a lousy life of rotten fortune and broken dreams but still made the most of every God-given day.

Not only did Rachel have a canny outlook on the world and its people, but she could also cut through a quarrel between neighbours with a one-liner to stop them in their tracks, and have them laughing or ashamed of themselves. And even more poignant where Anna was concerned, the old girl was always there for her when she was feeling a touch on the lonely side and in need of a friend to talk to over freshly drawn tea in a china cup.

Living on a state pension, the woman was excellent at making a small amount of money go further than anyone because she only ever shopped in the local markets, and always minutes before the stallholders were packing up. So instead of living hand to mouth, as most old folks did, her larder was stocked up for little emergencies – a habit left over from wartime. Sometimes she would come home from one of her trips to the local markets with her large basket on wheels crammed with vegetables of one sort or another that she would sell for a small profit to the corner shop at the end of the turning.

A widow of five years, she told warm stories of the man she had married some fifty years ago, who had dropped down dead in his vegetable patch. She was also good at giving gentle advice and, occasionally, Anna had been tempted to open up to her, but as it turned out there was no need because she had already worked out for herself that Anna was lonely. She had sometimes asked why the twins' father spent so much time away from the home and this, Anna felt sure, was Rachel's way of leaving her back door open should she need a shoulder to cry on at any time of the day or night.

With so much going through her mind and her resentment towards Frank growing, she couldn't bear to lie next to someone who had become like a stranger and smelled of someone else's scent. Drawing back the covers, she slipped out of bed, out of the room, and crept down the stairs so as not to disturb her sleeping twins. Collecting the spare quilt from the linen cupboard on the way, she felt sure that Frank wouldn't notice or care that her side of the bed was empty and going cold. Animosity wasn't the only reason for her leaving the room – she wanted to be by herself so that she could plan how to go about things the next day; what she would say and what she might do to Bridget when she paid her a visit at the restaurant.

After collecting some herbal pills that Rachel had given to help her sleep just before the twins were due, Anna went into the sitting room and made herself comfortable on the sofa ... her makeshift bed. Once

49

settled, she asked herself why she hadn't done this before: left Frank to dream and snore alone while she had the peace and quiet of the ground floor to herself. By the soft glow of her small table lamp, she curled up, pulling the padded quilt to her chin, and glanced at her Welsh dresser and the cut glass decanter half filled with sherry. She smiled wistfully to herself because the decanter had been a wedding gift from Ivy, her altruistic and doting mother who she would be leaving the twins with the next day.

Closing her eyes, she whispered, 'You'll make it all right, Mum, I know you will.' She then sank her head into her feather cushion and sensed a kind of intoxicating calm flowing gently through her as she closed her eyes and blocked out all thoughts of her long lonely evenings. Her sisters had told her that they had known for a while that she wasn't happy and that she spent most nights watching television by herself, because Anna's lovely old neighbour had taken them to one side and whispered it long before now.

So, as the quiet dark streets outside settled down for the night, Anna promised herself that she would get back to the person she once was – a light-hearted, fun-loving girl. She imagined herself going out to nice restaurants again, with her sisters, while Ivy looked after the twins. Earlier on, Linda had been firmer than Hazel, insisting that Anna put all that had happened between Bridget and Frank in the dustbin where it belonged and that it would be Bridget who would lose out in the end.

She had said the girl would not only lose her husband but get the push from Frank as well, once their little affair was out in the open and in the public domain. This was all pie in the sky as far as Anna was concerned, and by the time Linda had got round to telling her that she wasn't to torment herself over what Frank might be getting up to, she had already got to this point herself as if it had been written into her diary. She was ready for battle.

It infuriated her the way Frank walked around in a little world of his own, behaving as if she didn't exist and happier when getting ready for work in the mornings than when at home at the weekends when the restaurant was closed. Even when he *had* spent time with his family at weekends he was prone to singing along to a favourite LP, and often with those bulky black earphones of his on. With the herbal pills making her feel drowsy, Anna snuggled deeper into her bedding and told herself that she wasn't alone, that she had her beautiful twin babies, her family, and her lovely friend next door. Comfortable on the big squashy sofa that was her bed, she sank her head deeper into the silky feathered cushion and drifted off into sleep.

In his usual buoyant morning mood, Frank left the house at nine o'clock sharp to go to his brothers' restaurant at Tower Hill – as he did every Tuesday, their busiest day – not only to give them a hand but because he liked the change of environment. So, knowing that her husband would be working a full day in another area, it seemed a perfect time for Anna to pay her visit to Bridget. Frank had not asked her why she had slept on the sofa but, just in case he had bothered to ask, she had been ready with an answer, a deliberate cliché, that she had had a 'headache'. But he hadn't mentioned one word of it and she wondered if this was out of guilt. He didn't want to ask questions because he didn't want a confrontation. Anna couldn't quite work it out but neither did she want to.

She could no longer leave things be and wait to see how they panned out. Now she had to send the interloper packing. With all sorts of questions and worries flying through her mind, she went into the sitting room again and looked at the bedding. Since she was always the first one up so as to see to the twins, Frank could have been forgiven for not having realised that she had left their bed while he was still asleep, but there was no escaping the fact that the spare padded quilt was on the sofa.

'Forget it, Anna,' she told herself, as she went upstairs to gather a clean set of clothes for each of her babies from a large drawer in an old waxed pine chest. 'Don't waste your energy. If he wants to go then good riddance. If he wants to stay, then he has to come clean and make an apology. Enough is enough.'

Standing between their cots and looking from one to the other of her twin boys, she said, 'We'll be all right. We'll be fine. We've got your grandma and we've got your aunties who love you to bits.'

Smiling up at their young mother and gurgling, Oliver and James brought warmth back into Anna's heart as nothing else could. She leaned over to kiss one and then the other as she whispered, 'Your daddy's gone off the rails a bit that's all. It'll all come out in the wash.' She picked up Oliver first to dress him in his outdoor clothes and, as she held him in her arms, he looked at her amd smiled and she noticed that a first tooth was just beginning to show. This seemed like the best present she could have been given. A little pearly milestone.

An hour or so later, her mind flying from one thought to another once she had the twins dressed and ready and sleeping soundly in their twin pram, she relaxed in an armchair to enjoy a freshly percolated cup of coffee. Her view of her small walled garden lifted her spirits. There was a mass of beautiful forget-me-nots and some pansies opening up around the old gnarled apple tree. So, while the twins slept peacefully in the passage, Anna began to get herself ready in her own time, determined to look good. Once showered, she brushed her hair until it shone and spent more time than she had done in a while in front of the mirror putting on her eye makeup and, in particular, her favourite Corn Silk powder and lipstick chosen from her Avon catalogue. She wanted to feel and look her best when she faced Bridget.

In her pale tan leather boots with Cuban heels, flowing green and rust skirt with matching jacket set off by her black polo neck, and her chunky gold neck-chain, she felt as if she was almost back to her old self again. Checking her appearance in the full-length mirror on the passage wall, she realised that it had been a long time since she had been given a reason to get dressed up and memories of her days as a single girl came flooding back. A time when Frank hadn't been able to take his eyes off her when they were out and about, going to parties and nightclubs. A time when they were often on the dance floor until the band packed up and they then sat with the night owls drinking and chatting.

Since giving birth, she had simply pulled on a pair of corduroys or jeans and a sweater in the mornings before getting on with her role as mother, laundry maid and housekeeper without any thoughts of powdering her nose or swiping on some lipstick. Frank, on the other hand, had taken to primping himself and dressing as if he were a prince among men, wearing expensive aromatic aftershave to go to work and leaving the house as if it were a hotel and not a home.

Noticing the faint scent of his aftershave in the air, she put on her gold bangles and her rings, feeling how she imagined her sisters must do every day of the week. But Anna was happy enough if this one day of excitement was all she was going to get for a while, because she was about to shine a spotlight on the secret little love planet where Frank liked to escape. Ready to go on her mission, she eased the twins' navy and chrome pram out of the passage and into the tiny front garden with both her baby boys sleeping soundly. For a brief moment she thought about Frank as she looked from one little face to the other and it dawned on her that it was he who was the loser, not she. He was missing out on this very special time, especially today when that first pearly tooth showed itself.

'Your daddy's loss is not mine,' she said, and took a deep breath as she willed herself not to lose her confidence. This possible breakdown of her marriage wasn't what she wanted and was the last thing that she ever thought she would be doing. Going on a mission to sort out her husband's lover? No way. But if it was to turn out all right for her and the twins she had to try and keep her blood on the boil and be in the right mood when she walked into her and Frank's family restaurant to see off Bridget once and for all.

All she could hope for now was that some of her old regulars would be in today to silently will her on. Several of those who frequented Prima's had been there in the beginning when they first opened and knew Anna and Frank as the happy couple running their restaurant together and making a success of it. She couldn't imagine what they were making of Bridget who, from all that her sisters had told her, had kicked her shoes under the bed in the small flat above Prima that most knew Anna and Frank had onced shared. The bed in the little love nest that had been their first home after they were married – their cosy one-bedroom flat above their workplace, the restaurant which had previously been a truckers' café before they turned it into the successful friendly place it now was.

'Oh well . . . look what the wind's blown in,' said Ivy, glancing from her daughter's face to the twins in the pram. She then turned her eyes to heaven before cautiously saying, 'I take it your sisters paid a visit last night or you wouldn't be here?' She knew they had but was trying to make light of it.

'Well, if it's a problem,' said Anna, going along with the little bit of play-acting, 'I'll take Oliver and James over to Frank's mum. You know how much she loves having them to herself for a while.'

'Suit yerself,' said Ivy, from the doorway of her masionette in Peabody Street as she glanced from left to right hoping to spot a neighbour so as to show off her grandsons. All she could see was an elderly Asian couple in traditional dress coming along. She knew them quite well; they had four daughters who, between them, seemed to be forever pregnant and proudly pushing a pram or two. 'There won't be any white faces around here soon,' murmured Ivy as she waved her daughter through the open doorway and into the wide passage where she could park the pram as usual.

Easing the front wheels up and over the doorstep, Anna drew breath. 'You'll get done for being racist if you keep on saying things like that, Mum.'

'That wouldn't bother me, I'll be among friends in Holloway Prison.' She laughed, then looked over her daughter's shoulder, nodding and smiling at the old couple.

'Did it go all right down at the housing office, sweetheart?' she said, her voice raised and all friendly.

'Much better than so far!' said the gentleman. 'It looks like they will give us one of those lovely flats in skyscrapers. We are over the moon!'

'That doesn't surprise me,' said Ivy, 'and I'll tell you why! That little terraced house you're renting will be sold off to private buyers just like all the others round this way. They'll get a fortune for your place once it's been renovated.'

Laughing, the neighbours from along the turning showed a hand. 'We don't care what they do with it, Ivy! We are going to get a brand new council flat! And soon!'

'Good luck to the pair of yer! Don't forget to give me the address before you go!'

'We won't! Don't worry!' said Mr Dayjoo as he placed a hand on his heart. 'You, my friend, will be the first guest that we invite in for a cup of your favourite British tea.'

'I'll hold you to that,' said Ivy, smiling as she closed the door.

Anna slowly shook her head. 'You're so two-faced at times, Mum. And the word's renovated, not renoviated.'

'I know that. And as for the pretending to be racist, I just like to keep both sides of my friends happy, that's all.' She smiled at Anna and could see that her lovely soft eyes looked greener than ever with the sun coming into the room and shining onto her daughter's face. Coming up to her fifty-sixth birthday, even though life had been a little hard on her, Ivy was still a handsome woman herself, medium height and with a soft curvy figure and no spare fat. If push were to come to shove, she would have to admit that she, just like Anna, believed that there was a Lord keeping watch over the lot of them even if at times the Lord was dozing.

She pushed her fingers through her short wavy fair hair and said, 'Gwen from next door will 'ave been at the curtains eavesdropping when you arrived so my racist comment, as you call it, was to keep her happy. I told her not to knock once you were here but I bet she will.'

'Oh, right. So you sowed a nice little seed of mystery then?'

Ivy ignored that comment and leaned over the pram, slowly shaking her head and smiling at her grandbabies. Then in a whisper she said, 'Angels, sleeping angels.'

Anna, warm and comfortable in her mum's company and ever amused by her went into the kitchen and filled the kettle. She hadn't bothered to phone and tell Ivy that she was on her way over, nor ask if she would baby-sit, because her sisters had told her the night before that they were popping in to see their mother on their way home. She guessed they would have filled her in on everything. Hearing a low sigh escape from her mum as she came into the room, Anna turned and held out her arms for a hug. Obliging, and a little too choked to speak, Ivy squeezed her tightly and then looked intently at her youngest daughter. 'It'll all come out in the wash, sweetheart, don't you worry.'

'I know it will, Mum. And *you* don't have to worry about *me*. Not now that you all know and I don't have to keep secrets as if *I've* done something wrong.'

'Fucking men,' said Ivy as she set two big china cups onto saucers. 'They use their dicks like torches to hone in on a bitch on heat in the dark. They're worse than stray dogs. But I never thought that Frank would turn out like this. I suppose he's just forgotten how to behave decently, that's all.'

'You haven't told Frank's mum have you? Only I did say to the girls to tell you not to. I gave them that message. Did they remember to tell you? I don't want to upset her just yet.'

'That's not what you mean, Anna. I'm not daft. You don't want her to fly off the handle – which she will do once she does know. You've been more like a daughter to that woman than you have to me.'

'Oh Mum, please! I'm not in the mood for your baiting and I'm not stopping long. And it's not entirely Frank's fault all of this – it's that girl we took on in good faith. Now then, I've made the bottles up and all you have to do—'

'Is to stand them in a pan of boiling water to warm up.' Ivy cut in. 'I've done it before, you know. What time is their next feed due?'

Anna glanced at her wristwatch. 'In about an hour.'

'And if they don't wake up for it?'

'Give them ten minutes over and then do what you usually do, Grandma.' Anna smiled warmly at Ivy. 'I don't know what I'd do without you.'

'Nor do I,' said Ivy, keeping her emotions in check. Once Anna had gone, then she would shed a tear, or swear angrily and mentally throttle Frank before mentally squeezing the life out of the waitress who had got her claws into her son-in-law. The girl who dressed to kill and who had been taken in by his handsome looks, Italian suit, gold cufflinks and soft black leather wallet.

'I'm not sure now, though . . .' Anna sighed. 'I'm having second thoughts as to whether it would be best if you did phone Frank's mum today and tell her. But can we trust her not to phone Frank to give him a mouthful?'

'What if she did? He fucking well deserves it.'

'I know he does. But I want a whole day with him having no idea that I know.' She leaned against the kitchen sink and looked Ivy in the face. 'I'm angry, but worse than that I'm really hurt by this, Mum. It's that lush Bridget that's pulled him in by crossing and uncrossing her legs and showing off her fancy knickers. But I want to do it *my* way. Catch the bitch off guard and give her a good right hander.'

Ivy drew breath and then pointed a finger at her daughter, saying, 'Don't you dare lay a finger on her, Anna. From what I've heard she's a canny little cow—'

'Whose mouth wouldn't melt butter. I think I've got the message. But I will try not to leave 'er with a broken jaw.'

'Don't be silly. And besides, your sisters could 'ave got it wrong. Whenever I've been in she's been as nice as pie. And I've not seen 'er flirt once with Frank.'

'Of course you wouldn't have done! She's too clever for that. You're his mother-in-law for Christ's sake! She's hardly gonna squeeze up close to him while you're around, is she?'

'That's true. But I still don't think you should move too quickly, that's all I'm saying. And apart from that what if Frank doesn't take your side which … I very much doubt that he will if you show him up at the restaurant and in front of customers.'

'Frank's at his brother's place at Tower Hill today. I'm not daft – I wouldn't punch her on the nose if he was at Prima Pasta.'

'Well, if she is mostly to blame, you'll be playing right into her hands if you so much as touch her. She'll get Frank's sympathy whichever way it goes. This ain't the way to play it, sweetheart.'

'I'm not playing a game, Mum. And I know this must be painful after what you've been through. You still wish you hadn't broken Dad's tart's nose—'

'Too bloody well right I do. And you know why if you think back to all the rows. He wouldn't have left me for that ugly cow if I had played it differently, if I'd have acted the little girl hurt bit, shed a tear, said I could forgive and forget. He would have stayed with us if I had made me an easier option than him going off to Wales with her.'

Still leaning against the surface, her arms now folded, Anna said, 'And that's what you would have wanted is it? That's what you could have lived with? Dad here now and harbouring the over-romanticised thoughts that he'd given up the love of his life for you because you'd been so good about it all?'

'Bollocks to that. You know I wouldn't put up with that. Fucking liberty taker is what your father was.'

'Well, then?'

'Oh, do what you think is best, Anna.' Ivy dropped down onto a kitchen chair and held a hand to her forehead. 'I don't know who makes me more sick – dopey men or husband thieves.' She raised her eyes to meet Anna's. 'How can they sleep at night? Women who go out of their way to take someone's husband? I can't believe that anyone would do something like this. You've got twin babies between you for Christ's sake. And she's married to a lovely feller. You and the girls must 'ave got it wrong, love. Surely this can't be right?'

'I've seen the way she looks at Frank when I pop into Prima.'

'But she's never given you any reason to pull her up?'

'Of course not. She's too clever for that. Types like Bridget don't give a toss about anyone but themselves. By the time she's finished she will have turned his family against me. She must have seen Frank as a target when she first walked into our restaurant for that interview. The handsome, successful restaurateur that only need open up for five days a week? She was straight in. As soon as I was gone in *she* went, flashing her legs, pouting her lips, and fluttering the eyelashes.

'The thought of Frank holding another woman close wasn't even a tiny question in the back of my mind at that time. You know what we were like. We shared the same sense of humour; the same likes and dislikes. We had the same dreams. And we really did love each other, it didn't even have to be voiced. We just knew it. And, all right, he might not have been as over the moon about my being pregnant with the twins as I thought he would be, but deep down he was as proud as Punch.'

'I know, I know,' said Ivy slowly, the disappointment showing in her face. 'But I've seen Bridget in the restaurant and she doesn't come across as a lousy husband stealer. She obviously spends a lot of time in front of the mirror and she is nice looking, but that's no reason to be jealous of her, is it? I mean, we don't know for sure that he's been sleeping with her ... Do we?'

'Of course he has. And I'm not jealous! I'm angry! I've been totally humiliated! From the moment I set eyes on her I saw what she was up to by the way she looked dispassionately at me but smiled sweetly at Frank. I should have *known* she would be a marriage breaker. When that type wants something they just zone in and go all out, regardless. She all but lays her body on the bar and has the gall to act like a little girl, all sweetness and light, while doing so. It's *sickening* to watch.'

'Well, maybe I'm the fool for missing it then?' said Ivy, thoughtfully.

'No. You just weren't looking because decent people

don't. We don't expect women to perform the way that tease behaves. Frank didn't stand a chance, trust me.'

'Oh, give me a break, love. Frank? He's no different to the rest of 'em. Men can smell a bitch on heat from a mile off and then forget that they're married with—'

'Mum! Stop talking about the twins' dad like that.' Anna, suddenly on the verge of tears, went on. 'Why didn't you say something when that woman gave Dad the eye in the pub? Would you 'ave taken any notice of your mother if she had told you that Dad was being lured in by a charlatan?'

'No I wouldn't. I would have gone *potty* if she had of accused your father of being taken in by a silly cow. But now I know different of course.'

'Well, there we are then. Enough said.'

'But on the other hand—' The sound of the ding-dong doorbell stopped her short. Slowly shaking her head she said, 'I bet you my bottom dollar that's Gwen come to have a look at my grandsons. She can't resist little babies.'

'Well, don't tell her about Frank and Bridget,' warned Anna.

'As if I would,' said Ivy as she went to open the door.

Anna knew very well that as soon as she was gone Ivy and Gwen would be debating as to what either of the two of them would do to Frank if they saw him out on a dark night. But really, this didn't bother her as much as she made out. Gwen from next door was Ivy's best friend and the doting mother of John, the thirty-two-year-old who had at last told her that he was gay.

It had taken John two years to pluck up the courage

to stop dropping hints ever since the November of 1970 when the Gay Liberation Front was formed. When he did finally tell Gwen that he wasn't the marrying type, and explained why, she had surprised him. Even though his mother was every bit the old-fashioned housewife, she had simply shrugged it off, saying, 'I knew you was too pretty to be a boxer from the moment you opened your eyes for your first drop of breast milk.' She hadn't treated him any differently since, and continued to welcome his friends into her humble home whenever they knocked on the door.

When Gwen had moved into the maisonette next door to Ivy soon after her husband had passed away, she had been a touch isolated because her son and only offspring was a sociable, popular guy, always out and about with his fashionable friends. But at least she had a claim to fame. Every now and then John could be seen on the telly – on *Top of the Pops* – mingling and dancing with other young people.

Coming into the room followed by Gwen, Ivy was telling her friend that she was going to baby-sit for Anna, who was going out on a little shopping trip for some new clothes. A little white lie to appease her daughter, which Gwen accepted without much thought even though the rapid excuse had been a dead giveaway.

'Don't you look lovely today, Anna. You look prettier than that Jean Shrimpton,' said the woman, pulling up a chair and smiling. 'Look at that slimline figure – and you having lugged them twins about inside you for nine months as well.' She sat down and leaned forward to peer into Anna's face. 'You get your lovely looks from your mum, and thank God for it. Although I must say I have noticed a certain lack of interest lately where your mother's concerned. A bit of lipstick and powder goes a long way and you're the living proof of that.

'I had my hair curled and shampooed yesterday by Harry, the Jew boy in Becky Zeid's little hairdresser's in the Old Jago. You can't beat a Jew when it comes to a good cut and style even if most of them are manic, always shouting at each other. But put a pair of scissors in that man's hand and he works miracles. I keep telling your mother to go and get hers permed there but I think by doing that I was more of a hindrance than a help.'

'I don't *want* old-fashioned chipolata curls thank you,' said Ivy. 'Short and wavy with a few dark grey hairs coming through suits me fine. And it's natural. The colour and the waves. So don't keep going on about that fucking hairdresser.'

'See what I mean, Anna?'

'Don't push your luck, Gwen,' Anna chuckled. 'And anyway don't mind me – all this talk of a hairdresser is reminding me that I'm due for a visit. I might go to Vidal Sassoon's for a new look altogether.'

'Money for old rope,' said Ivy. 'Them poncey blokes haven't got a clue – West End salons or not.' She looked from Anna to Gwen and slowly shook her head. 'You can sit there pulling faces for as long as you like, it won't bother me.'

'I'm not saying that your hair don't look nice, Ivy. It's too short, that's all.' She glanced slyly at her friend. 'You look like a man when you're wearing slacks and a shirt blouse. I wouldn't be able to sleep a wink if I'd 'ave gone out looking like that in the daylight.'

Ignoring the baiting banter from her neighbour, Ivy poured her a cup of tea. 'I did dye my hair dark auburn once, to look like a movie star, but no sooner had I gone through all of that rigmarole than the blonde roots came through. Waste of time. So what do you think of them twins in the pram then, Gwen?'

Gwen stretched her body and neck to glance at them. 'They're the same ones I saw last week and the weeks before that. Why do you ask?'

'Our Linda reckons that they're gettin' to look more like me than ever.'

'She always did 'ave a sense of humour. No, they're beautiful, them boys. It's a good job you never 'ad quins like that woman in south London, Anna. She took one of them fertility pills as well, according to the newspaper. You might well 'ave delivered one of them who did resemble your mother if you shoved five babies out. I mean to say, you never know what's gonna 'appen when you start taking them new drugs, do yer?'

'Right, ladies,' said Anna, not wishing to be drawn in. 'I'm gonna love and leave you. Don't wake the twins up with your gossiping.' She then opened her tanned leather shoulderbag and took out her lipstick to swipe a little more on.

'That's a lovely shade of pink, Anna,' said Gwen. 'You'll have all the young men following you for a kiss on them cupid lips of yours if you're not careful.'

'It's the latest shade, Gwen. Pale Apricot. And thanks for the compliment. They've been few and far between lately.' Anna dropped her much-treasured golden-cased lipstick into her bag, then kissed her mother lightly on the cheek before squeezing Gwen's bony shoulder. 'Don't leave it too long before you come round to my place for a cup of tea with Mum.'

'Oh I won't, don't you worry. It takes me right back to when I was little and visiting my old nan, your house does. All right, so you 'ave got a fitted washing machine, tumble dryer and a fridge in yer kitchen, but your sitting room reminds me of all the dust that used to show up in my gran's house when the sun shone. I can't fathom why the young these days want old-fashioned brass ornaments and Victorian knick-knacks. Bloody dust collectors. The kitchens might be small in our maisonettes but they're streamlined – and with enough cupboards above and below the working surfaces. Who needs them bloody big old-fashioned oak dressers that take up space and light, eh?'

'I know what you mean. We're living in the bloody past, us young people.' Anna winked at her mother's friend and then, to cover the sick feeling in her stomach, smiled as she took her leave. This visit she was about to make was not something that she had ever thought possible.

'Shopping?' said Gwen, once she heard the front door close behind Anna. 'Pull the other leg, it's got bells on. I think she might have been telling you pork pies, Ivy. She's going to meet a feller on the sly if you ask me. I've not seen her looking so pretty like that before. And she touched up her lipstick before she left when it wasn't necessary. It's a dead giveaway that is. Applying fresh lipstick and powder during the daytime

67

every now and then. And I smelt that perfume . . . Well, good luck to 'er an' all. Good bloody luck.'

'My Anna's not like that. She's the rosy apple in the bowl that one. Her sisters are a different kettle of fish. And speaking of lipstick, you've not brought that Rose Red back that I let you try out last week.'

'Haven't I? Oh, I must have forgotten.'

'I'm sure,' said Ivy. 'It suits your face as much as it suits mine so you can borrow it whenever you want. But fetch it back!'

'Of course I will. Anyway, I still say that there was a certain look in Anna's eyes today that I've not seen in a long while. A kind of self-assertive smile, if you know what I mean. And if I didn't know better, I would say that she's got a bit of a grudge to bear. Not going to sort things out in the restaurant, is she? Cos no matter what's going on under the surface, she looked quite confident to me. As if she's gonna give the boot to that waitress you was telling me about.'

Gwen leaned back in the kitchen chair and undid a couple of big buttons on her thick apple-green cardigan. 'I'll be bloody glad when I stop having these hot flushes. I shall throw myself in the Thames if this goes on for much longer.'

Ivy quietly chuckled. 'You stopped having them years ago, Gwen. How old are you?'

'I'll be fifty-nine next birthday. I wonder if those foreigners work the same way as we do. I mean to say, you never see a West Indian woman breaking out in a sweat do yer? Lucky mares.'

'I expect they're exactly the same as us but they don't make a song and a dance and a show of it.' Ivy smiled.

'It's probably down to their black skin. I bet that's what it is. When they lived in the jungle in Africa their skin 'ad to adapt. That's what it'll be. Lucky bastards. *She* was a darkie – the woman my old man ran off wiv.'

Ignoring this because she had heard it all before, Ivy poured a little milk into each of their teacups while her friend fanned her flushed face with Ivy's rolled-up newspaper folded in her hand. 'We're all better off now even if there are more foreigners around. We've got central heating and takeaway Chinese shops. And look at the nice clean white baths we've got to sit in. Our maisonettes are lovely.' She glanced, with a touch of nonchalance, down at the kitchen floor.

'I'm not keen on these cheap tiles you've fitted mind you. I don't think you can go far wrong with lino on the kitchen floor, same as in the lav and bathroom.'

'Each to their own,' said Ivy. 'Each to their own.'

'I still use my old recipe for polishing the floors you know. You can't beat it. It gives a lovely shine and yet you don't slip arse over head.'

'I don't s'pose you miss having coal fires neither?'

'No, I bloody well don't. You can't beat an imitation electric flame. My chap's coming round later on to watch telly by the fire whether it's sunny or not. Ask him how our places compare to that grand old block of flats he lives in. All right, his is free and goes with his job as a porter, but I wouldn't want to live there.'

'Well, you've changed your tune,' said Ivy, topping up her cup with more tea. 'It wasn't so long ago when you was bragging about your new chap living in a grand block of flats up West that 'ad a posh reception, lift and porter.'

'Yeah, but at that time I never knew that he *was* the porter. Crafty fucker never told me that bit. The velvet lined curtains are dusty and faded and smell of stale pipe tobacco, and the glass shades everywhere are beautiful but thick with grime – and most of the bulbs are dead.'

'Just off of Tottenham Court Road by a tree-lined square is what I think you said . . .'

'I did, Ivy, but I don't think the rent is that much. Not by the type of people I seen coming and going. Shoddy old out-of-work actors is what they reminded me of.'

'So your chap's gonna move in with you one day is he? Into your little flat with a sparkling white bath to soak in?'

'No he fucking well ain't! I waited a long time to see the back of my old man and be a single person again. God rest 'is soul, the two-timing bastard. Couldn't keep 'is dick in his trousers for five minutes. The old tart he shacked up with was more than welcome to 'im. My new chap did once ask if he could stop overnight now and then and so I told him to sling 'is hook and not to come back any more if all he wanted me for was my body.'

'But he does 'ave your body, whether he stops over or not.'

'But I only do it to keep him happy and not give him grounds for complaint. He's got a mate you know,' said Gwen, sipping her tea. 'We could go out in a foursome. You look all right once you've put a bit of makeup on. His mate looks smart when he's wearing his suit and tie.'

'Oh yeah? And you've seen 'im have you? This mate of his?'

'Just the once or twice when I went on visits. He lives on the fifth floor, the top floor of the building. Horace. I think he comes from good stock.'

'Oh right. I've come across that type when I cleaned in a gentleman's club in Soho for a while. Black shoes polished so you could see your face in 'em but bloody great holes in the leather soles.'

Quietly chuckling, Gwen slowly shook her head. 'Who gives a fuck so long as they're good lovers? Mine is.'

'Is he now,' said Ivy, sensing a slight tingle inside which she hadn't felt for a long while. 'Well, you'd best ask your Wilfred if he's got a friend for me then, hadn't you? An ordinary good-looking bloke who's neither posh nor poor.'

'Posh or not Horace is a character, and just like you he can play a lovely tune on the piano.'

'Oh? Well that's different. I suppose I could go for a drink with him to see how we get on. How old is he?'

'Course you could. A nice little foursome. And I should fink he's about sixty-odd.'

'Suits me.'

'All right,' said Gwen, draining the tea from her cup. 'I'll broach my chap on the subject this evening before we make love. That kind of talk should turn him on. A lover for you and a lover for me and a foursome on the settee if he fancies it.'

'If your John could hear you now he'd blush redder than a rose. You're a filthy cow at times.'

'He can talk. Now, do you want me to feed one while you feed the other?'

'Could do,' said Ivy. 'Share and share everything alike, eh? Even our lipstick and powder – and you can't get more personal and friendly than that.'

Later on, around two-thirty in the afternoon, safe in the knowledge that her babies were in their grandmother's tender care, Anna made her way to Prima Pasta on a double-decker bus and was a touch angrier than she wanted to be for letting things go on as they had been for too long. As the bus approached Stratford East, she decided to get off one stop short of hers to give herself time to calm down a little and think things through logically as she walked through the back streets. So deep in her thoughts was she, that she hardly noticed the people around her or the traffic.

Her biggest regret was taking Bridget on as assistant manager. Other than a clairvoyant though, nobody could possibly have known that Bridget had been set from the very beginning on having her husband – with the restaurant thrown in as a bonus. But now that Anna did know what was going on, the anger in the pit of her stomach was actually helping her, as if it was a friend willing her on and there for the ride. She knew that what she was about to do could easily be a recipe for disaster where her marriage was concerned, but since that was already broken and being aired in public she felt there was more to be gained than lost.

Her sisters had pulled no punches when they gave her the sordid details the evening before. And now, in the light of day, she could see that they had known exactly what they were doing when they arrived at her door.

The three sisters were as close as they had ever been and this meant as much to her as it did to them and, of course, to their mother, Ivy. 'You have to *learn* to trust friends, Anna,' she murmured, 'but as sure as the moon will come and go family blood will always flow.' Her grandparents had passed away when she was a young girl but some of their old sayings, handed from one generation to another, drifted into her thoughts now and then. Lifting her eyes to the sky, she smiled to herself before silently asking her ancestors in the celestial world to give her the strength to carry through what she had set out to do: get her husband back on her side.

Chapter Three

Glancing up at puffy white clouds drifting across the light blue sunny sky, Anna slowed her pace as she neared the restaurant and remembered good times shared with Frank in the second half of the Swinging Sixties. That's when they had first met, at Tower Hill in his elder brothers' restaurant nightclub – the Lazy Blues. Being at an impressionable age, she had felt a rush of love whenever Frank had smiled at her from behind the bar where he mixed cocktails for customers. The spot had been a favourite of her sisters and it was they who had first taken her there to have a meal and then listen and dance to jazz in a fantastic atmosphere under subdued lighting. For Anna and Frank it had been love at first sight, and after a wonderful nine months of courting, a June wedding, and two years of glorious happiness, they had wanted the next good thing – to start a family.

Later on, once Anna was pregnant and had given up working in their small restaurant in Stratford East to stay at home with only herself for company, she had been thankful for the television and the radio because of the familiar voices of regular disc jockeys and newsreaders. She had often lain on the sofa in the evenings looking up at the ceiling, and the faint patterns cast across it from the rays of the street lamp, the old-fashioned street lamp that glowed through a small gap at the top of their William Morris patterned curtains.

For no reason that she could think of, Anna recalled the time when she had been trying for a baby. When their alarm clock had gone off at the crack of dawn one morning Frank had jumped out of bed in a rush because he had arranged to go early-morning fishing with a friend. Although only half awake at the time, Anna had tugged at his pyjama jacket and dragged him back beneath the covers to make love, because it was the right time of the month according to the chart she had been keeping. And this, of all the times they had followed the regime, was when she had successfully conceived. The one and only occasion when Frank had felt that he had to make love to order.

With all of this going through her mind, Anna willed herself not to weaken her resolve to save her marriage from complete collapse. She had every reason to be screwing her tissue into a tight twist because it did look as if she might have to bring her babies up as a single parent. The thought of being abandoned as her mother had been, terrified her. The day Anna's dad left for work one morning, with a wave and a smile, only to walk away carrying his suitcase and never be seen again was awful. This wasn't what she wanted for herself or for her boys, but she knew she couldn't take any more of Frank's excuses for being late, which had always been the same – the restaurant had been packed to overflowing with customers who wanted to drink and listen to music after time. The more Anna thought about it the more she berated herself for having let things go on the way they had for so long. Now, out in the real world, free from the confines of the four walls of her sitting room and her television serials, she could hardly believe that she had allowed Frank to get away with his lies time and time again.

When curled up in an armchair and watching television by herself, she had often wondered whether to tell her sisters how lonely and miserable she was. And now, because of them, she was going to give marching orders to the girl who loved to flirt. She recalled the day when there had been free drinks and canapés for the regulars at Prima as a kind of a leaving party for Anna. The toast given by Frank, though, had been to the promotion of Bridget from top waitress to his assistant manager, and this *had* hurt.

The regulars, men in particular, had been happy with Anna's replacement and who could blame them? Bridget loved to flirt with her naughty-girl smile and screw-me eyes when at the bar pouring drinks. The men knew that she was married to a decent guy, because Trevor was sometimes there during the evenings, eating pasta and enjoying a glass of wine while waiting for his lovely young wife. This was before Frank had insisted that he was duty bound, as Bridget's employer, to see she got home safe and sound at night and so a mini-cab was ordered especially unless Trevor called in unexpectedly to take his wife home.

Almost at Prima and knowing that Bridget would be there in her role as stand-in manager while Frank was elsewhere, Anna could now hardly wait to walk in unannounced. And why shouldn't she walk in out of the blue? This was her and Frank's restaurant, where they had once been happy to work side by side for hours on end, building Prima Pasta into one of the cool places to eat in the area – a bistro seating forty under subdued lighting and with the sound of love songs playing softly in the background.

At this time of the day it was normally a quiet spell, with mostly locals in for coffee and cakes, or simply lingering after a lunch of the pasta special chalked up on the blackboard as the meal of the day. Neither she nor Frank had set out to pretend that Prima was anything other than an atmospheric, small, family-run place. This had been their dream, something they had talked about for hours on end before they were married.

Anna wondered if her old friend, the palm reader Queenie Brown from Canning Town, had been bang on right when she had told her fortune and predicted that there was going to be a troublemaker in her life. At the time, Anna had laughed at the softly rounded woman with the big bleached white hairdo and old period fox fur coat, but now she wondered if it had been Bridget that Queenie had seen entering into her charts.

Her heart pounding faster the closer she got to the restaurant, Anna distracted herself by turning her attention to the oddballs around her – a singing drunk, a couple of touting prostitutes and the ordinary everyday folk. She knew that Frank was going to be livid with her for going behind his back, but still she was looking forward to it because the adrenaline was kicking in and she had never felt quite like this before. She arrived at the restaurant and pushed open the timber-framed glass entrance door of Prima Pasta to be welcomed by one of her and Frank's favourite records playing on the jukebox – the Kinks and 'Lola' – a song that had always made the couple chuckle whenever they heard it. Inside the small and cosy place, with its dark mustard and red décor, she saw the familiar faces of regulars and suddenly had no qualms about going behind Frank's back.

Nodding at the few relaxed lunchtime regulars, who were sipping coffee or something stronger, Anna showed a special smile to Detective Inspector George Blake, who looked a touch surprised to see her there at this time of the day. George was a warm and friendly guy in his mid-thirties, who also called into her sisters' salubrious home in old Bethnal Green on a regular basis. He, in his cheeky way, deliberately gave Anna the once-over and then winked and smiled at her.

'You're looking more gorgeous than ever, babe,' he said.

'I know I am,' she teased. 'You're not doing so bad either, all suited up and to die for.'

George chuckled as he watched her saunter, a touch sexily, through the restaurant, showing calm and decorum even though her heart was beginning to pound. She went into the small bar at the back and to the girl who she was about to send packing. A small burst of anger swept through her when she saw Bridget, who was dressed to kill. Anna's first thought was that she looked like a shop model except that she was pressing the keys of an adding machine and tilling up the takings. She was wearing a red silk dress with long tight sleeves and a full circle skirt, and her long ginger curly hair had been set to look as if it was tumbling naturally around her shoulders, perfectly dishevelled.

Anna stared at the back of her rival and so wanted to strangle her swan-like neck. 'You look glamorous today, Bridget,' she said, keeping her temper nicely in check while taking the girl by complete surprise. 'All dressed up with somewhere to go are we?'

The girl glanced sideways at her with an expression that was obviously meant to show that Anna looked like something the cat had dragged in. 'Oh, it's you, Anna. I didn't notice you come in.'

'Well, don't sound so surprised, I'm not a she-devil,' Anna laughed.

'You startled me, that's all.' Bridget spoke quietly and with a hint of practised superiority. 'Creeping about like Jesus himself. What brings you in today?'

'I wasn't creeping Bridget, I was arriving,' said Anna, and then, 'I'm not sensing a touch of dishonour am I? You didn't have your hand in the till perchance?'

With one eyebrow raised Bridet majestically turned her back to Anna and continued with the work in hand. 'I'll presume that was a joke,' she said, cool and calculating. This girl knew exactly how to put a person down.

'Presume away, sweetheart, but there's no need for you to look so anxious. It would come as no surprise to me. It's common practice, from what I've heard.' Enjoying herself now, Anna pushed her fingers through her soft blonde hair and then leaned on the bar. 'Quite a few of you temping staff steal a bit of cash from the till now and then, and who can blame you? Long hours and little reward. That can't be much fun.'

'You're probably right there, but I'm not temping, Anna. Let's not forget that I'm permanent staff. There's a huge difference. And in any case, I wouldn't touch a penny of Frank's money.'

'Permanent? Don't be *too* cocksure,' said Anna, her confidence rising by the second. 'You've not passed your apprenticeship yet. A year or so? That's nothing in the bigger picture, but don't worry. I'm not here to give you the sack today.'

'The thought hadn't crossed my mind.' Bridget looked far too cocksure for her own good. Throwing Anna a single look of derision, she turned back to the till. Speaking quietly so that she could only just be heard, she said, 'I think you're a little out of touch, Anna, and when I said you were creeping about – it wasn't meant as an insult. You're being far too sensitive and I'm not sure why. There's really no need for it.'

Allowing this to go above her head, Anna crossed her arms, narrowed her angry green eyes and looked intently at the cow. 'I told you, Bridget – I wasn't *creeping*, I was *arriving*. There's a big difference. But then you've got your mind on other things haven't you, and guilt is bound to fuck up your thinking.'

'My mind is on my work actually.' Bridget turned around yet again and looked directly into Anna's face saying, 'I can't say that I know what you mean by the word guilt?'

Anna laughed. 'I'm sure. And as for your mind being on your work – it's what you get paid for. And don't let's forget *who* it is that pays your wages.'

With the Cuban heel of her boot Anna then kicked

80

the bar door shut behind her. 'I think it's time that you and me had a little chat in private, don't you?'

'Really?' Bridget chuckled condescendingly. 'I hope you're not seriously going to try and give me the sack. I know that Frank likes to give the impression that this is a family-run business but he needs me more than even *he* realises, so if you're thinking of replacing me with a cousin or aunt or your own mother, I should forget it. And as for Frank, he's rubbish at keeping the books so as not to raise the eyebrows of the taxman. It takes a certain kind of a brain to keep this little business shipshape and looking as if it doesn't make too much profit.'

Then, just a touch too confident and a little too full of herself, she added, 'I wouldn't like to think of the state of the business if I were to leave it to Frank to keep the accounts.'

'Wouldn't you?' said Anna, smiling demurely. 'How generous you are with your loyalty towards your boss. And you don't have to tell me that my husband's not been keeping his mind on his work, Bridget, because I already know that. You'd be surprised just how many others know it as well. We'll have to run a few questions past him, won't we? Do you think he might have been messing with grubby little whores dressed in silk, satin and lace?'

'I hardly think so, Anna.' Bridget offered a patronising smile.

'Well, do you know what, Bridget? I couldn't give a toss what you think.'

'Oh dear, it's that time of the month is it? What we

women have to suffer. I can't imagine men putting up with the monthly curse, can you?'

'It's not *that* time of the month actually and you're not really listening. I *said* . . . we'd have to run a few questions by Frank. And the question number one would be why does he come home from the restaurant at the end of the day much later than he should do? And why do his boxer shorts smell of perfume even after they've been in the soiled laundry bin for a day or so? I think you know the perfume, it's the one you're wearing now.'

'I can't imagine Frank going anywhere near a local whore, if this is what you're getting at. I can hardly believe you would think such a thing. But then hormones when all over the place *can* be a puzzle at times.'

Anna took a breath and folded her arms as she fixed her eyes on her rival's back. She was determined to make her stop what she was doing of her own accord. 'You don't think he's screwing some dirty little tart on the side then? That the rumour spreading about Frank treating himself to a whore in his and *my* flat upstairs is unfounded?'

'Frank? Going with a paid whore? I hardly think so.'

'I never said *paid* whore did I? But then what does a bottle of that perfume you're wearing cost these days?'

'Very amusing, Anna.' Bridget turned to face her, slightly curling her lip as she raised an eyebrow. 'If you don't mind my saying so, Frank isn't the sort to pay for his privileges. You're being a touch too hard on him. He's good with the customers because of his personality – they love him to bits, as we all do – but I can't see

82

him wanting to touch the type of person you suggest. He's not like that. He runs this place as if he was born to it. He's hopeless with calculations and figures and keeping the books but that's what I'm here for. I was top of the class when it came to mathematics.'

'I bet you were,' Anna smiled. She then leaned forward and sniffed the air. 'Mmm. I think that's French perfume you've got on, isn't it?'

'It is French actually,' the girl said, lowering her eyes and focusing on her book-keeping. 'It was a gift.'

Anna laid a gentle hand on Bridget's silky soft padded shoulder and smiled at her, and she wasn't sure if it was an expression of fury that she saw in those soulless brown eyes or fear. Bridget, for most of the time, from what she had heard, behaved as if she was a simple girl up from the country, so it was hard to tell.

Carefully lifting thick strands of the girl's long ginger hair Anna twirled it around her fingers and held it tightly. Then, pushing her face up close to Bridget's said, 'You're nothing more than a tart really, but you set your sights high – I'll give you that. And you've got what you wanted. Frank. And he gets what he wants.'

The silence between the two of them for that split second could have been cut with a knife had it not been for the large, round, red wall clock ticking loudly. The clock which Anna had chosen, a bright and bold timepiece that was hung on the wall on the morning of the day that she and Frank opened for the first time. 'Pick up your handbag, Bridget,' Anna said quietly. 'Then lift your coat off the hanger and walk out of here with your head high if you want to save face.' She then let go of the girl's hair.

83

'I'll send your cards on and I'll leave it to you to tell that poor sucker of a husband of yours why you've been given the boot. You can tell him all about it yourself . . . how you've been sleeping with *my* husband in the afternoons, between lunch and evening shifts and then again around the midnight hour.'

Anna leaned closer as she whispered, 'Sleeping with Frank wasn't part of the job description. I know you've been sleeping with my husband and I know exactly how long it's been going on for. Frank's been giving you one while I've been in our house, our *home*, bottle-feeding one baby after the other. *Our* babies. *Mine* and *Frank's* twins. I wonder what your mother would say if she knew how disgracefully you, the good Christian girl, behaves? And what about your daddy, Bridget? Do you think he would be proud of his little girl?'

Bridget remained silent in the face of this onslaught, but Anna wasn't done yet.

'I suppose you do know,' she went on, 'that you're a running joke with the customers? My sisters tell me that the men have bets as to what colour silk knickers you'll flash when you're sitting on your favourite bar stool. You know, when you're in your teasing mood, and flippantly cross and uncross your legs while sipping a glass of white wine. You present yourself as the naive girl whose mouth wouldn't melt butter and then behave like a trollop. And you've been drinking too much white wine during working hours – or so I've heard. You've turned out to be a bit of a lush all round, really. Does that poor sod of a husband know what you get up to in mine and Frank's dirty old bed upstairs?

84

'I think you should talk to Frank, Anna. Not that he's going to be pleased about this. He won't be.'

'Go and get your coat and handbag, Bridget – and leave quietly. And don't ever cross this threshold again. I can't imagine what your family must think of you. I mean to say, you must have got some practice in back home for when you came to London for the big time. How many marriages did you wreck before you set your sights on Frank?'

Anna's angry green eyes bored into Bridget's dark brown ones as she said, 'Take your wages and get out of our lives.'

'But you've got it all wrong,' protested Bridget, determined to score a point. 'It wasn't me who did the chasing. It was Frank. I told him that it wasn't fair on you and he shouted at me, told me not to interfere in his private life.'

'You mean he's been horrible to you as well? Oh dear. That can't be right, can it?'

'Frank has *never* been horrible to me. But he wouldn't listen when I tried to tell him that we weren't being fair on you. You know what he's like once he digs his heels in over something—'

'There's no swaying the bastard is there.' Anna slowly shook her head as she said, 'You've been had, sweetheart. He's been using you.'

'Look, I know this is hard for you – but we are serious about each other. And you might as well know now that Frank wants the twins with us once we're settled into a new house . . . once they're old enough to go to a private nursery school.'

Anna raised her eyebrows in mock surprise. 'Really?

85

Well, he hasn't mentioned a word of this to me. And what about you? Once you're in this *new house* that you speak of? Will you want me to come and go? To visit my boys and their new mummy? Shall I be the one to baby-sit while you're in the restaurant working? Me and Frank by ourselves again and making love the way we used to? Me the rude girl and you the woman scorned? Of course – this is all presuming that you *want* my boys as part of the package?'

'God no! It's not what *I* want.' Bridget smiled as she raised a finely plucked eyebrow. 'I don't want to look after children thank you – my own *or* yours.'

'Oh, I see . . . and Frank knows this, does he? That you've got no maternal instincts whatsoever?'

'Not yet. But who knows?'

Flabbergasted by the gall of the girl and with no thought of the consequences Anna took hold of Bridget's thick wiry hair again with her left hand and clenched her right hand into a fist. As she pulled her arm back ready to land an almighty blow on that pert little nose, the door behind her opened and a much stronger hand gripped hers. The hand of Detective Inspector George Blake.

'This isn't like you, Anna,' he said, smiling warmly at her. 'No one's worth bruising your knuckles for, darling. Leave it be, eh?'

'I appreciate your concern George,' said Anna, staring into his face, 'but this is between us two. No doubt you've got your reasons for not wanting her face in a mess but there are plenty more where this one comes from.'

George's face softened as he looked into Anna's.

'Don't be daft. She's a married woman. And her husband's a nice guy, a good and honest working man. So leave it be, eh?'

A few seconds ticked by as she stared at him. He was giving her a message with just one look. A message that she had seen before. One of honest-to-goodness respect. She had known him for a long while and not only trusted him but liked him a lot. Respecting his timing, she slowly nodded. 'All right, George . . . I take your point. But leave us to sort this out for ourselves, eh?'

'Absolutely, babe – as long as you stop being silly and don't give me cause to have to call my boys in blue.' He gave her a friendly wink and went back to the lads at the table in the front of the restaurant. Bridget, still in Anna's grip, made the mistake of grinning slyly at her and it took Anna all her inner strength not to do what she wanted to do: slam Bridget's face down onto the bar.

'Lucky for me that our family friend George Blake stopped me from having to serve time because of you. And lucky old you that I've not splattered your feeble brains across the bar.'

She was about to slip down from the bar stall when Bridget pulled her arm back ready to punch Anna in the face. Had the girl not lost her footing an almighty blow would have landed between Anna's eyes, but wearing her red four-inch-stiletto-heeled shoes, it was hardly surprising that Bridget stumbled and fell. She crashed down awkwardly, her flailing arm catching a tray filled with empty wine glasses on the way just before her face hit the stone floor of the bar. Her scream mingled with the echoing sound of breaking glass as well as the song playing on the jukebox: Ray Charles singing 'Your Cheating Heart' – a record that George Blake had put on just for the hell of it.

As she leaned over the counter and looked down Anna saw blood trickling from Bridget's nose and, with false compassion, she asked her if she was okay. This could have been seen as a nice gesture had Anna not been smiling when she said it. 'That looks a bit serious to me,' she murmured. 'I hope you can find another over-sexed married man to bed you,' she added, 'because Frank won't want you with a crooked nose, sweetheart, trust me. He's a fussy fucker that husband of mine. You might be able to pick up one of his brothers though. They like a cheap Woolworths lipstick and powder whore now and then. I'd go for Johnny if I were you, not Alfie. Alfie has a penchant for pretty boys as well as girls. You might catch something you wouldn't want and pass it on to that poor sod of a husband of yours.'

Her head held high, her chin forward, Anna walked through the restaurant on her way out and gave Detective Inspector George Blake a wink and a smile and then blew him a kiss which he pretended to catch and put into his top pocket. He had been staring out of the window and looking the other way on purpose so as not to witness any bloodshed. He returned her smile with a look of gentle admonishment. He was a handsome sod and knew it. Handsome and sexy and someone who, for the cheek of it, had light-heartedly propositioned Anna more than once when she had served him at the table.

'Anna's a little cracker on the quiet,' said one cousin to the other. I wonder if she was one of them sixteen- and seventeen-year-old girls who wore no brassiere beneath their see-through blouses a few years back?'

'I very much doubt it,' said George, fed up with his younger cousin.

'Fancy one of your blokes arresting them girls for indecent behaviour. They brightened up our day, they did. I remember one in particular who worked on the forecourt of the Silverstone Garage in Finchley. I can't remember why I had gone to that area but a more beautiful girl you couldn't have wished to see. So what do we do about that little accident then?'

'Leave it be,' said George. 'Give her a bit of privacy to pick herself up. She's been humiliated.'

Exhilarated by having got rid of the tightness in her chest, Anna enjoyed the sense of being on top of things again. It was an incredible feeling. She didn't give a toss that George and his associates had heard all that had gone on. In fact she was revelling in it. She had known the small group since they were all rough kids on the street in and around Bethnal Green – a time when it was not unusual to see one of them with their arse hanging out of torn trousers. They were also the drinking partners of her sisters Hazel and Linda.

Once she was outside and walking away, George watched her through the window and then raised an eyebrow at one of his cousins who was grinning at him. 'What are you gonna do now, George? Strut out the back as if you're one of the Kray twins and warn Frank's lover off?'

'Do me a favour. One of the Krays? Neither of the twins would have known how to handle that little scene. They're not all they're cracked up to be you know.'

His cousin leaned back in his chair and laughed. 'You'd better not say that once they're out and about again.'

'I don't think they will be, David. They won't see the green green grass of home again. They were all right when they were kids on the street. They got too big for their boots, that was the trouble. They didn't live far from Mum and Dad once they moved to Valence Road – a three-up-two-down with an outside lavatory. Those back streets were a bit of a ghetto in them days for boxers, gamblers, hard drinkers and villains with one gang fighting another for competition. Mum and Dad moved out as soon as they could and got one of the first of those council flats to 'ave been built close to the Hackney Downs.'

'So you've said before. So what are you gonna do now, hero? Go and kiss the little tart out the back better?'

'Not yet. I know when to leave things be. I'll give her time to regain a bit of dignity.' He winked at the boys and lit a cigarette, a little more pleased with himself than he wanted to let on. It was Anna he was thinking about. He had just been her knight in shining armour and put a stop to something that could have seen her in trouble.

Once outside Anna drew in the fresh air and felt a tingling sensation in her spine . . . one mission was over and another more pleasant one was about to begin. A bit of shopping therapy in the West End where she would treat herself to an outfit or two on her and Frank's account. She hadn't been one for expensive designer clothes in the past, but having seen the way that Bridget dressed these days, in stunning clothes, she quite fancied the idea of spending time and money on herself. Especially now that she felt sure Frank had been treating his lover to the latest fashionable outfits on the sly.

With the sun on her face and her adrenaline calming down, Anna had a change of heart about her shopping trip for now and decided to postpone it for another day. She went into a phone booth instead, to call her sisters. It was them she wanted to be with right now, not pushy saleswomen. She told herself that she could always go on a spending spree up West whenever the fancy took her. She had been so maternal and housewifely since she had got pregnant that she had almost forgotten the old Anna that was tucked away. The Anna who had always loved to have fun and follow the fashion. She smiled as she remembered the daring mini-skirts she once wore when her hair was long and straight, her fringe thick and covering her eyebrows. A time when she wore dark eye-shadow and lash-lengthening black mascara and pale apricot lipstick.

In the Sixties, when it was a case of anything goes, Anna had bought herself a 1930s fur coat from Oxfam and big floppy hats in the Portobello Road market. Just one trip to Biba in Kensington High Street and she would be right back there – in the thick of it and with a little more money to spend now than she had had when she was a young and free single girl. She smiled as she remembered the times when she and her sisters enjoyed going to Sam Widges' coffee bar in Berwick Street, Soho, where senior citizens mixed with the new look beatniks who filled the place, all of them making a cup of coffee last a whole afternoon. It hadn't been a regular haunt of Anna's but it was a great place to pop into for a seat, a cigarette and a sandwich when her sisters had been in the mood to 'shop until you drop'. This had been a time when the upper-middle-class young were enjoying love-ins and burning joss sticks at Woburn Abbey and in Hyde Park. For a couple of years it seemed as if Flower Power and pop concerts were everywhere.

With these recollections floating in and out of her mind, as well as the vision of Bridget with a broken bleeding nose, Anna felt as if she was back to her old self again. And she had her adorable babies to love and care for. She had been shopping for her clothes locally, and mostly in markets, of late without a thought for fashion, but from now on she would use her and Frank's cheque book to equal the way he had been using it. She had been told more than once that she had a good dress sense and a flair for style and now she was going to make the most of it.

Her shoulder-length dark blonde hair, together with her big soft green eyes, gave her a kind of Swedish look and, even though she chose the new tailored style when going for a meal out, she was still comfortable in jeans and tops. She loved stiletto-heeled shoes as well as Cuban-heeled boots, especially the ones she was wearing right then, their heels tapping out a message as she walked – a message for Frank and his whore: Stuff you, stuff you, and stuff you.

Determined not to carry on trying so hard to be a mature woman but to get back to being a happy-go-lucky young lady, she was already on the road because she didn't really care what Frank was going to say once he had been told of the chaos that she had caused at the restaurant. As far as she was concerned Bridget deserved all she got.

'You've been a silly girl, darlin',' said George Blake as he kneeled on one leg behind the bar and briefly examined Bridget's damaged face, which was pale against the red blood trickling from her swollen nose. Handing her a second white glass-towel that he had soaked in warm water to wash away the blood from her face and neck, he did actually feel sorry for someone he had never been able to take to. Helping her up he spoke quietly, saying, 'I'm sure you must have been told before, sweetheart, to never take a leak on the boss's doorstep?' He then scooped her into his strong arms as if she were as light as a feather.

Her head flopped back and her long tresses soaked in blood, Bridget moaned as George carried her to a cosy corner out of sight of the lads in the restaurant and the harmless old tramp – also a regular – who had seen it all before during his lifetime in one place or another where he might have hung his battered hat. To George's way of thinking Bridget at least deserved privacy, and it would be too degrading for her if any fresh customers were to slip into the restaurant before

93

the open sign on the door was turned around to show *Closed until seven p.m.*

Gently lowering Bridget to the floor, George grabbed a small bundle of clean white tea towels from behind the bar to place under her head. Carefully studying the damage to her face, he placed the fleshy part of his palms on either side of her nose and said, 'Think of your mother smiling at you, sweetheart.'

Then, with a tried and tested jerk and a click, he fixed her together again as her echoing scream resounded throughout the small restaurant. 'It might swell up like a pumpkin, darlin',' he said, 'but at least you won't have to go to hospital.'

With her head resting on the makeshift pillow, Bridget looked up at him pale and in pain. She could feel the throbbing and closed her eyes, wishing that she could start the day all over again. The next thing she knew, the man who she felt sure had the hots for Anna was laying his cool wet sparkling-white handkerchief over her injury. 'Do you want me to give Frank a call or should I send one of the boys to get your husband Trevor?' he said.

'Neither,' was all she managed to say – but her mind *was* ticking over. She was not only in pain and damaged but humilated, and even in this state she vowed that she would use George Blake, the bent detective inspector, as her counter-attack. She would tell Frank a little white lie – that George had been sniffing around Anna and been familiar with her when she just happened to drop in for a drink and a bite to eat at lunchtimes while he was at Tower Hill, and when George just happened to be there too. And she wouldn't stop there. She was a good and convincing liar and always had been. She would then say that one or two of the older generation who came in for their discounted spaghetti Bolognese on Thursdays had been placing bets as to who the baby twins looked most like, Frank or George. Lies, all lies ... but, helped by her pain, she was already thinking about revenge.

'How about if I get someone to drive you home where you can sleep this off in the quiet, Bridget?' George offered, not because he wanted to look after her welfare but because he was protecting the reputation of a woman who deserved better. Six years older than Anna, George hadn't played in the streets with her as a lad, but he had seen her out and about when he was a fresh young copper on the beat and she was only seventeen, and he'd sometimes advised her not to go down the same road as her sisters, that she was too soft for their world. She had known exactly what he meant of course and appreciated his brotherly kind of protection. George had also sat chatting to her now and then when off-duty and when she had been with her sisters in Frank's brothers' restaurant. But now of course, even though she was younger than him, she was a mature woman and the mother of twins. Even so he still felt duty bound to watch out for her as if she was family.

Waiting for Bridget to say what she wanted him to do next, George could see that she would be all right once she asked for a bucket. Throwing up was going to be painful but from all he had seen before, it was the best thing she could do so as to shift any forming blood clots. As far as he could tell there would be no permanent damage. Carefully lifting her into a sitting position, he gently propped her against the wall and went to collect a slop bucket from behind the bar to leave by her side. Without saying another word, he left her to it and strolled back through the restaurant to his table and his cousins, Jimmy and David, every bit the true gentleman. He knew that the delectable Bridget would not have wanted him to see her being sick. It was far too degrading for a lady who sometimes behaved like a tramp by sleeping in other people's beds.

'She all right?' said Jimmy, containing laughter but grinning like a schoolboy all the same.

'Will be now. She slipped on the wet floor, on slops from the coffee machine. Her nose was put out of joint but it's back – just like Humpty Dumpty. So ... to business.' He couldn't be bothered to fill in the gaps and nor did he wish to.

'Don't you need another scotch after that little incident?'

'You're like a big girl at times, Jimmy.'

'All right, all right,' said Jimmy, knowing he had gone too far with the banter. 'It was a joke. All right? No sense of humour, that's your trouble.'

It was hardly a side-splitting joke but then Jimmy, the juvenile of the three of them, wasn't all that bright. But he was a relative and he was reliable and could be trusted – and that was what mattered most because this little firm of smalltime friendly villains only worked with mates or members of their own family.

George leaned over the table and kept his voice low as he said, 'So it's Sam's removal van then?'

'Yep – and that was one of the best ideas you've 'ad

yet, George.' David grinned. 'My cousin the detective inspector. All brains *and* brawn, not to mention sex appeal ...' Now it was his turn to torment their elder. 'Got that little bit of skirt from the Midlands tucked up nicely out the back 'ave yer?' He grinned. 'Gonna massage her pride once we've gone? A turn-on for you is it – a busted nose?'

'Watch your mouth,' said George, giving the fledgling one of his notorious icy stares. The lad had thoughts that could not be further from the truth. He had never taken to the girl and had had to bite his tongue once he realised that Frank was screwing her. He had seen her type before and kept at arm's length because of Anna being almost like family. George had had mistresses in his time, but if Bridget had come on to him he would have given her the cold shoulder. She reeked of trouble as far as he was concerned and now, if Anna wasn't careful, the tart would give her more grief than she could handle. He hadn't been far wrong of course, because when Anna finally gave up working in the restaurant, Bridget was straight in with not a trace of remorse in the way she calculatingly worked on Frank – the easy target. George and Anna had sometimes sat talking in the early afternoons when it was quiet in Prima Pasta and Frank was working at his brothers' restaurant or had gone upstairs to bed for a short nap, leaving her to run the place. His cousins Jimmy and David felt that they had picked up on stronger emotions than just friendship and liked to tease George a bit now and then. Giving him a knowing look David quietly chuckled.

'I know her out the back ain't your style. It's Anna

who's caught your eye.' He grinned, and thought he had managed to draw a guilty smile from George who he felt he knew inside out. They had after all played in the filthy back streets together as kids and were more like brothers than cousins. George raised one eyebrow and held his tongue.

'Right – back to business. The arrangements and expenses will cost us a grand but at least that includes the loan of the van as well,' said George, back on the subject of illicit business.

'More than worth it,' Jimmy replied, thoughtful and preoccupied. 'How many tea chests can you get into the van?'

'All four of them,' said Dave. 'You can leave the arrangements to me from now on. It's watertight. The gear will be in the loose tea leaves in the tea chests, nicely hidden should for any reason we get stopped en route. And each chest can take four gross, all nicely tucked away in the leaves. Two thousand, three hundred gold lighters at ten pounds a piece before expenses.' He sniffed and then raised an eyebrow. 'In a couple of days' time we'll be walking away with around five grand each I reckon. And that's why this will be my last involvement with you lot. You're younger than me. You can take over while I make the most of retirement.'

'Now when was the last time I heard that,' said Jimmy, chuckling. He slowly shook his head as a big smile spread across his face. 'Five fucking grand. I can't believe it. I could buy myself a little flat ... fly off for a holiday in Hollywood. And still have a bit of spending money left.'

'Don't be fucking stupid,' said George. 'Do any of that and the old Bill will grab you by the collar. Put it under the floorboards for a year or so and don't be flash with it. I won't come anywhere near you if you attract attention by being flash. The days of greasing palms for silence are over. That's why I'm getting out of the Met ... before the major clean-up campaign starts.'

David quietly laughed now. 'How many times 'ave we heard that. You won't quit. You were born to make and break the law.'

'This time I mean it. I'm getting out of the force. While I'm still young enough to start up my own business. A legitimate business.'

'Such as?' said Dave.

'Not sure yet. But I've got a few ideas I'm mulling over which is for me to know and you to find out.'

'Each to their own.' David grinned and then said, 'I take it the old farmhouse close to the barn is still vacant and all right for two days' storage with no nosy parker about?'

'I should say so,' Jimmy cut in. 'That farmhouse ain't fit to live in. It was nigh on derelict, with rats running all over the fucking place last time I was there. It needs bulldozing.'

'Don't bet on it. Some of them old farms are being bought up and renovated for anyone with an eye for a bargain and a bit of money in the bank.' George looked from one to the other of his cousins. 'The living-off-the-land lot who want the good life in the country are snapping up all the little bargains from what I've heard. Then there are that lot who like to squat and them who fancy a bit of communal living and a bit of love, light and peace. Pain in the neck they are. Kent should be all right for a while though. And nobody's got any reason or right to go near the barn we're renting. That's where you lads should be investing your ill-gotten gains. Old neglected cottages in the sticks, before the property magnates pick up on it and buy everything that hasn't got legs or wheels.' He leaned back in his chair and went all thoughtful. 'I wouldn't mind a country farmhouse to do up and retire in,' he murmured. Anna was still shadowing his mind.

'You must be kidding,' said Jimmy. 'Nostalgia and romance with the gypsies in their wagons and us lot living in the huts in days gone by has gone to your head, mate. Shame, though, that them hop-picking days are well and truly over. More's the pity.

'It'll be good to have a look at them old brick huts again. It was like a spooky little village the last time we went . . . that must have been a good year and a half ago. Even the old cookhouse was still standing. You remember that, George? Black corrugated iron roof and sides and a row of brick back-to-back fireplaces and shelter for cooking when it was pissing down with rain. All it needs is a young farmer to come along and plant the fields with vines and you'd 'ave plenty of London-ers more than ready to go hop-picking and fruit picking.'

'Never mind hop-picking. That's all in the past. I'm talking about the farmhouse and outbuildings,' said George. 'Maybe we should get in with an offer. We could take our time and turn it into a modest hotel once I've left the Met.'

'Whatever,' said David, a touch bored. 'The boys will pick up the tea chests from the barn and drop off the goods in Thetford. It can all be done and dusted within forty-eight hours and no trail left behind us.'

'And a brilliant bit of planning, even if I do say so myself.' Jimmy gave both men a wink. 'You won't find better brains than mine.'

'Keep your voice down, an' don't get too fucking loose with the tongue. And make sure the Thetford boys pay up on delivery. That, or no deal.'

Jimmy fell back in his chair and splayed his hands. 'What d'yer mean – loose with the tongue? There's no one in other than Tommy the tramp and he's too far gone on meths to make head or tail of us for fuck's sake. You're getting too paranoid, George. You never used to be so touchy. I think it must be time for you to get out and live with the carrot crunchers, my old son.'

'Your silly talk is getting on my fucking nerves, Jimmy. The slag's out the back don't forget, and she spells trouble.' George leaned back in his chair and rubbed his eyes. 'Anyway, this one will be a nice little earner and my last. You can all piss off to South Spain again for a couple of months while I stop behind and keep a straight face but then that's it. I'm packing it in. I can't go on working twelve or so hours a day on either side of the law.'

'Well, you would grow up to be a detective inspector,' Jimmy goaded.

George was in no mood for jest right then. He stubbed his cigarette out in the ashtray and checked his wristwatch. 'Right. I'm off to Tattler Street. Another midnight robbery to sort out.'

'Again?'

'Yeah. This is it though. Sammy isn't gonna get away with any more insurance claims. That's why he's made this the big one. Sly old fucker's gonna retire due to his heart complaint.'

'I'm sure,' said David. 'Nuffing wrong with 'is heart.'

'No. But there will be if he don't pack it in now.'

'Where's he gonna retire to then? Not fucking Spain I 'ope. Don't want the old fart out there chatting up the dolly birds in the beach bars. We'll all end up in nick.'

'No. He's off to Hawaii. It's been his dream for donkey's years and he can't wait to go. Give it two months and he'll probably drop dead from screwing every call girl going.' With that George got up and nodded towards the back. 'Stay until Bridget's okay. I'll drop in at Tower Hill and let Frank know there's been a fracas between the girls.' He winked at his cousins and left them to it.

All in all it had been a constructive afternoon and George had a good feeling inside, which he felt must be all down to the mention of the old farmhouse in Kent. He had always hankered after a place in the country, especially in that part of the world where as a kid he lived for five or six weeks of a year, picking hops and scrumping apples. He was more than ready to hand in his resignation and felt sure that now was the time to think seriously about making an investment for the future. He had had enough of living and working in London. On his way out of the restaurant, he slipped a five-pound note into the waiter's top pocket and told him to lock up and keep his mouth shut about the little dispute between the women. 'Bridget slipped on—'

'Sure, sure. I know. My fault,' the waiter cut in. 'I should've mopped up some drink I spilt behind the bar earlier.'

'Good man,' said George, squeezing the young waiter's shoulder. 'Keep the girls' conversation to yourself for now, okay? The little cat-fight's best forgotten.'

'Cat-fight?' the waiter smiled. 'Don't know what you're talking about.'

'Good man,' said George again, giving him a wink. 'Stay lucky.' Once outside in the street he glanced up at the sky to see clouds on their way over.

'Fucking weather,' he murmured. 'Fucking London.'

Chapter Four

Once she got out of the taxi at Victoria Park, Anna paid her fare and went through the large wrought-iron gates into the park gardens and boating lake. She was delaying the moment of going to pick up the twins from her mother's place so that she could have more time to herself to think things through. The echoing sound of stiletto heels tapping on the flagstones that was coming from the high-heeled shoes of three girls close by, reminded her of Bridget and the crack she had heard when the girl's face hit the floor in the restaurant. She felt a touch guilty at how painful it must have been but wasn't sorry that it had happened. She still felt sick inside but this was more to do with the reason she had had to go on her mission in the first place.

Ivy's flat was only a bus ride away from Victoria Park and Anna knew that her babies were being looked after properly, so she had no reason to worry or feel guilty and this comforting thought helped. All she wanted right now was to see her sisters and have them tell her that she had done the right thing. But she also felt the need for a stroll along a tree-lined parade, which brought back warm and comforting memories from her childhood. She wanted to be in Victoria Park and she wanted to sit on a bench overlooking the lake to watch the wildlife and the people she didn't know, coming and going.

She was calmer now, mainly because her anger and revenge had been spent at the restaurant face to face with the girl who Frank was possibly seeing as his future wife. Aware of her own footsteps now echoing on the pavement, she stopped to rest on a bench by the lake and, as she looked about her, she saw an old man walking slowly along with two sticks to help him and smiled hello. He smiled and nodded back and his efforts simply to get from one end of the park to the other made her feel humble. She began to think about the things that had been going wrong in her small world and how much of the blame might lie on her own shoulders. Questions began drifting through her mind: had she been so wrapped up in trying to get pregnant for all of those long months that she had killed off the passion Frank had once felt for her? And once the babies were born had she left him out in the cold? Or had she let herself go by always being in her dressing gown in the mornings before Frank left for work?

Her anger over her husband's affair now subdued, she was beginning to feel gutted inside. She only just managed to fight back tears as she tried to remember the last time Frank had hugged her lovingly. Her emotions all over the place, she measured his good points against his bad and a sense of fighting her corner for him was beginning to creep in. Ever since they had met as teenagers, she hadn't looked at another man – not before the ring was on her finger – or afterwards, when quite a few vain bastards had tried to win her over while she was working at the restaurant.

Of course she realised that she was young enough to marry again but this wasn't what she wanted. She and Frank had once been so happy and deeply in love that his indifference towards her still didn't seem possible. His loyalty and love towards her had all but come to a standstill since Bridget had stepped across their threshold to breeze her way into their world.

Leaving the park for her sisters' place, Anna strolled through the back streets into old Bethnal Green and passed boys kicking a football around. She tried to imagine a time when her twins would grow into lads and be doing the self-same thing. Now, with this peaceful time to herself, she began to relax more and more.

'It's partly your own fault, Anna,' she murmured. 'You should have read the signs earlier. You should have taken notice of the little warning bells in your head when you first saw the way she stood close, almost touching him, when they were having a conversation at the end of an evening shift at Prima and while a love song was played on the jukebox.'

Slowing down once she reached old Bethnal Green, she cleared her throat and braced herself for Hazel and Linda. They still looked upon her as the baby of the family, even though she was coming up to twenty-six. Just thinking about the way they were still over-protective brought a small warm glow to her heart. She of all people knew that, despite what others might think, they were good girls even though they loved the glamorous side of life, rubbing shoulders with the rich, the famous and a few carefully selected professional criminals. Criminals who paid for their pleasure out of the wealth they made on the backs of those richer than themselves.

The specially selected classy prostitutes on their virtuous list were not always from working-class backgrounds but came from all walks of life, and were chosen by Hazel and Linda for their beauty, intelligence and wit. They knew that most men liked or needed to escape from their humdrum lives and be pampered now and then and the girls were more than happy to fulfil their fantasies, weird or wonderful. Having been in this line of business for almost ten years Linda and Hazel had compiled quite a portfolio of men who totally trusted their integrity.

Nobody other than Anna's sisters got to see into the little red leatherbound book which held names and phone numbers of those gentlemen who wished to be fully protected from exposure: the titled, the famous, and one or two from the rich list in the Sunday newspapers. The reputation of Call A Girl Company was growing; it was becoming an exclusive gentleman's club in its own right for those who preferred to spend romantic nights in the house of assignation or in top-notch classy hotels in and around London. The company also catered for men who liked sleazy boarding rooms for their illicit nights of fantasy. It made no difference to Hazel and Linda so long as their clients treated the girls with respect and providing their wallets could allow them to be part of the exclusive club, which was now being praised in certain quarters, albeit in hushed whispers.

Hazel and Linda owned the detached building which

they had turned into a spacious, state-of-the-art Victorian house from a once dark sweatshop and boot-making factory. With a handsome loan as well as their savings, the girls had managed to see it renovated and refurbished until it resembled a palatial home which brought them considerable rewards. At the windows were beautiful drapes, which blended in perfectly with lighting and soft furnishings in all shades of soft gold and red, delivered mostly from Liberty's of London, or Harrods. So successful was their business that Anna's sisters had already cleared their loan and their bank balance was respectably in the black. They were going nowhere but upwards and onwards.

Ivy, choosing not to delve too deeply into what was going on in the house, was proud of her girls for having started up what she liked to refer to as their own dating company. It was a place that brought together lonely people. She thought of it as a kind of marriage bureau, where spinsters and bachelors met and found romance and a loving partner for life. All pie in the sky, but since this was the affectionate promise that the girls advertised in the Sunday newspapers, who was Ivy to question or to knock it?

Smiling to herself, Anna mused on the thought of becoming a hostess herself – to be driven around in a Mercedes or possibly a Rolls-Royce now and then. With all of this going around in her mind she told herself that she would be all right, that she wouldn't fall apart. In a feeble attempt to console herself she said, 'At least I won't have to put up with listening to you snoring in bed, Frank. Nor will I have to listen to your drawn-out drunken lies as to why you come home late at night.'

So deep in her changing thoughts and mood was she that the sound of urgent tooting from a car in the road that she was crossing brought her up with a jolt and her heart seemed to leap up from her chest. She nervously showed a hand and mouthed the word sorry. Sorry that she had almost caused him to kill her. Once safely across to the other side of the road, she burst into tears.

By the time Anna arrived at the wide stone steps leading up to the somewhat grand entrance door to the house that her sisters shared, Anna's mood had switched from melancholy to animated. She wasn't sure why this was the case other than it had slowly dawned on her exactly what she had done. She had been the cause of Bridget having had the accident. Not deliberately so, but it was because of her that she had ended up with her nose out of joint. She laughed inwardly at the memory of the expression on the girl's face just before she disappeared below the bar, as if she were a hand puppet in a Punch and Judy show.

Pulling at the old-fashioned and highly polished brass bell, Anna waited for the click-click of stiletto heels hitting the marble floor inside the wide hallway as one of the girls came to answer the door. She knew that it would be one of the so-called hostesses coming to greet someone she believed to be a client – who would no doubt have been furtively glancing from left to right had he been standing in Anna's place. A posh punter, hoping that there were no policemen or journalists around who might know this elegant building for what it was, a house of assignation. A brothel.

As predicted, it was one of the girls, a twenty-three-year-old known as Angelic who smiled broadly and waved her in with her long ivory and gold cigarette holder. 'The girls are out the back,' she said, happy that she didn't have to put on her mock upper-class accent. 'A right fucking pandemonium you've stirred up, madam.'

'You're kidding me,' said Anna, smiling. 'Word's not got through already has it?'

'Course it fucking well 'as,' said the girl as she closed the front door behind Anna. 'George Blake's bin in. You've only just missed 'im. His Mercedes pulled away not five minutes ago.'

'Oh. That's a shame.'

'He only stayed for five minutes. Lucky the woman who nails that handsome fucker, eh? There's nothing sexier than a man who works both sides of the law in order to fill his coffers – and a detective inspector at that. It's what sweet dreams are made of . . . a handsome fucking bent copper who drives a Mercedes. Brilliant.'

'If you say so. So what mood are Linda and Hazel in?'

'Who knows?' said the girl splaying her hands. 'Those two still change wiv the wind.' The doorbell went again, and the tall slim prostitute wearing a slinky calf-length powder blue designer frock, with long, soft, leg-hugging high-heeled boots to match, went to answer it as Anna slipped into the shadows of the grand hallway and waited to see who was at the door. She liked the idea of it being George making a return visit because he would have seen her coming along while in his car. She cautiously listened unseen, but once she heard Angelic speaking in her pseudo upper-class accent she went through to the room at the back of the house where she knew she would find her sisters.

Unable to resist taking a peep at the gentleman whom the courtesan was leading up the beautiful staircase, she felt sure she recognised him – a blond, brightly dressed hippy in tight silk jeans and shirt with a few clashing neckties thrown in. She thought she might have seen him on the television but couldn't be certain. She went to join her sisters and saw that some of the other girls were there too. Attractive and fun-loving, these elegant young ladies sipped champagne one minute and cracked dirty jokes the next.

'Your ears must be burning, Anna,' said one of the girls who went by the trade name of Mimi. 'George's not long gone. We heard about your poor waitress slipping on her stiletto heel. Didn't push the bitch over did you, darling?'

'No,' said Anna, 'but I would like to have done though.'

'I take it that Mum's looking after our twins,' said Hazel. 'Your old next-door neighbour is a lovely woman, babe, but too old to baby-sit.'

'You know very well that I took them to Mum. I expect she's been on the phone half a dozen times asking if I'm back and giving you a running account of what she's doing with the boys?'

'You lot know each other too well,' laughed another

of the girls, who was quite new and who went by the name of Eliza.

'We're sisters. We should know what each other is thinking because as sure as snow is white we'll never get to the bottom of men.' Anna took a cigarette from a beautiful large silver case on the table and lit it with a matching silver table lighter.

'I didn't fink you smoked, Anna. You 'ave surprised me, gal.' This was Mary, who had her feet in an aromatic footbath ready for a pedicure from the resident beautician. Mary was another kettle of fish – a blowsy bleached blonde with a French pleat hairstyle and big gold earrings. She had been at the top of the tree in her time, but nowadays she was there mostly for the gossip and the old timers who had been her regulars for years, long before she joined Call A Girl Company. It was mostly the old boys with old money that she attracted. They couldn't get enough of her special massage.

'I don't smoke as a rule,' said Anna. 'But sometimes there are exceptions and today is one of them.'

'I should fink so. Slipped? Do me a favour.' Eliza pointed a finger at Anna and narrowed her eyes. 'I hope that nobody saw you push the little fucker over. Her sort would go to a poor man's solicitor and try and sue you for every penny you've got.'

Anna laughed out loud. 'So George really did fill you in then? You wait 'til I get my hands on him.'

'He'd love you to get your hands on 'im. I reckon he secretly fancies you, Anna. Why else would he come and tell us what had happened if you weren't always on 'is mind?'

'You mean he didn't pop upstairs with either of my sisters or one of the girls then.' Anna smiled.

Coming into the room, Anna's sister Linda topped up her own glass with some tonic. 'George never goes upstairs, sweetheart. He might have a favourite that he takes out for a drink and a bit of nooky without us knowing, but he's not a client. A very good friend but not a punter. And Mary obliges now and then with a rub to his shoulders when he's in this room.'

'I don't fink so,' cackled Mary. 'Not with all of you girls around to cramp my style.'

And so the jokes and the banter and the drinking and eating of crisps, salted mixed nuts and any amount of assorted cheese on the board, continued. This scene was one that Anna had been part of several times and always enjoyed. A little and often of being in these surroundings with these girls around and she was guaranteed to laugh. In some strange way this place reminded her more than it had done before that life *could* be fun and life *could* be a lot less serious. She loved the over-the-top plushness of the drapes, carpet and sofas. It was Eliza who brought the attention back to Anna and deliberately so. As far as she could tell, this lovely young woman was in need of a treat – big time.

'So … my little cockney sparrow friend. What 'ave you planned for your birthday? Is it to be a show up West or knees up Mother Brown at your mother's flat?'

'I've not even thought about it, Eliza,' said Anna. 'And to be honest I'm not in the mood to plan anything.'

'Fair enough. But, if we was to get all the girls together and go out to the best restaurant in town, you'd put a bit more lipstick and powder on for that – wouldn't yer?'

Quietly laughing at this woman with the big heart and lovely smile, Anna shrugged. 'How could I possibly refuse?'

'Right well, that's that then. From what your sisters said I gather it's only a few weeks away?'

'That's right. Just a few weeks away.'

'Well, there you are then. We've all got summink to look forward to, haven't we? Now then, what restaurant is it to be? Chinese? Indian? Fish and chips? Or pie and mash?'

'Chinese, but only at Silverlakes.'

'Job done. I couldn't 'ave suggested better myself. Lovely old Chinese family and the best cooks in town. Now – d'yer wanna go there and eat in style or have them deliver in silver terrines?'

'I don't know. I'll tell you later. I don't really want to think about it right now.'

'Say no more. I'll arrange it with you when you're in the mood. And don't fink that I'll forget, because I shan't. Birthdays are important. And your sisters who're stinking rich can foot the bill.'

'Absolutely.' Anna laughed. She loved this place. This was her sisters' day-to-day lifestyle where they reigned supreme but behaved as if each and every one of their girls was equal to themselves. Their spacious sitting room had four luxurious feather-cushioned red and gold brocade sofas which were set around a large custom-made mahogany coffee table with polished brass corners. Above the table and in the centre of this magnificent room hung an exquisite Edwardian cut-glass chandelier, and hanging majestically at the long sash window were midnight blue and gold brocade drapes. The ambience of this drawing room was a match for any exclusive Knightsbridge hotel. The girls had managed to create an atmosphere of an elite residence-cum-cosy nightclub-cum-home. And it would take a miserable sod to think that this was not a fun place to be, with its mix of banter, jokes and discussions. It wasn't the kind of place to be found anywhere else in the world.

Relaxing more and more into the scene, Anna enjoyed sipping red wine and then looking through the profile album of the so-called hostesses who were not always chosen for their figures but the expression in their eyes. Some of the girls preferred to stay anonymous and this was the reason for such names as Glorious, Lolita and Honey, to name a few. Others had little they needed to hide or worry over and so used their proper names. As for some of the clients, especially those with political leanings, they preferred the secrecy of the lovers' nest rooms above, while others were happy to be escorted in their own cars or by black taxi to luxury hotels or sleazy boarding houses – according to taste in the city or West End.

'You know what,' said Anna, closing the photo profile album and chuckling, 'I think I could get used to this kind of a lifestyle.'

'No, you couldn't sweetheart, because neither Linda nor I will let you,' said Hazel. 'You're the good sheep in the family – and you've got our twins to think of.' She flicked her long thick black hair off her beautiful face and smiled. 'But if you were to come into the business, you, unlike the slag Bridget, wouldn't have to advertise what's under your skirt with your eyes. You're not only a natural when it comes to looks, Anna, but you've got a lovely nature to go with it. That's why God gave you a sprinkling of freckles, sweetheart. Freckles show innocence is what our old gran used to say – remember? Frank's lost the plot that's all. Silly bastard. He'll be on his knees begging you to forgive him once he knows that you know and that he could lose you. And you've got two beautiful babies, never mind your warm radiant smile. And look at your eyes for Christ's sake . . . they're beautiful! Round and doleful and a soft green that could light up the coldest man's heart.'

'Comforting words,' said Anna, 'and definitely what I need – but I've got to go back and face the music. Frank is going to go bananas over this.'

Linda came in and joined them, having just said goodbye to a client of distinction. She was just in time to hear Hazel say, 'The tart from the Midlands knew exactly what she was doing. Frank must have been guided by his dick and not his brain if he didn't see through that shy little girl act.'

'Absolutely,' said Linda, who had a fair bit of experience behind her.

Studying Linda's face, Anna looked puzzled. 'But I thought that you thought that Frank was just as bad as Bridget? That he might not 'ave been doing the chasing but he was up for getting her into bed?'

'Did I say that? I don't remember. Anyway, as with all affairs, it's a bit of both,' she said and left it there.

'Whatever we hinted at, it worked, sweetheart,' Hazel

smiled. 'You finally got off of your bum and did something about it.'

Anna laughed. 'I should have known that's what you were up to. Crafty cows. Anyway, that was last night and this is today. I don't want to think about horrible things now that I'm here and in this fab company.'

After an hour or so enjoying herself with the girls, Anna knew that it was time for her to go back to the real world, her mother and her twins. Checking her appearance in the huge antique mirror above the rococo fireplace, she was almost ready to leave when the sound of the doorbell rang through the house. She felt a ray of sunshine filter into her heart when she heard the voice of George Blake as he made his way through from the hallway. He came into the room and she felt a warm glow when he smiled affectionately at her. George then looked from Anna to the girls and gave a friendly wink before turning to Anna and saying, 'A black cab just pulled up outside and I told him to leave it once he gave me the address where he was going. If you can give me five minutes with the girls, Anna, I'll give you a lift to your mum's place.'

With his genuine smile, George removed all doubts from Anna that he was there to bed one of the girls but had seen her earlier on when he was leaving this little corner of old Bethnal Green as she was arriving. Whether he had come back just so as to give her a lift she wasn't sure and wasn't going to question it. His timing was perfect. Whether she would let him take her and the twins on from her mother's flat to home was another matter. For all she knew, Frank might have gone straight there and she didn't want to drag George into her mess.

She had little doubt that Frank would have heard through the grapevine, if not from Bridget, that Anna had been into the restaurant and caused havoc. She knew that he was going to be furious but she wasn't bothered. She didn't even care if he went into one of his sulky, silent, spiteful moods that he knew she could hardly bear. She would take a leaf out of his book and not say anything unless she had to. She would keep him in the dark, wondering what she might do next. She knew that he would want his twin boys even if he didn't want her but, as far as Anna was concerned right then, if there was going to be a separation it had to be all or nothing. In other words, he had either to leave and only see the twins away from the family home, or he had to really want to stay with her as much as she wanted him to. She thought of the gentle smile that she had sometimes seen on Trevor's face and the lovely warm expression in his hazel eyes. Trevor, the poor sod who was married to the ghastly tease. 'Never you mind, Trevor,' she said to herself. 'You're worth a dozen of her type of person.'

Cutting right through her thoughts a familiar voice said, 'So if you want a lift home, Anna, babe, I'm your man.'

Quietly laughing at him she said, 'Well so be it, George – so be it.' She was glad to see him because she had had enough of the Frank and Bridget scenario. Never mind Trevor who was caught up in the centre of it all. She might not have been so unconcerned had she known that her sister Hazel had taken it upon herself to write to Trevor's dad, Arthur Plumb.

When a letter from Hazel dropped through the letter box and onto the doormat in the front sitting room of Arthur Plumb's small 1950s terraced council house, he was giving his working boots a quick buff. It was seven-thirty a.m. Not many people wrote letters to each other in his neck of the woods so it was always nice to see an envelope that wasn't a bill and was without a window. The gentle man was puzzled at first because he didn't recognise the handwriting as that of one of his family or close friends. Hazel had, in her own special way, managed to get hold of the man's address by asking George Blake to do a little bit of homework on the quiet, and without letting Anna know what she was up to.

George had told Hazel and Linda that he had crossed paths with Trevor's cousins who lived south of the river. And that even though, just like several people he knew, they didn't always walk the straight and narrow line and could be a bit violent when push came to shove, they were decent enough guys and very family-orientated. The letter from Hazel had been penned and posted to Trevor's dad just before the girls had breezed into Anna's house armed with Chinese takeaway and the determination to get Anna off her backside and doing something about Bridget before she lost Frank for good.

Short and to the point, Hazel's letter told Arthur about his daughter-in-law's affair with a married man who was the father of beautiful twin baby boys and the husband of her own youngest sister. She also wrote that a mutual friend had given her his address so that she could let him know what was going on before Bridget ruined her sister's marriage and caused Trevor to go into a deep depression.

Having read the letter for a second time, Trevor's dad remained seated at his yellow and gold Formica-topped kitchen table and stared out of the open doorway into his small and tidy back garden in which he grew wall-to-wall vegetables. He didn't like the tone of this letter and he certainly wasn't happy with the content. To his way of thinking this note, short and to the point, was telling him in the nicest way possible to get his son and daughter-in-law back to the Midlands so as to sort things out. This bit of advice actually suited Arthur down to the ground because he knew that, apart from fulfilling his own desires, it would make Trevor's mother a very happy woman to have her only son back in the fold. As for Bridget . . . they would both be more than pleased to see the back of her.

In his mind's eye Arthur could see his wife planning a new look for Trevor's old bedroom, where the walls were still decorated with his swimming certificates and awards. He wondered if his son realised that his attractive young wife was two-timing him. Knowing him better than most, Arthur felt sure that the lad would know what was going on and was most likely waiting for the affair to fizzle out. Waiting – and suffering alone and in silence no doubt. He popped the letter back in its envelope and into his back pocket, where it would remain until he found the right time to let his soft-hearted wife know what was going on.

The fifty-eight-year-old thought about the letter on and off throughout his day at the local furniture factory where he worked as chief turner in the leg-turning section. Chatting and laughing during tea and lunch break with his pals, he gave away nothing of his inner worry, but then Arthur had never been one to hang his dirty laundry on the line. By the time he was walking out of the factory gates early that evening on his way to catch the bus which would take him the four stops to his home, he had almost made up his mind as to what he would do once his temper over it had settled down.

Once by himself, he again sat, staring at nothing and picturing his son in the London flat that he and Bridget had taken once they were married. The cheap rent was the main reason for the couple putting up with what they saw as a depressing little place. But at least it gave Trevor a chance to save for a deposit on a flat of his own, which had been the intention. Sipping a drop of his tea, Arthur allowed a few tears to escape. 'Life's hard,' he murmured, 'but so long as family sticks together it won't be altogether too bad.'

He pushed from his mind the image of his son sitting alone night after night while his flighty young wife worked as a waitress and then bedded her lover. At last unable to think about it any more, he switched on his wireless, if for nothing else but to have voices coming into the room to take his mind off things. He knew that he was going to have to show Hazel's letter to Rose, his wife, but felt that there was no rush. He glanced at the clock and knew that she would shortly be home from her work at Marks and Spencer, her uniform on under her coat so as to have saved time getting out of the building. The less time this couple spent apart the better they liked it. To stop himself brooding over his son, Arthur took his special mixture of vinegar and salt and a clean cloth from the cupboard under the sink and set about cleaning the brass and copper knick-knacks. After doing that, he went outside and parked himself in his old green foldaway deckchair to think about life in general.

If his son was to lose his wife to another man he didn't think that would be such a bad thing. Trevor had top-notch qualifications and an excellent reputation when it came to expertise and style. He had been a natural-born swimmer from birth and had grown into a natural-born teacher too. Arthur had taken him to the local swimming pool when he was eighteen months old to get him used to the water from an early age. This had been back in North London before he and his small family moved out of the capital to take the more modern council house in which they now lived. They had always dreamt of living in a more countrified part of England, so it came as no shock when they exchanged their old-fashioned late Victorian rented house in North London for one on a small and brand-new housing estate on the outskirts of Northampton.

Both Arthur and Rose had had to hide their feelings when Trevor, their only child, had said that he wanted to go back to London to live and work. They had been gutted to the core. Taking him aside before he made his departure, Arthur had told his son that should he, having spent a year or so in the smoke, wish to return home to the Midlands, he must never let pride stand in his way and that he wouldn't be seen as a failure if this were to be the case.

Arthur's only real concern during his son's first term by himself in London and living in a furnished lodgings, had been the girl he had met in a local café while in the East End – Bridget. The girl who, when Trevor brought her home, was seen by close friends and family as somewhat vain and supercilious. Neither Arthur nor Rose had felt right about the person from day one. Deep down he had always suspected that if another man with more shekels in his coffers came along, she might well switch her affections with no sense of guilt.

To Arthur, Bridget's working-class family had done their utmost to become middle class, but had failed in their aspirations before they emigrated to Australia, taking only Bridget's brother with them. His mind working overtime, Arthur had another change of heart as one of his familiar warnings to himself swept across his mind: 'Don't put off until tomorrow what can be achieved today.' He decided there and then that he would suggest to his wife that she take a break and go to London to visit her son for a few days.

He heard the key turn in the front door. Rose was home. 'My feet are killing me,' she said as she entered the room. 'I've been shelf-filling all the day long. Two of the youngsters were off with the 'flu.'

'Well then, sit down and kick your shoes off.' Arthur grinned. 'I'll make a fresh pot of tea while you rest, and you can think about the nice break you're gonna have.'

'Break?' said Rose. 'What break?'

'I've just this minute decided to take you to London

123

so that you can stop with your son for a few days. And I want no discussion on it. We're not so poor that you can't take a few days off work.' He got up from his chair and made for the kitchen, saying, 'I'm not going in to work tomorrow myself either. I'll phone my apprentice later on and tell him to let the boss know in the morning. End of story.'

Rose laughed. She loved it when her husband came over all bossy like this. Anyone would think that what he had suggested hadn't ever crossed her own mind. But she was content to let him think that this much-longed-for suggestion hadn't been a seed that she had sown over the past few months. She was already mentally packing her weekend case. She could hardly wait to see her son again, even if it did mean having to put up with Bridget – his young and flirty wife whom she could not abide.

The next morning the middle-aged couple were up at the crack of dawn. After a full English breakfast at home to line their stomachs, and dressed in their Sunday best, they set off for London. Once they were halfway there, Arthur decided it was time to drop the little bombshell about Bridget in the way he felt best. With one hand on the steering wheel he eased Hazel's letter from the top pocket of his suit jacket and said, 'This came in the post yesterday. Don't start doing your nut over it. Just take it in your stride the way I did.'

'Oh?' said Rose as she took the envelope and peered at the handwriting. 'So who's it from then?'

'A woman called Hazel. She's the sister of a girl

called Anna who part owns the restaurant where Bridget works.'

'The sister of Bridget's boss? What the hell is she writing to you for? You've not applied for a job there or anything, have you?' Rose enquired.

'Don't talk daft. Just read it – and don't do your nut.'

Rose eased the letter out of the envelope. She read it once, and then again, and then a third time before she murmured, 'Wouldn't you just know it, eh? The little scrubber.'

'We don't know if it's true yet, Rose . . .'

'Of course it's bloody true. You can tell from this. I'll strangle that skinny neck of 'ers, I swear to God I will.'

'You'll do no such thing. If you start shouting the odds you'll drive our son away from us. Never insult a man's woman, no matter what you've heard. You should know that by now. You stay quiet and you give your son a shoulder if he needs it. And if he does he'll make it clear to both of us.'

'I might have known you wouldn't come up with a sudden idea of a break for me for no good reason, Arthur.'

'What's that supposed to mean? You work because you want to. Always have done.'

'That's not what I meant. Think about it. How many times have I asked you to drive me to see Trevor? And all you can ever say is that there'll be too much traffic on the road. That he's younger than we are and should make his way to us. Well, from now on I'll take the train or a coach and visit him as and when I feel like it!'

'Finished?' said Arthur. 'Because if you are I

wouldn't mind a drop of tea from out of that flask. I'm parched.'

'You can't drink tea while you're driving. That's all Trevor needs is for you to have a crash and kill the pair of us.'

But Rose drew the flask from her shopping bag, unscrewed the lid and poured a little into a cup to hand to her husband the way she always did when they went out for a drive – after she had warned him in her own way to be careful with the steering wheel. They continued the journey in and out of silence, depending when either of them had anything of consequence to say. They knew each other inside out and both of them were upset by the contents of the letter, but pleased that the woman had written to them about it so that it could be dealt with.

When they finally arrived in Leytonstone and drove past the underground station, Rose took out the scribbled directions to the street where Trevor lived and read them to her husband. They had made this trip before of course, but it was always the last little bit with the many similar back turnings that had them confused in the past, leading to arguments as to who was right and who was wrong when it came to finding the way without getting lost. Today, though, they had little trouble because both minds were thinking as one. They couldn't wait to get to their son.

Once Arthur had parked in a back turning, they strolled towards the main road nearby and to the door to their son's flat, ready to use the spare key that Trevor had given them when he and Bridget first moved in. Their son had insisted they had this in case they fancied coming down to London on the spur of the moment when neither of them were home to let them in. Today they didn't quite know what to expect – whether he would be at work at the local school where he taught PE and sport or whether he might be teaching pupils at the local swimming pool. But after a couple of rings of the bell they heard footsteps from within as Trevor made his way down the staircase.

When he opened the door to them it wasn't his expression of shock, followed by a sigh of relief at seeing his parents, that caused each of them to want to weep. Their son looked awful. His face was drawn, he had lost weight, and it would have taken an idiot not to see that he was on the verge of tears. Hugging his mother first, Trevor held on tight to his emotions as his dad gripped his hand and squeezed it, saying, 'It's good to see you, son.'

They followed him up the narrow closed-in rickety staircase and when they arrived into his flat they were knocked for six at the state it was in. With the light shining through the window onto Trevor they couldn't help but notice the dark shadows around his eyes, or how unwashed his hair appeared to be – never mind the fact that he was unshaven and his clothes dishevelled. Clearly, he hadn't been to work that day and hadn't slept much during the night.

Looking half the man he was when they had last seen him, some three months since, they only just managed a smile. Rose was so taken aback at seeing her son looking like a vagrant that she could hardly speak, and all that Trevor was able to do was offer his open arms to his dad and hold him tighter than he had ever done before.

Feeling as if her heart was being squeezed to crushing point, Rose pushed from her mind the stuffy, narrow and dark rickety staircase they had climbed and looked around her, ready and willing to pull up her sleeves and get cracking. This wasn't the first time she had been to the flat so she knew where everything was kept; and she was used to the staircase, and the old three-storey building with another flat below Trevor's and an old-fashioned costermonger store on the ground floor. But now, inside this lonely-looking, furnished room, she had to summon every bit of her will not to weep. She was gutted to see that on the draining board in the tiny kitchen there was just one mug, one plate, one knife, one fork.

Looking from his mum to his dad, Trevor tried hard to stop his own tears from flowing. 'I'm sorry, Mum,' he just managed to say. 'I know this place looks a mess.'

'No it doesn't, son,' she said. 'It just needs a woman's touch that's all.' She immediately realised that she had said the wrong thing.

'I'll tell you what,' said Arthur, 'I'll put the kettle on and make a pot of tea and you sit down with your mother. We know about Bridget and what she's been up to so you don't 'ave to hold anything back to save our feelings.'

Dropping into one of the two old-fashioned and worn leather armchairs, Trevor sighed with relief and then covered his face with both hands. Once he had composed himself and had a cup of tea in his hand, he slowly started to tell them all that had been going on.

How lonely he had been and how heartbroken he was when he found out for sure that Bridget was having a full-on affair. 'I didn't want you to find out because I thought you'd be angry with me.'

'Don't be daft, son. Angry with you? How could we be? None of this is your fault, is it?'

'No. I've not strayed if that's what you mean. She's not just trying to get back at me or anything like that.'

'That's not what I meant, son,' said Arthur. 'You're not the type to two-time. So where is she living now? Because I don't see any signs of her lodging here.'

'She packed her suitcase two days ago and moved into the flat above the restaurant where she works. Anna – the wife of Bridget's lover, Frank, doesn't know this yet but no doubt she'll find out soon. Anna is part owner of the restaurant with her husband.'

'Yes, son, so we gather. One of her sisters wrote us a letter saying so. I don't know what she thought we could do about it but it certainly spurred me and your mother to come and see how you were coping.'

Trevor sighed with relief. 'I'm glad she did that, Dad. Really glad. It's much easier somehow now that it's out in the open.'

Leaving the men to talk in private, Rose wandered from the living room into the bedroom where the curtains were still drawn and it all seemed so dark and dingy. This room, just like the living room, was also dishevelled. Wandering back into the living room, she could hardly look into her son's eyes or his pained and tormented face in case she herself broke down.

Smiling faintly at him, she tried to ignore the half-empty mug of cold tea on a small grubby Formica coffee table by an old armchair, and the leftover cold fish and chips half wrapped in newspaper. She was so glad now that she had packed enough clothes for more than just a weekend because wild horses were not going to drag or chase her back home unless she was to take her son with her.

Sharing the fresh pot of tea as they made the best of the mangy sofa and armchair, Arthur and Rose learned just how much time Trevor had been spending in this ghastly flat by himself, with only a small black and white television set for company.

Chapter Five

Driving Anna from the girls' house to her mother's flat via the narrow backstreets of old Bethnal Green where the local whores hung out, George wasn't his usual self. The only reason for this that Anna could come up with was that he wasn't the flirt and womaniser that he had been made out to be. He really did seem quite shy now that he was alone with her in the car, and it was having a knock-on effect because she felt a little at a loss for making conversation. She didn't feel right about discussing the fracas in the restaurant between her and Bridget and yet it could hardly be ignored as if it hadn't happened.

'I didn't have any choice, George,' she finally murmured, right out of the blue. 'I had to find out for myself if Bridget was having an affair with Frank.'

'That's all right, babe,' he said. 'You don't have to explain anything to me. It's personal and private. I just didn't want you to go and cause bodily harm while I was in the restaurant. It could have been a bit tricky – to say the least.'

'Why?' Anna smiled. 'I wouldn't have been the first woman you'd have had to put the handcuffs on I don't suppose.'

George slowly shook his head and by the expression on his face he wasn't taking the incident lightly. 'You have to be more careful though, Anna. You've heard the expression *don't hang your dirty laundry on the line.* You'd be surprised how many people would put their hand up as a witness when a few ten-pound notes are skilfully shown.'

'I never touched the cow.'

'You had a grip on Ginger-nut's hair for Christ's sake. And if I hadn't have got the timing right you would have given her a right-hander. She ended up with her nose out of joint even though you let her go. It could have been a lot worse, with wineglasses flying and breaking. You could have been done for grievous, sweetheart.'

Anna found herself laughing. 'Did she break her nose then?'

'She pushed it out of joint and I clicked it back together again. But she could still have taken you to court for gbh.'

'And what about smh? Can I take *her* to court for that?'

'I'm not with you, sweetheart. Smh?'

'Shagging my husband.'

George laughed out loud and this in turn made Anna smile. 'I think the judge and jury might say that it takes two to tango, babe.'

'What about a jury of all women? They'd be on my side.'

'Listen,' said George, trying to pull this conversation back to facts. 'You've had your say and Bridget's come off worst. Leave it alone now and think about what you want. Either you want Frank back – and nobody's gonna argue with that – or you want a clean break.

You're a lovely girl and I can't see you being lonely for long.'

'It wouldn't make much difference if I were. I've been lonely for quite a while. I'd almost forgotten what it was like to be in company and laughing again. The girls at my sisters' place 'ave a great time, George, even apart from the different sorts of men they meet. The atmosphere there is fantastic. I feel as I've been stuck at home on my own for too long.'

George shrugged and then went quiet, concentrating on the route to Anna's mum's flat. Just as he turned into Ivy's street, he said, 'Listen . . . if you fancy a day out in Kent let me know. No strings attached. I want to go down and have a look at an old farmhouse that might be coming on the market.'

'At the place where you and your mum went hop-picking.' Anna smiled, all knowing. 'You want to claw back a bit of your childhood and the boy in you, and why not? Good for you.'

'It wasn't just me and Mum picking hops in Kent, Anna. My dad and two brothers were there as well.'

'I know, don't be so touchy. And yeah, if Mum will have the twins for me, I would love a day out. When?'

'This coming Sunday? I've already been on the phone and asked about it. Spoke to the owner in fact.'

'Amazing what a title does, eh, George. Detective Inspector.'

'It helps sometimes. The guy sounded distant at first but then once I said I wanted a place away from London to lay my hat he soon relaxed. So I take it that it's a yes then?'

'Providing Mum agrees to have the boys, it's a definite.'

'Good thing I stopped on the way to your sister's place and bought her a box of Milk Tray then.' George quietly chuckled, delight shining out through his eyes. 'And before the rumour gets up and running, my so-called wife is not around any more and it's come as no surprise to me. I gave her the freedom she wanted but kept it quiet. She's gone off to live God knows where. I don't know and I don't care, it's over between us. It was over months ago if I'm to be honest.'

'I'm sorry to hear that, but you won't be lonely for long. Or do you already know that? Have you got a sweetheart in the wings?'

Embarrassed by the question, George flushed. 'No I've not,' he said, and left it there. He then parked the car in silence.

Ivy was spooning some tinned peaches onto a layer of cold custard on top of the trifle she had made when Anna rang the doorbell. Knowing full well who it was, she asked her friend Gwen, who had been there all day and was now on her way out, if she would see them in as she left. Ivy had heard the car pull up and glanced through her net curtains to recognise George and his motor. She placed the trifle in the fridge, smoothed her skirt and quickly tidied her hair, speculating about the why and wherefore of George Blake. She liked him, and had known him a long while, but shadowing her youngest daughter and fetching her home made her think twice as to his motives. Men and their dicks spoke only one language in her opinion – but she was going to give him the benefit of the doubt because her other two daughters, who were experienced in the male species, were okay about him. If she found him to be a little too familiar with her youngest daughter she would give him one of her renowned black looks. She glanced through to the passage, and when he came in with a box of chocolates casually held out to her Ivy found herself blushing.

'You shouldn't have done that, George,' she said, all smiles. 'But they are my favourite so I won't tell you off for spoiling me.'

'You've never done so before, Ivy, when I've fetched you sweets – so why would you do so now?' He knew what was on her mind and wanted to clear the air.

She looked slyly at him while Anna attended to her twins and then moved closer to him. 'Don't you go and break her heart while she's on the rebound.'

'Come on, Ivy. Anna and I are old mates. Your daughters are more like my sisters than anything else.'

'If you say so, George. If you say so.' She checked that Anna was too preoccupied to take any notice of the pair of them and then whispered, 'What the fuck is Frank up to?'

'I'm not sure yet, Ivy. It might be a passing fling or something more serious. Time will tell.'

'That Bridget woman needs a bloody good spanking.'

'She'd probably enjoy that, Ivy.' George grinned at her.

'You're probably right. But seriously . . . why has she let herself be lured in like this by Frank when she's got a decent husband? I know what I would do if it were one of my girls behaving the way she is. I'd take the slipper to her arse.'

Slowly shaking his head, George quietly chuckled. 'Your Linda and Hazel are angels then are they?'

'I should say so! Look at the way they run their business. There's nothing shoddy about what they do. They provide a service for lonely men, young and old. You can't knock that.'

There was no answer that was going to appease Ivy so George kept his mouth shut. In any case, she had left him lost for words. Linda and Hazel were running a brothel after all was said and done. He crossed the room and looked out of the window, checking that there weren't any kids hanging around his treasured car. 'I was telling Anna about my hop-picking years on the way over. You never went down 'oppin' did you, Ivy?'

'No. We preferred fruit-picking in the summer time. Used similar huts to live in though. It was good but I wouldn't want to do it again. I like my home comforts too much.'

'I thought we might go for a drive this Sunday coming. A little nostalgia trip.'

'They don't do picking by hand any more though, do they?' said Ivy, quite fancying a day out herself. 'Machines are in full swing from what I hear and have been for a good few years.'

'That's right,' said George, keeping his eye on two lads admiring his motor. 'I'm kind of interested in a run-down farm near Tonbridge where we used to go as kids. The old farmhouse is a cracker but if left to itself it'll soon turn into a ruin. I think I could pick it up cheap.'

'What for? You wouldn't move out would you?'

'I might do. I was thinking of renovating it alongside a team of builders I know and turn it into a friendly type of small hotel and run it myself. Once I've packed in my job at the Met.'

'So you really do mean to leave the force, eh? Well, I don't blame you for getting out. London will end up like New York where crime's concerned according to a piece I read in the *News of the World*, never mind what goes on all around us.'

'Whoever wrote it wasn't too far out. But that's not the main reason, Ivy. I want out of the smoke. I want to live in the country and be stress free.'

'I can't knock that. So . . . Anna wants me to have the twins for the day then, does she?'

'I don't know,' he said, all innocent. 'It would be good for her to get away for a few hours though – after what she's been through. It's not very nice is it, finding out that her husband's been sleeping with another woman.'

'Keep your voice down, George. She might hear you.'

'So what do yer think then? You reckon it'll be all right if she comes with me for a day out?'

'So long as you're back in time to take her and the twins home, I can't see any harm in it. Christ knows what Frank's gonna do.' She turned from the sink where she was rinsing teacups and slowly shook her head. 'What do you make of all this, George? Is he serious about the tart or what?'

'You'll have to ask him that, Ivy. It's been going on

for a while though. They act as if they're a couple when they're in the restaurant.'

Ivy slowly shook her head. 'I still can't take it in. And what about her husband? What's he making of all this?'

'I don't know. He's a quiet kind of a bloke. Comes and goes when he's picking up Bridget and doesn't really say much. I shouldn't worry too much over it. It'll all come out in the wash.'

'Famous last words, George,' murmured Ivy. 'Famous last words.' She was thinking of the day when her husband walked away from her and their three girls. 'My only worry now is what's gonna happen when Anna gets home. Will Frank be there and furious? Linda phoned and told me what happened. I hope to God that Anna didn't cause that accident, that's all.'

'Of course she didn't. Bridget wears stiletto-heeled shoes for work. It was an accident waiting to happen. She's gonna have a swollen bruised conk for a while.' He chuckled at the thought of it. 'Let's see what Frank makes of that. Anyway, your Anna won't be lonely any more. Not now we all know what she's been going through. I'll drop in and see 'er every now and then – if that's all right by you?'

'Of course it is, George. You're as good as family. Well, almost.'

A couple of evenings later, with the twins bathed and asleep in their cots, Anna, even though she was by herself again, for some strange reason was not feeling too lonely. She had had a good cry that afternoon and this had seemed to help. She still couldn't get over the fact that Frank would leave her for another woman, but he had slept at the flat above Prima the previous night and now she had no idea whether or not he would do the same thing again this coming night. She thought the reason that he was staying away was because he was full of guilt. But now she wasn't too sure if he intended to ever come back at all. At least she had Rachel next door to one side of her and the young couple on the other and this helped. Curled up in an armchair in the quiet cosy sitting room, she could hear the muted sound of Rachel's television, which was comforting, and now that she had put the twins to bed she had time to herself.

She had no regrets about going to see Bridget, and didn't know whether Frank was angry with her and showing it by sleeping in the flat above the restaurant, or whether he feared that if he was at home he might be pushed into a confession that would be the beginning of him leaving. Anna sipped her milky cocoa and glanced at the small brass carriage clock which was softly ticking on the mantelshelf. Nine-thirty. She wondered how Frank was managing to run the restaurant without Bridget, who was hiding away until the swelling to her nose had gone down. Relaxed, and in a pensive mood, she was startled at the sound of her doorbell piercing through the quiet, especially at this time of night. She got up to answer the door. For the first time, she felt nervous in her own home and switched on the outside light so that she could see the shape of whoever it was outside through the frosted-glass panes. From the shape of the man outside it looked to be Trevor Plumb, Bridget's husband.

Cautious, just in case it wasn't him but a stranger, she

slipped the safety chain on and opened the door to see through the gap that she had been right. Opening the door fully to him, she offered a weak, almost apologetic smile and then shrugged as she waved him inside, telling him to go through to the back sitting room. The reality of all that was happening was really hitting home now.

In the back room where the last of the setting sun was casting lovely burnt orange rays into the room, Anna smiled warmly at the sad young man. 'I'm sorry about what happened, Trevor,' she said, 'but it wasn't my fault that Bridget slipped—'

'I didn't come round for an apology, Anna,' he said. 'Is it all right if I take my mac off?'

'Of course it is.' She instinctively squeezed his arm and looked into his pale freckled face. Beads of sweat were breaking out on his forehead. 'I'm really pleased and grateful that you've come. And please . . . feel free to visit whenever you want.'

'My parents are down for a day or so. I'm not by myself if that's what you think. I wanted to come and see you to ask what you thought of Bridget and Frank living together above your restaurant.'

'No, Trevor – they're not living there. I think that Frank's gonna move into his brother's flat above the restaurant at Tower Hill. Didn't Bridget stay at yours last night then?'

'No. Which was just as well because my parents arrived out of the blue and they're staying with me. It's a bit cramped, but Bridget wasn't there. She had already packed her bags and moved into your flat above Prima.'

'She did what! How dare she? Bloody cheek. I can't believe it. Are you sure?'

'It's what she said on the phone. I don't think she much cares what she does anymore so long as she gets her way.'

'And how long are your parents staying with you?'

'Only a short while – Dad goes back tomorrow because he can't take too many days off, but Mum is stopping on. I think she's worried about me.'

'Well I'll tell you what, Trev. Why don't you and your mum move into the flat above the restaurant? We'll shove Bridget out. She's definitely not going to stay there. No way.'

'I suppose she could nurse her nose back to being all right in our Leytonstone flat. If me and Mum did move into yours. If you really mean it.' He then broke into a soft and gentle laughter. 'You've got guts, Anna – I will say that.'

'She told you what happened then?'

'Yes. Over the phone. She said she couldn't stop herself falling in love with Frank. When I asked her if Frank felt the same she said that I was to ask him. That said it all really.'

'Yes, I suppose it did.' Anna felt a wave of pain grip her. 'I know she's a bit of a drama queen on the quiet, Trevor, but it all makes sense now. Frank's been walking about as if he's a hero in a romantic movie.'

'My mother once said that Bridget was the type who could become the village tart if we lived in a village. The marriage-breaker troublemaker.'

'Well, she's in a small corner of London now and one of a thousand of her type. I can't believe she's in my flat. Jesus. So what do you think? Will you want to move in? You can just turn up whenever you want and unpack your bags. I'll give you a key tonight. Then tell Bridget to move back into the so-called flea pit that she's always moaning about. She hates your flat from what she's said, so she can go and stew in it, can't she.'

Trevor laughed quietly again, and then said, 'Yes, she can. God, I'm glad that I came round, Anna. I feel better already.'

'Good. Now let's open a bottle of wine and celebrate your move in advance. It's hardly the end of the world is it? Sod the pair of 'em. Let's drink a toast to us, and others in the same boat! What d'yer fancy, a glass of red wine or something stronger? I've got some scotch.'

'That would be very nice. Scotch and water.' Trevor looked around himself and said, 'You've got a nice place here, Anna.'

'I know I have. And do you know what? I'm gonna hold onto it no matter what Frank tries to pull. Now then . . . are you hungry? It won't take a minute to make you a sandwich.'

'No, that's all right. For some reason I've lost my appetite.'

'Tell me about it,' said Anna. 'Sit yourself down and let's forget about my husband and your wife for five minutes. I'll get the drinks.' No sooner was she in the passage and going into the kitchen than the phone rang.

She hoped that it wouldn't be Frank's voice on the other end of the line. It was in fact Ivy, asking if she was all right. She told her that she was fine and made an excuse of having to go because she had just run a nice hot bath for herself. No sooner had she replaced the receiver than the phone rang again; this time it was George asking if she was still up for the day trip to Kent. She kept it short and told him she was. He then told her that he had booked off the day after the next. Sunday.

'I'll have to check with Mum,' she said. 'She'll baby-sit for me if she's got nothing else lined up.'

'I'll take that to be a yes, then, babe. Your mum would cancel a visit to the queen just so as to have her grandsons to watch over.'

'All right,' said Anna, 'take it as a yes — unless I phone to tell you that it's not.'

'Will do.'

'Sorry about that, Trevor,' said Anna, joining him again and handing him his glass of whisky and soda. 'Two phone calls in a row are out of the ordinary, but then the past couple of days have hardly been run of the mill.'

'You can say that again,' he said. They clinked glasses. 'Let's hope we'll come out of this happier than Bridget and Frank do,' Trevor went on. 'And if it's any consolation, I don't think they'll last five minutes.'

Looking into his soft hazel eyes, Anna shrugged. 'We'll see.'

'This isn't the first time she's slept with another man. It's happened twice before that I know of. And even though both affairs were a flash in the pan for the men involved, she languished over it for weeks. You're right, she's a drama queen on the quiet, is Bridget. But she also gets what she wants and doesn't much care who she hurts on the way.'

'Oh, well, that makes me feel better in a strange kind

of way. It couldn't have been easy for you to tell me that. I appreciate it, Trevor. And I do mean that.' She raised her glass and smiled. 'Here's to us.'

'Cheers. I hope she doesn't ruin your marriage that's all. She almost wrecked the two before yours, but the women saw the affairs as their husbands scoring with an easy woman who got off on having secret assignations with men who drove around in nice cars. One of her married men drove a brand new Range Rover and the other a red Jaguar. And from what each of the husbands told me, Bridget's preferred place to get screwed was in an expensive car.'

'She sounds as if she could do with seeing a psychiatrist.'

'She probably does need to but at least she gave the gossips something to talk about. They loved it.'

On the sofa now and drawing her legs up to be comfortable, Anna said, 'Will you take her back – if she gets down and crawls?'

'No. Would you take Frank back?'

'Probably. In fact – yes, I would. But I'll make him suffer for what he's done. I'll go out on a shopping spree.'

'Well, I wish I felt the same. But feeling as if your heart's been ripped out three times is not good. I'm finished with her this time. She can have her freedom and do what she wants with it.'

'Oh Trevor . . .' Anna reached out and took his hand. 'Don't go and do something you might regret for the rest of your life. You must love Bridget or you would have gone before now.'

'I *should* have done. I should have taken notice of the

hints being dropped here, there and everywhere by the parents of the children I teach.'

'Well, from now on you'll have a nice flat to live in. The one above Prima.'

'Mmm. But will I be able to deal with seeing her and Frank when I come and go?'

'Of course you will. It's got its own side entrance door don't forget.'

'Well, I don't want to leave London because of her. Because of Bridget. I'm not a bad swimming coach and my world is hardly empty is it? Not with all of those kids and their smiling faces. I taught beginners of around the age of six at local public baths until I'd cut my teeth. Then I was in charge of the more boisterous girls and boys from junior schools. After that I was moved on to the tough eleven- to sixteen-year-olds. Several of the youngsters that I coached swam in the area galas and won medals. My dream is to win the pools, buy a huge house in the country and turn it into a children's home and teach the underprivileged.'

'Oh, Trevor . . . that's such a lovely dream to have.'

'It won't happen, of course, but we all have to have a dream don't we? I *will* work for underprivileged children though. If I can.' Finishing his drink he stood up to leave.

'Let me know if you want to rent the flat. Once you've thought about it.'

'I have thought about. I would like to rent it.'

'Good for you!'

Anna could imagine Trevor and his mother living in the flat and looked forward to it. After all it would be a bit of a social life for the pair of them until his mother

145

went home and then it would be his very own pad. No one expected Trevor to be full of the joys of spring, for obvious reasons, but this opportunity to live in a much nicer home in a livelier area had come at just the right time for him, Anna thought.

Anna stepped forward to give Trevor a sisterly hug. 'I'm so pleased that you took the trouble to come round to see me. Thank you.'

Blushing a little he said, 'I wanted to. And in a way I suppose I felt obliged as well. I hope it wasn't too encroaching.'

'No, of course it wasn't.' Anna gently laughed. 'You got it off your chest and you've helped me get some of it off mine. And don't think that you can't ring on that doorbell again because you can. But I would prefer you to phone and let me know if you're popping in. Just in case I'm in the bath or something.'

'I will next time. I promise.' He squeezed her arm and said that he would see himself out. Brief though their time together was, it left Anna feeling as if she had just made a friend.

Settling back on her sofa with the cushion for a pillow, Anna looked through the *TV Times* to see if there was anything worth watching that would take her mind off things. The one thing she was resisting was playing favourite love songs of hers and Frank's. She wanted to get through the next few days as coolly and calmly as she possibly could. She thought about her babies, fast asleep in their cots upstairs, and asked God to at least help her look after and protect them.

Then, closing her eyes, she tried not to think about anything else. She was ready for a long soak in a warm

Radox bath. The house had always held a peaceful and calm atmosphere and she appreciated this now more than she ever had. But there was another ring on her doorbell to pierce through the quiet. This time it was Jackie the Avon rep on her doorstep.

'What a sight for sore eyes you are,' said Anna, pleased to see the fresh young smiling face. 'Come on in and tease me into spending some of Frank's money.'

'I won't be stopping long, and sorry I didn't come the other day,' whispered Jackie, as if Anna's sleeping babies were within hearing distance. 'I've got the new catalogue with me and you'll love the range of eye makeup. Three shades of soft gold that'll bring out the little hazel specks that I've seen in your green eyes.'

'Oh God, don't tempt me ...'

'You won't need persuasion, trust me. I'll leave you the catalogue and you can browse at your leisure if you want.'

'Good. That suits me fine. But come and take the weight off your feet for five minutes.'

'Now then, I've got two other clients to see this evening so no time to spare.' She smiled and her eyes lit up as she eased herself past Anna who was holding open the door. 'And one of them has a gorgeous young bloke for a son who loves the new range of products for men. Aftershave and the like.'

'They're the ones who'll spend the money, Jackie,' Anna laughed. 'Men love to pamper themselves on the quiet you know. More so than women I think.' Following Jackie through to the sitting room Anna listened to a running report on how well her sales were going and how she had half a mind to take this work on full time and give up her job in the city.

'I think I'm more cut out for this,' she said, flicking her auburn hair off her face. 'I'm earning nearly as much as I get for my proper job.'

'I would give it another few months if I were you,' said Anna. 'This might just be a flash in the pan.'

'No, I don't think so.' Jackie settled herself on the settee and smiled broadly. 'I love this work and it would be great to do it full time soon. If my orders keep going as they are, I can earn a lot of money in this game. Hard work, patience, and long hours are what are needed. And I can do that for the next five years – no problem. I would love to do it full time.'

'Well then, far be it for me to advise you otherwise. You seem to know your own mind, Jackie, and that can't be bad, can it?' Anna stopped herself from relating what had happened over the past couple of days because she had had enough of discussing it.

So, instead of being miserable again this evening, she was pleased to sit and choose presents – a lipstick and a powder puff for Ivy, talcum powder for Gwen and some crème perfume in a lovely pink jar with a delicately printed flowery lid for herself. And all paid for by cheque from the joint account. Once the order was made, her young friend was up and away and on to the next client. Closing the door behind the entrepreneur, Anna climbed the stairs ready for that soak in the bath and then a much-needed sleep in her comfortable bed all to herself. But, just as she reached the top stair, the phone went again and she was in two minds whether to answer it. This time it was Frank, and when she heard his voice every muscle in her body seemed to go into a spasm.

'It's me,' he said, his voice quieter than usual. 'I think I had better stay at the flat at Tower Bridge again tonight, don't you.'

Her heartbeat quickening, Anna said, 'I thought that's what you were going to do in any case, Frank. After all, you can't stay at Prima because you've moved Bridget in. Her husband came and told me so.'

'Oh well, that drip would have, wouldn't he? I'll be back some time tomorrow to fetch some of my clothes.'

Angry that he dared to talk to her like this, she forced herself not to scream abuse at him down the line. 'No problem. I'll put them in bin bags for you.'

'Good. Leave them in the passage if you go out.'

'As it happens, I am going out tomorrow. Taking the boys over to see their aunts.' She guessed that this would put his back up.

'That's not clever, Anna. You know I don't want them anywhere near that brothel. Not now – not ever. And you should want the same thing.'

'It's not a brothel, it's a dating agency. The girls are not sluts and there is a big difference. But then you'd know all about sluts. You having turned our first little flat into your own private slutting place.'

Ignoring this he repeated himself. 'I don't want the boys in that house, Anna. They might catch something for one thing.'

Anna laughed at him. 'I think that you should be more worried over yourself. I should get down to the VD clinic if I were you. Bridget's been passed around quite a bit from what I've heard. Ask her about it. And as for your clothes, you can take all of them while you're at it. Socks, pants, pyjamas, and the lot. I'll put them all in black bin bags, except for your underpants. I don't want to risk touching them. Not all bacteria come out in the wash you know.' She then gently replaced the receiver and felt so much better for the call. She liked the sense of getting back at him. She looked at the phone and said, 'You bastard.'

At least she had had the last word for a change and she had managed not to let him entice her into a row, which he could so easily do with just one of his timeworn sarcastic clichés such as, 'You need to get out a bit more with your friends,' or 'Why don't you get your mum to baby-sit while you go to a woman's evening class somewhere?' This was the kind of thing he would say when she had dared to ask why they couldn't go out together for an evening now and then. The worst of Frank's patronising suggestions was that he always spoke in a matter-of-fact tone while delivering them. And he usually delivered them while either watching the sport on the television or reading a newspaper. And now he was ducking out of a confrontation that he didn't want because he knew that he was as guilty as hell and Anna had dared to make it public knowledge. Whichever way it was viewed – this was the first step towards their separation.

Later on, once in her bed, as Anna had expected, she couldn't settle at all and didn't sleep well because she was crying on and off all night. Once dawn broke however, after hours of tossing and turning and fitful sleep, she dragged herself out of bed and went downstairs to make up the bottles for the twins, who would soon be letting her know that they were hungry. Looking out of the kitchen window and a little more alert, she could hear the beautiful sound of birds outside coming in through the small opening of the skylight. This was the time of the day that she loved most. The settling down of the wildlife after the first flush of activity from various town birds which followed the dawn chorus.

Lifting the white nursing chair, her first purchase of baby furniture from Mothercare in the early days, she carried it outside into the garden so as to be in the early morning sun and in the centre of nature itself – albeit in London's East End. After her first cup of coffee she went upstairs to the twins' room and found them awake and gurgling at each other through the bars of their cots. Had she left them waiting for five minutes or so longer, she knew that they would have been hollering for their feed.

Taking them below, one by one, she laid baby James on the settee and put on a clean paddy pad, then did the same with Oliver, and bottle-fed one after the other. She didn't feel anywhere near as lonely as she had done of late and appreciated the love and warmth exuding from her babies. Any leftover feelings of dread of the unknown and loathing towards Frank for all that he had done, simply melted away when she was holding either of her boys. She felt even better when she opened the drapes in the sitting room to let the morning sunshine flood in.

When she reopened the door leading out to the

garden after she had placed the boys in the playpen for a kick and a gurgle, she could smell grilled kippers coming from a neighbour's kitchen, which made her mouth water. Seeing that her babies were content enough in their playpen, she went into the kitchen again because she was hungry and ready for fried eggs and crispy bacon. Still in her pyjamas and dressing gown – her favourite pink and white candy stripe – she poured herself another cup of coffee when the sound of the front door opening struck through her as if she had touched a live wire. But then, as she drew breath, she told herself not to be stupid. If a burglar wanted to get in he would choose the dark of night to rob her and not broad daylight. It was now eight-thirty a.m. It had to be Frank.

Not knowing quite what she would say to him if he came anywhere near her, she peeled off two layers of bacon from the packet and laid them into the hot non-stick frying pan. Her heart beating nineteen to the dozen, she pretended she hadn't heard him and positioned herself at the cooker so that her back was to the open kitchen doorway. She didn't want to look at Frank. She didn't want him near her, and she could hardly credit that he was so thoughtless as to stay out all night after what had happened and then walk calmly back in through their door as if he had every right to come and go as he pleased. From his aura she knew that he was not here to apologise or explain. Old feelings of love had come and gone over and over again since the day before, but vanished when she pictured his expression of boredom whenever he had been in the same room as herself of late – when he could hardly wait to get out of the house, using any excuse possible. She moistened her dry lips with the tip of her tongue and braced herself for whatever was to come next.

Drawn perhaps by the smell of the frying bacon, Frank appeared at the open doorway of the kitchen, showing little other than a taut face – a defence tactic that she had seen before. He was as guilty as hell but not sorry for what he had done. She could read him like a book. She blanked her mind and thought of the birds, the bees and the flowers in her garden and ignored him. So as not to weaken, she reminded herself of what a self-centred, dour bastard he had turned into at home. Of course, once out at the restaurant or elsewhere, he was good old Frank, the easy-going, fun-loving decent guy who helped old ladies cross the road.

Glancing sideways at him, she could tell from his expression that he was going to carry on behaving as if he were the victim and not the *cause* of their marriage being blown apart. This was Frank playing the strong silent type, which was all bollocks as far as she was concerned. Once in the kitchen, he moved around in silence and opened the refrigerator to take out the milk and poured himself a glassful. He spoke not one word to Anna but she could tell that he was fuming inside.

He continued to behave as if she wasn't there and, because of this – not to mention his dark mood – she knew he was showing her what an ogre he could be when he was put out. She knew that he was waiting for her to come at him with questions and accusations. Having to be on the back foot was his problem. He didn't want her to question him as to what had been going on and for how long. She knew Frank inside out, whether he liked to believe it or not, and could tell that he had his rehearsed speech ready and waiting. Well, she wasn't going to oblige. Of course she wanted to hit him, to scream at him for being a selfish two-timing bastard but she was determined to keep control. Even though it was taking every bit of self control, she would not respond to his baiting tactic of silence. She had seen it too many times before, and in any case what did he think she would say? 'I'm sorry I upset Bridget. How is the poor dear soul? Did she break her nose or just put it out of joint?'

Gripping the wooden handle of the frying pan, Anna turned a slice of bacon over and wished that she had the guts to use the pan as a weapon and smack him round the face. Instead, just as if she were by herself, she opened the fridge, took out two eggs, and broke them into the sizzling bacon fat, humming a tune while doing so – a tune that Ivy had often sung to her when she was a child, 'Somewhere Over the Rainbow'. After all, it was Frank who had an apology to make and some explaining to do. She knew, of course, that this was not going to happen, because he was not the kind of man who could swallow his pride too easily, having been born with a stubborn streak. Inflexibility had always been one of his unpleasant traits.

What Frank didn't realise, or at least wouldn't admit to if challenged, was that he was transparent and not the deep and private man he liked to think he was. Even so, there was a side to him that she had never been quite sure about. If, for instance, she were to push him a little too far, would he give her a fierce slap around the face again? It had happened twice before within a year or so of them having been married. On both occasions, during an argument she had said things that had been a little too close to the bone when he had been in one of his dark and silent moods. And now he was there and in another one of them.

It seemed almost laughable that he was coming on with the strong and silent routine even though he surely knew that his sneak-around affair had been blown wide open and that people were now smiling behind his back. Since it had gone quiet in the sitting room, Anna knew that Oliver and James had fallen asleep in their playpen, so she went and collected them and took them upstairs to their cots. When she returned to the kitchen, Frank murmured, while opening his post, 'If you think you're being clever, Anna, you're making a very big mistake.'

He spoke as if he was talking to a business colleague and not his young and lovely wife. Taking no notice of him whatsoever, she spooned a little sizzling bacon fat over the yolks of her farm eggs. 'If Bridget decided to walk out on us after your little melodrama,' he continued, 'we'd be in real trouble. She practically runs Prima with me now.'

Still Anna didn't answer him or acknowledge his presence, even though it was filling the kitchen. She could hardly believe that he would dare to mention his lover's name within their four walls now that he knew that she had found him out. Even so, she wasn't going to let his patronising tone provoke her into losing her temper. He knew that she knew what had been going on and still he showed no signs of attempting to excuse or explain his behaviour. And of course no apology either. He and Bridget, according to what she had said to Anna, were making plans to buy a place together, weren't they?

'I'm gonna pack a few things in a bag and stay at my brother's flat until you come to your senses,' he said. 'You owe a member of our staff an apology, which I think, under the circumstances it would be better if you did in writing. You'd best not come to the restaurant until it all cools down. Bridget's not the type to bear a grudge but I think she might need some space for a while.'

Anna slowly turned to face him. She looked directly into his eyes and then, surprising herself, quietly laughed at the audacity of this man. '*What* did you just say? You want *me* ... to apologise ... to *her?*'

'I think you should, just to keep the peace.'

'Oh, do you?' said Anna, as she pushed her face up a little closer to his and spoke ever so quietly. 'Give me a break, Frank. The silly bitch buckled under her fuck-me four-inch stiletto heels. All I did was grip her hair a little while I was whispering that she ought to know that everyone's talking about her and the way she offers a shag with her eyes.' She raised one eyebrow and half smiled. 'I thought I was doing her a favour ... and you, come to that.'

'You're not funny, Anna. Don't you think I've got enough to think about – running from my restaurant to my brothers' and back again?'

'I'm *sorry*,' said Anna, now sporting a mock puzzled expression. 'But did you say *your* restaurant?'

'You know exactly what I said. What's with all the theatricals?'

Pausing for a moment, she looked him in the eye and could see that not only was his face taut but the little nervous tic that only showed now and then was going like the clappers. For a second or two, old feelings of love threatened to surface, but then he made the mistake of sporting his classic expression of patronising boredom. A look that told her that he wanted her to know that he couldn't wait to get out of the house and that he believed her to be incredibly thick.

She'd had enough. She moistened her dry lips with the tip of her tongue and said, 'Do us all a favour, Frank. Stop acting like Bridget's a brave soldier, it doesn't suit you. Fuck off and live with the girl if that's what you want. I don't need soiled goods around me and you have been reeking of stale scent for a long time.'

'What are you talking about? Soiled goods? Who've you been listening to?' Again Frank's anger broke through his matter-of-fact façade. The difference now though was that he was red in the face. She knew that he knew he was in the wrong, so why couldn't he just apologise and go?

'Everyone's been talking about you,' she finally said. 'I wasn't listening the way I should have been all of the time admittedly, but of course, now that I know everything, it all makes sense. I've smelled her perfume on your clothes and in your skin and hair. And *that* . . . is what *I* call soiled goods. Unlike you, I don't really need to listen to anyone else advising me what to do. I've discussed my worries with nobody. I didn't have to ask questions about what you were up to, Frank, because you talk in your sleep for one thing.'

Frank stared at her and she could tell that he was so filled with guilt that he had no choice other than to go on the attack. She now understood the saying, of not being able to change a leopard's spots. 'I'm not listening to this rubbish,' he said as he turned around and left the room. From the hallway he called over his shoulder: 'You should get out with the twins a bit more!' He then took the stairs two at a time and she knew that he was about to throw a change or two of clothes into his large, soft, tan leather holdall. This is what he had come for. A set or two of clean clothes and nothing else.

His high-handed tone infuriated her. He should have been full of apologies, of remorse. Fortunately, though, the melodramatic exit from the house that she knew he was about to make was adding fuel to her fire instead of bringing tears to her eyes. Taking a slow, deep breath, she brought Ivy to mind and could hear her quietly saying, 'Leave it be, darling . . . leave it be. Stay silent. Say nothing.' The sad thing about all of this was that there was a time when Anna would have done anything for Frank, and he would have bent over backwards to make her happy. That Bridget had so influenced him beggared belief.

With her mother still in her thoughts, Anna dished up her eggs and bacon to take into the living room. She settled herself at the old pine table and began to eat as if nothing untoward was happening. Then, with all the nonchalance she could possibly muster, she drew the Avon brochure close, ready to flick through it once she knew that Frank was on his way down the stairs. Whether he came into the room or not didn't matter, because the door was open and he would not be able to ignore the fact that she was seemingly unruffled. She blanked her mind until he left the house without a word, slamming the street door hard behind him.

She knew that he would go straight to Bridget and fill her in as to the kind of reception he had received, but what she couldn't be sure of was whether or not he had found out that George had given her a lift home from Ivy's flat. Innocent though it was, she knew that he would use this as a counter-attack in an attempt to pass the buck. None of this really mattered in any case, because a clear-cut message had been given. He had packed his bags. He had left. Going to the front-room window, Anna watched as he drove away without so much as a backward glance.

'You cold-hearted bastard,' she murmured. She could hardly take in what was happening. She had done nothing to deserve this. She had done nothing wrong.

Back in the kitchen, she poured herself another cup of coffee, but this time she laced it with a little drop of brandy. Ivy's smiling face and voice came to mind again. *Purely medicinal, sweetheart. Purely medicinal.*

Just as she was about to sip her warming drink there was a knock on the front door. She hesitated before going to open it in case it was Frank back to collect something he had forgotten. But when she did open the door, to her relief it was only Rachel, who had seen the car come and then go again, and noticed Frank carrying his bulky leather holdall. Standing on the doorstep, her expression said it all: I'm here if you need an ear and a bit of comforting.

Anna waved her in and they went and sat at the table. Before she knew it, she was shedding bucket-loads of tears while Rachel held her hand and gave gentle advice, which was exactly what she needed – another voice in the room, a soft and gentle voice. Once she had stopped crying, the old woman said, 'Do you know what, darling? I think you are going to have to fight for your man. Fight with every weapon you have, even though it might go against the grain and make you feel sick inside. Once he's back in the fold, then you bide your time and you ask yourself do you want to spend the rest of your life with him? Give yourself the right to choose what *you* want. Don't be impulsive. Be clever and come out of this feeling that you are on top of it.'

'I don't know if I'm strong enough a person to do that, Rachel,' said Anna, drying her eyes. 'I don't even know if I want to be bothered. I think I would rather change the lock on the door so he doesn't come in here again.'

'Listen to me. You have the babies to think about even if you don't feel that *you* need Frank right now. Him coming and going this morning was a rotten thing for you to have to go through. Mean. He should have stayed a lot longer and talked to you before he left with his things packed in that silly bag. I'm disappointed in him and I'm surprised. I take it that he's sulking and is going to sleep in that little flat above his brother's restaurant to sort out his mind?'

'I think so. But really, I know as much as you do, Rachel. I think he said that he was going to his brother's flat in Tower Hill, but he's a clever liar so who knows whose bed he'll be sleeping in tonight? And do you know what – I don't think I care any more. One thing is for sure – he can't shack up with Bridget in our flat because I've let Trevor and his mum have the keys. They are going to move into it.'

'Well, that's no bad thing, is it? In fact I would say that this is a clever move.' The old woman smiled and her face lit up. 'And of course you care where your husband sleeps. But *you* won't lose any sleep over it. That's what you tell him should he ask. So, listen ... I made some chicken soup first thing. You want that I should fetch it in around lunchtime? We could eat together.'

'No thank you, darling,' said Anna, squeezing the old lady's bony hand. 'It's enough to know that you're there for me. Right next door. But you mustn't worry – I will come through this, you'll see ... even if it does take a while to adjust.'

'Well, that makes me feel better,' said the old neighbour. 'But also promise me that you'll knock on my door, no matter what time, if you suddenly need a shoulder to cry on or somebody to talk to, even.'

'I promise,' said Anna. 'And I do mean that.'

'Good. Then I shall love and leave you.' Rachel pulled herself up from the chair and looked around the room. 'You know, I think you would be just as happy here – with or without Frank – once you accept the idea of it. I loved my husband but he got in the bloody way all of the time, God rest his soul.'

Once she was by herself again, Anna ran through her mind what the old woman had said, and the more she thought about it the more it made sense. Rachel had been short and to the point when giving advice: 'Give yourself the right to choose what *you* want. Bide your time and don't be impulsive. Be clever and come out of this the best you possibly can.' These were words of wisdom that she was going to tuck at the back of her mind and not forget. Since it was quiet and her babies, by the sound of things, were still asleep, she felt as if she deserved to go back to bed herself for another hour or so to catch up on the sleep that she had missed during her restless night. The worst of this morning's fiasco was that Frank had walked away as if he was the pained victim. 'You can be a selfish bastard at times, Frank,' she murmured, as she filled a glass with water from the tap in the kitchen, hardly able to comprehend that her world had tumbled almost overnight.

'I should have known you would try and make it my fault,' she thought. 'Make me look like the trouble-maker. But that's all right – I'll be your scapegoat for a little while longer. Blame me all you want. I know I haven't done anything wrong and so do other people. Especially those who eat in our restaurant.'

With a heavy heart she tilted her head to heaven as salty tears trickled down her cheeks, and whispered, 'Please, God ... please look after me and my babies. Help me to take care of them and keep all of this dark and horrible stuff out of their innocent world. I do realise that I badly need your guidance. Amen.'

Then, just as if her prayer had been answered, there was a short ring on the doorbell. Dragging herself to answer it and not really caring who it was this time, her face lit up when she saw her sisters standing on the doorstep with a bunch of flowers in Linda's arms and a big box of chocolates in Hazel's. Slowly shaking her head and laughing, Anna said, 'If you two are not witches then my name's not Anna. Your timing is perfect. Come on in.'

After hugs all round, the three sisters flopped down in the living room, their shoes off, their legs curled under them as they sipped their freshly percolated coffee and smoked their cigarettes. Linda and Hazel were getting exactly what they came for. Their sister was talking ten to the dozen and they were all ears.

'I don't want to be seen in the same light as hundreds of other women who this has happened to. I don't want to be talked about as the spineless wife and mother of two who needs to get off her arse and be shaken out of domesticity. But I do want to still get on with taking care of my babies even if it does have to be by myself. And I will carry on doing the shopping, cooking and washing and ironing and housework. It's not a hobby – it's a fact of life. These things have to be done.'

'No one's knocking that, Anna. Why are you being a touch defensive?'

'I'm not. It's just that earlier on I read an article in a magazine about men and their affairs. Statistics show that the "other women" are mostly the ones who get the boot in the end. Once the sex bit has been done to death. That's when the men usually get down on their knees to the wife and beg to be taken back. And most do take them back. It made me angry, that's all.'

'Mum didn't take Dad back though, did she?' said Linda, sadly.

'Good for her is what I say.' Hazel gazed at the floor, thoughtfully. 'You know what Mum's like. Too proud and too self-sufficient to have let him come back in the door. Plenty of men have found themselves out in the cold with the locks changed.'

'But that's not what I want to happen, Hazel. I want things back the way they were. And I'll go about that in my own sweet way. After all, I am partly to blame for all of this.'

'Rubbish. It's the Bridgets of this world and men like Frank who can't resist a bit of oats on the side. And let's face it, Bridget's been like a heat rash all over him from the start.'

'I know. She behaves as if they're a couple at times and in front of me. I don't know how I've kept my fist out of her face for so long.'

'That's why we're here again, babe. To goad you back into the right action.' Hazel looked at Anna. 'Just make certain that you do really want Frank back before you make a decision.'

'Absolutely,' said Linda. 'You just might start to hate him later on in life when you're lying awake in the night and he's asleep beside you and it all comes flooding back. It might just dawn on you that you don't actually want him any more.'

'Exactly.' Hazel smiled. 'That's that out of the way. No more talk about the bitch that seems to be permanently on heat. She's wasted enough of our sister-time together. Fuck her. She's doomed now whichever way it goes.'

Anna stretched her shoulders and breathed a sigh of relief. 'I do feel better about things. And I can see it in a different light now. Any woman working at Frank's side for twelve hours a day and on a regular basis was bound to get on friendly terms. The difference is that Bridget was set on having it all from the minute she walked into Prima.'

'I think you might be right, Anna,' said Hazel, pleased that their little bit of brainwashing had worked.

'I knew all along that Frank had been too tired at night once he got in. I know how the busy spells can be murder at Prima from when I did my two-year stint. But before she came along exhaustion didn't affect Frank's passion or performance in the bedroom. We were always at it. So by not bothering to touch me I think he was giving me a message to keep my distance. He was acting as if I had done something wrong. And do you know what? I was beginning to believe that myself.'

Hazel and Linda looked from their innocent fair-haired sibling to each other and half smiled. They had achieved their goal. They had arrived at the point where their Anna was not only facing up to what was going on but voicing it as if she had got to this turning point by herself. They couldn't have wished for it to have gone better. It was true that tears were in her lovely green eyes and her hands were trembling and she was twisting her handkerchief into a knot, but this was something that they had seen before, when she was at school and facing end-of-term exams. So rather than talk to her about her husband's affair, they coaxed Anna into talking about the twins. They asked questions to do with the stage they were at and gradually, the more she talked the more Anna relaxed and the more she relaxed the more she talked. Both her sisters had to hold tight to their emotions as they listened to her giving pathetic reasons as to why Frank had been disloyal to her. They were happy enough, though, to be the patient listeners as they waited for her to talk herself out. When she did finally lapse into silence Linda was straight in.

'Frank's just a stupid sod that's been lured in by a tempting arse and fuck-me expression. Bridget's just another ambitious little cow who wants it all. And in this case it's the man, the restaurant and the money.'

'Absolutely. I should have known she wouldn't have been able to fool the pair of you, but I bet the customers think that she's just a lovely girl down from the country.'

'I don't know about that, babe, but fool us? No way. We saw from the start what she was up to. And Frank won't have been the first married man she's got her claws into. This one was born to break up good marriages.'

'So . . .' said Linda, having heard enough, 'do you want all of this to work its way into boredom, babe, or do you want one of the boys to bring Frank up sharp?'

'How about we send Bridget packing?' said Anna, more positive. 'Wouldn't that be the most logical thing to do?'

'It would be the best thing but maybe not logical. What's to say that Frank wouldn't take a drive to wherever she goes next so as to meet her secretly in some little pub or club somewhere? Men are turned on by the chase don't forget.'

'I don't think that he would go that far.' Anna looked from one sister to the other. 'Would he?'

'Oh, I think he might, Anna,' said Linda. 'He'll be just like the caveman pursuing the woman on heat. And let's not forget that Bridget hadn't been working there for a week before he was lured in by her little-girl smile when she posed in her flowing fuck-me frocks and high-heel shoes. The men could smell her from a mile off and Frank was only a few feet away.'

Anna's sister could be crude but she got to the point. 'You're right, Linda,' she responded. She *was* up for it. She was after Frank and only Frank. Frank the owner of the restaurant. The one with the money. If she wiggled her backside at any of the male customers it would have been to torment Frank and nobody else. It brings back a sickening picture in the mind – but it's true. It's all true.'

'Give her the fucking boot,' said Hazel. 'I can't see Frank going looking for her. She's just been a cheap thrill, that's all. I reckon he'll beg to have you back once this comes out into the open. And when this does happen, no more playing the perfect wife and mother. You're coming out with us now and then for a bit of fun. You're getting back out there again and shaking off the dust!'

A deep sigh of relief escaped from Anna. 'God! I think I might just be ready for that. Just one night a month would do. I want to rock and roll again.'

'Rock and roll? I don't think so.' Hazel turned to Linda. 'She's living in the fucking past.'

'You know what I mean,' Anna said. 'One of *your* haunts. A nightclub with a live band and lots of fantastic atmosphere.'

Quiet and thoughtful, Linda, out of the blue, said, 'Do you know what the most sickening thing of all is? Bridget never stopped talking to us about her husband when we were in there now and then for a quick bite at lunchtimes. Her Trevor. Her Trevor the swimming instructor. The poor bastard that she's been two-timing for God knows how many years. So what is that all about?'

'Ask a psychiatrist,' Anna said. 'As for me, I'm not all that sure what makes her tick and neither do I care. She's got our undivided attention and she's not even under our roof!' She looked from one to the other as she slowly shook her head and smiled at them, saying, 'I can't tell you how much I appreciate the pair of you coming round to give me another kick up the bum. I'll sleep better tonight having had it reaffirmed that I'm not on my own in all of this.'

'On your own? No way. And as for that girl getting her grip on the daddy of our twin nephews . . . forget it. Frank's been sucked in by someone who deserves a good slapping before she moves on, and if that's what it takes that's what she'll get.'

'Exactly,' said Hazel. 'Now let's get off the subject.' She leaned forward and brushed strands of hair off Anna's face affectionately. 'Would you like us to come back and sleep over tonight? Me on the sofa and Linda on the foldaway bed in the twins' room?'

'No. Thanks anyway, but I think I need to be by myself. I want to think how best to play this. If we're to get rid of Bridget for good it would be better if it was Frank's idea that she goes and not mine. I don't want to play it wrongly and kick myself for it later.'

'That sounds sensible,' said Hazel, even though she realised that there was a possibility that Frank might not choose Anna and the twins over Bridget. He had looked every bit the man in love when speaking intimately to the girl behind the bar at Prima.

'God,' said Anna quietly. 'I feel as if a weight's been lifted off my shoulders again by having you to share this with.'

Glancing at each other, Linda and Hazel knew that enough had been said all round. 'Well, don't forget that if you want to get out on a Saturday night with old friends, we'll be only too pleased to baby-sit.' Linda smiled.

'I won't forget and I'll be all right. I'll be more than all right.'

Happier now that their sister was in this frame of mind, the girls relaxed and stayed for a little longer, drinking coffee and tactfully filling her in as to just how much private time Frank had been spending with Bridget in the small cosy flat above Prima Pasta. Once they had said as much as they thought she could take in this second session of brain bashing, the girls promised every bit of their support before hugging their sister and then leaving her to herself.

With a glass of water in her hand, Anna slowly climbed the stairs as fatigue washed over her and a calm of sorts spread right through her body. She was tired, ready for her feather pillow and the quiet of her bedroom, where she doubted she would ever see Frank sleep again. Once beneath the covers, she drifted off into a light sleep feeling better for the fact that she had Rachel living next door. When she woke from her forty-minute nap she knew she had been dreaming of herself and George, in the thick of the Kent country-side by a river, with sheep in the background and hop vines all around her. She was looking forward to her day out in Kent while her mum, the doting grandmother, looked after the twins.

Chapter Six

Choosing to kick off with an early start, George had arranged to pick up Anna and the twins at eight o'clock on Sunday morning to drop the babies off at Ivy's flat before heading for Kent. Tonbridge not being that much of a distance, Anna knew that once they had got through the traffic leading into the Blackwall tunnel and out again, it wouldn't be much more than an hour or so before they were at their destination. From all that George had said, and had shown her on his map, the tiny village that they were heading for had only one shop and one pub. Up early as usual, Anna saw to the twins then got herself ready. Once dressed – in her favourite sandy-coloured corduroy flares with matching jacket and a soft multi-coloured blouse – she had time to spare.

In her hold-all she had packed a clean set of clothes for each of the twins as well as all the other paraphernalia that went with not just one baby but two. Now she had plenty of time to relax with a cup of coffee before George arrived and while the twins, dressed for outdoors, were asleep in their carry cots. Why her stomach was turning over at the thought of this outing she had little idea other than she hadn't had a day out in a long while and was excited by it. She realised that some people would see this as her going on a date with George, but this didn't bother her too much.

Checking her appearance in the mirror above the fireplace she smiled, then quietly laughed, at the image that greeted her. Her impromptu visit the day before to the new hairdresser's on the Mile End Road, with the twins in tow, had given her a new look. As suggested by the owner, a young woman of thirty, Anna had thrown caution to the wind and had one of the latest styles, referred to as the shaggy dog cut, which didn't alter the length of her hair but had changed it from one length to several layers – and she loved it. Adding to this sense of a new beginning and trying to sort out her life, she had accepted some of Rachel's old-fashioned herbal pills to help her relax.

Having been a family friend ever since she could remember, George was proving to be a tonic and she was seeing him in a slightly different light. Before now he had been one of the good guys who worked on both sides of the law and kept his private business to himself. Apart from the fact that he had lovely light blue eyes and a smile to die for, he was also six feet tall and attractive in a rugged sort of way. She wasn't sure what Frank was going to make of them having a day out together and wondered if, by doing so, she was making things worse between them. Even though he had treated her badly, she did still love him and still hoped that he would come to his senses and ask her forgiveness. From the way he had behaved when he came to collect his things, she could imagine him seeing her day out as revenge. She knew that Frank would have heard that George's wife had left him and so was now considered single and free. She didn't think for one minute that he was going to be happy with her being chauffeured around like this.

With this and other worries floating in and out of her mind, she sipped her coffee in the quiet until the bell rang and she opened the door to George. Standing on the front step dressed in his casual clothes she thought he looked more handsome and cuddly without the suit and tie. Cuddly – in a brotherly sort of way, of course.

Once they were settled in the car the couple chatted quietly as George drove the little family through the back turnings to Wilmot Street in Bethnal Green, and during a spell of comfortable silence, George had to admit that he rather liked this role of a father figure to the twins, which was how it felt to him right then. He was touched by the fact that the babies, who had woken up when he placed their carrycots into the back of the car, hadn't started to cry but had gurgled and smiled at him.

'What a lovely life, eh?' George smiled as he drove. 'Clean and warm and loved. I wouldn't mind swapping places with one of your twins.'

'Yes you would,' said Anna, smiling. 'Just think about having to start all over again ... going to school for the first time; having to do homework; being told that you're too old to scramble about on old ruins or too young to play kiss chase ...'

George chuckled. 'Fair enough. We've come this far in good nick, babe, so why turn the clock back?'

She looked sideways at him. 'Exactly. My marriage is on the rocks but look what I've got on the back seat. Not one carrycot with a baby sleeping soundly but two.'

George smiled warmly and continued on his way to Ivy's flat in a comfortable, placid kind of a mood. He and Anna were easy in each other's company and he put this down to the fact that they had known each other for a long time and so spells of silence were bound to be relaxed with no awkward moments.

Once they had dropped off the twins and were driving away from Ivy's, George said, 'Your mum's a good woman, Anna.' He then switched on the radio and tuned it, searching for some easy classical music on Three. 'She thinks the world of you girls.'

'And we think the world of her, George. She's a one-off who'd do anything for any one of us. But she's also a crafty cow.' Anna started to laugh as she remembered what Ivy had said as they were leaving her flat, *I wouldn't mind a little quiet drive out into the Kent countryside myself*. 'Mum reckons that she wouldn't mind moving out into the countryside. She reckons that by pulling the old terraced houses down to build blocks of flats in their place, the planning department are ripping the heart out of the East End.'

'She's probably right, Anna.'

'If you say so. She's gonna take you up on your offer to take her for a drive to Kent you know.'

'I don't mind if she does. I work long hours, Anna, and I work hard, so to sit in this driving seat and make for the countryside is a pleasure.' He smiled. 'In any case ... your mum and her mate, Gwen, are free entertainment and better than theatre comedy. They make me die.'

'I know. Gwen's funnier than Mum though ... the things she comes out with.'

'They play off each other just like any good comedy duo.' George laughed and then went quiet as he concentrated on his driving. Whether the two friends would have been so relaxed and in such a lighthearted mood had they known that Frank had arrived in Anna's turning some ten minutes or so before she and George left with the twins, was something else.

Frank's reason for being there was to pick up some more of his things but now, still in his car, he was seething. Having recognised George's car parked up outside the house on arrival, he had reversed until he was at a space that he had spotted on his way in. This had been an ideal spot because he was obscured between a lorry and a van and there he had sat and watched the pair of them. Frank had always seen George as a bit of a mate as well as a good customer at Prima, but now, still parked, he was wondering if perhaps George's car had been there all night.

Sitting back and watching for any sign of action, he had been in two minds as to what to do next when the front door had opened and George had come out with the handles of a carrycot gripped in his hand. Once he placed this on the back seat of his car, Anna had followed him out with his other baby son, in his makeshift bed. Frank had been livid when he saw Anna get into the front seat to be driven away. A little happy family scene was what it had looked like.

Still parked in the same spot and seething, Frank was having a one-sided conversation with himself. 'What a fucking bastard. What does he think he's up to? The shit-faced turncoat! The two-faced bastard.' His mouth dry, his anger burning deep, Frank could hardly believe

175

that he had watched the car pull away with his family aboard and George the bent copper in the driving seat. 'Well, it didn't take *you* long, did it Anna?' he fumed. 'It didn't take you long.'

Filled with rage and what could possibly have passed for jealousy, Frank couldn't quite bring himself to get out of his car and go into his house to make a cup of tea which he badly needed. He also wanted to sit down in his living room and have a cigarette in the quiet. He was so put out that he was trembling with what he believed to be fury. Shock and dejection, of course, were furthest from his mind. He wasn't the kind of guy to be jealous and never had been. At least this is what he was telling himself. The worst thing of all as far as he was concerned was that both Anna and George had been laughing. There were no signs of heartache coming from his wife over their impending separation, only laughter. He now wondered if they had been seeing each other and if so, for how long?

George, from what he could tell, had been sharing a joke with his Anna. Sharing a joke after possibly sharing a bed. His bed. He felt sick. He didn't know what to do next. After a few minutes of sitting in the car with not much going through his mind he badly needed some fresh air. Getting out of the car, he leaned over as he rested a hand on the bonnet and drew in long slow breaths of fresh air that tasted sweeter than it had ever done before. This done, he collected himself, locked the car door and crossed the narrow road to unlatch the little gate that led into his tiny front garden. Seeing Rachel, their neighbour, snipping and clipping bits off her tall neat privet, he nodded and just about managed to say a civil hello. Rachel had in fact come out of her house once she had seen, from her upstairs window, George pulling away in his car just after she had spotted Frank manoeuvring his so as to park and watch the comings and goings.

Pretending she knew nothing, Rachel smiled at Frank. 'What have you forgotten this time, scatter-brain?' she said.

'Oh you know me, Rachel, I'd forget my head if it wasn't screwed on. I didn't see you there when I just came out from inside the house,' he said, testing to see if she had any inkling of what was what. She was old and senile after all. 'Gardening already, are you? You'll get green fingers ...' he gently teased as he just managed a smile. 'I forgot to take this week's menu list that I worked out last night before bedtime,' he said.

'You men,' she said, 'you're all the same.' With that Rachel smiled and gave a little wave as she went back inside her house and closed the door.

'Well, well, well,' she murmured. 'What next? He is prepared to tell a lie so as not to fall out with me. So? What can this mean?' She laughed quietly to herself and went to put the kettle on the stove. 'He'll be back, Anna ... but you must make him suffer first if you take him back. As I think you will. But who knows?'

Frank let himself into his house with a very strange feeling inside – it was almost as if he didn't belong there any more. When he picked up on the awesome silence with no sound of the radio, TV or stereo and worse still, no sound of Anna or his twins, James and Oliver, tears came into his eyes. Drawing a deep breath, he told himself to get a grip before strolling along the passage and into the kitchen. His intention had been to come in and collect the rest of his clothes and let Anna work it out for herself that he was leaving her. But now, he was having second thoughts. He was in a bit of turmoil. He felt as if he was going from a dream into a nightmare. The dream was of he and Bridget living in their fantasy world, and the nightmare was Anna letting him go without so much as a goodbye. Never mind that she was already out there with George Blake . . .

He poured himself some lime juice and added water from the tap and felt as if he was doing all of this in slow motion. Then, when he strolled into the living room and saw a tiny sock on the floor close to the twins' playpen, reality kicked in. He looked from this to the window and into his small lovely back garden where washing was hanging out on the line to dry. Some of Anna's laundry, some Babygros and nappies. Nothing of his was out there blowing in the warm breeze. Then, catching a glimpse of Rachel clipping dead leaves off her climbing ivy and clematis, he realised what he had done – and what he had been slowly doing for a year or so. He shook his head and swallowed against the lump in his throat as he murmured, 'You stupid bastard, Frank.'

Anna and George's outing from the East End to the countryside seemed to be taking no time at all because the friends were so comfortable in each other's company and could chat about this, that or the other without touching on the more serious side of life. George had freely opened up with his reasons why he was looking for a place in the countryside to restore and renovate as a going concern for the future.

Consumed by his dream, he opened up to her more and more. 'To be honest with you, babe,' he said, after a short spell of silence, 'a little bit of work on the side that me and the boys were recently involved in is the last as far as I'm concerned. I want out of the Met as well . . . while the going's good. We did have a nice little earner from the gold lighters, which I think you might have picked up on in the restaurant when you were in—'

'I did as it happens,' said Anna cutting in. 'One of your cousins needs to realise that even his *hushed* voice is loud enough for anyone in the close vicinity to hear. I did think about mentioning it to you but thought better of it. Male pride and all that.' She smiled.

'So long as I've got my male pride, that suits me fine,' said George. 'We delivered the goods and we've been paid out, but there are still a few loose ends to tie up.'

'Such as?'

'Paying off one or two people who played a small part. There's a grand in my pocket right now – believe it or not. And yes, I had already arranged to go to Kent to sort that little bit of business out before you ask. But you weren't an afterthought, Anna. When I made the arrangements over the phone you came to mind. I thought a day in the countryside and the fresh air would do you good.'

'Well, we're not even there yet and I already feel good. I'm in a nice comfortable car, sitting next to a handsome man. What more could a girl wish for?'

He smiled as he looked sideways at her and seemed a bit shy as he said, 'Thank you for that. But I do need to be in Tonbridge at one point, babe, and so I'm gonna have to nip off by myself. To see two guys in a pub. It shouldn't take long and there are some nice little tea rooms in Kent where you can wait for me.'

'Sounds idyllic. Afternoon cream tea. Lovely.'

'Good. That's settled then. I was worried that you might get the 'ump over it.'

'Don't be daft. And I'm pleased that you're getting out of the Met. And I think that your idea of buying a cheap rundown old mansion to do up is brilliant. Enough said?'

'Absolutely, babe. Spot on. I want to do something completely different that's all above board. I'm not the type to go into the protection racket lark that some coppers who've got out of the force have done. It's not only the Kray twins who went down that road. Although as well as making money from their protection racket, the Krays must have been running over thirty different clubs and pubs all around London. It's a shame that they went from lads who loved the sport of boxing to lads who thrived on terror and risk. But there you go. They fell into the trap of needing to sleep with guns under their pillows.'

'It's their parents I feel sorry for. What must it have been like to see their baby twin boys growing into evil criminals?'

'Don't even think about it, Anna. There was something wrong with the pair of them. There had to be. I just wonder if their mother was actually pleased when they moved out of their family home in the mid-

Sixties to a lavish apartment in Clapton. From what I heard they did it up as if it was a wing in Buckingham Palace. And then of course, in time, Reggie got married ... and didn't we all pity that poor cow. She didn't know what she was letting herself in for.'

'George ... don't talk about it any more. It makes me feel sick to think about the underworld not that far away from where I'm living. Don't let's spoil our day out.'

'Sorry, babe. I do go on a bit.'

'It's understandable. You knew the Krays before and after their stroll into crime.'

'But we'll change the subject. Tell me about your dad and what you remember of 'im.'

'I would rather tell you about my gran and granddad before they died, if that's all right. They were like second parents to us girls.'

'Fair enough. Off you go.'

Anna began to voice her favourite recollections during the rest of their journey. They laughed and joked and discussed all kinds of things – except each of their failing marriages. On the last stint of the ride to the small and old-fashioned village of Hunston, George was reminiscing about when he was a lad and had come down to this neck of the woods for hop-picking.

'The little butcher's shop is still there and run by the same family can you believe?' He spoke as if it were a miracle.

'I think that might be the case with most butchers and fishmongers, George,' she said. 'They tend to be passed from father to son, don't they? Even in the East End. But it's lovely that you can come back after ten years or so and still see the same name above the shops.'

'They're not really shops though, Anna, are they,' he said, steering his car around the tree-lined narrow and curling lanes. 'Not the way we know shops in London in any case. In Hunston was the post office and store that was the bottom half of a cottage with living space above.' He slowly shook his head as he recalled it all. 'Do you know what I used to love as a kid? The bare floorboards in the village store. Varnished . . . but bare floorboards all the same. I loved the sound our boots made on 'em. Daft things you remember . . .' he murmured, and then went quiet.

'When was the last time you paid a visit to the farm?' Anna asked, touched by the sensitivity of this man who dealt with hardened criminals every week of the year. He was one of the few who enjoyed the thrill of keeping law and order one week and bending the rules the next to meet his own ends, and he was not the only officer within his realm or outside it to do so. To some, it was all part and parcel of the job when working in major cities where life was fast and risky and the workload heavy.

'I was down nigh on twelve months ago to the day as it happens – to see to a little bit of business with some gear we had stored in the barn that we've been renting at a cheap price for a few years. I just go along with them, or by myself come to that, for the ride every now and then when needs must, but only when I think the cousins need the boss to hold their hands.' George chuckled.

'Oh, so you're their boss then, are you?' Anna teased.

'It was meant to be a joke, Anna.'

'I know it was, George.'

He glanced sideways at her and smiled, and as she smiled back at him he felt his heart beat a little faster. Drawing breath, he spoke to her as if she was a mate and not the woman that he thought he was in love with. 'Once we're in Tonbridge, I'll leave you in a lovely little tea room for fifteen minutes, enjoying the best fruit and malt bread going and the best pot of tea you'll find anywhere.'

'Oh . . . and will this be after we've visited your old farm where you picked hops or before?'

'Afterwards, babe. But it won't take me much more than twenty minutes or so. I've got to see a man about a dog. You won't mind sitting by yourself will you?'

'No, I don't think so. So long as I'm not stuck there for hours waiting for you to come back.'

'I wouldn't do that to you, Anna,' he said, as he turned into a long winding lane. 'And now . . . I'll show you the huts we used to live in and then, if we've got time, we'll go and 'ave a look at the farmhouse that's up for grabs.'

'How did you know about it in the first place?' said Anna.

'I put some feelers out months ago and it turns out that the wealthy landowner's gonna move to Ireland where he's bought acres of land, and an entire little village by the sound of it.'

'And you fancy the idea of living in Kent, then? Or would you just come down for nice weekends?'

'I don't know. It's not cut and dried. And it'll take a couple of years to get the place into shape from what I hear. But it's a fantastic house. Must have about eight double bedrooms. Colonel John Knight and his wife had all kinds of staff living in, and there was a small family who lived in a little cottage that went with the job that was a part of the estate. It's an old titled family that goes back years and you couldn't wish to meet nicer aristocrats who are nowhere near as wealthy as some people think. They were good to us hop-pickers. Treated us as if we were no different to them. Well, almost.'

'Do they still grow hops on the farm?' said Anna enjoying this little outing that had been mentioned in passing one minute and was happening the next.

'I'll tell you what,' said George, smiling, 'if they did still have pickers coming down I would sign up.'

'Oh, shut up.' Anna laughed. 'You're too used to home comforts just like the rest of us now. You wouldn't live in a tiny hut and sleep on straw. Give me a break.'

'Well, maybe you don't know me as well as you think you do because I think I would.' To the sound of Anna's soft laughter, he turned into a narrow lane just wide enough for two cars but not a car and a tractor should one happen along. He remembered it well.

'And to answer your question, no they don't grow hops anymore. The farmer turned all of that in once picking by hand was done and dusted. Once mechanisation and modernisation found its way on to the hop fields.'

Going all quiet and thoughtful as he drove slowly and soaked in the silence of the gentle countryside, George saw in his mind's eye another way to try and resurrect that style of living – without the hop-picking. A holiday place that had more to offer than just camping out in tents or huts but still with the great communal way of life. 'Do you know what I reckon, Anna,' he murmured. 'I reckon that the farmhouse, which is more of a rambling mansion, would make a fantastic up-market bed-and-breakfast place for holidays. That's what I can see – a brilliant place in the thick of the Kent countryside, with one section rigged out for the wealthy to luxuriate in and another part for the not so highly paid townies. A little bit of country living and an escape from the mad world in the fast lane. I reckon me and the lads could pick up that rundown estate cheap. It was in a dire condition when I last came down.'

Anna slowly shook her head. 'You've got great ideas, George, but if you wanted to do what you've just said you'd need a huge loan from the bank for the development.'

'Yeah ... and so did Mr Taylor and Mr Woodrow. The market boys who grafted their way to success from running a stall selling any end-of-the-line goods they got their hands on in the Roman Road and became property developers. Little acorns and big oak trees, Anna. Little acorns and big oaks.'

Turning into yet another long and winding lane, George smiled and slowly shook his head. 'I love this bit of the journey. It takes me right back to when we were kids on the back of the lorry. Happy as Larry we were once we finally arrived, belting out old-fashioned songs with the older generation.'

'I can remember the kids around our way getting

excited when September came round,' said Anna. 'We never went hop-picking ... I don't know why not though. A lot of our neighbours did. Even if Dad hadn't left Mum when we were little, I don't think he would have taken us. We all went to a holiday camp once a year up until I was about eight or nine.'

'That's odd,' said George, a puzzled expression on his face. 'That's *really* odd. I can see smoke which I can only imagine is coming out of the chimney of the old cookhouse on the common.'

'Maybe some squatters have moved in,' Anna said. 'And who would blame them in this little bit of heaven.'

'No one. Tramps have been doing the self-same thing for donkey's years. They get away with murder if they have a mind to,' said George. 'The boys in blue leave them alone in and around London. Long may that last.'

The closer they got to the common and the row upon row of brick huts with black tin rooftops glinting in the sunlight, the more excited George became and he didn't mind showing it. He was like a boy who had gone looking for a lost shilling and found a pound note. He could hardly believe what he was looking at. People were living on the site, which now resembled a medieval village, and were meandering around camp-fires on which they were cooking their Sunday dinners.

'Bloody hell ...' said George, steering with one hand and running the other through his hair. 'They've knocked two huts into one in every row and turned 'em into little country cottages. I don't believe what I'm looking at.'

'I wonder why David and Jimmy didn't tell you. You said they came down recently.'

'Not to this part, sweetheart,' said George, still a touch dumbfounded by it all. 'The barn we're renting is on the acreage around the old farmhouse that I was telling you about.'

Overwhelmed by all he saw, he drove slowly and in silence towards a nearby oak tree and parked beneath it without saying a word. He then got out of the driver's seat and looked around him as he went to open the passenger door for Anna and found his voice again.

'I can't believe that the farmer would 'ave sold off the huts to Londoners, Anna. It would only have been for peanuts if he had've done. I would 'ave been in like a shot and bought the lot of 'em.'

Looking from the little commune to George's face, Anna hoped she wasn't about to discover a side of him that she had not seen before – greed. 'Maybe the fact that you would 'ave bought them in a job-lot was the reason why it was kept a tight secret? Maybe those that have bought a little bit of nostalgic heaven for themselves didn't want someone like you to approach the farmer.'

George looked sideways at Anna, frowning slightly. 'I'm not a developer, babe,' he quietly said.

'But you would 'ave been … if you had bought up the job-lot though, wouldn't you? You would have been just as bad as those who would want it all for themselves with nothing other than profit on their minds.'

'Point taken.' He looked into her lovely face and those big soft green eyes and drew a breath. He then

187

spoke with a touch of shame in his voice. 'Seeing all of this brings back memories, Anna, and yes, you're right; if I'm honest I would 'ave loved to have been the creator of the scene we're looking at as well as being part of it now and then.'

Sorry now that she had doubted his integrity, Anna slipped her arm into his and smiled. 'Come on then, Mister Amazed-Man. Let's go and get a slice of nostalgia for you to take back as a nice memory to tuck under your pillow tonight.'

George peered under his hand to see that just across the field, which had been patterned by nature with wild flowers and weeds, there were well-kept vegetable beds. 'Jesus Christ,' he murmured, 'they're growing Mary Jane, Anna.'

'What are you talking about?' Anna laughed. 'Mary Jane?'

'Just another name for the obvious, sweetheart – marijuana.' He glanced at her, his eyes twinkling with amusement. 'It's in the herb garden – the patch that's closest to us.' He then burst out laughing. 'All neat and tidy like Hampton Court and nurturing drugs among it all. Brilliant.'

'Well, it wouldn't be the first time I've heard that, George. According to my mum – and you can ask her yourself – her gran, just like other housewives, used to grow something similar in their herb bed. For soups and stews.'

George looked sideways at Anna and waited for her to say that she was only kidding, but she simply laughed at him. 'Don't tell me that you've never heard that before?'

'I've not as it happens,' he said. 'I suppose none of them knew what it was?'

'Oh of course they did! It was a herb they used in cooking and by the look of things still do. They made nice hot bedtime drinks with it as well. But mostly it was used to lift someone's spirits if they were down in the dumps or in shock over something or the other.'

'Pull the other leg, Anna ... please.'

'I'm not making it up! You must know about the old herbalists? Mum used to go over to Wapping to Mary Reeder, who was married to a lovely West Indian guy. They grew all kind of things in her back yard. We used to have hot peppermint tea, spearmint tea ... something to make you go if you were constipated ... and something else if you had the runs.'

'Yeah, all right, babe, point taken.'

He shook his head slowly and then nodded towards the campsite. 'We'd best go and let them know who we are. I'll avert my eyes from the herb garden that's smack bang in the centre in this nostalgic little universe where pensioners grow cannabis.'

'Stop calling it that,' said Anna. 'Let's go and see who it is that's peering at you peering at him.'

George nodded and then went and locked his car out of habit. 'I hardly expected this, on my life. I can't tell you how much it means to me to see people living in the huts again. Amazing.'

She took his hand in hers and they walked along a dirt and gravel track towards the homesteaders – just two good friends from the old days. He was enjoying a bit of childhood nostalgia and Anna was relishing this little bit of freedom.

Coming towards the couple from the village-like scene was an old-fashioned chap in his seventies, who was peering at them under his hand even though he was wearing a docker's cap on his head to shade his eyes and his bald patch. George, still smiling, said, 'If this is a picker from the old days that I know, Anna, get your hanky out because I'll need that as well as my own.'

'You old softie,' she said. 'Men are worse than women, I swear it.' She liked the way he sometimes showed the feminine side of himself – whether he knew he was doing it or not.

As they drew closer to the old man he stopped shielding his eyes and looked at George as if for a split second he recognised him. He then straightened, placed his hands on his hips and said, 'Are you visiting family or just being nosy parkers?'

'I'm not visiting any of my family and, to be honest, I'm still a bit too overwhelmed by all of this to recognise who you might be.' He offered his hand saying, 'My name is George Blake.'

The old man rubbed his chin thoughtfully and then shook his head. 'That name rings a bell.' He then looked George straight in the eye. 'Did your family used to come to this farm to pick hops in the old days?'

'For nigh on ten years or so. Probably further back if you start to think about great-grandparents.'

'Oh ... right ... well, I probably will 'ave known them then. The memory ain't all it used to be but it'll come to me soon. Course it will. Now come and meet the missus. The kettle's on the stove so you're just in time for a mug of tea.'

They followed him to a row of brick huts – one which George had shared as a bedroom with his two brothers when they were kids. His emotions all over the place, he looked at Anna with tears coming into his eyes and murmured, 'You're gonna have to help me out here, babe.'

Anna took hold of his hand again and gave it an encouraging squeeze. The gentleman, who was clearly one of the governors of the commune, showed his importance in his stride, which was not as stable as the old boy would have liked to think, and since it was too early in the day for beer, George assumed – correctly – that it was the old boy's hunched back that was a little incapacitating. Even so, he was wiry enough, and a bent back for the older generation from the East End or south of the river was not unusual because they had either worked in the docks or the markets, from boy to man, carrying heavy loads.

'We don't keep coffee in the hut because we're tea drinkers in the main,' said the man as he glanced over his shoulder at them. 'But if you like you could buy a bottle of Camp coffee from our little on-site shop.'

'Tea's fine by me,' said Anna, secretly amused at this comical sight of someone who made her think of a favourite television programme – *The Beverly Hillbillies*.

'Tea sounds lovely,' said George, also stifling a giggle.

'It's all right, our little shop. It does us nicely. We all take turns to serve on a kind of a rota system.' He stopped in his tracks and almost had Anna and George bumping into him. Staring down at the ground he shook his head. 'Now, what was I about to do?' He nudged his cap back a little and scratched his head. 'I'll be blowed if I can remember.' He turned and stared at Anna. 'Just remind me, ducks ... do I know you?'

'No,' said Anna, warming to this old boy. 'But your family or one or two of your friends might know George. He used to stay in these huts when he was a kid – at hop-picking time.'

'That was it! That's what he said, wasn't it? Bloody memory's playing up today.' He held out his hand to George and clicked his false teeth. 'Welcome back, son. Welcome back. The name's Ernie.' Then, chuckling to himself, he turned around and continued leading them to his hut in one of ten rows. 'Yes,' he said, 'having our own little shop saves us walking up to the village every time we need something. And it saves us 'aving to listen to the plumber who's always going on about how much it costs in petrol just to turn on the engine of his car. You can't blame him though. This lot would have him running about like a delivery boy on wheels if he didn't put his foot down now and then.'

Then, as if he had somewhere important to go, the old boy stepped up his pace, swinging his arms like a man in a hurry to get to the pub before it closed. Doing their best to keep up, Anna and George glanced at each other while the old-timer stopped again to have a think. 'A lad comes on a pushbike with the newspapers most days,' he murmured, 'and sometimes fetches a choice of damaged paperbacks for us to buy. I mostly use the library in Tonbridge myself – when I can get someone to give me a lift there. That's where my favourite pub is – the Gudgeon. We all go together in Willy's converted ice-cream van every fortnight on a Tuesday. He's put wooden benches in and his wife Rosie made some lovely long cushions to fit the length of 'em.'

'You seem to have thought of everything,' said Anna. 'You've created your own tiny village by the sound of it.'

'Oh yes, we don't want for much. It was our resident plumber's idea to convert two huts into a launderette. He fetched down a van filled with six second-hand machines that he'd rebuilt. It makes a decent laundry room, that conversion. I made the surface for the washing machines to go beneath. Lovely bit of old pine that was.'

Walking on again, he continued his running commentary. 'I'm the resident carpenter. We used to do our washing by hand years ago in one of the old tin baby baths. We've still got one hanging up somewhere that one of the Romany gypsies painted for us the last time they set up camp in the field. Beautiful it is – with lovely flowers all over it. Laura Leigh, who married out and settled in the village, comes around the huts with 'er basket every other month selling pegs and that. Sight for sore eyes she is. She can tell fortunes so they tell me, but I don't believe in all of that.' He stopped again and stretched his back. 'Now whatever made me tell you all of this?'

'A bit of local history's no bad thing,' said Anna, wishing this man would not keep on stopping short.

Setting off again he said, 'We only used paraffin lamps and lanterns at first. And candles of course. But then we got electric lines connected. We had to give up our little council house for this way of living, but fair exchange is no robbery is the way I see it.'

'Did you honestly do that?' said Anna.

'Oh yes ... and it was the best thing we ever did do. The borough council of Hackney and Poplar paid for the renovations of the huts by all accounts. The farmer wouldn't 'ave made a loss, you can bet your life on that. But the point is we *own* the huts, you see. Oh yes ... we're all property owners now. We each privately own two and joint own the communal building where the washing machines and that are. Some chose to 'ave back-to-back huts knocked into one and some, like me, took a pair next to each other. The Stepney Council wanted us out of our old tenement houses so they could sell on or knock them down for new estates ... or, as my missus would say, rabbit warrens. It was a nice little deal that's paid off all round, you could say.'

Ernie's wife, Betty, a nicely rounded woman with soft grey curly hair showing beneath her knotted paisley turban which matched her wrap-over pinafore, was checking her pot roast over the open fire. Once her husband had seen to the introductions in his own muddled way, she said, 'When I heard your car I thought it was the postman. I look forward to Paul coming down the track in his little red van. He's from the village. His father used to come onto the common, and his father before him, with the letters and little parcels when we were down here for the hop-picking.'

'Betty's the presser,' said her husband proudly, placing an arm around his wife's shoulders. 'Trouble is, she prefers pressing the men's trousers if you know what I mean?' This brought a small burst of polite laughter.

'I'm in charge of the laundry rota, thank you very

much! I do most of the ironing because I *love* ironing,' laughed Betty. 'But I make them all pay me. It's a nice bit of pocket money for the piggy bank. I usually take somewhere around four to five pounds a week, which is very good money for doing something that you enjoy.'

'Hard work brings its rewards,' said Ernie. 'Mind you, standing outside in the sunshine and ironing? That's more of a leisurely thing to do if you ask me. Mind you, I don't do so badly – I get a free ride *and* my ticket for the pictures in Tonbridge paid once a week for organising the work rota and that.'

It was fun listening to these folk, who clearly were in their seventh heaven in what seemed to have become a retirement home in the country, camping style. Others soon gathered around Anna and George, and the more Anna heard the more impressed she was. When a nice fresh cup of tea was offered to her she took it gladly. The folk then told of how they went fruit- and pea-picking during the seasons and how, other than potatoes and most root vegetables, which were delivered in sacks from a local farm at a knockdown price, the men mucked in and grew most of their vegetables and salads. An acre of a ploughed field had been given to them when the huts were sold off.

'We all muck in, this is the point. Some of the work is a bit too much for some of the men.' The woman lowered her voice saying, 'It's hard work for Ernie but we don't let on that we think so.' She winked and smiled at George. 'Pride is important – so long as it doesn't come before a fall.'

'I couldn't agree more,' said George, wishing that he

had been in on this little project. He hadn't been slow in clocking that some of the residents had built little brick extensions onto their huts and planted climbers in pots here and there. The once plain brick constructions were already beginning to resemble little cottages and, from what they had gleaned so far, the settlers spent most of their time outside, often until dark unless there was something worthwhile on the television – each of them had a set inside their own cosy dwelling.

Looking around her, Anna quietly said, 'George ... this scenery is incredible. I feel as if I'm in the centre of a landscape painting.'

'I know what you mean. Can you imagine what it's like when the sun's setting? What the evenings are like? With this lot sitting round their campfires? I can just picture it ... and it takes me right back to the old days.'

'I could stop here for ever.' Anna sighed.

'I know, but we're gonna have to make a move to Tonbridge, sweetheart, and to that café I was telling you about. I don't want the bubble to burst either but business is business.'

'I know. And anyway, we could come back another time, couldn't we?'

'I don't see why not, babe.' A touch moved by the whole scene he said, 'I'm just gonna have a quick nostalgic wander around the huts – I won't be more than a few minutes.'

Anna watched him go, guessing that he would be looking to see if there was an old unused building that he could lay his hands on so as to be part of this little world at weekends. He was looking across to a field in the distance. She followed his gaze and could see a small herd of cows that looked so perfect in the setting. She loved it. She was in the centre of a medley of old-fashioned Londoners enjoying their little bit of this old-fashioned heavenly place. Coming along the dirt track was an old boy who was red in the face as he struggled to push his bike. Blowing and puffing, it was clear that he needed to rest, so Anna walked over to him and took hold of the bike while his wife saw him into their hut and sat him down on an old feather-cushioned armchair. None of the others seemed too concerned, and Anna gleaned that the old boy frequently returned exhausted. Sitting down on a simple wooden chair by the campfire with a few of the women, Anna felt happier and more relaxed than she had in a very long time.

Content just to let the heart-to-heart chinwag go above her head, she thought about Frank and the twins, and how lovely it would have been for them to spend a bit of leisure time in such a place as this every now and then. There didn't seem to be any one of the folk who didn't bring something to the table – or in this case the fire. Each had something to offer in the running of this little commune of Londoners.

One of the men had been an electrician, man and boy, and another could boast a plumber's certificate. A couple of the women, who weren't old enough to get a state pension, worked in a biscuit factory in the small town of Yalding and fetched back bags of assorted broken biscuits. Broken, but as fresh as the day they were baked. And another woman told Anna that she loved housework and did a bit of cleaning for most of the others as her way of making a little spare cash.

'I love housework so much that I would clean and polish for nothing,' she said. 'But they will insist on paying me, which suits me fine because I put it all away for Christmas and that way I've got a nice little bit to spend in London.'

'So you do go back to your roots from time to time then?' said Anna, finding this little oasis pulling her further in by the minute.

'Oh yes, we all do. It makes a lovely day out. My son comes and fetches me now and then. Lee's a carpet fitter. He fitted out most of our cottages with carpet or lino. Well, when I say cottages, really and truly they're only huts. But then we don't spend many days indoors in any case.' The bright and breezy woman looked at Anna, a knowing twinkle in her eye. 'I can see that you wouldn't mind one of these places,' she said. 'And I don't blame you. But I don't think there's any going spare now.'

'Oh, I'm just soaking it all in really. I love to hear the birds singing and cows lowing in the distance. I love it.'

'It is a good way of life, and we get to go to the pictures and to see shows in village halls around and about us. I couldn't ask for anything more really. Except coming up on the blooming pools!' She suddenly burst with laughter. 'Now that *would* be lovely, because you know what I would do? I'd have a really nice long hut built for my son and his wife to use at weekends. That's what I would do. That'd be lovely!'

Picking up on her contagious laughter, Anna only just managed to say, 'How do you get your washing dry on wet days?'

'We don't do washing on wet days. It's as simple as

that. But if it's dry weather but cold and damp we use one of the two dryers in the laundry shed.'

'And do you know, we nearly always get to go and see the West End Christmas lights by train, even though there's plenty to entertain us around this way. And we go along to the local little chapel of a Sunday *if* the sun's out. The church is a bit of a long walk for most of us but we do go sometimes for a bit of a sing-song. We all love to sing, whether it's by the campfire or in the church. The best times are when the Girl Guides or Boy Scouts come all dressed in their uniforms to kick us off. That's smashing, that is. They volunteer to do little jobs for us and they're good company.' The woman became thoughtful. 'You see, there always someone to chat to. This is my point. And I s'pose that's what keeps our brains alert.' She smiled sweetly at Anna. 'I'm sixty-seven but do I feel it? Course I don't!

'Now some might call this little place a retirement home, but so what if it is? We can all tell each other our little problems, and if a row breaks out it's usually forgotten within the hour unless someone is really put out over something, then it takes a bit longer.'

Her face broke into a lovely warm smile again as she lowered her voice and looked cautiously around. 'There has been a few romances between widows or divorcees and one or two have knocked dividing walls down between huts and set up home together. Happy as larks they are. But don't let on that I told you so.'

This was wonderful. The older generation were behaving worse than the so-called promiscuous young. Anna said, 'So you never get bored then?'

'Bored? No dear. There's always something to do or something happening. And I'll tell you what else ... we've got a doctor that will come out if we're not up to going to the surgery. We've even got a resident healer as well. Can you believe that?'

'I can,' said Anna. 'I can believe anything in this place.'

'She lays a hand on top of your head and she can tell if there's anything wrong, and I'll tell you what – she's never far out. You get a lovely warm glow going right down your spine when she lays a hand on you. She's got rid of a migraine for me more than once. She's got the gift, and you can't bottle that, can yer? She can bring a temperature down quicker than medicine will.'

Anna nodded attentively, even though she was now caught up in her own thoughts. She felt as though the ancestors were showing the twentieth century how things could be without all the trappings of the modern world. She wondered if it was feasible for her to bring up her twins in the countryside. She could just see them when they were older – running around on the grass and laughing.

'I would never go back to the way I was living before this,' continued the woman, bringing Anna back to the here and now. 'I can't imagine living back in our old turning in Hackney with all of the traffic and the markets and crowds of people everywhere. London born and bred until you're dead?' She slowly shook her head. 'No ... I realise now that you can easily pull up your roots and start all over again.' She grew pensive again. 'It's been a wonderful new beginning.'

'I'm sure it has,' said Anna, her heart sinking a little.

She was thinking of her own predicament. Then, pushing her troubles from her mind, she drew a slightly trembling breath and said, 'You know what you've done? You've created your own little village by the river. Just like the first settlers who came from overseas.'

'Yes – I suppose in a way we have, dear. I can't say that we're totally self-sufficient mind you, but we don't go short of much. We go to the village fetes in the summer and that's lovely. And then there might be a Country-and-Western dance on in the village hall that we'll attend. My husband used to play in a band years ago, so he gets to have a go on his saxophone now and then.

'He also teaches music part-time to the children at the home just outside of Hunston. We helped to run a fete in the gardens last year when we saw the piece asking for volunteers in the local paper. And we've been doing our bit one way or another ever since. We must have had about thirty children here on Guy Fawkes last year. Most of the villagers came too. It was lovely. A lovely big bonfire and a little firework display.'

'I bet the orphans loved that.'

'It was a joy to see the expression on their little faces. I don't know how many sausages and beef burgers we cooked on a grill over the embers. They loved it – and so did we.'

'And they go to the local school do they?' said Anna.

'No ducks. No. The home has its own little school ... a proper school with desks and that. I suppose in a way it's like a private boarding school except that it's not full of the posh children with wealthy parents going in to visit with hampers and that.'

Trevor immediately came into Anna's mind. She could imagine him here – resident PE teacher and swimming coach – which was his lifelong dream. To work with underprivileged children.

'I think there are a few such places spread around the country. Few and far between but at least they've not all been closed down.' The woman glanced at Anna. 'There's another site similar to this one if you're thinking of moving out of London. I don't think they would let you have it as a weekend kind of holiday home though.'

'No, I wasn't thinking of that,' Anna smiled. 'I've got twin babies. But I can see my mum and her friend Gwen living here. They would love it. But wild horses wouldn't drag either of them from the East End. London's in their blood. No, it was the children's home that made me think. I know someone who might just be interested in being a resident sports and swimming coach.'

'Well, remind me to give you one of their leaflets before you go. You can give that to your friend as food for thought.' The woman then nodded in the direction of George, who was making his way back. 'Your husband looks as if he likes it here as well.'

This made Anna laugh. 'We're not married. We're old mates from when we were kids on the street.'

'Oh, now you *have* surprised me,' said the woman, as she watched George looking into the open-fronted bike shed. 'You seem like the ideal couple. But do you know what? A good friend is often better than a mediocre husband – but don't repeat that or some around here will get the hump over it.' She laughed.

'You could be right there,' said Anna. 'I think that George has been turned on by the bikes and the thought of riding along a gravel lane. Look at him. Miles away in dreamland.'

The woman glanced at her watch. 'Oh look! It's time for my programme. *Crossroads*. I must love and leave you.' With that she was away, back inside her hut. Staring after her, Anna couldn't resist the urge to follow and take a peep inside her home.

Standing in the doorway she spoke quietly, saying, 'I don't suppose I can have a little look inside can I?' She smiled apologetically for intruding.

'Of course you can, dear! It's only two huts knocked into one at the end of the day, but you can go through and have a look at our bedroom, bathroom and kitchenette if you like. But you must excuse me if I don't show you around because I never miss an episode. Go on – go and steal a look at my kitchen with all its mod cons. It might be small but it's functional.'

Anna accepted and crept past to the kitchen; she was impressed at how neat and tidy and yet homely it was, with enough room to take a fridge, electric cooker, sink and floor cupboards with work space above. Through the small window she could see a view of the wooden bridge over the river and black and white cows in the background chewing the cud.

The small double bedroom reminded her of the old people's ground-floor flats that had been purpose built on the new council estates in and around Stepney and Bethnal Green. There was enough room for a bed for two people, a double wardrobe and a chest of drawers – and just enough space to walk from one bit of furniture to the other.

Her lightning view over, Anna was back into the cosy living room with its small three-piece suite and an old-fashioned dresser holding an accumulation of china. In the corner of the room was a pre-war oak dining table for two that could be extended to sit four. The walls had been decorated with a floral wallpaper which went with the old-fashioned mustard gloss paintwork. And on the walls hung an assortment of framed family photographs, going back a decade and coming to the present day. This little home was lovely. It was welcoming. And it was a sight for a townie's sore eyes. A bit of old-fashioned London life in the heart of the countryside, in the middle of a field by the river. And there was George, tall, broad and handsome, chatting to the old boy who had struggled home on his bike. She felt like weeping and didn't know why. But it was time for her and George to leave and head for Tonbridge, where she was to wait while he conducted his little bit of business.

Chapter Seven

Anna, relaxing in the quaint little tea rooms in Tonbridge while waiting for George to return, was enjoying her afternoon tea which consisted of delicate sandwiches, home-made cakes and a fresh pot of tea. Her table for one was at the front of the Elizabethan building and in these surroundings she felt as if time had stood still. She watched through a small leaded glass window as a young couple on the opposite side of the cobbled street fussed over their baby in a pram. She could picture Ivy, with her twin grandsons, in the same place loving the life and the fresh air.

The difference between Anna and the young mother, of course, was that the girl had her husband beside her and he was holding firmly on to the handle of the pram. Smiling at him, his wife was pointing out a nice summer dress displayed in the shop window. Nodding agreeably at her, the man looked so relaxed that Anna, for the first time in her life, knew what it was like to feel envy. This is what she so wanted and yet it was just a simple everyday family scene, nothing out of the ordinary but certainly no longer within her realm – not where she and Frank were concerned in any case.

Out in the real world, away from the comfort of her four walls hugging her like a big security blanket, and with more time to think, it was becoming clearer that during the past year or so she had cut herself off from almost everything. She wondered again if she had been so wrapped up with trying to get pregnant that, once she had finally achieved her dream and delivered her babies, she had built invisible walls around herself and them.

She had done everything she possibly could to protect the twins from the dangers of the outside and all of the germs on planet earth. But had she, without realising it, cut the babies off from Frank too? Guilt swept over her like a fierce heat rash. Guilt, mixed with a fear of the unknown that she was facing.

Shaking off this mild panic attack, she reminded herself that earlier on at the converted huts she had realised that this outing with George had restored some of her self-esteem, so all was not lost. She didn't know why it had but she wasn't going to question it. She turned her attention back to the couple across the street and watched as they happily sauntered off together. They had reminded Anna how she had imagined that she and Frank would be once the twins were born, but he hadn't once gone for a walk with her when she took the babies out in their pram. Not once. Not even on his days off from the restaurant, preferring to watch sport all afternoon of a Saturday and play golf on Sundays in order to unwind.

Frank, having gone from his house to the flat above Prima and then to his brothers' restaurant at Tower Hill, was now on his way to Ivy's with every intention of collecting his baby boys. After what could only be described as a fit of rage coming from bruised pride he was still in a sorry state. He had wanted to be in his brothers' restaurant, which opened on Sundays, so that he could sit for a while in a place that was familiar but which meant nothing much to him, but he hadn't been able to settle. Having driven through the back streets, a touch too fast, he arrived in Ivy's turning and parked just around the corner, out of sight of her kitchen window in case she happened to be looking out. He didn't want her to see him pulling up in his car because he knew that if she did, by the time he was inside her flat, she would be ready with a bit of rehearsed preaching about right and wrong. He wasn't in the mood for it and, apart from this, he couldn't be sure if George was inside with Anna and the twins, or if they had gone out for a nice lunch somewhere. In short, he didn't know what the fuck was going on and this didn't sit right with him. Frank wasn't used to being on the back foot like this.

He could hardly believe that George would be straight in with his wife before his own side of the bed had gone cold. He rang the doorbell, aware that he was grinding his back teeth, a dead giveaway that he was angry, but even so he couldn't stop himself. His face set, his mood dark, he listened for the sound of his wife's voice from inside. When Ivy opened the door she gave him a kind of all-knowing, all-scolding look, as if he were still a boy, but she stood aside to let him in.

'I was hoping you'd come round to see me for a chat,' she said, as she pulled the door wide open. 'Go on – in you go. Into the kitchen. I'll put the kettle on.'

'I'm not stopping for tea and a chat, Ivy. I've come to pick up my boys.'

'And what makes you think they're with me?' she said, as she filled the kettle. She then told him to sit down for five minutes and, surprising her, he did so in a quiet, humble kind of way which didn't square up to the fierce expression in his eyes. She knew him from old and could tell that he was in what she would call a bit of a rage.

'Rachel told me that Anna and George were on their way over to you,' said Frank. 'She was quite casual about it as well. Almost as if it was an everyday occurrence. She said that your place was where I might find Anna and that she was dropping our twins off here. I take it that she's gone out for the afternoon with an old friend of mine.'

'George? An old friend of yours? I didn't know that. Of course Anna's known him since his arse hung out of his trousers and he searched for pennies in the gutter with the other kids his age.'

Settled on a kitchen chair and leaning back with his legs stretched and crossed he said, 'I don't know what they think they're playing at, Ivy, and I'm not all that bothered, but I don't like the idea of my wife and my best friend going out behind my back.'

'I don't think they're playing at anything, Frank. But I do think that you're being a bit of a drama queen, if you don't mind my saying so. George is a close friend of our family. We all go back a long way, son. So what is your problem?'

'Oh right ... so they've done this before then, have they? Gone on an outing and left my boys with a baby-sitter?'

'Baby-sitter? I'm their grandmother! And those

babies are safer with me looking after them than they would be with you. You wouldn't even know how to change a fucking napkin. And before you ask, they're upstairs, sound asleep.'

'You know what I'm getting at, Ivy. Stop trying to be funny because you're not amusing me and I am very annoyed over this.'

'No, as it just so happens, Frank, I *don't* know what you're getting at! If you're asking me if Anna has gone for a nice day out the answer is yes, she has, and good luck to 'er. If you're wondering if she's made a habit of it the answer is no. If you ask me if I think it's a good thing – again the answer is yes, it most definitely is a good thing. She deserves an outing, which is more than I can say for you. How's the little tart managing without you pandering to her every whim? Are 'er knickers in a twist – or didn't you stop to 'ave a look before you left her to come round here?'

Pushing his hands into his face and rubbing his eyes, Frank spoke in a tired voice. 'I work bloody long hours, Ivy, and I get a bit exhausted now and then. All right? So stop having a go at me.'

'I should think you would be exhausted.' She poured boiling water into her brown teapot and then said, 'Did you know that statistically men are known to 'ave less energy than women even though they are all brawn and body? So I should think that's why you're tired ... working all day long and then shagging your waitresses for hours on end once you've bolted the door.'

'Oh right. So Anna's been telling you pork pies has she? Your baby daughter's been laying it on your shoulders again. You're gonna have to let go of your girls, Ivy. They're all grown women now.'

Ivy turned her back to him as she took a bag of sugar out of the kitchen cupboard and topped up the sugar bowl. She couldn't stop the smile that was spreading across her face and had to will herself not to laugh at Frank. He was on the attack, which was a first. From what she had seen in the past, if even a tiny bit of criticism was fired at him he would go quiet and walk out of the room.

'I don't think my Anna does tell lies. And I thank God for it because do you know what, a lie is the lowest form of defence and often used simply to score cheap points.'

Turning to face him, her smile now dissolved, she said, 'Frank ... don't ask me all the ins and outs. Go and see our Hazel and Linda and ask them what's what. All I can tell you is that Anna's none too pleased with that girl you took on. The one who's married to that lovely feller called Trevor.'

'She's been listening to silly gossip, Ivy.'

'I don't think so, son. And if you don't mind my saying, it's a bit too late to deny anything. If you want her back you're gonna have to play your hand honestly, and with more than just a little bit of discretion if you don't want to be left the joker. I saw the look in Anna's lovely eyes this morning and it wasn't green for envy, sweetheart. There was a relaxed expression that I haven't seen for a while. I won't say it didn't please me because it did. And do you know why? Because my girl is back in there – and in her own calm way, she's fighting fit.'

'Well, I hope she finds a battle then because I don't know what you're going on about. And if you all think that I'm having an affair with my waitress—'

'Assistant manager. And as for me . . . it's hear no evil, see no evil, and speak no evil. That's me, sweetheart. Always has been. Always will be.' She spooned three sugars into his tea because she knew this was how he liked it.

Having got nowhere with Ivy, and once back at his and Anna's house having almost crashed into another car when he had gone through a red light, Frank couldn't wait to get comfortable and chill out. He poured himself a glass of red wine, and then opened the door from the sitting room into the garden and welcomed the sound of the birds calling to each other, with the only other noise coming from the distant hum of traffic.

Easing himself down into the cushioned armchair where he had a better view of the garden, he soaked up the sunshine coming in through the windows. He glanced at the brick barbecue that he had built when they first moved in and remembered the dinner parties they had thrown. He could almost hear the sound of his and Anna's friends laughing and talking as the wine flowed and records played – friends who had slowly dropped off over the past year or so since he had spent ever more time at the restaurant.

Trying for the umpteenth time to think what to do for the best, which he had been doing since the moment Bridget dropped the bombshell just a couple of weeks ago that she was pregnant, he could come up with nothing. Nothing other than to let other people toss the whole thing up in the air and see which way the cards fell. Then he would make a decision whether to stay with Anna, who he thought that he probably did love, deep down, or move in with Bridget, who really did know how to make a man feel like a king in the bedroom. The excitement and secrecy of their affair had been intoxicating, and better than anything he had experienced before. Bridget could be a very naughty, rude lady when she felt like it and brilliant at taking the piss out of morons when they frequented his restaurant. She made him laugh, and laughter as far as Frank was concerned was all-important – one of life's best tonics.

Shaking his head as if trying to bring himself out of a drug-induced state, it dawned on him that the girl had actually been like a drug ... one that he had tried just for the fun of it and then found himself hooked. Bridget made him feel like a prince among ordinary men, especially when they were between the sheets. But then his Anna could sometimes melt his heart with just a smile. What would be perfect, he thought, would be to have the two of them rolled into one. He tried to think which of the two he was going to have to let go. Weighing it all up, and especially when it came to this house that he loved and that he knew he would have to sign over to Anna for her and the boys, he felt himself go cold. If push came to shove and a divorce was on the cards he stood to lose a lot more than he would gain. A hell of a lot more. He could hardly bear the thought of it.

He was so deep in his self-inflicted troubles, he was pulled up sharply when the shrill sound of the doorbell broke through the peace and quiet. Rising from his chair, he surprised himself at how eager he was to see who was on the doorstep. He was half wishing it would be one of their old friends dropping in after a long gap. But it wasn't an old friend – quite the reverse in fact – it was Bridget's husband, Trevor, standing there. The two young men stood looking at each other in silence until Frank stepped back and opened the door wide. A touch sheepishly he said, 'You'd best come in, Trevor.'

'No, I don't think I will thanks. I wasn't expecting you to be here. I came to see if Anna was all right. And to ask if she knows that Bridget's carrying your baby. She told me so this morning. Bridget that is. I'll be in touch with her through my solicitor from now on. You're welcome to the whore.' This said, he turned away and got into his second-hand light blue Anglia that meant even more to him now, and drove off.

'Fucking hell,' said Frank, as he shut the door and leaned on it. 'What the fuck 'ave you done, Frank?' Feeling as if he had just woken from a long sleep he went into the back room and withdrew a favourite bottle of his Scotch whisky, that was thankfully still a quarter full. He felt as if his brain needed a quick zap. Apart from anything else, two men had come to his house today, one for a little tête-à-tête with his wife and the other to take her for a drive into the countryside. He wondered what the hell he'd done to deserve all of this.

Later that day, when George pulled up outside Ivy's flat and went inside with Anna for a cup of tea, Ivy was only too pleased to be able to pass over her treasured grandsons to their mother. Her cheeks flushed and her pulse racing a little faster than usual, she fancied she was starting to go through her second menopause. 'I've loved having my grandsons, Anna darlin', don't get me wrong, but Christ Almighty; I'd forgotten what a full-time job looking after babies is.'

'Tell me about it!' said Anna, with feeling. 'Feed, bathe, change, play, sleep, feed, change, get their wind up again . . .'

'Yeah, all right, don't remind. I'm dog tired, and I'm supposed to look my best tomorrow. I shall have to have an early night with my curlers in, that's for sure.'

'And why have you got to look your best?' asked Anna, looking from one of her sleeping babies to the other while George filled the kettle from the kitchen tap. 'Going to Buckingham Palace to get your OBE are you? Your award for being the top best grandma in the world?'

'And pigs might fly . . .' Ivy sighed. 'No, I'm going on a blind date, that's why. A blind date at my age must be the best one to go in for with no reason to explain, I shouldn't think.' She quietly chuckled at her own joke.

Anna smiled, and nodded knowingly. 'So . . . you are gonna go and see those old boys of Gwen's then, are you?'

'Not so much of the old, young lady. The chap's only in his early sixties. That's not old these days.' She turned her back on Anna to mouth the words to George: 'Frank's fuming!'

Then, turning back to Anna, she said, 'Oh and by the way, love . . . our twins' daddy came round to see me earlier on. By all accounts he went home to pack a few more of his things and Rachel from next door told him that you and George had gone for a ride and that I was baby-minding.'

'And?' said Anna, looking up at her mum. 'What else is new?'

'No more than this as far as I know. He came round to ask if he could be of any help in looking after them and I said I was coping all right. I told him that the pair of you had gone to Kent for the day.'

'And?' said Anna. 'Come on, spit it out, Mum. I can tell by your face that there's more to it than this.'

'Well . . . he wasn't any too pleased—'

'Oh really? He wasn't any too pleased because I was having a few hours off for a change and going for a ride into the countryside? He begrudges me that after all he's done?'

'No, I don't think that was it. I would say, if anything, that it was more from jealousy than anger that he chewed the inside of his cheek and went pale . . . when I told him that the pair of you had gone out for the day.'

'Can you believe that man?' said George. 'What a nerve! After all he's been getting up to? And then he's got the nerve to play up because she took a day off, Ivy?' George went quiet and thoughtful and then said, 'I'll go and see him face to face and just let him try and throw a wobbly. We've had a lovely day out and he wants to cast aspersions because of his own guilt? No way!'

'Oh shut up, George,' said Ivy, wearily. 'Carry on like that and you'll have me thinking there's more to it than you and Anna being just good friends.'

215

'Come on, Ivy, even you've got to see that he's taking a liberty coming here to check up on her after what he's done.'

'Oh, stop it, you two. This is daft,' said Anna. 'You're letting him do it again. Here we are – the three of us having enjoyed a lovely day, one way or another – and even though he's been and he's gone he's left something behind for us to feel bad about.'

'Maybe you feel bad, Anna, but I don't,' said George. 'No way, sweetheart.'

Ivy slowly nodded because they were both bang on right and she knew it. Frank had come into her little domain where she was happy as Larry with her baby grandsons to look after, and he had managed to pull her down and make her feel a touch sad instead of angry with him by the time he left. She had enjoyed her day though, before he arrived, and once he had gone again. 'It's strange how just one person can, without meaning to, change the mood in a room whether he's present or not,' she said.

She then remembered the look on Frank's face when he left and it made her stomach turn over. 'The silly man is all at odds with himself – and with the rest of the world I should think.'

Pushing it from her mind, Ivy looked from George to Anna and said, 'Well you can love and leave me, now. I'm gonna put my curlers in and set my hair ready for my day out with my chap tomorrow.'

The look on her daughter's face made Ivy smile. 'Good for me, eh, love? Bloody well good for me. I'm looking forward to my blind date.'

'Definitely good for you, Mum. And you should be

looking forward to it.' Whether it would go well or not really didn't matter too much. A day out was what Ivy needed – a change of scenery, a change of people, with a little bit of romance thrown in as a wild card.

That evening, tired after the travelling, Anna was only too pleased to be back home, relaxing on the sofa after putting her babies to bed. Appreciating the silence and her own company, she had no desire to watch television or listen to music; she just wanted to enjoy the peace and quiet. Sipping a glass of sherry, she kicked off her shoes with a sigh of relief and pulled up her legs to recline full length. She was tired but not yet ready for her bed. She had so enjoyed her time with George and had got to know him better. She thought about the people she had met who lived in the huts – it all seemed so unreal. But her contented solitude was not to last because the sound of the street door opening told her that this was Frank who, clearly from what her mother had told her, was confused as to what he wanted or what he expected of her.

Coming into the doorway he looked around almost as if he was checking to see if anybody else might be in the house. He tried to seem casual as he said, 'I take it that my boys are asleep in their cots?'

'No, Frank, they're not. They're out in the garden pulling up the flowers.'

'Very funny, Anna. So ... you've told your mother that I'm having an affair with Bridget, so I might as well fucking have one, mightn't I? Because she is very attractive. So I'll take it that I've been given free rein, and – if she still wants me – I'll move out of our house for good and in with her to the apartment above my brothers' restaurant in Tower Hill. Okay?'

'It's up to you, Frank. I don't think I much care one way or the other now. Sadly.' She wasn't going to let him know that she had found out from Trevor that Bridget had moved into their flat. And neither was she going to mention the fact that she had said that Trevor and his mother could move in there.

'And actually, Anna – you're hardly ever in the restaurant to see what's what. So if it's not the gossips that have lined up at our front door to fill you in then it must be Hazel and Linda that's been poisoning your mind. Or George of course . . . just so that he could get his end away. Some men are like that. They like to fuck a woman who's not long delivered a baby – or in your case, two babies. Maybe the hero George is a bit of a perv on the quiet, eh? I mean – if you're so close to each other for him to be taking you out for a day in Kent while your mother baby-sits – the little love affair can't only just be starting, can it?'

'If I didn't know you better, Frank, I would say that you've got a sick mind. I think you're letting your imagination fly a bit *too* fast. How dare you tar me with the same brush as Bridget and, as for George, he is a lovely man. He doesn't seem to mind what he does for any one of us girls. But then, of course, he knew all three of us long before you did so I s'pose we're like close family really. Not that I'm suggesting that you never was like family. You were – once.'

'Was?' said Frank. 'Were? So I'm past tense now, am I?'

'You tell me,' said Anna sipping her drink. 'You tell

me what your plans are because I don't know you any more. Are you going to buy a house with Bridget? Because this is what she said. Or was she just being nasty to me? And if she was – why? I've not done anything wrong. She has.'

'If she said that to you, Anna ... *if* she did ... then she was getting carried away. I've flirted with her a bit, I admit that, and I shouldn't have done because she's gone and got a crush on me.'

'Oh really?' said Anna. 'So you've not been having an affair with her? You've not been having sex in our old flat above Prima?'

'It was a fling, not an affair.'

'Well, that's not the way she told it. She's a liar as well then? But then again – what about the gossip that's been up and running that I've only just picked up on? Is she spreading poison everywhere? Telling people in the restaurant that you're leaving me for her? If so, we had better give her the sack. And if you're not careful, she'll be the cause of you losing access to your sons. But then maybe that won't bother you now? Now that there's another rumour floating in the breeze. And if you don't know what that is, I'm not gonna tell you.'

'Who has been told what and what has she told them, Anna?'

Looking at him, she almost felt a touch of sympathy when she saw that he was chewing on the inside of his cheek, a habit from childhood according to his mother. She had to be strong though and get him to do the talking if she was to find out just how serious the affair was.

'Well, she laid her cards on the table and told me everything when I popped in for a little chat with her.'

'Told you what?'

'I think that you should ask Bridget that. It was a shame she went and twisted her ankle, but what could she expect wearing those high-heeled shoes for work. Anyone would think that she was employed there to model the dishes rather than deliver them to the tables. How is she now? I think her nose must be black and blue and swollen. Was she on her feet or on her back when you last saw her?'

'You're not funny, Anna,' said Frank. 'What exactly did she tell you?'

'Oh . . . far be it for me to interfere between lover and mistress. You must ask Bridget. But don't you go and fret over this because of me. I'll be all right. I'll be fine. In fact I'll be more than that. I've come through all the lonely nights by myself, never mind the sleep I've lost for months on end. I was stupid to suffer in silence but that's over now. My sisters know about you shagging Bridget and so do most of our customers, so don't worry if you want to go off and buy that house that Bridget mentioned – you carry on, Frank. I've got my family and I've got my friends. I'm thinking of throwing a party. A kind of a get-together of all my old mates that I've neglected since I got pregnant.'

'And what's all this with you and George? How long's that been going on for?'

'Me and George? Oh years. I thought you knew how close we were. He took me for a lovely drive to the countryside today. We had a fantastic time. And of course – as you've probably heard – he's split with his wife, so really . . . we're both in a nice little rowing boat at the moment, me and George.'

Frank leaned back against the wall and folded his arms as he stared at Anna, trying to face her down. But he saw a different expression on her face than the usual compliance. He saw guts and determination. 'I don't know what you said to your mother but she seems to think that we're gonna get divorced.'

'Well . . . Mum, as you know, does form her own opinion at times, and especially now that she thinks you've treated me like a toe-rag for God knows how long. She can forgive a little bit of steering off the road now and then but you've taken liberties. You've gone too far. Shagging that silly cow in our flat that we first lived in? Even I think you should be ashamed of yourself, never mind the older generation.'

'So I'm being seen as a bastard all round then, am I?'

Anna shrugged and showed an expression of uncertainty. 'I'm sorry that I can't fight your corner, Frank. You have been a rotten bastard and it's gonna take a lot on your part to gain your respect back. I'm easy-going as everyone knows, but you've rocked our boat a little too much and do you know what – I can be more stubborn than my sisters when something just doesn't sit right with me.'

'So what am I supposed to think about you going off for a day to the countryside with George? For all I know you could have been at it in a haystack for hours. Some men love that kind of thing.'

'No. No, we didn't do anything like that. We had a lovely day out. To Kent. To where George and his family used to go hop-picking. He wanted to show me what he loved about it when he was a boy.'

'Anna – you're not clever. Stop talking about the prick.'

'But you asked me,' said Anna, all innocent. 'And it was a lovely day. Our family never went hop-picking, but we did go fruit-picking, but then that was only for two weeks of the year whereas hop-picking—'

'All right, Anna! You've made your point!' Frank glared at her. 'You were sharing a bit of romantic nostalgia. I don't need a chapter from one of those romance books you've always got your nose into.'

'I suppose . . .' said Anna, gazing up at the ceiling and ignoring the jibe, 'that it was a kind of a romantic place. Hops are a kind of herb that goes into making the best beer . . . and you can't beat a river and fields and cows. I think nature couldn't have made a better setting for romance.'

Frank knew that she was reeling him in like a fish on a line and it grated. He didn't like this new Anna, even though he knew she was acting. 'I want to spend a day or so with the twins,' he said.

'Oh . . . that's nice. Just let me know when you want to take over and I'll make sure I'm out for the day. And if you get stuck you can always call Mum. She'll give you all the advice you need as to how to feed two babies when they're both crying from hunger and thirst. I'll leave a list for you on how to make the bottles up with the Cow and Gate and how to test the heat just before you feed. You drip a little onto the back of your hand and only feed them the milk when it's blood-warm. And once you've winded 'em, give 'em twenty minutes or so in their playpen to have a kick around before you change their napkins, so they'll have filled them up good and proper before you put them down. And don't throw the paddy pads down the lavatory whatever you do, no matter how much they smell. You wrap them in newspaper and then put 'em in a plastic carrier bag tied up so that flies can't get in. If you get stuck, just ask Rachel next door what to do. She may be long in the tooth, but she knows all the tricks in the book. She'll help you out if you can't cope.'

'You've made your point, Anna. You keep the boys under your wing.' Clearly gutted, Frank turned to leave and then turned around again. 'I didn't want this, Anna. This isn't what I wanted. I've always known what Bridget's been up to – what she's after. But if you force my hand I won't have any choice but to leave you.'

'And why's that?' said Anna.

'Because Bridget stopped taking the pill. She's missed a period and if she is pregnant it won't be Trevor's baby but mine in there.'

'Well, that *is* a fine mess you've got yourself into. A fine old mess,' said Anna, longing to get up off the couch and slam her fist in his face.

'It's my own fault for trusting that she wouldn't forget to take a pill. I was careful, doubling up by using a condom, but Bridget couldn't see the point in using both, so we decided to stick with the pill.'

'Close the door after you, Frank. The street door, that is. And all I'm gonna say about your little bit of news is that you're one hell of a stupid bastard. You've fallen for the oldest trick in the book, she's got you right where she wants you. And don't slam the front door.' Frank looked at Anna, and realised again just how stupid he had been. He drew air in through his nostrils and then slowly exhaled, and looked to be on the edge of shedding a tear or two. He then quietly turned and left Anna to herself.

The house suddenly seemed too quiet. She was alone again, but for some reason that she couldn't be bothered to fathom she didn't feel lonely. And the fact that Bridget was pregnant with Frank's baby left her cold. Whether he realised it or not, Frank had just damaged their marriage beyond repair. She wasn't angry. She wasn't even sad. She felt nothing. But strangely enough it was George who came to mind. She felt like phoning him and saying that she and Frank were over, but she knew that this was not the right thing to do.

Chapter Eight

The following day, Monday, Ivy and Gwen set off on their arranged outing into the West End, wearing their best frocks and summer coats and a little more lipstick and powder than usual. And while they were changing from one bus to another on their journey, their dates were waiting in the spacious sitting room of Horace Travers-James' flat, which was crammed with old-fashioned furniture, antiques, and several Persian rugs on the polished oak floorboards. This flat, just off Tottenham Court Road, was absolutely charming, though it couldn't have been in a more archaic Victorian building. The gentlemen waited patiently for the girls to arrive for afternoon tea. Horace, an upright man of around six feet had thick silver-grey hair and light blue eyes, and what Ivy would term a Roman nose – long and straight. He had chosen to wear his black and gold 1930s silk smoking jacket, while Gwen's chap was in his usual smart attire, except that he had treated himself to a new navy and white spotted tie for the occasion and had left off the cap which usually covered his thinning hair.

Horace, sitting on a faded red velvet sofa with a carved mahogany frame, was idly thumbing through a weekly journal taken from the neat pile of magazines on a low table in a corner of the room. He stopped at the astrology page, about to read aloud to the annoyance of his friend. 'I am correct in my assumption that you are a Gemini, Wilfred dear boy, am I not?'

'You are,' said Wilfred, 'and you know it. Don't start reading that bloody rubbish to me. I'm not interested in what's to come and you're not interested in what's been and gone. So why torment me now with star signs and predictions?'

'I wouldn't dream of tormenting you, dear boy,' said Horace, giving his friend a sly look. 'Although I must say that this week's is rather interesting. It says that we Leos are in for a bit of an illuminating few days. Maybe this woman friend you are introducing me to is not a born and bred Cockney after all, and we may have at least something in common. Anything in common would help.' He shuddered melodramatically. 'But how rude of me to read out my own horoscope. Now then, let's see … Gemini …'

'I would rather you didn't read out mine, thank you very much. I don't want to know what is gonna happen to me, as I've said a thousand times before.'

'How can you possibly mean this, my dear Wilfred, when you've no idea what is in your stars for this coming week? What if they were to tell you that you're in for a windfall? I presume that you did fill in your football coupons, as usual – wouldn't you like to know if you are to become a millionaire overnight? Or do you already know this? Have you already taken a little peek at the horoscope?'

'You realise that the horoscope you're reading is a year or so out of date,' was Wilfred's response.

'Well, it matters not one iota. It is the day of the

226

week in which it is read that counts – in my humble opinion, that is.'

· Continuing to read, but barely audibly now, Horace glanced over his spectacles at Wilfred. '"Immediate developments when you will embrace romance are not far away . . . but conflicting loyalties leave you uncertain of what to do . . . for the best. You have the time to learn more about those around you so—"'

'The ladies will be here soon,' interrupted Wilfred, stopping his friend in mid-flow. 'Read your horoscope in bed tonight before you go to sleep when nobody else is around for you to bore to death.'

'If I must, then so be it.' Closing the magazine, Horace sighed loudly. 'We don't get anywhere near enough visitors coming into this building – this is the problem. Not that it surprises me in the least when you consider the sort of people you normally find in abodes such as this decrepit Victorian prison-like place. I mean to say . . . it's bound to put some people off, is it not? Do you not agree with this one tiny observation, Wilfred? I mean to say, the others who live here do tend to offer only false smiles, and false promises of neighbourliness before disappearing into their lavish apartments. It is all a perfect setting for a murder mystery – I would have thought. What we could all do with from time to time is a visitor or two for afternoon tea who, out of good manners and a gesture of good will, would bring a fresh Victoria sponge from the food hall at Harrods.'

'You're harping on about your two cousins from the country I presume?'

'Yes, I suppose in a way I am. They were more like

227

sisters to me when I was a boy. I lived with them for a while once Mother ran off with her fancy man. Then I came back to London, to be with Father, of course, but mostly so that I could work in the best of our British theatres. I was terribly lonely at first, what with my father getting on with his own full social life and letters from my aunt and cousins not arriving as often as had been promised. None of the family wanted me to go on the stage, you know.'

'So you've said.'

'It was hard to know what to do for the best at times ... follow my heart or the well-meant advice. I don't suppose I would want to live anywhere else if I am to be honest with myself. I've been happy enough in this modest abode.' He withdrew a beautiful old gold fob watch from his waistcoat and sighed theatrically.

'Where on earth could your lady friends have got to?' He glanced wistfully at his chum. 'Let us hope that the exterior of this place has not unnerved this blind date of mine. This female who comes to me straight from the very heart of Charles Dickens territory.'

'Dickens never did live in the East End, Horace.'

Ignoring the interruption as he was apt to do, Horace continued his flow. 'They are, nevertheless, from the poorer parts of London, are they not? In such parts where only the Cockney will survive. Where thieves and rogues continue to kill each other in dark alleyways ...'

'You had better not start all of that acting malarkey once they are here. We'll go out for a walk if the pair of you finds that you can't fill a silence.'

'If my blind date and I have little or nothing in

228

common, you mean? This of course could very well be a problem.'

'You might be like chalk and cheese but you've got nothing to lose. It's just a bit of fun, that's all. If it doesn't work out, we'll stroll to the park and then see them to the bus stop. Nothing lost, nothing gained, and there are seven days to a week and fifty-two weeks to a year.'

'Indeed. So what are a few hours of discomfort in one's somewhat lonely life? Although I will say that I have always got on with the Cockneys. This is probably because of the war, when we all rubbed along together regardless of creed or breed.'

'You've been on your own for too long, Horace, that's your trouble. You've got used to the solitary life and that's not good for anyone. You've been lonely I expect. You need a good woman to help you enjoy your money.'

'That is as may be my dear friend, but I think I would rather be lonely than risk being miserable with somebody else. Did I tell you that two out of the three of my fiancées were also in the theatre?'

'Many times, Horace, many times.'

'Oh . . . well, then, do please forgive me for being so tiresome!'

'Just don't go and mention your fiancées once the ladies are here.'

'I'm not a complete fool, dear boy. But there – we shall see what we shall see. Maybe this woman whom you seem to think is a match for me will get little dicky rearing its head again to see what is what?' He glanced at Wilfred and raised an eyebrow. 'I've put on a clean shirt, clean socks and brand new underwear that my sister gave to me several Christmases ago. I do believe they are called Y-fronts these days and not short Johns.'

'Short Johns?'

'Yes, dear boy. Long Johns cut down.'

'And that's what you usually wear is it?'

'In the summer it is. I have four pairs of the originals for the winter, and five pairs of the older originals cut down for the summer so as to let air into one's private parts that never get to see the sunshine. And each garment is still as white as the day it was purchased. Bleach and cotton go hand in hand, dear boy, hand in hand. I have always said so and shall continue to say it.'

'Fascinating,' said Wilfred as he gazed out of a window. 'That kind of talk should turn the girls on.'

Horace chuckled as he looked out of another of the grimy, almost ceiling to floor windows fringed by fading, dusty red velvet drapes. 'Do you know, if either of us were a cat or a dog, I do believe we would have been put down by now.'

'Don't start all that again.' Wilfred looked across at his friend and smiled. 'You look handsome in your Somerset Maugham attire. Quite the gentleman. So try not to be too Jack Blunt when the women arrive, eh?'

'I? Jack Blunt? Dear boy ... you surely confuse me with some other person. I have always prided myself on being discretion itself.' He straightened the perfectly pressed white handkerchief that just showed above the top pocket of his quilted silk smoking jacket. 'I was brought up by a wonderful nanny, you know.'

'I do know. You told me already. You're always telling me. You should have stayed on stage. You're a good actor.' Wilfred wandered about the room and then went back to the window and looked out to the pretty back garden below. 'If you didn't live on this top floor we could 'ave 'ad our tea outside.'

'We'll save that for another time, old chap. Not tea though, it would be far too much trouble having to take down a tray et cetera. Cold beer and cut sandwiches would be the ticket — should it all go well this afternoon, that is.'

'At least it's a nice quiet afternoon. I like it when it's quiet. That's why I suggested the women come on a Monday.'

'Not for long will it be quiet,' said Horace. 'I do believe I can hear footsteps in the corridor, Wilfred. Our visitors have arrived. We are about to have female company, dear boy.'

The tapping on the big heavy mahogany door confirmed his supposition. With a theatrical wave of the hand, Horace urged Wilfred to open the door while he stood up and glanced at his reflection in his ornate, if rather tarnished, mirror above the white marble fireplace. He felt that he still cut a dash, and winked at himself before breathing deeply and arranging a pose next to his high-backed armchair. He clasped his hands together, and waited demurely to see whether it was to be a beauty or a beast entering his lonely yet quite contented world.

'Bloody tourists . . .' moaned Ivy, as she came into the room. 'I've never known the roads in the West End to be so packed, or so many of the bloody things on the road all at once. I would 'ave like to have jumped off our double decker and got onto one of them open-topped sightseeing buses and gone on a little tour myself on our way here.'

Having cut right through the silence, she looked straight at Horace and smiled broadly. 'You look very smart, sir, I must say.'

'Really? How very good of you to pay such a compliment to an old veteran.' He smiled. 'And you look a picture in what I can only describe as a *powder blue* costume that matches your lovely eyes.'

'I've seen you on the telly, haven't I?' said Ivy, a twinkle in her eye.

'Possibly,' said Horace, smiling back at her. 'I have been in one or two of Harold Pinter's plays, to name just one playwright.'

'Well, I'm proud to be in your company, sir,' she said, offering her hand to shake his with the elegance befitting an actor of standing. She was lying through her back teeth about having seen him before, but wanted to cut to the chase so as to break the ice and soften the atmosphere. Gwen's chap Wilfred knew exactly what she was up to. He turned a blind eye and helped Gwen take off her lovely lightweight primrose summer coat.

Looking about the room, Ivy said, 'Do you know I feel sure that I've been in this building before, years back, when I used to clean and disinfect telephones for a company called Micro Clean. We mostly went round offices, but the company had a few contracts for these big types of residential places as well.' She crossed the room to look out of the long sash window at the grounds below and the gate which led out to a small garden, and silently told herself that she could live in such surroundings.

'This is a lovely place,' she said, turning to find that Horace had quietly moved and was standing behind and quite close to her. 'The name's Ivy, by the way.'

'And mine is Horace, I am sorry to say. I can't imagine what my parents could have been thinking. Please, do sit down.'

'Thank you very much – I will take the weight off my feet.' She looked around the room again and felt comfortable in her surroundings. 'It's a nice flat,' she said. 'Very nice.' She sank into a faded armchair and looked at Gwen, waiting for her to say something.

'Yes, I suppose it's not a bad place you've got here,' said Gwen, picking up on her friend's unspoken request. 'You know, you could bring that old Persian rug up a treat if you were to grate two raw potatoes into a basin of cold water and let it stand for a few minutes—'

'Oh here we go,' said Wilfred, cutting in. 'Another of her old-fashioned ideas she won't let go of. Well go on then, get it over and done wiv.'

'It might be out of date but it bloody well works.' She gave Wilfred a look of remonstration and then continued. 'Once you've strained off the liquid, Horace, you dip a dry old rag into it and rub the rug all over. Then go over it again with a cloth that has been wrung out in clean water.'

'And it really works?' said Horace, sounding truly fascinated.

'Indeed it does. And if you can be bothered to clean your cut-glass decanters, when they're empty, cut up potato into small bits and drop this into the top of the bottle and then swish it around in a little cold water. Or you could cover some eggshells with lemon juice and stand for forty-eight hours. The eggshells should have dissolved by then and so you pour the liquid into the decanter and shake occasionally.'

'Shake what?' said Wilfred. 'Himself or the mixture?'

Ivy found this amusing, as did Horace, but she saw Gwen giving her man friend another dirty look. 'The mixture, Wilfred, the mixture.'

'Actually,' said Horace, 'I do sometimes use such old receipts myself, which are far cheaper than those in the supermarkets and far more efficient if you were to ask my opinion. For instance, did you know, ladies, that to look after leather upholstery as it should be looked after, one boils a half-pint of linseed oil for one minute and then have it go cold before adding a half pint of vinegar? All that is then required is to give it a thoroughly good stir. Then one takes a clean piece of rag to rub it into the leather – another soft piece of rag is then required to polish it up – and this will also prevent cracking.'

'So you kill two birds with one stone? Very good. I would definitely try that if I had leather furniture, but mine's mostly Dralon covers that come off and go in the washing machine.' Ivy smiled fondly at him. 'But I shall remember that and pass it on to my daughters.'

A touch put out at just how Ivy was sailing through all of this, Gwen sniffed and, turning to her friend, said, 'You look very much at home, Ivy, I must say.'

'I feel very much at home as it just so happens.' She glanced at Horace, who politely nodded to acknowledge the compliment, and she couldn't help feeling a slight tingle in the crevice of her womanhood.

'My father was rather a wise man,' said Horace. 'Being a sporting gambler, he took a chance when purchasing this lavish apartment – a very long time ago. He dealt mostly in stocks and shares during the weekdays and gambled at Newmarket and such racecourses at weekends – when he wasn't playing golf. He would have been so proud of our Tony Jacklin for winning the British Open Championship in '68 and then the US Open in 1970.'

'A sporting man as well as someone who kept his eye on the property market? That's no bad thing, is it, Horace.'

'Indeed not, Ivy. Had he not have purchased one or two properties such as this one, he might well have been penniless when he passed on to the world beyond. But he could die with dignity because he had left to me, his favourite child, this apartment, which I believe would now fetch a pretty penny or two. I can't imagine what he would have made of the many changes we have seen.

'It is now a case of anything goes, with the scruffy young wearing old fur coats and animal skins when they sit in one of my favourite little coffee shops in Berwick Street, where we seniors are now made to feel as if we are strangers. The so-called new-style beatniks fill the place, all of them making one cup of coffee last a whole day. And the only thing one hears when it comes to conversation is talk of legalising marijuana. Not that I'm old-fashioned mind you. I have always prided myself on moving with the times.'

Ivy was surprising herself. This tall and handsome gentleman in his early sixties certainly was warming parts of her where the sunbeams hadn't shone in a very long time. She liked him. She liked him a lot. 'You must be very happy living here,' she said.

'As a matter of fact I am,' he said, looking into Ivy's smiling eyes. 'We do have a communal garden at the rear of the property with a gate that leads into a small grassy square, which has benches and beautiful shrubs. It is a small public park of sorts, which not many seem to know about, thankfully.'

'Now then,' said Wilfred, 'what's it to be? We've bought some cakes and I've set a tray with a china tea set, so who's for a cuppa?'

'Smashing,' said Gwen, easing off her shoes as she rested back in her armchair. 'I didn't know there was a gate leading into a park. I shall 'ave to investigate that, Horace.'

'You do surprise me, Gwendolyn,' said Horace. 'I would have thought that our mutual friend here would have taken you for a stroll around by now. There used to be a mass of bluebells out there but the children would pick them and so they eventually gave up I'm afraid. As a matter of fact, my father planted two beautiful shrubs in the little green and now they are quite established. So we have red berries in the winter and white flowers in the summertime. And do you know what I love the very most of all, Ivy?'

'No, but I would like to know, Horace,' she said.

'The smell of rain on warm damp earth.'

'Yes. Yes, I know what you mean. Has your father

been dead long?' Ivy was giving him her complete attention.

'Oh, about six or seven years ... Ivy,' he said, his voice dropping to a whisper.

'And what about your mother?' she continued.

'Mother? Why, she left long before Father passed away. Ran off with her titled lover I'm afraid. I've not heard a whisper from her since. She may not even know that her husband, my father, is no more. It was I who looked after him towards the end, you see. We lived here together in this apartment.'

Ivy was surprised at how easy it was to talk to this lovely gentleman, who she would have thought to be snooty had she met him outside in the street. She smiled at the thought and silently berated herself for being more of a snob in her own way than he was.

She was just about to ask if he had been given help with looking after his father when he said, 'Death is not so bad, you know, if getting to it isn't too unbearable. If there is someone there to assist ... if you get my drift.'

'I do, Horace, and I agree wholeheartedly. I was by my mother's side for the last three weeks of her life and, do you know, I can't remember her being sad even though she knew she was going. She seemed ready for it – as if it was all part of her travels – if that makes sense.'

'Oh, indeed it does, Ivy. Indeed.' Horace was clearing enjoying himself and was in full flow as if he were behind the footlights. 'Sadly, Father was incontinent towards the end,' he continued, 'but even that wasn't anywhere near as bad as I imagined it to be.'

He replaced his handkerchief and drew a quivering

breath before letting out a long sigh. 'I can see it now as if it were yesterday. My father would be in his bed and I would roll him against the wall, ease out the soiled sheet, and then let him roll back onto the rubber. Get a dry sheet, push him towards the wall again, hold him there, and get the dry one on as best I could. He would then roll back and rest, and I would sit on a chair by his bed and he would look at me and only just manage to whisper the words, "Thank you my boy." I truly never minded one bit. And the good thing about it all was that he knew I wanted to be there doing this for him. It went fairly well, all things considered. When the weather was fine I managed to get his wheelchair into the lift and out into the garden. He adored the sunshine in the summer and coal fires in the winter. Sometimes he sat by the fire with his legs stretched out so that his feet almost touched the flames.'

'And you say that he was a gambling man?' Ivy smiled. 'Did you manage to place a bet for him while he was bedridden?'

Horace became thoughtful and then slowly shook his head, saying, 'Do you know, he never ever asked this of me. It was as if that part of his life had already gone on to the ever after. I expect he imagined that there would be a racecourse in heaven awaiting him.'

Tenderly laughing, Ivy felt more and more relaxed in his company, as if she had known him for years. 'You paint a lovely picture, Horace. A kind of a watercolour painting of a heavenly place that we'll all go to one day.'

'Do I really?' He looked pleased. 'Well, that's very sweet of you to say so, Ivy.'

'He never 'ad a bad life though, your old man, did

he?' said Wilfred, feeling a touch left out. 'I mean to say, he drove around in an old type of a car, right up until he was in his mid-eighties. He was dead within a year of knowing, wasn't he, Horace?'

'I should think it was about a year, yes.' Gazing down at the floor he slowly shook his head. 'It takes a year for any of us as a baby to learn how to walk and feed ourselves and it takes a year to forget again. At least, that's how long it was with my father. A year to the day almost. Until the body, mind and soul finally slept for the last time.'

Touched by this, and a little saddened, Ivy crossed herself and whispered, 'May he rest in peace.'

'Oh he will, my dear, don't you fret. My father was ready to meet his maker. My father was everything to me. Perhaps this was because I never married and so therefore had no offspring of my own to worry over. Who knows?'

'And why was that, do you think?'

'Why was what?' said Horace, a glazed look in his eyes. 'I'm so sorry I've lost the thread . . .'

'I asked why it was that you never married.'

'Oh, I'm not entirely sure if you want the honest answer.' He smiled ruefully and shrugged. 'Always the best man but never the groom.'

'Were you ever engaged?'

'Yes. Three times as a matter of fact. But I could never quite take that next and final step. The trust wasn't there you see. I couldn't trust that a woman wouldn't do to me as my mother had done to my father. He wouldn't have admitted it to anyone, but I saw what a broken man he was once she left. He spent a very long and lonely time on his own ... before he went out and about again. Then he made up for lost time and became a bit of a playboy.'

'Well, all I can say to you, Horace, even though I've not known you for five minutes, you're a lovely gentleman. And I expect that your mother was a fool to walk away from your father. You can take me to the pictures any night of the week. We'll try our hand at courting and see how it goes – if you would like to, that is.'

Breaking into a lovely smile and then a laugh, Horace slowly nodded. 'I think I would enjoy that very much – but you'd have to show me the ropes.'

'I'll do my best,' said Ivy. 'I can't say more than that.'

'I can,' said Gwen. 'You're a bloody fast worker!'

Chapter Nine

Anna, while her mother was being entertained in Horace's West End apartment, was making the most of the time while her twins were contentedly asleep. Her eyes were closed and she was enjoying the warm sun on her face as she lay on one of a matching pair of foldaway sunbeds, almost drifting off into a light doze. In her back garden at this time of the afternoon it was usually quiet. Almost asleep, she hadn't heard Frank come into the house, and her heart felt as if it had leapt out of her chest and back again when, from the open door and right out of the blue, he said, 'If you're thinking about George, Anna, you're wasting your dreams. He'll go back to 'is wife again. They're like yo-yos, that pair. So I would stop fantasising if I were you.'

Willing herself to stay right where she was and not respond, Anna put into practice a relaxation exercise she remembered from her afternoons at the ante-natal clinic. 'What is it you want, Frank?' she finally said, her best bored tone to the fore.

'A cup of strong coffee would be good. But don't get up, I'll make it myself.' He went to the kitchen, leaving her to marvel at his audacity. He had moved all of his things out and into the flat at Tower Hill where he was now living with Bridget, and yet he had the nerve to walk in as if nothing had changed, as if he had been nowhere. She so wanted to tell him to fuck off, but her inner voice was telling her not yet, that it made sense for her to remain silent, keep her eyes shut and wait to see what it was that he wanted. What he had to say. She knew that he would be able to see her through the kitchen window, but he couldn't see inside her mind and this was what would be getting to him more than anything else. She had learned to imitate him by giving little or nothing away.

'I know you're not asleep, Anna,' he said, once he was back with a mug of coffee in his hand. 'So you can stop play-acting because it doesn't wash.' He spoke in a softer tone than usual. She realised of course that he had previously been covering his guilt by playing the sometimes angry, sometimes silent man who had a load on his mind and on his shoulders. Turning her head ever so slightly she peered lazily at him and said again, 'What do you want, Frank? Why are you standing there? Bridget gone off with an older and wealthier man, has she?'

'No. Why do you ask?'

'Just curious, that's all. Take whatever it is you've come back for and go. I really don't want any horrible discussions today. Go away and live your life the way you want to and leave me to lead mine.'

'This is still my house and my home, Anna, as well as yours. I suppose you think that you're clever letting Trevor and his mother move into our flat?'

Anna did her level best not to smile. She was proud of just how easily she had been able to slip back into her nice relaxed mood again, even though he was still there. She kept her face to the sun and her eyes closed, and spoke calmly to him. 'When you say *our* flat, Frank, what exactly do you mean? Because, as far as I'm concerned, until Trev's whitewashed all the walls and ripped up the carpets and torn out the curtains, it's yours and Bridget's shagging place. The sheets on the bed reeked of the pair of you. They'll make good dusters though, now that they've been ripped to shreds.'

'I don't remember signing a contract to say that the drip and his mother could rent the flat,' Frank retorted. 'I want any signs of Trevor out of there so that I can move back in when I'm good and ready. Tower Hill is all right as a place of work – but to live? No. It doesn't entirely suit me.'

'There isn't a contract, Frank. I'm letting him and his mother stay there for the time being. Do anything daft or cruel, like chucking their things out, and the law will be down on you like a ton of bricks. Even squatters have rights these days and Trevor and his mum are my guests. So forget trying to stir up trouble and go back to your little sex den at Tower Hill with your little whore. Or is she too busy with other clients now that she's in that rich tourist area?'

'Very funny, Anna. I'll tell her you said that. And what about George, who you seem to have taken a fancy to all of a sudden? Don't forget that he's my friend as well as yours. I can read him like a book and I'm telling you – he'll drop you like a hot potato should another free fanny come by. You'll soon be yesterday's fish and chip paper.'

Ignoring his crude and insulting remarks, Anna sighed loudly and pretended to shut him out. She knew that he was using George to bait her, but since they had been more like cousins than friends even when they were kids on the street he was wasting his breath.

'Stop making up stories about people, Frank. And before you go on about his wife, she's on a world cruise.'

'Well then, she must have decided to cut it short and jump ship, mustn't she, because she's back in his realm.'

'George would have told me if this was the case. We're good friends. I played with him and his brother when I was a kid – as did my sisters – so if his wife is back on the scene I would have heard. Go away, Frank. Back to Tower Hill. The tourists will be about and Bridget's on the loose. You've got to keep an eye on girls like her. *She'll* be coming home in the wee hours next, smelling of aftershave.'

Anna heard his deliberate angry sigh but she was enjoying this new experience of speaking up for herself, of baiting him for a change. It was fun. 'If I'd thought that you were gonna come in and out disturbing my new way of life,' she said, 'which doesn't include grief, I would have changed the lock on the street door.'

Frank's silence proved that she really had got to him this time. A few seconds passed before he said, 'I came to see my twins. But before I go up and take a peep I'm gonna make myself another cup of coffee in my kitchen. All right?' He then stepped out onto the small crazy-paved patio to inspect an old-fashioned, over-grown rose bush which he had never pruned in his life. Anna was the one with the green fingers. 'This is in a bit of a state,' he said. 'You're letting the garden go to pot as well now are you? Too busy going for outings in the country and leaving our babies with one baby-sitter or another. Is this what it's come to?'

'So far I've only left them with their grandma and I've only had one trip to Kent, Frank. Although more are planned. Jackie along the turning has offered to have them for a few hours whenever I want. And she said she'll baby-sit in the evenings for me as well. She's a lovely girl. And she does seem to love the twins. She could easily get work as a freelance nanny to release young housewives who don't want to give up work once married.'

'Well, that's something at least. Jackie could have them for, say, three days a week, and you could go back to work as a telephonist part-time. Put a few quid in the joint account for a change instead of taking it out. I might go and have a chat to her about that.'

'Don't bother . . .' Anna yawned. 'I shan't be going back to work until the boys are at school. In five years' time. Now, I just want to drift off for ten minutes, I'm tired. Both our babies are teething and I was awake half the night. But you don't wanna hear boring old stuff like that.'

'So you don't want a coffee then?'

'No.'

'Or a cup of tea with a drop of brandy in it might be better. You seem a little uptight.'

She wasn't uptight and he knew it. She didn't want him there, especially not if he had come to try and woo her back into his good books for his own selfish reasons. She just wanted him to go. 'Just do me a favour and leave me to catch up on a little bit of sleep.

And don't slam the front door of the house when you leave, the way you've slammed it on our marriage.'

He was getting on her nerves but she was now going to hold her tongue to put a stop to any further dialogue. He had come around because he realised what a fool he was making of himself. Gossip spread quickly in their close-knit world. She knew him like the back of her hand and could tell at a glance that he wanted her to feel sorry for him. But this was Frank all over and he was too far gone to change.

She had been hurt by him many times during the past year or so, and she knew what he was like when he was sorry and wanted to make up. But this was different. Much different. He was now living with another woman.

'I'm all right, Frank,' she finally said. 'And the boys are fine apart from the teething. Mum's being a brick and my sisters fantastic. And I *have* phoned your mum, before you ask, and I've told her that I'll take them over to visit soon. She was all right about it. She apologised for you of course but, as I said to her, we can't be responsible for the way our children turn out. She and Mum are keeping a little bit at arm's length for a while until we've sorted things out between us ... you and me that is. They agree that this is for the best. It won't be long though, until they're back having pie and mash together with Gwen and John from next door to Mum.'

'John?' Frank sniggered. 'You'll be linking arms with 'im next and strolling along the Bethnal Green market or going to Columbia Road to buy some pretty flowers.'

'Yeah, that's a nice thought. We get on well. Always have done. I might even go out with him and his chums one night. They have a fantastic time when they're out dancing from what I've heard.' She turned her face to the sun and away from him.

'I don't suppose there's any point in us talking?' he said, after several seconds of silence. 'I'm not really bothered one way or the other what either of our mothers do or don't do. It's my twins I'm thinking about – especially once you go clubbing with the "boys who will be girls."'

'Us talking about what, Frank?' she said, ignoring his sarcasm. 'Divorce?'

'No. Not divorce. Us. Just talking ... about what's best for the babies for instance. Or don't their welfare come into it?'

'Don't you mean what's absolutely the best for you, Frank? That's what you'll be saying next, and do you know what? All I'm thinking about right now is what's best for me, because I'm not completely off the page am I? I *am* still breathing.'

'Stop trying to make this harder than what it is, Anna. I meant ... is there any point in us trying again? And before you ask – and in case you've not heard – Bridget's definitely not pregnant. She just missed a couple of periods, apparently.'

'I couldn't give a monkey's what she is or what she isn't. I don't even want her name around me. All right? So just take it, put it in your trouser pocket, and fuck off.'

'Oh, right. So you're not pleased then?'

'Pleased? Because that silly cow all of a sudden isn't having a baby?' She let out an exasperated sigh. 'Give me a break, Frank. And to be honest, I really couldn't care less one way or the other now. Pregnant? That's the oldest trick in the book. Go away Frank, I don't wanna hear any more. I can hardly believe that anyone would try that these days – even that sly cow. And before you start to defend Bridget, what exactly do you mean by us trying again? I don't remember having to *try* before she arrived on our doorstep fluttering her eyelashes. I thought that we were in love. No sorry, not "in love" – that we loved each other. There's a difference. So I don't go for "trying again".' Anna was delivering her words with no hint of sentiment but, inside, in the pit of her stomach, she felt as though there was a ball of fire.

'What I'm trying to say is – is it worth us wiping the slate clean, Anna?'

'You make our marriage sound like a dish chalked up on our menu board, Frank. One that hasn't been all that tasty.'

'And you sound as if you've been around your sisters too much.'

'So what?' said Anna, yawning again. 'I'm sorry, but I was just sinking into a lovely doze when you arrived.'

'I'm not finding this easy, you know. I'm trying to patch things up, here. We've got our sons to think of.'

'Well, that's really good of you, Frank, but I shouldn't bother yourself. It's far too soon – and possibly far too late as well.' This was her leaving the door ajar, and if he picked up on it fine; if not, enough was enough. She had flogged her emotions to death and all he was serving to do was to remind her of how drained she was, and how fed up with him and his self-pity. She wondered if he had forgotten that he had telephoned a few nights earlier when his speech was slurred from drinking. Missing the point she had made about it being too soon, he continued with his usual rhetoric.

'I'm not stretching your brain too much am I, Anna? It's not as if I'm trying to have an intellectual conversation or anything. I'm just asking if you want us to try again. It's up to you.'

'I'm tired, Frank,' she said a touch condescendingly. 'Go away and leave me in peace.'

Frank pulled a packet of cigarettes from his trouser pocket and lit one with what looked like a new slimline gold lighter. 'I'm gonna make myself another cup of coffee. Do you want one or not?'

Anna knew that this was a very big step for Frank. He was eating humble pie. She just wanted him to leave; grief was building up again and she was too drained to cry any more. Her pillow had been soaked with tears too many times.

'I don't want anything to drink, Frank. And I'm not in the right mood to discuss us, I need time and I need space.' She could smell the familiar scent of his aftershave, and this of all things almost had her break her resolve as she felt tears welling again. 'Please go away now, Frank. Leave me be.'

'I need to know if you want me to move out permanently. If you want your freedom, I can't say I think much of your choice, but I s'pose that George is a good-looking bloke even if he is a bent copper.'

Placing her hands over her face as if she were shielding it from the sun in order to hide her expression from Frank, she forced herself not to let his galling attempt at patching up their marriage make her scream. Right then, she didn't think that she could forgive or love him the way she used to. The daft thing about it all was that Frank was focusing on George when it was she and Trevor who, without saying it aloud, were perhaps having to keep a check on their emotions. Of course she loved being in George's company because he was fun and he was attractive in every sense of the word, and this alone had told her to be on her guard from the very beginning of her break-up with Frank. She wasn't made of stone and she didn't want to be hurt again.

And as for Trevor . . . she didn't think she would ever forget how awful it was when she had seen the state of the poor sod when the muck had hit the fan.

'You're gonna have to accept that this is all going to take time, Frank,' she finally murmured, hoping this might be the end of it and he would go back to Tower Hill. 'I need time here in the house by myself with my babies to get over what you've done. You've not only been sleeping with another woman, but someone who everyone knows. Even my own mother. How do you think this makes me feel? I've got my pride, if that's all I've got, and I'm protecting that in the same way as I would protect my babies. Go and stay with your mum if Bridget is getting on your nerves.'

'Why would I want to do that when I've got the flat at Tower Hill that you seem to think is good enough for me? And Bridget's *not* getting on my nerves.'

'If you needed to get away from Bridget, is what I meant. You owe your mother a bit of time as it happens. You can take the twins to visit her whenever you want.'

Appearing not to have heard the suggestion, Frank sighed loudly and then said, 'So what's this little whisper I've heard about you and Trevor being all matey then?'

'Exactly that, Frank. So leave him alone and let him stay in the flat with his mum for a while and let's see how it all pans out. If it wasn't for his mother coming down to stay with him I think the poor sod might have topped himself. Bridget's a selfish, self-centred bitch for leaving him like that.' She adjusted the cushion under her head. 'I don't want to talk or think about any of it any more. I'll phone you.'

Waiting for him to start up again, Anna breathed a sigh of relief when, after a short spell of silence, she heard the front door open and close again. He had gone. 'Don't you dare let go, Anna,' she murmured as tears filled her eyes and her throat seemed to close up. 'Don't you dare let go.' She was determined not to let his intrusive arrival upset her because, as far as she could tell, the only reason he was behaving like this was because his precious Bridget wasn't the be-all and end-all as he had first thought. Well, that was his tough luck. If anyone was going to get her sympathy it was Trevor who, unlike Frank, didn't show any signs of self-pity whatsoever. He was gutted over Bridget behaving like a slag, but he had kept his feelings to himself. His wife had trampled all over him and the pain sometimes showed in his eyes – but that was all.

She and Trevor had something in common – their partners had shacked up together and they had both been humiliated. Somehow she felt responsible for the poor sod, and when she had mentioned this to Linda and Hazel, they had applauded her suggestion that Trevor move into the flat above the restaurant. Anna had already slipped in the side door of Prima on the quiet to see Rose. She was received with warmth and the two women had got on like a house on fire. She liked his mother a lot. And as for Frank, she knew that he would have to let things stand or else be seen in a very bad light by everyone if he turned Trevor and his mother out.

Closing her eyes again, content on her lounger with the comforting early summer sunshine on her face and a soft rug over her legs, Anna, within seconds of closing her eyes, was drifting off to the distant sound of the birds as a lovely familiar background. As far as she was concerned right then, even though her marriage was falling apart at the seams, the song of the birds would always be there, no matter where she lived. And if Frank thought that it was always going to be the East End of London he was mistaken. She was beginning to think that she might let her house to her eldest sister, Linda, who had now touched on the subject more than once; she was looking for a two-bedroom place like Anna's nearby so that she didn't have to live above the shop any more. The shop of course being the grand House of Assignation. So, not only did Anna have a ready-made tenant in the wings, but her home would be kept in the family and she would be able to come home and visit and stay whenever she chose to.

She had no real plans yet, of course, but she hadn't been able to get out of her mind the little commune in

Kent where huts had been turned into homes. She had loved the sense of the ex-Londoners living as if they were on a permanent holiday. Nor had she forgotten the quaint tea rooms where she had enjoyed watching people through the window – especially the happy young couple who were out for the afternoon with their baby.

She wondered what Frank's motives were. Had he expected her to fall into his arms? One thing was clear – he was not too surly over Trevor and his mother moving into the flat. Even though he didn't know what was going to happen next, he wasn't as angry as he should have been. The plan was for Rose to stay for two weeks or so to keep her son company, and Anna was more than happy with the arrangement of cash in hand of forty pounds a month to include electric, gas and water bills.

Holding the image of Trevor and his mother living in Frank's secret sex den, Anna drifted in and out of a light sleep with a smile on her face. She was turning the tables on the bastard and she was relishing it as she luxuriated in the peace and the sunshine. How long this mood would last was another matter, but she intended to make the most of it. She hadn't felt this light inside in a very long time – no longer the downtrodden victim, tossed aside like a bundle of old clothes for the ragman any more, and she so welcomed the new feeling.

She could imagine Rose and Trevor living in the flat and possibly making new friends. No one expected Trevor to be full of the joys of spring, but this opportunity to live in a much nicer home in a livelier area was his just reward.

Rose, having ignited the old spark of home decorating, had inspired Trevor to paint the walls of the spacious one-bedroom flat a brilliant white, and she had gone out straight away to purchase bright and cheerful readymade drapes in rust and red that she had seen in a shop window in the Stratford East market. And so, right at that moment, as Anna sunbathed in her back garden, mother and son were in the flat above Prima Pasta, having washed away any sign or smell of Bridget.

Later that evening, while watching a Harold Pinter 'Play For Today' on television, Anna smiled at the thought of the look on Frank's face at Prima, knowing that Trevor and his mum were settled above while he and Bridget were working below. She had to admit that there was possibly a little more than just kindness in her motives when she had come up with the idea – a touch of malice had its place in there too.

While she was enjoying the irony of it all the phone rang, interrupting her lovely mood. She couldn't believe that this was going to be Frank in a telephone booth shooting his mouth off again. It was in fact Trevor. He asked her if it would be all right for him and his mother to come around with a bottle of sparkling white wine as a thank-you gesture for letting him move into his new home. Naturally, she wanted the company and a bit of celebration, no matter what the given reason. She replaced the receiver and immediately went next door to Rachel to ask if she would like to pop in and join the small family in their little revelry.

Half an hour later, Anna was opening the door to Trevor and Rose, both in celebratory mood, as well as her lovely neighbour. She welcomed them in, and once in the sitting room Trevor took over. He insisted that the women sit down while he found everything he needed in Anna's kitchen – a corkscrew and four wine glasses, and little dishes for the crisps and peanuts that he had brought with him. And to help it all go with a bit of a swing, Anna put on one of her and Frank's latest long-playing records – Cat Stevens' 'Teaser and the Firecat'.

Chapter Ten

With Trevor and Rose settled in the flat, Anna was beginning to feel on top of things. Today, Rachel was baby-sitting the twins for a couple of hours and she was getting herself ready to hail a cab and pay a return visit to Rose. After that, she was going to a street close by to the restaurant, where she knew that her and Frank's car would be parked. She had broached the subject with Frank of them buying a smaller runaround car for her so that she could move about more freely with the twins and visit her family. She gave him what she considered to be sound reasons for needing it now that they were separated, but he had simply shrugged it off, saying that it was an unnecessary expense.

Anna wasn't sure whether he just wasn't prepared to pay for a second car from their joint account, or whether he simply didn't want her to be too free to come and go. Clearly, he intended to continue using their dark blue Volvo Estate himself. She knew he wasn't using it to travel to work from the Tower Hill flat because her sisters had told her that he was still taking black cabs – as he had always done so as to be able to drink while working. Knowing that it would be difficult for him to park long-term in the tourist area of Tower Hill, where he was working today, she felt sure that he must have left the Volvo in a back street close to Prima. She couldn't fathom what was behind his behaviour, other than his stubbornness in not letting go, and she wasn't prepared to ask him for a third time to return the car to where it was usually parked, in a turning near their house, so that she could use it.

So, with the lovely Rachel coming in, and with Jackie in the wings to help out should the need arise, Anna was all set. Jackie the entrepreneur was now working on a part-time basis as a copy typist in the city, and getting stuck in to her growing business of not only selling Avon products from home, but jewellery and fancy lingerie too.

George had told Anna that she could phone him if ever she needed a lift anywhere, but she was too independent for this. She knew he would understand because he had been brilliant about everything since the day she went to Prima to sort Bridget out. He had called round now and then, as well as phoning, to make sure she was all right. His support was a comfort to her, as was the fact that she had her babies and no one could take them away from her, and she was no longer crying herself to sleep at night.

On her way to Prima in the taxi, Anna was not only relishing the fact that she was about to hijack the car, but was also looking forward to seeing Trevor's mother – after she had enjoyed a cup of frothy coffee in the restaurant below. She couldn't wait to stroll into her restaurant to meet up with her sisters as arranged, and then click her fingers at Bridget for attention. She had phoned her sisters the previous day and told them her plan, and they were only too happy to come along and give her some moral support. She also knew that George would be there at this time of day.

Anna got out of the cab in warm sunshine and strolled towards the entrance of Prima Pasta. She couldn't have been more pleased to see her sisters with George at their usual long table by the window. Greeted by a song from Simon and Garfunkel playing on the jukebox, she looked at George, and from the way he looked back at her, it seemed that he was conveying a message through the lyrics that filled the space between them: 'If you need a friend I'm sailing right behind. Like a bridge over troubled water I will ease your mind.' This brought a lump to Anna's throat and tears to the back of her eyes and she wasn't sure why.

The blood rose to her cheeks when she caught sight of Bridget, who was leaning against the bar and sipping a glass of white wine while looking from George to Anna with one eyebrow raised and a sly smile. Her expression said it all. She would report this little intimate cameo to Frank when she got back to Tower Hill that night.

'Take the weight off of your feet, sweetheart,' said Linda with a welcoming smile. 'And once you've ordered something to eat you can tell us why you're looking a touch on the smug side.'

'I don't want anything to eat.'

'Are you sure? Because this pasta with mushrooms and fresh prawns is delicious.'

'I'm not hungry. And as for looking smug . . . once I've been up to see Rose I'm going to search the little side turning for our car. And if it's not there I'm taking a cab to Tower Hill, where it might be. Once I find it, I'm driving it back home.'

There was a silence all round as the other three exchanged looks. This was the kind of thing that any one of them would have done themselves without batting an eyelid. But Anna? The most docile of Ivy's three daughters? It didn't sit right.

'You won't have to search far, babe,' said Hazel. 'It's been parked in the same place for days, halfway along the turning. And you'll know why if you think about it. Frank likes his daytime drink and I guess he's been sipping more wine than usual lately. I hate to think how much he's paying out in taxi fares with his toing and froing, but then that never did bother him in any case, did it?'

'He can do what he wants,' said Anna, 'so long as I've got my transport back. He's kept the car away from me deliberately to get his own back. He's still livid about Trevor moving into the flat.'

Linda chuckled. Whether she agreed with her sister or not didn't matter. She had a lovely determined expression on her face and that was what they had been waiting for. 'You're bang on right, sweetheart. Let the bastard stew in his own juice and good for you for waking up at last. It's about fucking time. Now then, wave Fanny La-La over for today's menu and get some food inside yer. George is entertaining us with more stories about the Krays.'

'As if you don't know already.' Anna was amused. 'And I told you, I'm not hungry.' She looked at George and said, 'Well, go on then, storyteller. I haven't seen you for days so now you can entertain me as well as my sisters.'

George looked away from her gaze and picked uncomfortably at his pasta. 'It's not that interesting, babe, I was just killing time that's all. I was just about to tell the girls about the Krays' first fight in the ring when they wore old worn-out boxing gloves. They gave such a good show by all accounts that their wages for a fight went up to seven and sixpence.'

'It's a pity they didn't stick to professional boxing then, isn't it. Then they wouldn't have had to face a murder charge, would they?'

'Maybe not. But the twins were known as tough gang leaders by the time they was sixteen, babe. They used knives, choppers, swords – you name it. There were a lot of rival fights in those early days.' Sighing as if he was bored with his own conversation, he leaned back in his chair and looked away. Just seeing Anna sitting there was pulling at his heartstrings. 'They were heroes to us younger lads, even though they were five-foot nothing.'

'It was the way they walked about as if they were kings of the patch that made others of their kind fear or respect them,' said Hazel. 'Reggie was the better boxer of the two, but they both fought at the Albert Hall at one time or another apparently.'

Anna received this information with a quizzical expression, then said, 'Changing the subject to something a bit nicer, I would love a frothy coffee.' She smiled, and winked at George who was looking at her again, and then clicked her fingers for attention. The look on Bridget's face was priceless. As much as she wanted to ignore the summons, even she knew that she had little choice other than to be at the beck and call of the customers. Very slowly, she slipped off the bar stool with anger blazing in the dark brown eyes that went so well with her bright ginger hair.

'She's gonna love the clicking of fingers, Anna,' said Hazel. 'Mind she doesn't accidentally spill hot coffee over you when it comes.'

'Don't bank on her coming over,' said Linda. 'She'll send one of the kitchen staff if necessary because there's no way she's gonna wait on *you*, sweetheart.'

Linda wasn't far off the mark, but even though Bridget was desperate to click her own fingers at one of the other waiters, they were all far too busy serving at their own tables. She had little choice but to stroll over in her high heels and take Anna's order. She looked at Anna with apathy bordering on insolence – and might have got away with this and managed to provoke an angry response – but her nose was still bruised and a bit swollen, and Anna could hardly stop herself from grinning as she ordered her frothy coffee with a small brandy on the side. Once Bridget had gone off to the back to place the order, George spoke.

'Come on, girls,' he said. 'Give her a break for Christ's sake.' He then gave Anna a meaningful look. 'She coped with having her nose put out of joint. Now lay off.'

'Well, you would side with her, George, wouldn't you.' Hazel smiled. 'She's done you a favour where our Anna's concerned. When's the next little trip down to Kent for the pair of you, then?'

George took a gulp of lager and said, 'It's the sign of ageing, Hazel – gossiping like old women.'

'As it happens,' said Anna, 'we had a lovely day out. I loved it down in Kent. And you'll never believe it, but there's a vacancy at a children's home close to Tonbridge for a secretary-cum-matron.' She looked at Linda and shrugged. 'Life in the country has to be better for the twins than life in the East End.'

This bit of news out of the blue went down like a damp squib and brought instant silence. 'And what about your little house?' said Linda, coldly. 'Frank will be in straight away with you know who. You're living in a dream world, Anna. Get real.'

'And how do you know all of this about this children's home?' said Hazel. She hated the idea of not only losing her sister to the sticks but her twin nephews too. 'Been down there again by yourself, have you?'

'Trevor picked up some leaflets from the library to do with schools all over England looking for resident sports teachers. And there it was, children's home and boarding school. The very one that we learned about on our day out, George. Remember?'

'No, I can't say that I do.'

'Trevor's gonna look into it for himself, and while he's at it he'll find out about the secretarial post for me.'

'Did you say it was close to Tonbridge, Anna? This school?' said George, still picking at his pasta even though he had lost his appetite.

'I did indeed, George. When Trev showed me the leaflet I could hardly believe it.' Anna suddenly seemed to be glowing. 'Ever since you took me down there I've not been able to get that bit of the countryside out of my mind. Then Trevor goes and picks up a leaflet about a boarding school-cum-children's home that are looking for staff no more than fifteen minutes away from where the converted huts are.'

A silence fell, and again the others looked sheepishly at each other, wondering what was going to come next. As it turned out, it was Bridget, with the coffee and brandy. Placing it in front of Anna, she stared at her and managed a condescending smile before she walked away, wiggling her arse more than usual.

'It's not as exciting as George's news,' said Linda, cutting through the silence while making a brave attempt to get her sister off the subject of the children's home and Trevor. She wasn't the only one at the table who was gutted to think that Anna would even consider the thought of moving out – never mind shacking up with Bridget's husband. Which is how all their minds were working.

Anna turned to George. 'What's your news then? Come on. Out with it. What's the secret you've deemed not to tell me?'

'I've handed in my notice at the Met, babe. That's all. No big deal.'

'And the rest,' said Linda. 'He'll soon be off to the South of Spain to live like a lord.'

'Give it a break, Linda,' said George, clearly uncomfortable with his life being discussed as if on the open market.

'You're going to live in Spain?' Anna could hardly believe it. 'How come you never told me? Is this why you've been keeping yourself out of the way? I've not heard a peep from you nor seen hide or hair of you for days.'

'I thought that Trevor and his mum were keeping you company, Anna. You've been busy helping them get the flat up there all nice and cosy. Anyway, Spain's out of the picture, but I am going to see someone about the Kent project.'

'Oh my God! Is that the time!' exclaimed Linda, giving Hazel a gentle slap on the shoulder. 'Come on you. We've got clients due in thirty-five minutes. You're gonna have to put your foot down and show what that red Jaguar can do when push comes to shove, babe.'

'Christ Almighty. Why couldn't you 'ave made the appointment an hour or so later?'

'Because when a judge who stands at the Old Bailey whistles his tune for a naughty dance, we jig to it.' Linda laughed. With that she brushed a kiss across Anna's face and told her to listen to what George had to say about the Kent project.

Once by themselves, Anna, a touch shy all of a sudden, glanced at George, the man who she used to blow kisses to when a young teenager, and smiled. 'I'm not sure what to ask about first. What a dark horse you are.'

George leaned back in his chair and studied her face. 'Ask me whatever you want, Anna,' he said, his voice a touch deadpan. 'I've got no secrets, darling.'

'Are you really gonna leave the force?' she said.

'I've handed in my notice so I suppose the answer to that is yes.'

'Right. So does this mean that you've managed to get a good price on the crumbling mansion in Kent?'

'It's not a mansion and it's not crumbling. And yes, in the end I did get it for a good price. After a lot of negotiating. I'll 'ave to borrow a few grand but it'll be worth it. The bank's gonna give me a loan and keep the deeds of the property as collateral and that's always a good sign.'

'But won't you miss all the excitement?'

'Of being a DI? Not really. It's time for me to go.'

'You might end up twiddling your thumbs.'

'Not me, sweetheart. I've seen too many men who've left the force to take early retirement turn into heavy drinkers or lazy bastards because they've got too much time on their hands. That's when friends fall away. And I don't want that. I don't want to turn into a man who drinks on the sly. You can spot them a mile off. Dark anger just beneath the surface and shifty glazed eyes with guilt written all over their puffy red faces. It's sad to see good people go down that road. A tragedy in fact.'

He raised his eyes and met hers and felt as if his heart was melting. Collecting himself, he got back on track. 'I will be taking a risk with the Kent property but I'm used to taking risks every week of the year in my job. I reckon I could sell it on after three or four years without touching or laying a penny out. But I don't want to do that. I want to work and make a profit at the same time as living out my dream. And I don't care who has a laugh on me if I come unstuck.

'I'll turn that place into a small hotel or upmarket holiday flats. There's a big change on the way, Anna, where the future new rich are concerned. It might take another ten years but at least by then I'll have my place up and running. And if those of us who've got a few bob saved up now don't get in quick and invest, we'll not only miss a golden opportunity, but we'll be out in the cold in a decade or so when it all starts happening. Land is still cheap in East London. In twenty years or so we'll be surrounded by sky-scraping tower offices for people to work in. Now, if I was to find one or two of the old-style hotels in Spain that are run-down and pick them up dirt cheap, I would convert those into holiday flats as well. And before you tell me that I'm running before I can walk, I know I am. But that's how I've been brought up to do things.'

'You'll never be a lazy bastard, George,' said Anna. 'You'll work things out to the nth degree and then go in as if you're a novice and a bit green. I've known you for a long time, don't forget.'

'Anyway ... enough about me. What about you and lover boy?'

'What lover boy? Trevor?'

'If the name fits ...' George shrugged.

'What makes you think he's my lover?' she teased.

'The gossips are not always wrong. And your mum told me that you've been seeing him.'

'She would – and you know why.'

'Do I? I'm not so sure. Anyway, from the look on your face sweetheart, you're happy. So let's leave it at that. He seems a nice chap.'

'Your wife seems a lovely woman.'

'Touché.'

'So she *is* back then?'

'Been and gone. It's over for us, Anna. I won't say it doesn't make me feel sad, it does. But it's all amicable.

She's going off to live on the Isle of Man with her new bloke. Good luck to 'er.'

'The Isle of Man? Isn't that where the rich go so as not to pay too much tax?'

'Exactly. I can't match the pocket of someone who can afford to live there. She's caught herself a millionaire. He's an ugly bastard but a lovely man according to my ex.' After a few seconds of silence George checked his watch as if he had somewhere to go.

'Don't let me keep you,' said Anna, half joking.

'Wouldn't dream of it, sweetheart, but I do have a little appointment to keep. I'm going round your mum's place.'

Taken aback for a second, Anna looked at him puzzled. 'Are you? What for?'

'I'm meeting Horace there to go over a few figures.'

Anna could hardly believe it. She knew who Horace was because Ivy had told her. And, of course, she had kind of hinted that they were in the early throes of courtship. But why would George be meeting up with him?

'I don't get it, George. Did you know Horace before Mum did, then?'

'No. I popped in to see Ivy the other afternoon and he was there with a mate of Gwen's from next door. There was a foursome – the girls were just going out with the boys, and they were about to show the old chap the real East End – especially the pie and mash shop in Bethnal Green.'

'Oh? I don't remember Mum mentioning that to me.'

'Why should she? What's up with you today, Anna? She's in her fifties, for Christ's sake. I think she knows what she's doing, and from what I could see of it the old boy is really taken with her. You haven't got a problem with it, have you?'

'Of course not.' She looked at him, all but staring him out before saying, 'I loved our day out in Kent and I would love to do it again sometime – when you're free that is.'

'When *I'm* free? You've been busy, sweetheart. Sorting out Trevor and his mum.'

'I have been a touch busy, it's true, but I've also been under stress.'

'Course you have. And as for Horace, I like him and I trust him. When he asked what I was in, I told him that I was just about to get out of the police service and then I bent his ear about my pet subject. His attention was grabbed straight away. In fact he was keyed up over it. Thought it was an excellent project. We got talking and he asked if I was looking for a silent partner.'

'And?' Anna was a touch bemused by all this.

'I told him he could be as noisy as he liked because he looked keen.'

'And?'

'I've never seen a more genuine smile in my life. He was so happy at the thought of it that a little tear trickled from the corner of his eye. I burst out laughing and offered my hand and he shook it passionately. He's all right, Anna. A good bloke. Posh but down to earth. The best of his type.'

'So . . . Mum's found a friend that might turn out to be your business partner? I've lost a husband. Trevor's got rid of his whoring wife. You're getting out of the force – and the world goes round and round.'

'And so does money, babe. And as for the Kent project, a bit of old money influencing the horoscope is no bad thing. Plus the old chap wants to do something interesting at sixty going on seventy. And if that's not a man after my own heart I don't know what is.'

Looking into George's handsome smiling face, it dawned on Anna that she had possibly hurt his feelings by not getting in touch enough. She now wondered if she had been too wrapped up in her own little world and her involvement with Trevor and his mother and the flat. Glancing at George's face, she felt as if she was about to lose a friend and this made her stomach churn. 'It seems that some grass has been growing under my feet with all of this going on. I'm sorry, George, I—'

'Don't worry about it, babe. We know each other too well for that.' He stood up, straightening his shoulders, and took a deep breath. 'I'll see you around. You take care of yourself.'

Anna looked up at the tall and handsome sod and said, 'If you walk out of here and leave me feeling like this, George, I don't ever want to see you again.'

'Feeling like what, Anna?' He was getting impatient with her.

'I don't *know*!' She then lowered her voice to a whisper. 'Sit down, for Christ's sake.'

'What for? You're going up to see Trevor's mum, to have a cup of coffee with her until he gets in, and then I suppose you'll come back down here for a candlelit dinner.'

'George, please . . . sit down.' She was close to tears.

'No. I don't think I want to hear what you feel you've got to tell me. Do what you want, Anna, but don't forget that you're on the rebound from Frank. Stay lucky.' He then walked firmly out of Prima Pasta without paying his bill. He hadn't done this intentionally but once outside, when it dawned on him, he smiled to himself and quietly said, 'Fuck you and thank you, Frank. It was a good pasta. Eat your heart out.'

But Anna wasn't going to leave it at that. She was up from the table and outside in a flash, ready to run after him if necessary. She called out to him in a tone of voice that ordered rather than asked him to stop, and her shrill voice was enough to affect even the most hardened plainclothes police officer. But he shrugged it off. 'George! Don't you dare ignore me! Don't you dare walk away from me!' she screamed. 'Wait!' He didn't look back and nor did he show a peacemaking hand.

Standing there as if she were frozen, there was nothing that Anna could do to stop those tears rolling from her eyes and down her cheeks, to then trickle the length of her neck. 'What is it with me?' she asked herself. 'What am I doing wrong?'

It was then that she realised just how much George meant to her. She didn't want him to walk out of her life the way Frank had. She didn't want to wake up in the mornings without his image ever coming into her thoughts – his smiling face and his affectionate wink. She went back inside the restaurant to collect her handbag and saw Bridget leaning against the bar with her arms folded, smirking. She had seen and probably heard it all, and it took every bit of Anna's strength not to rise to the bait and go over and punch her in the face, as she'd wanted to do in the first place when George had stopped her.

Staring back at the girl who had turned her world upside down, she restrained herself from giving Bridget something further to gloat over. Instead, she put on a patronising smile and slowly shook her head, as if she were looking at someone who seriously needed to see a shrink. She then walked out of Prima with her head held high and went up to see Trevor's mother – before going to take from Frank something that she felt sure he treasured more than the silly cow at the bar. His precious car!

Once in her old flat and in the company of Trevor's mother, Anna began to relax again. Knowing this woman the way that she now did, she knew that she would ignore the fact that Anna had shed a few tears and no doubt smudged her mascara.

'The kettle's just boiled, love. Tea or coffee?' Rose asked.

'Coffee please.' Anna smiled warmly at her and then dropped into one of the comfortable arm chairs in the light, bright sitting room. 'I don't know about you, but I'll never fathom men.'

'More importantly, Anna, they'll never fathom us. Bear that in mind and you won't feel quite so bad when you've upset one of them for one reason or another.'

To Anna, Rose seemed as if she had been born to comfort people. 'You and Arthur seemed so easy and happy when I saw you together,' she said. 'Is it an art or does it come naturally?'

'It takes time, Anna. Years. But then, as we know,

not all marriages are made in heaven and those that are don't always stay there, love.'

'Trevor and Bridget's didn't and neither did mine and Frank's. Thanks to Bridget.'

'It takes two to tango, sweetheart. Sugar and milk?'

'One sugar and a little milk. Thanks.' Anna went quiet, because even though she knew that Rose was right and that Frank was just as much to blame, at least he hadn't slept or flirted with women before Bridget came along – as far as she knew. 'The thing is, though, Rose,' she said, a touch wary. 'This isn't the first time that Bridget's all but destroyed a marriage, is it?'

'Ah. So you've found out about the other two men in her life.'

'Trevor told me. At least you can rest assured that he won't ever take her back. You've got a really good son there, you know. I wish I had met him before I had met Frank.'

'Oh?' said Rose, placing the small tray with their hot drinks on the coffee table. She sat down in the other armchair. 'And what makes you say that? You've not fallen for him, have you?'

'It would be hard not to love someone like Trevor. I don't mean in a wild romantic way. He's such a lovely guy. A best mate type that you know you could rely on.'

'Exactly. So what about Frank? Do you think he'll stay with Bridget for long? Or is this just a fling he's having? A fling that's destroyed a marriage.' The tone in Rose's voice had changed from friendly to accusing.

'I don't know. I don't think he so much as looked at another woman before she came along. But then she was a practised man stealer by then from the sound of it, and a clever flirt too – with a smile that's full of promises. Never mind the way she sits, long flowing cheesecloth skirt or not. She might just as well have put a sign up saying, Welcome to the Inn.'

'Really? From what I've heard Frank was all over her from the beginning. But like I said, it takes two to tango.' She glanced covertly at Anna and then said, 'Will you take him back?'

'No. I don't think so. I might have, for the sake of the twins, but I don't think I like him any more. He's changed. I think I still love him though. But hopefully this will wear off as the memories of good times fade into history.'

Rose shook her head thoughtfully. 'That makes me feel better, but I don't know why.' She smiled and shrugged. 'I suppose I was hoping that you and my Trevor might fall in love.'

Taken aback by this confession, Anna let her guard down. For some silly reason she thought that she had been under attack. 'Oh Rose, that's a lovely thing to say. But even if we did feel that we were right for each other, he would be taking on twin babies. Frank's sons.'

'True. I suppose it was just a silly fancy of mine, love, that's all.' She shrugged and gently laughed it off. 'I was being a bit selfish. I'd love you for a daughter-in-law and, if truth be told, I suppose I was kind of trying to engineer things this way. I think that Trevor is going to apply for the position in that children's home you know.'

'Well, if he does, Rose, I might well apply for the position of secretary and matron. So we'll be living under the same roof for a while if we are both accepted. My sister and her chap would rent my house while I gave it a try.'

'I would love it if you did, Anna. Trevor is wonderful with disabled children as well as those with no problems. I've seen him working with them in the local swimming baths. He's got medals for coaching you know.'

'I know he has and I'm sure he deserves them. So who knows? Maybe we *will* be living under the same roof. We'll just have to see how things pan out won't we?' For some reason it was George who came into Anna's mind as they laughingly clinked their coffee cups in a kind of a toast to the future.

'I'll live in hopes, Anna. I'll live in hopes. You're a lovely girl.'

'Thank you, Rose. And you're the best mother that Trevor could have asked for. One day he'll have a family of his own. There's more than one lovely single girl out there that would melt under his gaze. He's tall, broad and handsome, don't forget. Never mind that he's a swimming coach with medals under his belt.'

'We'll see,' said Rose. 'The wind will blow the way it wants to and sow the seeds near, or far and wide. Love for my son might be in the heart of the Kent countryside or right on his own doorstep. Who knows?'

'Nobody. And that's about it really. None of us know, but right now I'm about to go and get in our car and drive it home, come what may.'

'Come what may? Why do you say that, Anna?'

'I'll be doing it behind Frank's back. I want the car. He took it. Now I'm taking it back.'

'Rather you than me,' said Rose. 'Rather you than me.'

Chapter Eleven

As Trevor pulled away from the house Anna glanced sideways at her and Frank's car parked on the opposite side of the road and smiled inwardly. She brought to mind the evening when Frank had phoned to ask if she had dared to take it from where it had been parked up, close to Prima. She had so loved that moment. Immediately her ex had discovered it gone he had put two and two together because he had been told that she had been into the restaurant that day and in a fairly buoyant mood. The best of it, as far as Anna was concerned, was that he hadn't been able to vent his anger openly because even he knew that nobody in their right mind would question the fact that his young wife, the mother of twins, had to have a vehicle so as to get from one place to another.

A fortnight seemed to fly by in Anna's busy day-to-day life as a mother of twins. With the car at her disposal she felt as if she had been liberated again and it felt good – not only that, but it meant that she could go to and from her sisters' place as well as taking the twins to see their grandma. She still hadn't plucked up whatever it needed to go and see Frank's mum. Deep down she didn't want the gentle woman to be dragged into the dirty mess of it all. In an attempt to get some kind of a routine back into her life without a husband there for her, she found an inner strength that she hadn't realised she possessed.

And now, with her babies in Rachel's good hands, she was sitting next to Trevor in his car on a Friday afternoon while hers was parked near her house. They were on their way to the children's home in the heart of the Kent countryside and just a few miles from the small and lovely town of Tonbridge. Anna had purposely timed the day of the interview to coincide with George and Horace's visit to the farmhouse some fifteen minutes drive away from where they were heading. After some discussion, Anna and Trevor had agreed that they really had nothing to lose by applying for the posts, and each had written off to Wymark Hall, mentioning that they knew each other – even though it might have sounded too chummy for comfort. But this didn't seem to have mattered and, as luck would have it, the interviews for both situations were being conducted over two days and it proved easy to arrange things so as to be there at the same time.

With Trevor driving and Anna map reading, they found the boarding school for waifs and strays quite easily and when they arrived at the entrance into the long, wide and curving driveway they were more than impressed by it all. A touch blown away in fact. They reached the grand and beautiful mansion house, which was tucked away and set within glorious gardens, and had to admit that neither of them had expected to find such a magnificent old building or the beautiful sloping grounds, which were almost enclosed by various types of tall trees.

'You *are* sure that we're in the right place, Anna?'

asked Trevor, a little uneasy at these plush surroundings.

'You saw the sign at the entrance gates, Trevor. Wymark Hall.'

He broke into a lovely smile. 'But it's not what I expected. I think I could live here, Anna.'

'You and me both,' she said. 'You, me and probably hundreds of other people. I wonder how many interviews have been held already. I don't think we should get our hopes up.'

'I can't keep them down.' Trevor drove slowly towards the black and white sign which pointed to the parking area. He turned at a wide bend to the rear of the building and was delighted by the sight of boys and girls, in their red and white lightweight summer uniforms, playing on a grassy slope that was interspersed with lovely flower beds filled with different kinds of roses in bloom.

'This looks more like a private boarding school for privileged children, not a home for orphans. We *can't* be in the right place ... can we?' said Anna in disbelief. 'But wouldn't it just be fantastic if we were. If we are looking at orphans ...'

'We are, Anna. Have a bit more faith. There are some people around who've got money and do good things with it.'

'We'll see,' said Anna. 'We'll see. But don't hold your breath.'

No sooner had they parked and got out of the car than two thin little girls, aged about eight or nine, their arms linked, came up to them and showed lovely smiles. One girl had white-blonde hair cut in a bob and the other long, dark brown plaits. Both had rosy cheeks and wore white socks and black plimsolls with their red and white checked cotton frocks. They spoke almost in unison as they said, 'Hello – we're pleased to meet you.'

Laughing appreciatively, Anna said, 'How long did it take you to practise that?'

The girls looked at her for a moment before saying, 'Would you like us to show you around?'

'I'd love it,' said Anna, 'but we have an appointment and we're only just on time.'

'Oh well, thath's all right,' said the blonde girl with a lisp. 'We're allowed to show people to the thecretary'th offith. Come on. It'th thith way.' The girls then did an about turn and walked in step as if they were keeping time.

Anna glanced at Trevor who, like her, was doing his utmost not to laugh. The girls led them through to the gracious entrance hall with polished wooden floors, and an ornate marble fireplace filled with an arrangement of lovely dried flowers. Next to this was an oak door with a black and white sign that said Secretary. One of the little girls knocked on the door and opened it to announce that two visitors had arrived. She then waved Anna and Trevor inside and closed the door after them.

The woman who was clearly in charge of conducting the interviews wore a black and white dogtooth jacket and skirt and a pretty red blouse. As she rose from her seat behind the polished mahogany desk, her rather serious face broke into a warm smile. She held out her hand to Anna, and said, 'Hello. I'm Mrs Page. How do you do.' She then shook Trevor's hand, invited them to sit down, and immediately reeled off what the work involved with no hint of a question as to why the couple had chosen to come together for the interview. When she had finished giving what she obviously felt was a true and honest picture of the hard work and long hours required by both jobs, the woman waited for their reaction. It was Anna who spoke first, asking if she thought that it was feasible for her to carry on the duties involved as matron and secretary even though she had her twins to take care of. Mrs Page smiled at her and nodded.

'I can assure you that you will have many volunteers who will want to wheel your babies around or keep them amused one way or another. Even though we keep strict rules when in the classroom, once outside it, our boys and girls are encouraged to treat this place as if it were home, and I am very happy to be able to say that, believe it or not, they have little trouble in doing so. Grand houses and grounds or not, this place means the same to those from poor backgrounds as it would to those who are, shall we say, more used to grandeur?

'Our children, when they first arrive here, might be a little intimidated at first, but give them an hour or so and they are outside exploring the grounds with those who know all the secret hideaway places. And the swings of course. No matter the colour, creed or age, most of our children settle in very quickly.'

She looked from Anna to Trevor. 'You seem a little taken aback, Mr Plumb. Are we not quite as you expected here at Wymark Hall?'

'You're everything I could possibly have hoped you would be – but I hadn't held my hopes too high. I thought I was going to find shy and sad unwanted children who looked as though they felt they had been dumped.'

'And this disappoints you?' asked the woman.

'No, of course it doesn't disappoint me,' said Trevor, a touch offended. 'I'm not on a mission to save the destitute. I'm here to see if I would fit in as a swimming coach and sports teacher. I would very much like to work with under privileged children but, equally, if this were somewhere for the more fortunate, providing it had the ambience that this place does, I still wouldn't be disappointed.'

'That's a good answer and one I would have hoped to hear. And what about you, Mrs Watson? What are your thoughts on what you have seen so far?'

Anna looked thoughtfully at her and then said, 'I'm impressed – and I'm a little bit overwhelmed if you want the honest answer. The grounds are beautiful and I didn't expect this. The children that we've seen so far, and especially the little girls who showed us the way, seem very much at ease. Very much at home in fact.'

'And this is exactly what we aim for.' She looked from Anna to Trevor and then leaned back in her chair. 'May I presume that you have come on this trip together because you are a couple?'

'No. We're friends,' answered Anna. 'Good friends. But we're certainly not a couple and we would certainly need separate living quarters. It's just coincidence that we've both arrived at a time when we want to work with children. And for my part I know I would fit in here because, from what I pick up, the children that we've seen so far look relaxed and happy and that's the kind of environment I would like my twins to grow up in. There seems to be a lovely atmosphere here.'

'You're right, there is. Our policy is to adhere to the wishes of the founder of this institution who donated this building and the grounds to the poor children of London. We do put character before anything else when inviting people to work with us because, after all, the children who come here have very sad backgrounds, as a rule. They have been either abandoned or beaten or, in some cases, not fed properly and some, although not many, thankfully, have been used as house slaves of one kind or another. Our Victorian benefactor wanted this building to house suffering young souls who could be offered the same opportunities and education as those who have been brought up with a loving family, rich or poor.'

Mrs Page looked from one to the other and smiled. 'If only there were more such gentlemen prepared to give up second homes to neglected children rather than leave everything to their own families, it would be a far better world that we live in – don't you think?'

'Of course it would be,' said Anna. 'I don't know anybody who would argue with that.'

Mrs Page proceeded to ask questions of each of them as to their previous occupations and, where Trevor was concerned, his present work as a sports coach, and before they knew it an hour had flown by. They were then given a lightning tour of the school, the dormitories, and the sickroom and, of course, the enclosed swimming pool and PE hall. After shaking hands and saying their goodbyes Anna, from the expression on the woman's face, felt sure that each of them had come up to expectations.

Once on their way back to the parking area, she was touched by the way the same two girls who had escorted them to the secretary's office were waiting to escort them back to Trevor's car. It was obvious that these two skinny waifs who, she had learned from Mrs Page, had no family coming to visit them at any time, were eager for both Anna and Trevor to return. The shyer of the two, without the lisp, having said goodbye through the open window of the car, quickly added, 'I hope you come and work here. It's really nice and I think you'll like it.'

'We'll just have to wait and see how it pans out.' Anna smiled. 'We may not have passed the interview.' She then looked about herself and lowered her voice to a whisper. 'Have many people been and gone for the position of swimming and PE coach?'

'Yes. Quite a few.'

'And for the job as secretary and matron?'

'No. Not many for that one. A couple of older ladies, that's all.'

'Well, thank you for letting me in on that,' said Anna. 'I won't say you told me. It's our secret.'

'Do you want to come and live here then?' said the girl with the lisp, all hopeful.

'Oh, I shall have to have a good long think about it. I've got twin babies you see and—'

Before she could say any more the girls squealed with delight. 'We could wheel them about in prams!'

Gently, Anna said again, 'We'll just have to wait and see. My mind's not made up yet.' She then climbed into the front seat of the car and waved through the window as Trevor drove slowly through the tree-lined grounds along the wide drive.

'That was a bit mind blowing wasn't it, Anna?' was all he managed to say.

'You're not kidding,' she said. 'I kept feeling on the brink of tears and I'm not really that sure why. I think there are a lot of people out there who would be willing to visit those kids and be adopted parents from afar. I learned from my days of trying to get pregnant, that there are hundreds of couples who, for one reason or another can't have children, and who would love to foster a child.'

'I'm sure,' said Trevor, 'I'm sure there must be.'

Both of them were silent as they rode out of the wide entrance of the majestic grounds and continued on through the winding lanes of Kent, heading for the little commune of Londoners who lived in the huts by the river. Anna wanted to show Trevor another side of life that seemed a million miles away from the East End. She also wanted to look at the property that George was in the process of purchasing.

Of course, George would be there with Ivy's new friend, Horace. Horace the backer, who would be part-owner of the property and who, according to what Ivy had told her, was keen to move out of London himself. It seemed to Anna that fate was playing a very interesting, even bizarre, hand. If she were to be offered the post and accepted it, she could easily end up living just ten or so miles from where George might begin a new life, once he got his dream low-cost holiday hotel up and running.

'I wonder how this is all going to pan out,' she murmured, deep in her own thoughts.

'I'm not with you,' said Trevor. 'Pan out?'

'Will one of us be offered a job and not the other? And if this is the case – should we make a pact now as to what we'll do if this does happen?'

'Of course not. I don't see it as a problem whether both or one of us are accepted. I would be disappointed if I wasn't, but I wouldn't want to stand in your way if you were to be invited back and not me. I think it would be great for you and the twins to live in this environment. Who could wish for a better setting? And if it did turn out that it's just one of us they take on – and if it were me – you could visit at weekends every so often. The cottage that comes with the position is tiny but there are two bedrooms from what I remember of the details. And if this were to be the case, you could leave your car parked at the boarding school and I could drive us out for a Sunday lunch or afternoon tea in Tonbridge. Us and the twins.'

Anna smiled. 'That's a good second option to pave the way for disappointment. I know that you would really love to work there, Trevor, whereas with me . . . well, it's a lovely idea, but that's all at this stage. It's a bit like a fairy story to be honest and I have to keep my feet firmly on the ground.'

'I *would* love to work there myself. You're right. Let's wait and see whether it is an option or not.'

'Absolutely. But I do want you to know that I won't be put out if you are recalled and I'm not. I've got baggage as far as the authorities are concerned, don't forget – and you haven't. You're more or less single and with no ties. Whereas I've got the twins.'

'And a husband who might want you back.'

'Well, he'll be whistling down the wind. It would take a long time for me to be able to trust him again after what he's done.'

Trevor nodded thoughtfully but gave little away. In truth, he desperately wanted this appointment more than anything else in the world and, if he was honest with himself, now that he had seen and listened to the woman who had given a picture of something that dreams were made of, he was ready to give up everything.

Once they reached the little oasis of Hunston, Anna had to rely on memory to direct Trevor along the narrow winding lanes that led to the commune. 'We'll know when we're close to the place, because we'll see smoke rising into the sky from the chimney of the old cookhouse on the common,' she said.

'You are kidding me.' Trevor smiled. 'You told me that the huts had been converted and that they had been fitted out with kitchens.'

'They have been, but they often use the cookhouse when the weather's fine. I told you – it's like up-market camping and they love living this way. It's their bit of paradise and long may it last. George reckons that they grow marijuana in their herb garden. Purely for medicinal purposes of course.'

Trevor slowly shook his head. 'I think he might have been having you on, Anna.'

'No, he wasn't. And why wouldn't they grow it? As I

told George at the time, my gran always used to have a plant on the go in her back yard for medicinal purposes. She was given seedlings as a gift by an old-fashioned herbalist who used to live in Wapping before she passed away, aged ninety-eight.'

Peering into the distance while driving and not really taking notice of what Anna was saying, Trevor murmured to himself. 'I can't see any smoke but I can see the sun glinting on some long black corrugated tin rooftops.'

'That'll be it then. We're here. Drive slowly in case any of the old boys are pedalling their ancient bicycles.'

'It's a bit out in the sticks for pensioners isn't it? How on earth do they manage?'

'Well, it's hardly in the outback and there's all the amenities just a car ride away. Wait 'til you see them and then you'll know. They've adapted to the life like ducks to water. They've knocked two huts into one along each block and turned them into little country cottages. You can pull up and park under that big oak tree.'

Sinking into a mood of regret at not having headed directly for London after the interview, Trevor parked and looked ahead at the commune. 'Are you sure that they don't just use the places as holiday homes, Anna? I can't believe they live here season in, season out.'

'Of course they live here. Come on. You'll understand once we're there in that little oasis.' She got out of the car and waited for Trevor to lock the door while she, just like George had done, peered under her hand at the huts and the surrounding fields where masses of wild flowers were now opening. Beyond, in the distance, she could see the river twinkling under the sunshine.

'Come on.' Anna turned to Trevor and smiled at his mystified expression. She couldn't know, of course, that he was at a complete loss as to why Anna and George had been so taken with this place. To him this was just a bunch of people – the older generation – staying on a camping site.

'Are you sure we won't be intruding, Anna, if we go trampling on their privacy?'

'No, of course not, Trevor,' she said. 'It'll be fine. Come on. They'll have seen us by now and will be wanting to know who's arrived.' She gave him a fond nudge with her elbow. 'Come and have a glimpse into what you could be living like once you're a pensioner.'

'I'm not sure that I really want to, Anna – to be honest. I've got the picture from all you've told me and from what I can see. It reminds me of a camping site in the South of France that Bridget and I once drove to for a week's holiday. It was good, but not exactly incredible. And I don't think that I would have liked to have people coming and going and watching us as if we were prehistoric.' He glanced at his watch as if he had somewhere more interesting to go.

'I never saw it like that, Trevor, but I suppose you're right. They don't want us gaping at them.' Disappointed that she wasn't going to enjoy a chat and a cup of tea with the lovely old folk, she shrugged it off and suggested that they move on to the next port of call and look for the farmhouse that George and Horace would be exploring. She couldn't help wondering what the thatched cottage on-site that George said he might move into was like.

'To be honest with you, Anna,' said Trevor, with a faraway look in his eyes, 'I would rather go to a pub on the way home for a pint and a sandwich and chat quietly about the children's home and my future there. Whether you think it would be a good move for me when it really comes down to it. Would I miss London too much for instance?'

This second change of plan was worse than the first. 'You mean that we're not going to try and find the old mansion?'

'Mansion? From what you've told me it's an old farmhouse, Anna, very large and very dilapidated.'

'Well, whatever it is, I really did want to see it. It means a lot to George and to Mum's friend, Horace. George worked really hard to finalise the deal for something they have great plans for. And I know it's not far from here, Trev. I think it's only about ten minutes away from what I remember George saying. We could ask someone. I've got the address in my handbag. And we needn't stop long, just have a lightning tour.'

'But then we'll be shown around, Anna, and by the sound of it both men will want us to see every inch of the place which to them is exciting, of course it is – but to us?'

'Well ... Horace is Mum's friend, so it is important to me. She could even end up living and working there once they've got it up and running.'

Trevor checked his wrist watch and sighed. 'Well, I don't know about you, but I could really kill a pint and a sandwich. Why don't we head for a pub en route home and maybe come down another day as a treat?'

'Okay,' said Anna reluctantly, her desire for excitement now waning in the face of Trevor's lack of enthusiasm. 'Let's go.' She managed a weak smile and followed him to the car. Once they were slowly pulling away she said, 'George was over the moon when he found the place where he used to go hop-picking as a kid. To find that it was being used again, that is. And used in such a terrific way.'

'Nostalgia.' Trevor smiled. 'A trip down memory lane which is great until all the leaves come off the trees in winter. Then it would all look a touch bleak. I'm sorry to be realistic, but facts are facts, Anna.'

'But winter doesn't last for ever. Think of all the blossom in spring and then the fruits in late August and September. Apples, plums and damsons. You can't beat an apple straight off the tree.'

'I think you can. I tried one once and it put my teeth on edge.' He shuddered at the thought of it as he drove along the gravel lane, homeward bound. 'Now, raspberries and strawberries freshly picked is another thing altogether. If you like I'll take you soft-fruit picking. That's a lot of fun. Last year, on a trip back to the Midlands to see Mum and Dad I must have picked about five pounds of raspberries for the freezer. I spent a whole day out there in the sunshine picking. It was wonderful.'

'Mmm . . . Perhaps I'll have a try at that one of these days. It sounds really healthy – being out in the fresh air like that and for all those hours.' She said this simply because she couldn't find anything to talk to Trevor about. Not that it mattered too much because he had been more than content to drive in silence for most of the time on the way down. Other than *The Archers*, which he told her he never missed, the radio was switched off. There were no songs from the hit parade belting out and no half-hour comedies to smile at.

She recalled her day out with George, when they had walked along the dirt and gravel track towards the huts, holding hands – two good friends on an outing. He had been enjoying a bit of nostalgia and she had been taking pleasure in having a day off from motherhood and the role of a housewife.

'I'm surprised that George can afford to buy such a large property. If it is as good as it's been made out to be,' said Trevor, as he softly filled the quiet space. 'I know it will need a lot of work to bring it to what he wants it to be, and where will all the funds come from? He can't earn that much as a policeman and he's too young to collect a pension – I would have thought.'

'He's a detective inspector, Trevor,' said Anna. 'I daresay he's got some savings.' Of course, she well knew that he was a bit of a bent copper, but from what she had heard so were others who worked in and around London. It was perks that made up for the long hours and low pay is how most people saw it. It was also exciting, and a little bit of that did nobody harm in the general run of humdrum life. 'I think that George might dabble in a little bit of business that's not strictly above board when working with his cousins.'

'I might have guessed,' said Trevor, slowly shaking his head.

'He risks his life keeping the drug dealers out of the

East End. He's not only hated by the dealers but feared by notorious villains.'

'A bit of a gangster movie star then?' Trevor laughed.

'And he's loved by the old people he keeps an eye on. I've seen for myself how kind he is to them.' She brought to mind the comical sight of George with the lovely old boy who had shown them around the site when they had been there, the one who had reminded her of *The Beverly Hillbillies* on the telly.

The space in the car went quiet again and Anna didn't mind one bit. She was thinking about the place that she had arrived at and then left without saying hello or goodbye to the affectionate people. The old folk had, without doubt, in their own special way created their own tiny village. 'You've got to take your hat off to the people living in the huts though, Trevor, surely. I mean to say, they even turned two of them into a laundry room using six second-hand washing machines that the resident plumber repaired and fitted. And they've got two old tumble dryers donated by a launderette somewhere in South London.'

'Of course I take my hat off to them. It's just that I don't see it through the same eyes as you do. It's a campsite and no more than that.'

'Well, I think that it's romantic. The last of the Romany gypsies in their painted horse-drawn wagons still turn up for the potato and fruit-picking seasons, and they still dress in their traditional clothes from what we were told.'

'Of course they would do. Those that turn up every now and then in the Midlands paint a lovely picture as well, but they also leave an ugly one behind – old rubbish of all sorts. They're a bloody nuisance. Not all of them clear up after themselves.'

'Well, maybe the ones you're referring to are a different kind of travellers and not the Romanies, who always clear up after themselves.'

'Gypsies are gypsies, Anna.' He smiled.

'I suppose so,' said Anna, ending it there. All that she wanted now was to get back home after being more than disappointed at not having another look at the huts or taking the ten-minute drive to see George and Horace in their exciting new world. She wasn't quite sure what excuse she was going to make to them for not turning up. She could hardly say that Trevor couldn't be bothered and that the high point of this trip for him once they had been to the children's home was to go to a pub for a pint and a sandwich. She couldn't help but compare it to when she had been there with George, before he had dropped her off at the lovely tea rooms in Tonbridge while he went to do a bit of business. She had loved everything about that day. She could have stayed for ever with the hotchpotch of old-time Londoners who loved their new life, not to mention her time in the olde-worlde tea rooms.

'A penny for your thoughts,' said Trevor as he glided along the wider road to pick up a bit of speed and get them back into suburbia and a pub for a bite to eat.

'I was thinking about the cottage that was mentioned. I should have asked if I could see it really . . . but then again, if that woman thought that I was what she was looking for, she would have offered to show it to me, wouldn't she?'

'No, I don't think so. The interview was the first

step, Anna. You've got to think about whether it would suit you.'

'I know. I need time to think about it. About everything really. It all sounds idyllic but would I want to move away from my friends and my family? It's not as if I'm unhappy where I am.'

'You need time, that's all. Time to adjust to the fact that you're no longer living with your husband. You're probably still in shock.'

'Do you think so? And what about you, Trev, are you still in shock?'

'No. Don't forget that Frank's not the first. Deep down I think I knew it was only a matter of time before she would leave for good. I just wish I had been the one to make the move, that I had thrown her out before she chose to go of her own accord.'

Anna slowly shook her head and sighed. 'If someone had told me a year ago that this was all going to be happening to me I would have laughed in their face. I suppose this is what people refer to as the twists and turns of life.'

'I think so. And there's nothing we can do to stop what is coming because we have no idea what the next day will bring. For all we know, right now we could be lying in a mortuary tomorrow having been killed in a car crash – in this very car.'

'Well, that helps,' said Anna in a wry tone. 'A right bundle of laughs you are today, Trevor, I must say.'

'I'm being realistic. And my feet are firmly on the ground. I'm not one for dreams and never have been. All I hope now is that I will get that position at the children's home. I really want it, Anna. It's as if it's already written in my stars, but I can't begin to make plans in my head in case something else happens to stop what might be on the cards right now.'

Anna slowly nodded. He was right. Life did seem to be a lottery – just like her old neighbour had told her more than once. Not in her wildest dreams would she have imagined that she would be sitting next to Bridget's husband having this conversation – never mind that she and Frank would split up. Even so, she couldn't be too down about things; at least she had learned a lot in a short space of time rather than being cheated on and kept in the dark. She had also seen how the children she had met today, who had mostly been born on the poverty line, were now living in a beautiful mansion house, albeit an orphanage, that they could call home. Really and truly, she had seen enough for one day now that she thought about it. More than enough.

'I don't want to be a killjoy, Trevor,' she murmured, 'but do you think we could go straight home without stopping off at a pub? I've got a headache.' This was a white lie but she couldn't help it. She just didn't want to sit in a pub, surrounded by strangers and with little or nothing to say to Trevor, who was totally preoccupied with whether he would be accepted as swimming instructor and PE coach or not.

'You're not being a killjoy,' said Trevor. 'Don't worry about it. We've had a lovely day out.'

'Yes, we have,' said Anna, relieved that they were heading straight for home. London was where she belonged. London was where she had been born and bred. She did admire the old folk who had opted out in Kent, but she would always want to be able to hear the sound of the hooter from the local beer-bottling factory in the late afternoons telling the workers it was time for them to clock off.

She loved the quiet back street that she lived in and she loved her neighbour Rachel, the woman who had come through two world wars and still had no chip on her shoulder. The woman who was playing grandma to her twin babies. The only thing that was niggling at the back of her mind now was that Ivy might be tempted to move out of London if the romance between her and Horace strengthened. Life wouldn't be the same without her mother there for her and the twins. She checked her wristwatch and then asked Trevor to drop her off at Ivy's flat.

Chapter Twelve

'Oh ... look what the wind's blown in,' said Ivy when she saw her daughter standing on the doorstep. She then looked over Anna's shoulder at the car and the man at the steering wheel. 'He can come in for a cup of tea, you know, Anna. He might not be one of us exactly but that don't mean I can't get to know 'im.'

'He doesn't want to come in, Mum.' She turned to Trevor, smiled and raised a hand, and he waved back at her before pulling away.

'What is he then? Just a friend who don't mind chauffeuring you around or is he a man with a guilty conscience? I hope the fresh air didn't get to the pair of you. It's too soon, Anna. It could be out of the frying pan and into the fire, sweetheart.'

Anna followed Ivy into the kitchen and flopped down onto a chair. 'He gave me a lift to a children's home in Kent, that's all. I was considering Linda's offer. Of renting my house while I languished in the Kent countryside for a while. But I've changed my mind. I would miss you lot too much. You, our friends and my sisters.'

'I could have told you that. Frank's been on the phone by the way.' Ivy filled the kettle. 'He wondered if you were here. Then, when I told 'im you weren't, he asked if I was looking after his twins again.'

'Oh Christ! What did you tell him? I hope you didn't mention Rachel, did you? He'll use that against me if you did.'

'I said that Jackie was baby-sitting them – which she is – with Rachel keeping an ear should she be needed. He's still livid over you taking the car back.'

'Oh really? Good.' The room went quiet as daughter and mother looked at each other. Anna could see that Ivy was worried that she might be pushing Frank just a little bit too hard. She kept her thoughts to herself though.

'He asked if you'd gone to the woods with George or with Trevor. I said you'd gone for a ride out to the countryside with Trevor and that George was with my boyfriend, looking at a property investment in Kent.'

'And what did he have to say to that?'

'He burst out laughing and then said he had to go because one of the two of you had to look after the welfare of the twins. He said he was going in to Jackie's house to see that she was coping all right. Then he put the phone down.'

'Really? So what was he laughing at? Or was it a sarcastic chuckle?'

'I've no idea. He's acting selfish, I think. Doesn't want to think of you having a lovely time, never mind what he's been up to. He phoned ten minutes later to ask if my boyfriend was a gangster – just like George. I said George wasn't a gangster but a detective inspector and that he'd got his facts wrong again. I also told him that George was leaving the force and going into property development with a friend of mine.'

'And?'

Ivy sat down at the table and looked Anna in the face. 'He didn't like that one bit. I don't think he knows who to be jealous of – Trevor or George. What do you think, Anna?'

Anna shrugged with a touch of nonchalance. 'Trevor has really got his heart set on working with underprivileged children Mum. And I think he'll jump at the chance to live and work in the home in Kent. As for George, he isn't in the least bit interested in me other than as a pal from the old days. And that counts a million times more than what Frank's accusing him of. He hasn't come on to me at all. Okay? I am Nora-Nobody's-Sweetheart. All right?'

This brought a lump to Ivy's throat and she swallowed hard. Her youngest daughter, her baby, meant everything to her, and here she was feeling as if she was on the rubbish heap and she was only in her mid-twenties. And the worst of it was there was nothing she could say or do to make her lovely daughter feel better about herself. It was the wrong moment to give her the praise that she so deserved. Ivy felt sure that Frank would want her back but she also knew that Anna had pride – and that pride had been badly bashed about. As for Trevor, she had prayed that he would go off on a mission and not draw Anna into a relationship that to her mind would be one of utter boredom that her youngest in the flock would live to regret. Nice enough chap, though, he was.

George, on the other hand, was the one that Ivy chatted about to the good Lord before settling her head snugly into her pillow. She felt that he would love, cherish and look after her Anna right the way through life and into old age. But dare she try and match-make? No way. She held the silence which hung in the room and reached out to the kitchen dresser for a small tin of shortbread biscuits. She was biding time and giving Anna the opportunity to talk if she wanted to. Her patience paid off, because not only was her daughter ready to talk but tears were softly trickling down her face – and this is what Ivy had been waiting for. Anna had been holding in her emotions so that no one would know what she was going through for far too long. Ivy was no fool. She knew that her daughter had been broken-hearted when she found out about Bridget, never mind the fact that Frank had now left her and the twins and shacked up with the little bitch. Still Ivy said nothing as she sat down at the table and gently pushed the tin of Anna's favourite biscuits towards her.

'This time last year everything was so wonderful,' Anna only just managed to say. 'We were looking forward to the twins and we loved each other. How can it all change in such a short time?'

'This time last year you were five months pregnant and Frank was fucking that woman in the flat above the restaurant, Anna.' Ivy was determined not to let this opportunity slip by, even though the stance she was taking was tearing her apart.

'If you hadn't had a visit from your sisters to urge you on, Anna, he and that waitress would still be laughing behind your back. As it is, as it's turned out, this isn't the case. Frank's ashamed and wants you back. Bridget's had a smack on the nose and she's lost Trevor for good. She must know that her days are numbered and that Frank will sling her out with the rubbish. All that he's hanging around for is to see you weaken and forgive him and forget what's happened.'

'Well,' said Anna, between sobs, 'he's got a long wait. I won't ever be able to get it out of my head that he was fucking that woman in *our* bed, time after time. He was touching another woman's body and she was touching his. I hate him, Mum. I hate her. I don't ever want to be in the same room as either of them.'

Ivy got up from her chair again, speaking quietly and saying, 'I think it's time for something a little stronger than coffee. A drop of best brandy will do you the world of good, sweetheart.'

'Yes please, Mum.'

This is what she had been waiting for. This is what she wanted. An hour later Ivy was still in the kitchen and still having to watch her daughter languishing over a lost way of life. And then, to top all of her wishes, she heard George pulling up and parking outside. She could recognise the sound of his beautiful car anywhere.

She glanced at Anna and could tell that she wasn't in any fit condition to hear anything other than her own crying, and her cursing at her swine of a husband. She didn't stop her and she didn't say why she was leaving the room. She just left her to get on with it. As quietly as she could, she opened the door and waited for George and Horace to arrive on the doorstep. She placed a finger on her lips to give them both a clear message not to say anything.

Once they were in the kitchen, Ivy leaned on the dresser, her arms folded and looked sadly at her daughter who was now sobbing into her hands again. This emotional scene was too much for George. He was pinching his lips together tightly, trying to contain his strong feelings of sorrow at seeing the woman he loved in this much misery and pain.

'Oh dear, oh dear, oh dearie me,' said Horace, all fatherly. 'We can't be having this, dear child. Dear me no. At this rate you'll be having us all in fits of tears and crying rivers.' He then winked at Ivy and gave George a look to say, *Leave this to me. Leave the kitchen.*

Ivy nodded, led the way out and into the sitting room. And George was only too pleased for the chance to escape from the kitchen that was so charged with emotion – in particular, uncorked grief.

Once alone with the daughter of a woman he thought was just wonderful, Horace sat on the kitchen chair, held out his hands to Anna, and cupped hers in his own. He spoke gently to her, saying, 'My dear sweet girl … you have every reason in the world to cry and I cannot think of a better place than around your mother's kitchen table because, for one thing, you are quite close to the sink should the tears become a flood.'

This brought a feeble smile from Anna, who tried to say something but just couldn't get her words out – it seemed as if her throat was closing up. She shook her head miserably and the pained expression on her face and in her eyes was more than even an old acting veteran could cope with. Horace did his best to stay his own tears and, without thinking, he picked up Anna's glass of brandy and drank it down in one. This unintentional diversion made her giggle softly through her tears. Whether the kindly gentleman had done this deliberately or without thinking really didn't matter. It had done the trick. Horace in his own way was bringing her out of her misery.

Reaching across the table to take her hands again he looked into her eyes and said, 'Now I know you will think this an old and worn-out cliché from an old and worn-out actor, Anna, but please do believe me that this little honest outburst of yours is part of the beginning of healing your broken heart. Not one soul whom I knew in or out of the acting profession, but especially those in the theatre, who had gone through what you suffer now, did not escape without a sudden rush and flood of tears every now and then. Anger is actually the best of all cures, sometimes, and this no doubt will follow quite soon – which is possibly why your mother as well as the man who I believe loves you dearly, have both run for the comfort of the living room.'

This made Anna laugh as well as cry. 'Oh, Horace, I do hope that you don't walk away and hurt Mum the way she's been hurt before. Because this dark feeling of pain inside is awful.' The tears trickled again, but she carried on. 'I know you're only friends, but she does like you a lot, and I don't want her to go through this. I don't have a cut or a bruise to lay a wet flannel or wrap a bandage around but I hurt so badly inside at times.' It was now as if a tap had been turned on full because there was a steady stream of tears.

Anna placed a hand beneath the centre of her ribcage. 'This is where it's worse. It feels as if there is a dark sickening hole and the feeling of dread keeps on coming and going.'

Horace offered both arms and Anna was ready for

them. She stood up and fell into them, holding on tightly as he patted her back the way a caring father might. He spoke very quietly, saying, 'I know you won't be able to absorb any of my well-intentioned words at this moment in time, dear child, but please do try and trust me when I say that this awful unendurable pain *will* ease, and you will feel better for having suffered it now and not later on. Deep down, you will have known what was going on between your husband and that hussy all of the time – but you weren't brave enough or ready to accept that one of your worst nightmares was a reality. So *do* be angry, Anna. Be jealous. Be vengeful. Be anything that will help to shift that dark knot of pain until it gradually fades away altogether.'

Drawing breath and gently pulling away from him so as to look into his face, she managed to say, 'What on earth must I look like?'

'As beautiful and as innocent as the day you were born into this world. And in any case, who gives a monkey's great-aunt what you look like, my dear. It is you, Anna, who this family and fold of friends love and want so much to see happy. And if I may be so bold as to give advice, I would say to you: pay attention to the fact that under this roof and within just a one-brick wall division, is a very good and decent young man who loves you as no other could.'

'George?' said Anna, dabbing her nose with her handkerchief. 'No. He's a family friend. I suppose we've always loved each other, but more like cousins than anything else.'

'I could not disagree with you more, child,' said Horace. He then eased her back down onto the kitchen chair, and sat himself down opposite her. 'This is all I will say on the subject, Anna. But you know . . . George was very disappointed that you didn't turn up at our beautiful old tumbling manor house.'

'Tumbling? Oh, Horace . . . it's not really that bad is it? You and George haven't made a big mistake, have you?'

'No, indeed we have not. And if you will forgive an old veteran for repeating himself, George was so looking forward to you seeing it. He wanted to share a glass of sparkling champagne with you – and of course the person called Trevor.'

'Trevor wasn't interested, Horace. He wouldn't even walk with me to the old folk from the car, once we'd parked. Those who were living in the huts that I was telling you about the other day. He just wanted to get away from it all.' She started to shed a tear or two again.

'I presume you mean the huts which I have already seen?'

Anna could hardly believe her ears. 'Have you seen them? When? And why would you want to?'

'Why? Because George wanted me to see how simply people could live.'

'Well, it sounds as if you had a better day than I did then. We did go to the children's home for the interviews though and that was very nice. A bit sad and happy all rolled into one. But I'm really glad I went.'

'I can't imagine how you coped. It must have been emotionally charged, Anna. You were in an orphanage after all is said and done. Do you not think that your tears might well have been brought on by all that you saw and heard while there? You have just come from a place where there are children who have no parents to love them, after all. And you, deep down, of all people must know a little of what this feels like. Your mother told me about your father leaving you and I can see for myself how close to Ivy you and your sisters are. This is something that cannot be matched by anything. Wealth and notoriety kneel at the feet of this kind of precious love.'

'We are close, it's true,' Anna murmured as she dried her eyes. 'Look at me. What have I got to cry over? I've got my family and I've got my babies. And soon I'm going to get back in touch with all of my old friends. And I won't be ashamed to tell them that I'm a single parent now. That Frank's left me. That we're getting divorced.'

Horace drew a slow and trembling breath as he leaned over the table. 'I shouldn't start to use that divorce word yet, Anna. I wouldn't trouble trouble until it troubles you. Your husband has separated himself from you. Leave it at that for now. But enjoy this time of changing fortunes and just wait and see how things pan out.'

'"Don't jump in – or out, as the case may be – with two feet," is what you're saying?'

'Well, not exactly. I think it's more a case of just don't jump out of anything yet. Take it easy and bide your time. Legal matters and court procedures and divorce papers … let it lie. Enjoy life and see what drops onto your doormat in the mornings. I never pay a bill, you know, until the very last red warning letter.'

This made Anna smile. 'No wonder you get on so

well with Mum. That's just what she does even though she's got the money in the post office ready to pay.'

'Well there we are. When you're in bed at night and can't sleep, mull this kind of an attitude over and I think you'll see what I'm trying to say, even though I'm not making a very good job of it.'

'You are doing *very* well, Horace. I do know what you're saying. Live and let be?'

'Whenever possible – yes. Now then, why don't I run you home in my car? How does that sound?'

'Perfect. If you're sure you don't mind?'

'I would not have suggested it otherwise. From the East End I shall drive homeward bound to the West End. From East to West.' He chuckled. 'It sounds like the title of a film, doesn't it.'

'It probably is,' said Anna, as she stood up to leave. 'I'll just go and say bye-bye to George and Mum. I can't wait to hold each of my babies. I miss them even after just a half day or so. It's a funny old world, isn't it? Sometimes I feel as if I can't keep up with what's going on inside my own head, let alone out there. I used to be ahead with the fashion and what was going on but not any more.'

'This is because you don't need such trivia, my dear. And you are not as behind as the debutantes who attend Ascot when it comes to fashion. They do not seem to have caught on to the new fashion. The new look – hot pants. The Chelsea Pensioners have little else to gaze at with joy. Long may hot pants survive and swiftly may the memory of flower power and men in girls' clothes die.'

The ride through to Stepney Green and to Anna's house had been really pleasant. Horace entertained Anna with amusing stories from his theatre days, and before they knew it they had arrived in her street. She didn't have to ask if her knight in shining armour wanted to come in for a cup of tea because he had already assumed that he would. He was out of the car and opening her door before she could even begin to thank him for the lift.

Gently holding her by the arm as he saw them both across the quiet narrow road, he admired the tree-lined pavements on either side. 'I had no idea that the back streets of the East End were so pleasant,' he said.

'What were you expecting?' said Anna as she pushed the key into the door. 'Thieves and vagabonds?'

'Well, as a matter of fact, in a way I suppose I was. Not quite true Dickensian in this day and age, but where are the shifty people with shifty eyes?'

'Here, there and everywhere, but spread out all over the world, Horace.' She opened the door wide and waved him in. By the look on his face she could see that he was not only impressed with the inside of her house but a touch amazed.

'Why, Anna . . . it's such a lovely little house. And I do so love the way you've decorated it. William Morris has always been a favourite designer of mine.' He stood and admired the pale pink and green honeysuckle wallpaper in the passage, reflecting the beautiful coloured light coming from the stained-glass window above the doorway. He then drifted into the kitchen where Anna said, 'I'll put the kettle on for a cup of tea while you sit in the sunshine in our back garden. It's small but lovely.'

'I should like that. I shall think of the new designer Zandra Rhodes in Notting Hill and the clothes she designs for the hippy generation, and thank God for Jean Muir who continues to produce the best of English clothes. Classic, simple and elegantly expensive.' Horace was deliberately side-tracking because he had seen through the window exactly who was in the garden. 'This is how I see you, child.'

Anna switched on her chrome electric kettle, feeling lighter and happier now that she was back in her little house. 'You didn't expect to see an overflowing dustbin and rats running around did you?' she joked.

'No Anna, I did not. But then neither did I expect to see who I can only presume to be your husband ... who seems to have the undivided attention of a beautiful young girl.'

Anna spun around and felt as if an icy electric shock had struck right through her entire being. She stared at Horace and then slowly stepped to the window to see who was in her garden. Surely to God he wouldn't bring Bridget here!

It *was* Frank – but it wasn't the whore with him. It was Jackie, her young friend the Avon rep. They were each in a deckchair and almost close to touching and she was looking into Frank's face and smiling. Smiling, and by the look of things, hanging onto her husband's every word.

'Now let's not jump to any conclusions, Anna ...' said Horace.

'I don't need to.' She turned to face him. 'I'm going

to go out there and very quietly ask him to leave. I don't want to know any ins and outs, and until Jackie's explained herself I'm going to give her the benefit of the doubt. Please don't feel you need to stay, Horace. In fact, if you wouldn't mind too much, I would really prefer it if you left now because I don't want Frank to see you here. He'll use you as a diversion and probably even accuse you of being my sugar daddy just to get himself off the hook.'

'I shall leave, and absolutely agree that this is the right thing to do. But please don't be too irrational. That is a very innocent scene. Don't give him any reason to accuse you of being a nasty suspicious wife.'

Anna sighed deeply. 'You are *so* on the ball, Horace. You're absolutely right. The twins are probably upstairs fast asleep. This is still Frank's house as well as mine and he's entitled to be in the garden with Jackie.'

'My thoughts entirely, Anna,' said Horace. 'Well done, you. Play this impassively and without suspicion.' With that he quietly took his leave.

Anna turned to look at the innocent scene again and suddenly felt as though there was another hand at work here, that maybe one of her guardian angels wanted her to see Frank in action. He was pulling in someone as lovely and innocent as Jackie – she could tell by the way he had just leaned closer and taken her hand in his. She wondered just how long he had been reeling her in, baiting her with his good looks while going through the Avon catalogue with her.

With a sudden urgent need to get out of the house before her presence was felt, Anna left and closed the door silently behind her. She only just managed to catch the attention of Horace who was pulling away. She waved her arms to get his attention and he made an excellent emergency stop. She opened the passenger door and slipped in beside him short of breath. 'Another thirty minutes away from my babies will be worth what I'm about to do. Drive off, Horace. Please take me back to Mum's place.'

He said nothing, and drove away with no intention of asking what she had in mind or what had gone on in the house once he had left it. But he could see the determined look on her face that had replaced her earlier sorrow. Fate had a very strange way of working, he thought.

Ivy was in the sitting room enjoying a cup of tea with George, Gwen, and her chap, Wilfred, when Linda opened the door to Anna. She hadn't expected her sister to be there and smiled as she fell into Linda's arms. 'You don't know how pleased I am that you're here,' she whispered.

'Really?' said Linda. 'Why? I only popped round to give Horace the once-over.' She looked from her baby sister to her mother's boyfriend. 'Well, you look all right, but are your intentions honourable is what me and Hazel need to know.'

Horace was amused and touched by her forthright manner. 'Scratch the surface, my dear sweet child, and you will find that I am dreadfully sensitive. Please *do* be nice to me.' His acting ability was to the fore and he was enjoying himself. 'See me off if you really feel you ought – but don't hit me, I beg you.'

'Silly bastard.' Linda laughed. 'You'll do. Go on, get

into the sitting room, the pair of you, and give us the latest. Frank's been on the phone.'

'What?' said Anna. 'Already?' She looked at Horace and shrugged. 'I didn't think he even realised that we were there. What can he be up to?'

'You tell us,' said Linda. 'He just asked if you were back from the trip out to Kent with Trevor, the budgerigar who you're training to talk in long sentences.'

'Oh right. He was possibly making sure that I wasn't about to disturb him while he was making a move to shag Jackie in our house.'

Horace left the girls to themselves and made his way into the sitting room, thinking to himself that life in the East End was certainly stranger than any play that he had ever been part of. And certainly stranger than any fiction he had read.

'Listen,' said Anna, lowering her voice and taking both Linda's hands in her own. 'I'm gonna have to work like lightning. Frank's up to something. And I'm not talking about the flirting that's going on right now with young Jackie. She'll be all right. She'll see right through him. But he's gonna move back into the house if I'm not careful, and from the way he's been behaving lately it wouldn't surprise me if he changes the locks.'

'Oh come on, Anna. He wouldn't dare do that. Lock out his twins and their mother? No way.'

'That's not what I said. He'll lock me out but keep my babies with him. He's already hinted that he'd report me to the authorities as a bad mother who keeps leaving the twins with strangers to look after.'

'I'll fucking kill him if he even hints at that. The fucking little toe-rag.'

'Never mind all that. Just listen and do as I say.' She looked directly into her sister's eyes. 'I'm deadly serious here, Linda. Keep on track. Right?'

'Well, go on then ... what do you want us to do?'

'This week you move into my house with me. Then, together we'll pack up mine and the twins' things, hire a van and a driver, and then later on we'll move me temporarily into the flat above Prima.'

'Get off it! You're not living with that jerk, Trevor.'

'No I'm not. And he's not a jerk. He's a lovely guy but not one of us, that's all. He's different and we mustn't knock that. He's already looking for another flat for himself. He doesn't want to live up there any more while madam is down below crossing and uncrossing her legs at the bar. And anyway, I think he'll be taken on for the job at the children's home.'

There was a pause while Anna allowed Linda to take it all in. 'Go on then,' Linda finally said. 'So you'll live in that one-bedroom flat ...'

'Yes. You live in my house and pay me the rent we mentioned. I'll be more than happy, living above the shop as it were. And I'll have company in the evenings, won't I?'

'What? You're gonna sit in the restaurant in a corner like a sad old bag lady are you?'

'No. I'll be upstairs and I think that George might come and go more than he feels he can if I was to stay at the house.'

'That makes sense.'

'I know you're gonna say that this is all on the

rebound, but it's not. I don't think that either of us realised it, but we've always kind of loved one another. Even Horace in there picked up on it. The old boy saw it straight away.'

'But you're more like brother and sister. George is our adopted brother.'

'Neither of us knew what the other was thinking, so for all of these years we've left it at that. I do love George, and do you know how I know this?'

'You're obviously gonna tell me, sweetheart, so spit it out.'

'Because the thought of maybe never seeing him again if he were to go and live in Spain, which he's mentioned as part of his plan to do with property and all that – I would be gutted. Heartbroken. Whereas if Frank was to go off and marry Bridget I would feel really hurt, but it wouldn't be as bad as George never being there again for me. I don't want Frank to get my house. I want you to be living there and guarding it for me.'

'And where is Frank supposed to live?'

'The flat at Tower Hill where he's living now with the slut Bridget. Why change it? Once we get divorced, the courts will decide how things are divided up. Let them do the dirty work.'

'And George? What if he wants you to move into his house in Chigwell now that his wife's gone? He's yours if you want him – but don't go there if you don't feel the same way about him. Don't break the poor sod's heart, Anna. We already love him as if he's one of the family.'

'So do I – and more. I thought that I'd lost him the

other day when he walked away from me at Prima. I all but begged him to come back and talk but no way.'

'And do you know why? Because actions speak louder than words. Get in there and let the bloke know that you love him or back off.'

'Shush! Someone's coming.'

'Anna, do you want me to run you back home?' said George, deadpan. 'I'm off back to Chigwell and the old boy's going back to his pad.' He looked from her to Linda. 'Or are you gonna give her a lift, Linda?'

'Whatever fits in,' said Linda and left the kitchen to go into the sitting room.

George studied Anna's face as she looked at him and smiled. Neither of them said a word and the atmosphere could have warmed butter straight from the fridge. Emotions filled the small space between them and it was all that George could do to stop himself shedding a rare tear. Still neither of them said anything. Then, drawing in air, Anna pinched her lips together and slowly nodded her head as a few special words drifted into her mind. But could she say them aloud? No. Instead, she blew him a kiss, the way she used to many years back when she was just fourteen . . . and he caught it in his hand and placed it in his jacket pocket, the way he used to do.

Clearly doing his best to control his emotions, George was lost for anything to say, but it was all right because Anna was taking those all important first steps towards him and only stopped once their hands touched. He cupped her face, looked into her lovely soft green eyes, and then murmured, 'I love you, Anna.'

The seconds ticked by and, with a solitary tear rolling

down her cheek, she only just managed to whisper, 'And I love you, George Blake.'

'Good. Because your birthday is only a few days away, and so we can have a double celebration.'

'And what might the second celebration be for?'

'Well, if you say yes, I would like to slip a diamond ring on the third finger of your left hand.'

'And if I say no?'

'I'll slip it onto the third finger of your right hand . . . and wait patiently for you to say that you will marry me once your divorce comes through. Yours and mine.'

'Put like that – how could any girl in her right mind say no?'

'Good. I'll take that as a yes, then?'

There was no need for Anna to say anything, which was just as well because she was too choked up for words. She closed her eyes and hugged him and that faint smell of aftershave that she had picked up on so many times before was now against her skin. 'I think I've always secretly loved you, George.'

'Well, then you should have said, because I've loved you since you were only sixteen.' He cupped her chin and kissed her lightly on the lips. 'Dreams don't normally come true, babe, but mine has. Don't break my heart, will you.'

'No, George. I won't break your heart. Kiss me again.'

So there, in Ivy's kitchen where many problems over many years had been discussed many times, there really was no need for words and no more to be said.

Handbags & Gladrags

Acknowledgements

I would like to thank Charlotte Plater and Mark Dickenson at Hudson Property Services for coming to my rescue with this book when my printer stopped working. They were my knights in shining armour.

Chapter One

Coming out from under the railway arch and into a quiet and familiar cobbled turning which led out onto a main road, shy and sensitive thirteen-year-old Nathan Cohen screwed up his eyes against the glare of the bright July sunshine. He pushed his round, loose National Health glasses up onto the bridge of his nose and did his best to focus on a small group of lads who attended the same school as he – lads who were known as bullies. In the midst of them was not one but two local ruffians who loved to pick on boys who were loners through no fault of their own, and who unintentionally invited humiliation of one sort or another any day of the week.

Too late to turn around and make a cautious retreat. Nathan, who was overweight and a touch short for his age, felt a rush of fear sweep through him as he realised that he was already the focus of the gang's attention. His lips beginning to quiver, he felt his throat go dry. The boys were forming a kind of human chain across the worn cobblestones and each one, arms folded, was grinning at him – bar one, who hunched his shoulders and splayed his arms, palms upwards, as if to mimic a

1

distinguishing posture of an East End Jewish elder. Clearly, he was mocking Nathan's grandparents, who ran a small local grocery shop-cum-Jewish delicatessen in a back turning.

Nathan knew from experience that it would be folly even to try and retrace his steps, never mind run for his life as he had done before, only to be chased and caught. It was certain that there was going to be no escape from humiliation of one sort or another, perhaps a good thrashing, for they saw only that he was faint-hearted and fat and an easy target. So, trying to act natural and friendly even though beads of sweat were breaking out on his forehead, Nathan did his best to keep an easy pace as he strolled closer to his five would-be tormentors, who were at a loss to do much else with their time other than taunt those weaker than themselves.

On his way to visit his grandparents who lived close by, Nathan was in his faded spinach-green school blazer and an open-necked cotton shirt tucked into his grey school trousers. These were the clothes he wore day in day out, come rain or shine. His only pair of stout black shoes was a touch shabby but, as ever, had been highly polished by himself that very morning while his mother, Lilly, was at work in the local umbrella factory. Nathan's father Jacob, an accomplished tailor, worked in a small sweatshop in the back and beyond of old Aldgate East and had done for several years. Jacob had always taught his three sons and his only daughter that they should make the best of whatever talent they had and work hard so as to achieve a more comfortable way of life. He had also drummed into them the most important thing of all – that they should take pride in having been born Jewish.

Nathan's elder brothers had taken their father's lessons to heart. They had gone into the print business together some years back, and had managed to climb the ladder of success. They both now lived in Golders Green on the border of Hampstead, and only came into the East End to be with their parents and younger brother for Sabbath on a Friday afternoon or evening, depending on the time of the year. Of course they would then stay overnight because of the strict rule of no travelling after the sun had set. These close-knit family gatherings were part and parcel of the Orthodox Jewish way of life, as was the written law of not working on a Saturday. Their observance was also something that rewarded Jacob and Lilly for having been good parents.

Sadly for Nathan, his sister was no longer a part of the gatherings. Jacky Cohen had married an American Jew when she was only eighteen and had gone to live in the States. Nathan had missed her so much at first that he had cried into his pillow night after night, but now, six years later, he had learned to live without her. She had left the country in 1953 when he was seven years old and just before he and his family had joined in the street parties on the day that a princess had been crowned Queen Elizabeth II. It was a day when there had been a national celebration the like of which had not been seen since VE day. Had it not been for his close friend Charlotte, who lived in the same block as himself, Nathan would not have joined in the celebrations. Charlotte was his one and only best friend and it was she who had got him to join in the spirit of national unity, when Union Jacks decorated every street, every child was given a Coronation mug, and schoolgirls – rich and poor alike – wore red, white and blue ribbons in their hair. Together they had watched the Coronation on a small black and white television set in his living room with his parents, and had sat next to each other at the street party later. The second of June 1953 had been a day to remember always, despite the rain that came down on the spectacle.

Nathan's dad was a young unmarried man during the battle of Cable Street in London's East End in 1936. He joined Jews, and other groups such as communists, in protest against a march by Oswald Mosley's British Union of Fascists, the Blackshirts. That experience taught him a lesson which he now passed on to his son, that he would be better served if he kept his eyes lowered when approaching a group of lads who were not of the same beliefs as himself. And that, even though he should always return a smile, to be on the safe side, he should never invite one.

Good though Jacob's advice was, Nathan knew that it wasn't of much use when a gang such as he was approaching was bored and looking for a bit of fun. The small menacing group was now spreading across the cobbled back turning, which was hemmed in by lock-up storage space beneath the railway line on one side and black iron railings and a park on the other. There

4

really was no choice for the thirteen-year-old in this deserted street other than to turn around and run or steel himself for their goading and then a beating – unless an adult happened to come by.

The sweat trickling down his forehead had all but plastered his black wavy hair flat and his spectacles were more steamed up than usual, but he knew this was no time to take them off and dry them with the big white handkerchief that he kept in his trouser pocket. It was no more than seventy degrees that day, but to Nathan, who had never been good in heat, it felt like a hundred. A worried frown creased his forehead but he forced a nervous smile and he nodded hello to the intimidators, who smirked sarcastically.

'Here he comes, the fat Jew boy who's in the A-stream class wiv all the other fucking clever dicks,' said the leader of the pack as his lips parted in a detestable smile. 'Don't he make yer feel sick. Look at him. Fat 'n' Jewish and he stinks of herrings. And he's in the fucking clever A-stream.' He looked from his followers to Nathan. 'I bet you he still ends up in a suit factory what's run by Jews. *You want a good suit?*' He mimicked the lad's father, Jacob Cohen, by hunching his shoulders and splaying his hand. '*If you want a beautiful suit then go see the boy's father. He makes such a beautiful suit you couldn't believe it.*' The boys laughed as Nathan flushed with humiliation and suppressed anger. Still doing his utmost to appear unruffled, Nathan could see the louts closing in with the same menacing look he had seen before. Tears welled behind his eyes and he could feel his heart beating so rapidly that he was afraid they would hear it. Taking a deep breath, he forced back the tears and waited for the assault that would no doubt begin with him being forced to the ground and end with a good kicking, accompanied by insults to do with his religion or his weight.

This was not the first time he had stepped into their realm, only to receive a hiding. From experience Nathan knew that all he could do was clench his fists, close his eyes tightly, and take whatever came. But luck was on his side this afternoon because suddenly another person had caught the attention of Kenny, the ginger-haired leader of the pack. He now peered over Nathan's shoulder with a different kind of smile on his face, and an expression now much softer and, for the moment, quite normal, even warm.

Following his gaze, one of the others – the tallest youth – licked his lips and then quietly chuckled. 'Lucky day . . . see what the wind's blown our way.'

'Charlotte the virgin,' sneered another. 'Charlotte who likes to hang around with weirdos. Given 'er one yet, 'ave yer, Jew boy?'

'Watch your mouth,' said Kenny, glaring at his mate. 'I wanna keep this girl sweet. I've marked 'er out. I fancy 'er rotten.'

Knowing when to keep quiet, Nathan chose to ignore the comment about his best friend. At least the immediate attention was off him and he could breathe a sigh of relief even though he had every intention of staying right where he was. Reaching the gang, thirteen-year-old Charlotte, with her lovely natural blonde hair cut into the new urchin look, narrowed her wide blue eyes as she summed up the situation. She then winked at Kenny, who was wearing his brother's hand-me-down black leather biker's jacket.

'How hot is your blood today, Kenny?' she said, doing her utmost to behave as if she hadn't picked up on what was going on.

'At boiling point, and hot enough for you any day of the week, babe,' was the cool reply.

'Good. Because the leader of the Roman Road gang and a few of his crowd are on their way. You've been a naughty boy and gone and upset them from what I heard.'

Chuckling, and looking from her to the lads and back again, Kenny raised his eyebrows in derision. 'The Roman Road gang? Do me a favour. We saw 'em off wiv a good kicking weeks ago. They know not to come onto our patch.'

'I just did you a favour by telling you, but it's up to you whether you believe it or not. Your mum wasn't best pleased to see them on her doorstep – not from what I could hear from the stairs on my way down from our flat.'

'Listen to it.' The lad with the ginger crew-cut chuckled. 'On my doorstep? No way! They wouldn't dare step on Bethnal Green territory.'

'Please yourself,' said Charlotte, 'but don't say I didn't warn yer.' With that the slim, shapely girl, who was tall for her age, slipped her arm through Nathan's and gave a gentle tug. 'Come on you or we'll be late. Move yerself.'

Kenny was by now too preoccupied with what

Charlotte had told him to care about his victim any more. 'So, Charlie, where are they now then, the cretins?'

'Looking for you lot. And especially *you*. And my name is Charlotte to people I don't like. You'd best get home and find out what's what.' She then pulled on Nathan's arm, saying again, 'Come on, we'll be late.'

Staring into her face with a hint of fear in his eyes, Nathan slowly nodded as the penny dropped. 'Time waits for no man,' he said, relieved that he had an escape route. Charlotte had sidetracked the gang with her fib about them having to be somewhere else and he was off the hook. This time . . . Talking over her shoulder as she walked away, she boldly advised the lads to keep a low profile for a day or so. The couple hadn't got far when Kenny's voice pierced through the air.

'If that was a lie and you did it to get the fat Jew off the hook, Charlie, I'll find you and I'll take yer while the others hold the Jew nice and tight. He can watch the free show. I reckon he'd like not having to *pay* for a ticket!'

Charlotte stopped in her tracks and glared at him. 'Go fall in the cut, Ginger! And watch your vile tongue or I'll start telling tales. Your dad's fitting carpet in our front room next week. You wouldn't want me to tell him about your strange hobbies, would you?'

'Hobbies? What fucking hobbies? I live on the outside,' said the bully, going pink in the face. 'I hang out in the snooker clubs and on street corners—'

'Whatever you say, Ginger. Whatever you say!' She

8

then quickened her pace, whispering to Nathan to do the same. 'Don't look back,' she said. 'Just keep on walking.'

'I fully intend to,' said her friend, embarrassed at the way she had stood up to one of the most notorious bullies around, making her braver than he was. 'Tell me about his strange hobbies later.'

'I made that up, but from what I heard from the girls at school most lads have the same one. But we won't go into that. He did go red in the face though, didn't he.' She giggled. 'So perhaps I pressed the right button.'

Looking sideways at Nathan, Charlotte could see that he was blushing. 'It's all right,' she teased. 'Just so long as you don't do it in public.'

'I don't know what you're talking about,' he said, a touch haughtily, and then changed the subject. 'Ginger's no more than a little boy in a big boy's jacket.'

'Maybe, but you should try and stay out of his way all the same.'

Nathan shook his head with a jerk. 'I can't believe that you said that to him. The bit about his strange hobbies.'

'Everyone's got a secret. Especially lads of his age.'

Still blushing a little, he nodded. 'Yes I suppose so.' He glanced over his shoulder and drew breath. 'Shit. They're following us.'

'It's all right,' said Charlotte, squeezing his arm. 'We'll be fine once we're out on the main road and by the entrance to the park.' She looked back to see that the boys were now milling around their leader, who stood all macho with his hands on his hips.

'See you in the classroom, schoolboys!' Charlotte called back to them.

'Oh for fuck's sake, Charlie. You shouldn't have said that, you're asking for trouble. I learned long ago not to rise to their bait. It's not a game of tease and chase. I used to have to hide in the boys' toilets. That lot can be right bastards when they want. You should watch your tongue.'

'Don't be mad. I'm a girl! It wouldn't wash if Ginger Kenny were to lift a hand to me. He'd lose too many Boy Scout points.'

Still perturbed by her lack of respect for a gang with a reputation, Nathan glanced over his shoulder again and saw that they were half loitering, half inclining towards them. 'They're gonna come after us.'

The boy then took a grip on himself and encouraged her to step up the pace. 'You shouldn't antagonise that kind of person,' he said, slipping his arm out of hers and taking off his glasses at last to give them a wipe and dab his perspiring forehead.

Charlotte tenderly punched him on the arm. She could tell by the look on his face just how scared he was. 'They're wastrels, Nathan. Nothing but loud-mouthers.'

'I know that, but they take pleasure in beating me up. You don't know how hard it is for me to stop myself from running but I know that would be worse than anything.'

'Oh come on, you know that I know that. Why do you think I just dragged you out of that little trap?

You've got to stop trying to get on their side. They won't let you in so don't even *try* and be their friend.'

He looked back nervously once more. He could still see the lads, but at least the space between them was growing. 'I don't think they *are* going to follow us,' he said, in a tone of relief.

'Seems not.' Nathan looked as if he had just escaped a fate worse than death, and quite possibly he had. Charlotte slipped her arm into his again and they walked slowly along the path. 'I wish they would all move out of our neighbourhood.'

'Me too.' Nathan just about managed to smile at her. 'They were only loitering because they've got nothing else to do.'

'Exactly. Whereas you've always got somewhere to go because of your relatives being close-knit. And anyway one day you'll be able to jump all the hurdles that they'll baulk at.'

Nudging his spectacles back into place, the lad drew himself to full height, took a deep breath, and pushed his shoulders back. He wanted to walk proudly beside his friend, who was not only pretty, but everything that any boy could wish for in a girlfriend. She was all that his honeyed dreams were made of, but he had never said so – and never would, because he felt that they would only ever be friends. He was shorter than she, he was fat, and he was Jewish. Mixing religion when it came to marriage wouldn't go down well with his parents, never mind hers. He had felt warm and brotherly love towards her since they first got to know each other at the age of five, when his family moved

11

into the block of flats where Charlotte was already living. On the first day that he started at the same school as she, they had partnered each other when forming a queue to move from their classroom to the art room. It was one of her favourite places; there, they were allowed to use primary colour powder paints and were given their own paintbrushes to clean and keep in their school desks.

Aware that he now had sweating armpits, Nathan slipped his hands into his trouser pockets and kept his arms straight and close to his sides to try and hide the damp patches on his cotton shirt. Certain that the gang really had gone, it was with a thankful sigh that he strolled with Charlotte in the park. They rested for a while on a park bench.

'We're very lucky to have these gardens, Charlie,' he murmured. 'Who would have thought it? A beautiful place like this in the heart of the most feared and dreaded East End.' He quietly chuckled. 'That's what others from better parts of our city think, you know? That here we live as if it's still Dickensian land, but look at our surroundings. What more could you ask for?'

'A pair of slingback shoes and a matching handbag.'

'Oh, not that again. If your parents think you're too young for that kind of thing then that's all there is to it.'

'Others in my school year have got them. I've seen them all done up on a Friday night, going to the local dance halls. Dad doesn't seem to realise that I'm a teenager, he still treats me as if I'm his baby girl and I'm not even allowed to wear stockings. Mum said she'd buy me some, and a pretty suspender belt to hold them up once I've turned fourteen, but that's nearly a year away.'

'I'm not interested in girls' fashion fads, Charlie,' said Nathan, a touch self-conscious to hear her talk about her underwear. 'And anyway, you shouldn't walk through the back streets by yourself at night and you would have to if you were going to any of the youth clubs that hold dances. It's dangerous. Especially in old Bethnal Green, around by the old Jago.'

'The old Jago? I wouldn't go there anyway. It's all old factories and workshops now. But it's all right where my great-aunt and uncle used to live. Broadbent Road is okay, and there's a smashing dance hall for young people close by. I went there one summer evening to see what the girls at school were getting excited about.'

'And was it any good?' he asked.

'From what I could see from the doorway it was fantastic,' Charlotte replied. 'It was dark, with red and blue light over the dance floor, and there was a stage where a band was playing and singing songs from the hit parade.'

'Why didn't you go inside?' he said, his elbows now resting on his podgy knees and his hands cupping his face.

'Because I was wearing my gingham check frock with the white Peter Pan collar that would suit a six-year-old. My parents just won't accept that I'm a teenager. That's what comes of being an only child, I s'pose, but I *will* get my slingbacks even if I have to get a Saturday job and buy the shoes myself.'

Charlotte turned her head towards the open gateway

to the park, and felt an icy chill shoot through her: the boys were coming their way. 'We might be through the gates, Nathan, but we're not out of the woods, as my grandparents would say. They're still hanging around. Let's head for the park-keeper's little wooden hut and hide in there. Come on.'

'Won't he mind? The park-keeper?'

'I doubt he'll be in there on a sunny day like this. And anyway, no, he won't mind, he's nice. I often sit with him when he's in Queen Victoria's open-fronted shelter.'

Nathan laughed. 'Queen Victoria? I doubt she ever sat in our park.'

'Course she didn't, but it was built to commemorate her coronation so the adults have always referred to it as her shelter.'

'I know that. I know my local history.'

'So you should. Come on.' They made their way to the little tucked-away place where the kindly man in his uniform and peaked cap usually sat when having his packed lunch or taking a tea break. They passed through heavenly flowerbeds where scented roses, ranging from pale apricot to deep velvety red, were in bloom. They could see that the hut door was open but there was no sign of the keeper.

Charlotte turned and looked to the entrance again. She could just see through the shrubbery and the iron railings that the gang was either about to enter the park, or carry on across the main road that led to the Mile End Gate. Whatever the case they were hovering, and clearly looking for something – or someone – with which to kill time.

Not wishing to risk any trouble for Nathan, she turned her attention to her friend, who was now sitting on the bench inside the hut. He was in full view of any passers-by, and she quickly went to him, pulling at his arm and ordering him to get behind the shed and duck down behind the thick foliage. The thicket, with its leafy screen, had always been a favourite of Charlotte's when she was a child playing hide and seek with friends.

Doing as he was told and once hidden, Nathan didn't move a muscle as they watched from their hiding place. The gang were now sauntering along in their direction and Charlotte's own heart was beginning to beat faster. She clasped her hands together and silently prayed to God to make the boys turn back or walk by without searching for them. They were now sitting targets and it had been she that had led them into this corner. Nathan, realising that this could be the lull before the storm, removed his glasses and rubbed his eyes but gave nothing of his terror away, and Charlotte couldn't make out from his expression whether he was troubled or not.

But she *could* see the lads were looking about them and sniggering at a tall, upright man with greying black hair slicked back. Definitely a gentleman, he was wearing a shabby, old-fashioned suit, frayed at the edges, with a gold fob watch and chain in his waistcoat pocket. He had the air of a man who had once had money, but it was impossible to tell if he was from a posh or poor background. Linking arms with him was a woman of similar age; her thinning, almost transparent, blue-rinsed hair shone in the glow of the afternoon sun. The boys did no more than snigger at the couple, and Charlotte could see that Kenny was peering in their direction but, fortunately, didn't spot them through the screen of foliage. 'I think they're going to turn around,' she whispered.

Nathan wiped his brow with the back of his hand and breathed a sigh of relief. 'Yes, I think so too.' The boys sauntered away, going back through the open gateway and leaving the park with an air of despondency. This patch of greenery was not one they could be bothered with.

'The trouble with that lot is they're now finding out about the birds and the bees at school and it's messed up their thinking. They don't know what to do with themselves now that they're meant to be thinking about the facts of life,' said Charlotte.

'What are you talking about? I don't understand.'

'Well, up until recently any talk about sex at home just didn't happen, but not any more. Our parents are being encouraged to talk to us about things, aren't they.'

'I don't know,' said Nathan, 'but then my dad never held back where sex was concerned. I know most of what I need to know already.'

'Perhaps Jewish families are more open about that kind of thing. But now that we've got this education at school, these boys don't know whether they're supposed to be kicking a football or kissing a girl. Before now we were brought up to be ashamed of puberty. My mum still hides her box of sanitary towels even though I'll soon be starting my periods.'

Nathan was aghast at the thought. 'Urrgghh. You're making me feel sick. For God's sake, shut up.'

'Why? We shouldn't be ashamed. I read an article about it in a girl magazine. It all made sense so my fivepence wasn't wasted.'

'My grandmother once told me that I was never to have anything to do with girls and I passed out when she explained what she meant and why she had said it.'

Charlotte laughed. She could see that Nathan was embarrassed and tried to think of something to change the subject. But then, all of a sudden, there came from the overgrowth a pattering of warm raindrops that had settled on broad leaves earlier on after a light July shower. Laughing as they came out into the open to shake off the rain, they dusted themselves down then strolled through the grounds towards the public library. There, a glass of welfare orange juice and a biscuit were served at this time of the day to school children, pensioners and tramps.

'I really wish I didn't have to hide from those fucking bastards,' said Nathan, pulling both hands into tight fists. 'It's bloody well getting on my nerves. I'm sick of them calling me a fat Jew boy and then putting the boot in.' He looked sideways at Charlotte to see that she was trapping laughter.

'Well, three cheers that you find it so amusing.'

'Oh shut up. Of course I don't. I'm just relieved that they've gone and you've got away without a kicking. It's when you swear that makes me want to laugh. I can't help it. You're just like your dad when he sounds off at you sometimes. And something else – I think you should tell your parents what's going on with the bullies.'

'There's no point. I think if I told Mum she might feel that I was making up stories and if I told Dad he would want to go up the school and let them know what's going on, and I don't want that.'

'I don't know about your dad, but your mum would never think you were making it up. She's not like that.'

'I don't care what you say, I don't want them to interfere. And as for swearing, my dad hardly ever says fuck in front of me and would go mad if he heard me saying it. He only does it when my brothers come. They sit and talk in the kitchen and swear. My mother would go potty if she heard what I hear at times.'

'Men always do that when they're together with no women about. You hear it going on all over the place. It's the way it's said I s'pose. Not angry but just part of the language.' She smiled. 'You did remind me of your dad though when you said it.'

'Well, I'm *bound* to, Charlotte! I'm his son! The only difference is that I'm a young Jew and he's an old one.'

'Oh, for Christ's sake! Will you let go of all of that Jew boy stuff? And it's not because you're Jewish that *they* start on you, it's because you react as if *that is* what they're doing. I remember right back to when we were six and you had a row with one of the boys in the playground. He called you a fat Jew boy and you went berserk in front of all the other kids watching. You ranted that if anyone else called you that you would

18

pulverise him or her. So what did they do? They all chanted fat Jew boy. Remember?'

Nathan sniffed. 'I don't recall that. You must be thinking of someone else, it wasn't me.'

'Yes it was. And it was your own fault that they did it more and more. That lot behave like big kids and you should walk the other way when you see them. You should turn around and leave. They'll soon get bored with trying to lure you in. We've all turned thirteen going on fourteen, Nathan. We're not kids any more.'

'Tell me about it. I've not long since been through my barmitzvah.' He held up his hand. 'Don't ask!'

'I wasn't going to. And listen . . . I'm not gonna say it again after this. Right?'

'Whatever,' said Nathan, fed up with it all.

'You can't do anything about your religion but—'

'I don't *want* to do anything about it, thank you,' he snapped. 'I like being Jewish. All right?'

Looking into his face she could see that he was grinding his back teeth and her heart went out to him. 'Of course you do. Why wouldn't you? But you don't like being fat, so do something about that. Every time I see you at school, in the playground or whatever, you're putting something into your mouth – a sand-wich, sweets, crisps. You and a bag of chips go hand in hand.'

'That's *my* expression. You shouldn't steal other people's expressions.'

'Hand in hand?'

'Yes.'

'My grandparents have always said it. Don't change the subject.'

'I didn't know that your grandparents also said it. So you think I eat too much?'

'You *know* you do. And I've seen you hiding behind the caretaker's shed at school.'

'What if I was having a pee?'

'The boys' toilets are closer to the school than the caretaker's shed is. And before you make any excuses about the boys teasing you in there being the reason for you not using it, I've seen you go in and out lots of times.'

'So you've been spying on me then? Thanks. And if you really want to know, I would rather die than go on a diet. My mother keeps saying I should and my dad tells her to leave it be. He says that once I shoot upwards I'll be lean like him.'

'Well, it's up to you, it's your body. But I'll help you if you want me to.'

'You don't have to worry over me. You're not responsible for my welfare. It's not as if we're boy and girlfriend, is it?' He glanced slyly at her face hoping that she might blush, which would give him a little hope.

'We're mates, Nathan. Good friends. We go to the same school and we live in the same block and that makes us neighbours as well as best friends. Just because we're the opposite sex it doesn't mean to say that we've got to be going out together.'

'Who said it did? Did I say that?' Shaking his head in despair Nathan then gently laughed, and said, 'You are *so* old-fashioned at times. I can't believe that you just said that. You watch too many free films at the cinema where your aunty works. Complimentary tickets might be your downfall.'

'Well, you don't turn down an "entrance free" when I get a spare one, do you?'

'That's true, but it's because I need to study all aspects of drama. I would rather your aunty worked in a local theatre that she could get free tickets for. But we can't have everything go our way.'

'Oh, not that again.'

'I can't help it. I've dreamt of being part of that world ever since I helped put on a children's show for parents at our Stepney Jewish club. You know that. I loved it. I was assistant stage manager, don't forget. My dad said that that was quite an achievement for an eleven-year-old.'

'Maybe it was, but rather than harp on about it why don't you join a young people's theatre group? They run something like that at a disused church hall in Wapping.'

'We'll see,' said Nathan, 'we'll see.' He then broke into quiet laughter and said, 'Going out together? You and me? As if . . .' He gave Charlotte another sideways look, then, trying to make light of it, he fooled around by holding his arms out to her and singing loudly, 'Let me call you Sweetheart.' This was a line from a song that his father liked to sing to his mother now and then when larking around in the kitchen while she was cooking.

'You're mad, Nathan. Do you know that? Stark

raving bonkers, and what's more I've got something to tell you.'

He waved a theatrical arm and said, 'I am all ears, your majesty . . .'

She gently took hold of his hand and smiled warmly. Then, swallowing against a lump in her throat said, 'It's a secret that my mum and dad don't want to get out. Not yet anyway. It's all to do with my grandparents and aunts who might start shouting the odds, saying that family should live where their roots are.'

Nathan showed a puzzled expression. 'Are you mad or what? Who gives a shit about roots? Especially those around this way. We live in a dump, Charlie.'

'It's not a dump but I'm glad you're okay about it.'

'About what? What are you talking about?'

Charlotte sucked on her bottom lip and then said, 'In a fortnight's time we're moving. Out of the East End. We're going to Norfolk. To live in a small country town called Bridgeford.'

'Norfolk? Bridgeford? Where in God's name is that?'

'I just told you. In the countryside, miles away, where they've built brand new council estates for Londoners. And from what I saw of the stuff they sent about it, cheap private houses are planned for people who want to buy their own property.'

Nathan slowly shook his head. 'Bridgeford? It's not even on the map.'

'Yes it is.' She stood looking at him as a few leaves swirled in the warm breeze. 'Mum and Dad are over the moon about it so I'm trying my best not to be down. I won't be going back to our school next term.'

After a horrible silence the two best friends looked at each other while a desperate thought ran through Nathan's mind. *What will I do without her?* 'If the piper calls,' he finally said, speaking in a quiet and croaky voice, 'then the troupe must follow.' He couldn't believe that the same thing could happen to him twice. The only other girl that he had cared about was his elder sister, Jacky, who had left him as well. He had missed her so badly it hurt. Now all that he could hope was that the old-fashioned saying where love was concerned – *Absence makes the heart grow fonder* – was a load of rubbish.

'Some friends of my parents are doing the selfsame thing,' he murmured. 'Except that they're going to Suffolk. To a town called Bury St Edmunds.'

'Well, that's not far from where we'll be living. Dad mentioned it more than once in the past because the firm where he works as an electrician will have a branch there too. Dad reckons that he'll get a bit of private work as well. Because of the new estates that are being built. He wants to work for himself eventually. We're going in for a transfer from our borough to Norfolk, so we'll be on a brand spanking new council estate. Can't be bad, can it?'

'No. My parents' friends will be living on a small quiet estate in a terraced house. They'll be getting a mortgage and all of that stuff. Barratt Homes I think is what my dad said. Maybe your parents should talk to them about where they'll be going?'

'There won't be time, Nathan. There's so much to do and arrange.'

Holding out his hand so as to shake his best friend's, he only just managed to say, 'I hope you'll find it over the rainbow. The pot of gold.'

Charlotte pulled back and narrowed her eyes. 'I'm not gonna shake your hand, you daft sod. We're friends not business people. But promise that you'll get yourself on a train and come to visit me?'

'I won't make promises. I hate it when people do that. Make them, and then break them.' He pinched his lips together and tried his best to smile as tears welled behind his eyes. With a broken voice he just managed to say, 'God go with you and your family.'

'And I wish the same to you and yours.'

'I think I'm going to need it,' he all but whispered as the recurring thought rolled across his mind. How could he possibly live each day without her being there? 'Will I see you before you leave?'

'Of course you will. We're not doing a moonlight flit. I just wanted you to know before the other neighbours. Mum will only have to tell her friend from next door and it will be all round the block.' She looked into his big, round and doleful warm brown eyes. 'Don't tell anyone though. Because of our relations.'

'I won't say a word. Although I might get the local paper to broadcast it.' He felt like crying but laughed a touch nervously instead.

'I'll write to you. You don't have to write back if you don't feel like it. I won't be offended.'

'I'm pleased to hear it because I won't write back. Old people send letters, not the likes of us. I will jump on a train and come visit you though.' He looked into her face again and pinched his lips together. 'It'll be a nice trip out for me. A few hours in the countryside. That I *can* cope with. Just.' He pushed his hands into his pockets and looked down at the ground as he slowly walked onwards.

'You realise that you'll be leaving all of your old friends behind, Charlie,' he murmured, 'and so will your parents be. But I'm sure they must have considered all of this.'

'Probably, but I'd rather not think about it. I've always hated change of any kind. They plan to get rid of Trinity Square you know. Knock down my aunt Sheila's house.' Her gaze fell to the ground. 'They're going to pull all the lovely old almshouses down to make room for another small council estate.'

'There's nothing wrong with that. It's called progress. We all have to move with the times. As a matter of fact, I'm going to join the local drama group next week, so in a sense I'll be taking a step forward. I've always fancied the idea of being somebody else on stage.'

'I didn't know that – why didn't you say earlier when I suggested it? I think it's a great idea. You'll make new friends.'

'Maybe.'

The two of them went quiet and little else was said as they made their way towards the library, each of them immersed in their own thoughts. Thoughts of how it was becoming a scary and fast-changing world. More importantly, where Nathan was concerned, very soon he would only be able to murmur Charlotte's name to himself because she would be gone. And while he was thinking this, she was trying not to think about the sad fact that she was going miles away – and not just for a fortnight or so, but for ever.

A silence hung in the air until she spoke in a quiet husky voice. 'I can't say that I won't cry because I will. I'll miss all of this, Nathan. I'll miss you as well.'

Too gutted to think straight he held firmly onto the only bit of bravery that he could muster. 'Everything, with the exception of a ring, comes to an end at some point. None of us will be in this area for always I don't suppose.' He slipped his hands into his pockets and looked anywhere but at her face. 'And we're all bound to miss each other. You'll be gone for too long but there's nothing we can do about that. You'll be gone for ever in fact.'

'Maybe. But I might not like living in the sticks very much.'

'You're bound to like it.' The lad pushed a hand through his short black curly hair and forced back the tears. 'Write me a letter as soon as you get there.'

'Of course. I'll write straight away. You're my best friend.' Her lips parted in a smile, and Nathan wasn't sure whether this was purely from friendship or whether the expression might possibly be laced with love. But the look on *his* face as they observed each other said it all. He worshipped her.

'The only good thing to come out of this is that Mum whispered to me that if I was good and didn't make a fuss and kept the secret then she would buy me some slingback shoes and a handbag to match – once we've settled into the new house. But what good will they be then? I'd look daft walking along country lanes and rivers all done up with nowhere to go.'

'You don't have to go. You could live with your grandparents, you know how fond you are of them. And you never know . . . when you leave . . . it might be the last time you'll see them alive.'

'They're only in their early sixties. That's not old.'

'Well, maybe not, but you won't be seeing much of them, will you? Not with all of those miles in between. It stands to reason.'

'You don't have to tell me. I already know it. I'm just gonna have to make the most of things. Mum and Dad can't wait to go. I've never seen them as happy as this before, so if they think it's a brilliant thing to do it must be . . . mustn't it?'

'If you say so.' He shrugged exactly the way his father did. 'Then it must be. But don't abandon me altogether.'

Charlotte could see that he was crushed by the whole idea of her not being there for him. She didn't want to leave. She didn't want to say goodbye to any of it. She didn't want to have to get used to different grocery shops and markets and a baker who probably wouldn't be Jewish so there would be no beigels for tea. No more beigels and no more going into the local sweet shop with the wooden floor that she had been in and out of since she could walk with reins. She could hardly bear the thought of it, but she was going to have to. It was now set in stone.

'You make sure you join that drama group like

you said. You love being in the school plays and the Christmas shows.'

'That's true. And it's what the drama teacher keeps on saying as well. Maybe that's what I'll do. Act my way through life.'

Charlotte laughed fondly at him. 'No. Act your way through plays on the stage and live your life the way you want to.'

Chapter Two

Five Years Later

Enjoying a pint in a nearby pub in Bridgeford where he, his wife Rita and daughter Charlotte now lived, Eddie Blake thought that he recognised someone across the bar from back home in London. Peering discreetly over his pint glass at the lad, who looked to be about the same age as his daughter, he tried to think where he might have run into him.

The tall, skinny youth, with dark auburn hair cut in the Beatles style, seemed a touch on the flash side and wasn't the type that Charlotte would have had as a boyfriend, but for some reason when Eddie looked at him he thought of her. He wondered if the lad had been part of their earlier life in the East End. Resting his elbow on the bar and leaning discreetly forward so as to catch his accent, Eddie smiled inwardly. The kid was a true-blue Cockney all right and a Jack the lad with it, and as far as he could tell he had cold-hearted thief written across his forehead.

'Live and let live,' he told himself as he drained his glass. But then, when he glanced across the bar again, the penny dropped as to just who it was in the same pub as himself so many miles from both of their roots.

It was that flash little bastard Kenny Wood, always known as Ginger, who had lived in the same block of flats as his own little family. He wasn't best pleased to see him there. Kenny's dad was a good bloke, but the lad had spelt trouble since he had been knee-high. Bridgeford was a small town, and Eddie hoped that this young man, who had always been a lying little toad, hadn't settled here. His hair had changed with age and was now a dull red but he still wore the same old troublemaker expression. He decided not to let on to Rita that Kenny used the pub because she would only stop going in there. As much as he loved his wife she was a bit of a worrier, and a snob on the quiet.

Catching Eddie's eye, Kenny peered at him and then half smiled as he showed a hand, saying, 'All right, mate?'

'Good as gold, son. You?'

'Not so bad.' Kenny grinned. 'You look familiar. Do I know you?'

'I don't think so.' Eddie placed his empty pint glass down on the bar and winked at him. 'Stay lucky,' he said and then turned away and sauntered out of the pub. He didn't want to get on friendly terms.

'I'm sure I know that face,' murmured the eighteen-year-old to one of the men that was keeping him company – a professional gangster who wore a dark blue serge suit and heavy gold cufflinks.

'Well, maybe – just like you – he's moved up 'ere to find out what a fucking dump it is,' said the man as he narrowed his eyes and drew on his small cigar.

'Each to their own, Albert,' Kenny chuckled. He was

a touch miffed by the way the two men he was drinking with were knocking the town into which he had recently arrived. 'What's it to be then, boys? Chinese takeaway or fish and chips?'

'Neither.' One of the partners in crime shook his head, sighed, and then said with a smile, 'You should 'ave moved to Haverhill, son, instead of this fucking dump. What on earth brought you up 'ere?'

'What brought me up 'ere? What d'yer think? Or can you see the Old Bill crawling all over the place?'

'Get to the point, Kenny.'

'I am getting to the point, all right? The country coppers are just as slow on the uptake as the country bumpkins are. You could rob a fucking bank in broad daylight and they wouldn't notice. And anyway, an old mate of mine who joined the army is stationed close by. He put me on to a cheap flat and I've not looked back.' He grinned. 'I'm on the dole, you know, and I get quite a bit of work painting and decorating, cash in hand. And I do big favours for the local criminal fraternity when they can't find anyone wiv guts and a bit of *savoir faire* . . .' He tapped the side of his head and grinned to get his point across. The point being that he thought he was brighter than they were. 'I pick up a few nice little earners that keep the pockets lined, and as for that shit hole Haverhill, don't be too sure. You can't always tell a book by its cover you know. There are more pubs in this town than there is there.' He saw the guy glance up at a sign on the wall and then smile wryly.

Kenny turned to look at it and then shrugged. 'Who the fuck wants to jive or bop in any case.'

'That's my point, son,' said Albert. 'Even the outdated sign is a turn-off. You need to go elsewhere at your age. This is a pub for thirty-year-olds and over.'

'What, and you reckon that Haverhill's full of night life, do yer? You'll be lucky.' Kenny sniggered.

'It's a lot closer to London, son, and that was the point I was making.' Albert checked his gold Rolex wristwatch and then eyed his friend. 'We'd best be on our way.'

'And don't forget, boys,' said Kenny, with an overly familiar wink. 'If the post office job goes well you can count me in for other work in London or in Essex. I'm not fussy. And I can handle a shooter, no problem.'

'We'll bear that in mind,' said one of the men with a knowing look at the other.

'Good.' Kenny winked again and grinned. 'Because I'm not as wet behind the ears as I make out. I can't please everyone all of the time it's true . . . but can any of us? But I won't let you down.' He smiled at Albert and then gave a cheeky wink at the other, Tony, who was an Italian born and bred in London and who, from the expensive perfumed aftershave he was wearing, Kenny presumed had a penchant for toyboys . . .

'We'll see. You've not got your diploma yet, sunshine.' Albert looked from Kenny to his Italian friend, who was also wearing a made-to-measure suit and handmade shoes and who now had the look of murder in his eyes. 'In this game big fish eat little fish. Don't forget, it's the way of the world. Take it slow, son, and take it easy with the mouth.'

*

In the eyes of the two professionals, lads like Kenny were two a tanner unless they showed promise: that they would be able to shoot to kill should the need arise. Each of them was of the opinion that most dogs had the right to at least one bite – but not this flash little upstart. The expression on each of their faces told the other that they should give this one the elbow. Leaning towards his friend, Tony whispered in his mate's ear. 'It's true you can't always tell a book by its cover, but I think we can with this moron. Come on. Let's get out of this pisshole. I'm starving.'

With just one look his friend told him that he couldn't agree more. Leaving the pub, all three of them got into a brand new Jaguar saloon, with Kenny in the back seat. The upstart still had Charlotte's dad, Eddie, on his mind. 'I'm sure I know that bloke from somewhere,' he said.

'What bloke?' Albert asked as he pulled the front passenger door shut.

'The one I spoke to at the bar! Who else? I just can't place 'im. It'll come to me though. In time.'

'If that's the case,' said Tony from the driver's seat, 'you'd best leave Bridgeford. Forget the post office job, you don't want to risk anyone sucking up to the country coppers. The bloke had a good view of all three of us which would 'ave been fine if you hadn't started to rabbit like an old woman. Fancy asking if you knew 'im. You've got a lot to learn, son.'

'Nah, I was acting natural. You two need to chill out a bit more. Take a leaf out of my book.'

Sighing loudly, Tony slowly shook his head and

pulled away from the pub car park. The silence that filled the space said it all. The kid was no more than a tadpole in a pool of sharks. He had a long way to go before they would even think of letting him go on a job with them, never mind arranging one himself, which had been the suggestion thrown at them. After this drink with him, set up by the boy's father, they were already striking him off their list. He couldn't even be trusted as a messenger any more. The boy had been useful in the past as a kind of runner, but it was time to give him his marching orders. It also seemed prudent to give his dad a bit of advice as to the way his son behaved. His dad, who was a distant cousin, needed to be told that his son would be better sticking with the family tradition of carpet fitting.

The flash little sod was, after all, from a different era to these men. They had been through the Teddy Boy period of rebellion; they had drunk at Ronnie Scott's jazz club and smoked marijuana through all-night sessions of trad and modern jazz. In the afternoons they had enjoyed Italian-style espresso in coffee bars while listening to the jukebox or live music. They had been there in the early Fifties at Mocha in Frith Street and then in Heaven and Hell in Old Compton Street. They had mixed with young aspiring actors, artists, designers and students, and the only difference with them and their own kind was that they sat back and inwardly laughed at those demonstrating around Trafalgar Square and campaigning to ban the bomb.

They still drank at Ronnie Scott's and spent time in the all-night coffee bars, rubbing shoulders with the rich so as to be able to steal from them. They pretended to be cool while they weighed up how best to extract wealth from the wealthy – and it had paid off. And because of all of this, they, and several other gangsters like them, had got used to a certain way of living and their standards were high. Fledglings like Kenny from the old East End were seen as boy servants until they had proved themselves, and very few ever did. To make it as professional and respected criminals, who could mingle with society and the famous, it took more than a decent suit and polished shoes. Men and women of their ilk had to have that extra something that couldn't be bottled or go on sale in a supermarket. And the kid didn't have it.

The telling thing about Kenny, as far as they were concerned, was that he had told them in the pub that he liked the old town of Bridgeford and loved the ancient buildings and narrow back streets. He had whispered that it reminded him of Dickens and pickpockets and Fagin. He was no Oliver Twist, he had said, but he fancied himself as Fagin, all nicely set up with a team of thieves to steal for him. Even apart from these infantile fantasies, he was right out of the picture where they were concerned.

But Kenny wasn't quite as wet behind the ears as he had made out. The two men, comfortable in the front of the dark blue Jag with the leather seats, had not picked up on the fact that he had no intention of working for them. It had been enough for him to be seen in their company in that popular pub where some of the flash boys drank and the old locals kept away. He felt that he had notched up a gold star or two by drinking with London gangsters of their ilk.

He had had no intention from the start of arranging a post office break-in, but had simply dangled the idea as a carrot. He had merely been laying the foundation for his own plans. He wanted to be in on their little meetings when strategy was being worked out and listen and learn from it. Then, after a short spell, he could back down and show fear and trepidation or whatever else would convince the jerks that he was too young and too chicken for them. He had wanted to spend as much time in their company as he could. Then, when the time was right, he would grass on them before an important bit of illegal business took place. He would take a nice little earner from one of several palm-greasers in the London force. Men who he had been tipping off about certain planned robberies since he was fourteen, and from whom he had received decent pocket money for his efforts. And the best of it all, to Kenny's mind, was that he knew he had one up on the flash boys who saw themselves as top-notch gangsters. Yes, he had every intention of grassing on them when the time was right. How could he be blamed for grinning into their faces in the pub? He had been one step ahead of them all along.

Smiling in the silence that the two in the front were creating, he had to stop himself from laughing out loud. He knew that their minds were turning over the question as to whether or not to take him on. The joke was that people in their profession needed faceless risk takers and the stupid bastards, from what he could tell, had him down as someone they could use. Just so as to keep them in an easy mood Kenny sighed contentedly and then said, 'This is a nice car, boys. It's always been my dream to own one of these. I don't care what task you set me. Nothing's too risky where I'm concerned. I respect you two more than I respected the headmaster at senior school. And I'm telling you – he was a wicked bastard with that cane. Hard as nails. I loved 'im.'

This final spurting of verbal diarrhoea from someone who the men saw as a little shit slammed the door shut as far as these two timeworn villains were concerned. They glanced at one another and then at Kenny via the rear-view mirror to see that the lad was, in his own pathetic way, gloating.

'How's the carpet-fitting business going, son?' said Tony as he glanced at him in his rear mirror.

'It's all right. Keeps a bit of butter on the bread and the law off my back.' He grinned and then chuckled in his usual irritating way. 'It's an honest to goodness trade, innit? And an easy way to suss out who's got what tucked away in the bottom drawer. Some of them Jews that me and Dad work for are fucking loaded. Wads of notes in the bottom drawer. Money they've earned but not paid tax on. I do all right on the quiet. Don't tell the old man though or he'll cut me dead. Too fucking honest for 'is own good at times. He'll die a poor man if he don't wise up a bit.'

The somewhat hushed atmosphere in the car, reminiscent of a church before a service, was sending the wrong message to the eighteen-year-old. He actually thought that he was winning the hardened criminals over and that they were all ears. 'I'd rather work for you two than fit carpet for Jews. Their houses stink of fried fish. But there you are. If I hadn't of been born on the border of Stepney and Bethnal Green I would never 'ave met the likes of you two. We're third cousins removed, ain't we?'

'If it wasn't for your old man, son,' said Albert, 'you wouldn't be sitting in this car. Show a bit of respect.'

'My dad's all right,' he said, missing the point. 'Goody two shoes, but there you go. Someone's gotta walk the straight an' narrow, ain't they?' He went quiet and thoughtful. 'Mind you, he and Mum are not as innocent as he likes to make out. The cupboard in their bedroom would make your eyes pop out at times. A dozen solitaire diamond rings was brought in last year. I sold on three of 'em in a week. I 'ave to be careful though. I'm the sort that them fucking newspaper writers love to get an angle on when they wanna write about the criminal fraternity in the East End. Dozy bastards.'

'They weren't diamond rings, son – they were zircons and sold out at a fiver each.' The driver quietly laughed. Tony and Albert knew his dad well and liked him. They glanced at each other and contained their frustration with each of them thinking similar thoughts, that Kenny was either a penny short of a shilling or totally full of crap. 'I don't know why I've lost my appetite,' said Tony, 'but I have.'

'Me as well,' said Albert. 'We'll eat once we get to Haverhill.'

'Ah well, you'll 'ave to count me out on that little

trip. I can't stand that place. Fucking Haverhill, do me a favour.' Kenny started to snigger again, and when he heard the despairing sigh of the driver he let it go over his head. He was enjoying his own little bit of games playing with two men who could put the fear of God into the criminals in the underworld but couldn't ruffle his feathers. He returned the sound of clearing of the throats from the elders with more irritating quiet laughter and only just stopped himself from calling them jerks.

Needless to say he wasn't in the least bit put out when the car pulled up outside the dingy wireless shop in a side street beneath the run-down self-contained furnished flat that he was renting. A flat that consisted of a box room with an old-fashioned bed and sagging mattress and a single wardrobe, as well as a tiny sitting room and a makeshift kitchen on the landing. This was his home. His castle. A place where he could be self-sufficient and answer to no one, and be able to pay in advance the rent of two pounds a week all inclusive. His dad, not knowing that his son earned a decent bit from grassing to the law, had been more than pleased to lend him some money to start a new life in Norfolk. Or Suffolk. Or Kingdom Come. He had been glad to see the back of him in the same way that he had been glad to see the back of his mother when she walked out on them earlier on in life. She soon drifted back into the fold, though, once she started to miss her son and heard that he had been pining for her. Kenny had been a bit of a mother's boy and still was, if truth be told.

Kenny had loved his mother so much when he was small and it hurt worse than anything could when she left him. He was just seven at the time. The only reason he caught the train back to old Bethnal Green now and then was to see her. His dad was all right. He liked him well enough, but he just couldn't forgive him for encouraging his mum to go out on the game earlier on in life. She had earned good money though – before age caught up with her and younger prostitutes took over her patch.

Looking from one of the London gangsters to the other Kenny detected a sense of boredom. He knew that the swanky bastards were about to dump him without an offer to work for them, but decided he didn't give a fuck. To his mind they would always be morons and not worth his time and attention.

Coasting past the Bridgeford post office about which he had already given them details as to when cash was normally delivered, the two men burst out laughing. It was useless information and a joke as far as they were concerned, but the trip had not been a complete waste of time. They had wanted to check out this small town that was now being whispered about as being the next generation small-time underworld and a place to lie low when the need arose. It was no more than a backwater town as far as they could see but they weren't sorry that they had made the journey. The men owed a favour to the lad's father, who sometimes did a little bit of work for them on the quiet and had asked if they might think of using his son Kenny for better paid work. They had seen him, bought him a drink or two and had a chat, and that was more than enough. They didn't like the way he was turning into a self-opinionated little upstart and they couldn't wait to get on the road back to the East End.

Chapter Three

One week later, and Charlotte was waking up to the familiar sound of a squirrel that came and went from its nearby habitat, the grounds of a boarded-up mansion house that had seen better days. She smiled sleepily and peered at her bedside clock. It had only just turned seven a.m. and she still had thirty minutes or so before her alarm went off. Snuggling down into her bedding she slipped back into a light sleep. She felt sure that she had been dreaming about the little furry creature, as she had done several times before at this time of the morning. She knew that it was a squirrel scrabbling on the roof tiles that had woken her but she didn't mind in the least bit. The furry creatures that reminded her of the Beatrix Potter picture books was something that had helped her bond with her surroundings ever since the day that she and her parents had moved into this old Victorian terrace house, three up, two down. A house that had an old-fashioned kitchen with a scullery attached.

Charlotte made a mental note to place a few more dried shelled walnuts, left over from the previous Christmas, into a cracked dish that she had placed at the very end of their back garden, and then pulled her white cotton sheet over her head. She wanted to stay in this cosy half-awake mood, trying to picture what her surroundings might have been like when the grounds on which her parents' house now stood had been part and parcel of a mansion house – a building now in a dire state and badly in need of restoration. The one good thing that she could say about the small town in which she now lived was that it was steeped in history and, from what she had read and heard, it had once been a much livelier place.

She had learned from an old boy called Eric, who was born and bred in the area, that there had once been a theatre in the centre of the town, opposite the Queen's Head pub, which had been built in the distant past by a large family of actors and comedians. Her thoughts turned to Nathan, and she recalled how he had often said that he would rather be involved in the unreal world of theatre than the cruel world of real life. The last time that she had heard from him a couple of years since, he had written to say that he had joined another theatre group and spent his free time and most weekends working with actors and others involved in little theatres. He had started as a runner and was, according to his final letter, an assistant stage manager during weekends and some evenings.

The lovely small theatre in Bridgeford had closed down a century and a half ago, but by all accounts it had boasted a good company of excellent actors from all over the country. She hugged her warm pillow and tried to imagine her lovable friend in costume, giving his all on stage. She made a vow there and then to get in touch with Nathan sooner rather than later to see what he was up to. She wondered if he was now frequenting discotheques and nightclubs like others of their age who lived in the capital. She couldn't imagine him on a dance floor. The thought of it made her smile.

With one picture of her old life coming after another, she felt a glow spread through her. No matter how unhappy she was at times, nothing and nobody could take away Charlotte's memories. Even though she had been out of the East End and living in Norfolk for five years, she still pined for everything and everyone she once knew. The truth of the matter was that she had never got over having to leave London, but she did have those treasured memories. They were hers, and they were tucked in a safe place inside her head and in her heart. Wrapped in her warm bedding and submerged in reminiscence, she didn't hear the bedroom door open. It was her dad coming in to get her up.

'Time to get up, sweetheart. I've just made a fresh pot of tea. D'you want your mother to fetch a cup up?' Eddie said with his usual smile on his face and warmth in his voice, even though his thoughts were with work and the jobs that he had lined up for the day: fitting in private work in between the hours he put in for the company he worked for. His dream was to be his own boss and have his own successful business one day.

'I'll be down in a sec,' said Charlotte, slow and sleepy and not best pleased with the intrusion. 'Is there any cut bread for toast in the bin?'

'No. Your mum used the last of it for my sandwiches, but there's still a loaf of uncut that she bought at the bakers yesterday. You're a big girl now. You can

44

cut a couple of slices with the big bad bread knife.'
Quietly chuckling he left her to her early morning
pillow.

Downstairs, Eddie downed the last drop of tea from his
cup and checked himself in the large modern mirror on
the wall in the passage. He had fitted it himself, and
loved the way that it reflected light from the stained-
glass panels in the top half of the old pine front door.
He was smartly dressed and smelt of decent aftershave;
he took pride in his appearance and outfitted himself
according to the day and the customers that he would
be looking after. He was also proud that his daughter,
his only child, took after him where looks were concerned. His blond hair had, of course, darkened a little
over the years, but there was no doubting as to where
his Charlotte had got her colouring and her light blue
eyes.

Always ambitious and heading for the top of the tree,
Eddie had been pleased enough about his recent
promotion to a managerial position for the electricity
board. Even so, to him this was just another stepping
stone to the top. He spent most of his working days
going from one site to another, inspecting the work of
less experienced electricians until his day ended around
four o'clock. He would then return home and change
from his suit into smart casuals and spend another
three hours or so with his private customers. After
that, he would pop into his local and favourite pub for
a pint or two before going home for his evening meal.

This was Eddie's routine and this was what kept the bank figures in the black.

Rita, his attractive wife, had lovely green eyes and dark auburn shoulder-length hair, and was employed as a receptionist with plenty of clerical work to keep her busy. She loved her work at the nearby Bridgeford Cottage Hospital. When the family had first moved into the small town, Rita had passed an interview for the position with flying colours. She almost lived for her work and, more than anything else, had enjoyed going around in her free time to chat with and cheer up the in-patients. Then, a year previously, the wards were closed down to allow the hospital to cope with the ever-growing influx of outpatients who were coming with their families to settle in the town.

Still in her dressing gown, Rita was carefully painting her nails a creamy orange. Glancing at her wristwatch to check that time was not running on too fast, she went to the bottom of the staircase and was just about to call up to Charlotte when Eddie said, 'I've already nudged her, she'll be down in a minute. I'll see you around seven.'

'No you won't. I'm going to the indoor swimming pool, remember?'

'Oh yeah, keeping fit and all of that. It's a pity you don't get Charlotte to go with you. She spends too much time on 'er own.'

'If she wanted to come with me she would, Eddie. She enjoys her own company. You should know that by now.'

Looking into his wife's face, he sighed then turned to

leave. They had been down this road before, but the more often he said that his girl needed to get out and about, the tetchier Rita would get. Just as he was about to open the front door Charlotte came down the stairs and said, 'Hang on a minute, Dad. I've got something for you.'

'Oh? And what's that?' said Rita, who was now standing in the open doorway of the kitchen.

Paying no attention to her mother, Charlotte put her arms around her father and spoke in a quiet voice, saying, 'I haven't got anything other than a kiss for you, Dad, but I wanted to say stop worrying about me. I'm all right.' She then kissed him on the cheek and could see that he was a bit choked. 'Honest to God – I'm fine.'

'I know that, sweetheart.' He smiled and winked at her. 'I'll be in my local around seven if you fancy popping in for a Babycham.'

'All right,' she said, returning his smile, 'I just might do that. If I've not turned up by eight o'clock you'll know I'm not coming. Is that okay?'

'Good as gold. See you later.' With that he nodded at Rita, opened the street door and left the house.

Looking into the hall mirror now that her nail varnish had dried, Rita swiped on her favourite pale apricot lipstick and glanced sideways at her daughter. 'Cheeky sod. As if you'd walk into a pub by yourself as bold as brass. What if you missed one another?'

'You mean if I went in and he wasn't there?' Charlotte shrugged. 'I'd walk out again, Mum. I'm not eight years old, I'm eighteen, and I have got a brain between my ears.'

'And you've also got something between your legs that men in pubs would like to have a go at.'

'Cheers for that. It's nice to think of myself as a walking come-on for dirty old men.'

'A horny young man is what I meant. It wasn't intended as an insult. You're too sensitive, that's your trouble.'

'So you've said. I'm gonna cut some bread and make some toast. Do you want some?'

'No, I had some Weetabix. And anyway I promised to go into work a bit earlier than usual. One of the girls is out sick.' She dropped her lipstick in her make-up bag and snapped it shut. 'Right. Just enough time for me to go up and throw some clothes on.' She gave Charlotte a peck on the cheek and then smiled at her. 'Would you like to come swimming, sweetheart?'

'Maybe. I'll think about it. I used to hate going with the school, you know I did, but . . . now that I'm free of rules and regulations, maybe I would enjoy it. Free will and all that.'

'Well, the offer's there. It's up to you. The group that I meet up with would like to meet you, I'm sure, and a bit of fun gets the boring jobs done – as your gran always used to say.'

'She still says it. And thanks, Mum. I'll dig out my old swimming costume next week and see if it still fits me.'

'Even if it does, Charlotte, I think it might be time for a new one. A good one that shows off your figure.

We don't want the swimming club to think that we can't afford to move with the fashion, do we?'

'No, that would never do!'

Tilting her chin, Rita narrowed her eyes. 'Don't be facetious. Your dad relies on the sort of friends I make for us. Some of them have very big houses and some have husbands who run their own companies, and your dad needs all the right contacts he can make.' She then cupped her daughter's chin with her hand. 'One day we'll be living in a big country house, babe. You see if we won't.'

'I like this one. It's homely.'

'It's a stepping stone, Charlotte. A stepping stone.'

That lunchtime, with the sun on her face, Charlotte sat on an old bench on the river bank, eating her cheese and Branston Pickle sandwiches and fancying herself on a narrowboat with a handsome guy at the helm. She imagined herself with a good-looking young man wearing a straw boater and striped jacket, just like she had seen in films. Daydreaming herself into one romantic flight of fancy or another was a way of passing time as well as blocking out the reality of her life in this small town where nothing ever seemed to happen. She was taking her lunch break from the local borough offices where she was employed as a copy typist for little more than half as much as she would earn in London, her hometown that she still so badly longed for. Shuddering as if a ghost had walked across her grave, she pushed all thoughts of her old life from her mind as she had done a thousand times before. She knew from experience that wishing to turn back the clock only served to make her feel as if her childhood and upbringing with her cousins, her aunts and uncles, her grandparents and friends, had been obliterated in one clean sweep.

A touch on the low side for no apparent reason other than that she was lonely, she told herself to get a grip. Even though she had been on a few dates soon after a four-month uneventful courtship had ended, she still felt as if there was something missing in her life, but didn't quite know what it was. Looking about her, she tried to shake off another wave of the loneliness that came and went but always left a horrible empty void in her chest. She could see couples, and others in small groups, sitting on the grassy banks on either side of the river and deep down knew then – as she had known for a while – what her problem was. She also knew that wishing was not going to make a dream come true. Ever since she had come to Norfolk with her parents, she had hoped that sooner or later some of her old school chums from the East End would leave London for a new life and come to Bridgeford. But this, it would seem, was not meant to be. Five long years had already passed and there had been no sign of a familiar face from back home.

When she saw the lovely smiling face of Mavis, a village woman who was strolling towards her and who worked in the same building as she did, Charlotte felt a grey cloud lifting. Smiling back, she raised a hand in greeting.

'I'm just on my way to the post office, Charlotte. Did

you want me to get you anything while I'm by the shops, dear?'

'No, thanks,' said Charlotte. 'I thought you was gonna sit by the river and eat your lunch.'

'Well, I should like to, dear, but needs must. I shall tomorrow though, and that's a promise.' With that, the woman, who always seemed to be smiling, continued on her way with a wistful Charlotte watching her go. So in need of someone to talk to, Charlotte quietly repeated something that she had heard as a child, which kept her going when she was in this lonesome kind of mood. 'No one feels sorry for those who feel sorry for themselves.'

Swallowing against the lump in her throat, she looked around at the trees and the riverside shrubs and reminded herself that she was lucky to be living in beautiful surroundings in the heart of old Bridgeford. Her grandparents, Nell and Johnny, had told her more than once that, if she found that she couldn't settle in Norfolk, she could return to the East End and live with them in Bromley-by-Bow once she was eighteen. Deep down she knew that they had always felt sure that she would want to return. Just thinking about her nan made her smile, and she remembered what she had said to her on the quiet: 'Even if your mother and father are as happy as pigs in shit living as if they was countryside born and bred, you don't 'ave to put up with it. Get yourself back down 'ere before depression sinks in if you don't like the life up there.' Thinking about the few words that had followed this, Charlotte smiled as it all came flooding back. 'Bridgeford? It's not even on the fucking map,' her nan had said. But then she always did have something to say.

Of course Norfolk was on the map and of course her nan knew this. But at the time of their departure, even though on the surface she had shown a temperate face, Nell's heart was breaking. On the occasional visits that Charlotte had made with her parents to London during these last five years, they had gone down in her dad's van and then later on in his new grey Anglia car. It was at such times that Nan had taken her to one side and hammered it home that if she missed the atmosphere that she had grown up in and the people that she had lived among, she would get her granddad to wallpaper the spare bedroom. And not only this, but to lay new carpet. This comforting thought of being able to go back home to her roots had kept Charlotte going, but recently it was doing more than this. It was becoming more and more likely. A day didn't seem to pass when she wasn't seeing herself back in the capital, living and working in the centre of things. This dream was consuming her thoughts when alone and was becoming more of a fact of life rather than an option to be considered. Deep down she knew that she was going to have to go back home if she wanted to wake up content in the mornings.

Chapter Four

Charlotte was the only grandchild from Nell and Johnny's only daughter, Rita, who had married her childhood sweetheart, the lovely Eddie. Nell was of the opinion that her granddaughter would return, but would not necessarily want to lodge with her and her granddad. She was prepared to accept and settle for this. If her beloved Charlotte wanted to share digs with people of her own age, Nell was prepared to swear with a hand on the Bible that she would not interfere in her life. She might drop in once or twice a week to be certain that the place was being kept clean, and maybe bring one of her famous steak and kidney pies, but this, she had told Charlotte, would be all.

Nell's husband, Johnny, had hardly ever missed a day in Spitalfields where he had worked, man and boy, since the age of fourteen. Now he was more than content to help out locally in the nearby markets – Whitechapel, Roman Road and Bethnal Green – ducking and diving and paying no tax. He always had been, and occasionally still was, happy enough to travel to and from Spitalfields in the wee hours of the morning for cash in hand. Charlotte's grandfather was as fit and active as a man ten years younger than he. He wasn't alone: there were several old boys like himself who, having worked since they were thirteen years old, were now garnering a bit of untaxed money. He had run his own little stall a few years after the end of the Second World War but it was too much like hard work. And now that the mood of being self-employed and independent was creeping through the working-class sector, he was leaving it to the young to go upwards and onwards.

Londoners had been, and still were, uprooting from war-damaged or run-down areas east, south and north of the Thames to go and settle in new houses in new and old country towns where housing estates were being built to accommodate the London overspill. And the evacuation was continuing as families were moving in their droves to Essex, Cambridge, Suffolk and Norfolk.

Even though Eddie and Rita had moved on since their arrival in Bridgeford and were now living in their own Victorian terraced house, they knew very well that Charlotte was not happy. She had said many times that, unlike them, she badly missed the atmosphere and the buzz of London, but for the first few years she had tried to keep up a pretence of liking Bridgeford for their sakes. She knew they were enjoying their new way of life and she didn't want to put a damper on it. They had, after all, joined a few groups and clubs and made friends of their own age and both were working full time. Her dad was taking on more and more private work as well as holding down his position as master electrician with a small team of younger men in his charge.

It had only taken her parents a year or so of living in

a council house to save enough for the deposit on the modest house in which they were now living, one that was close to the railway station. Of course, there was still a huge gap between the affluent who didn't have to rely on work, and the rest of the country who did. Nevertheless, the mood was that the dream of a change for the better for the working classes was actually becoming a reality. Charlotte had heard the familiar Cockney accent here and there from the very day they had moved into the town, but still this hadn't compensated for her missing the buzz of things. Back home was where she wanted to be; shoulder to shoulder with those she had grown up around. She had tried to stop thinking about the simple things that she had once pined for since the day she left the East End as a thirteen-year-old.

Lying in bed at night listening to the sound of the sleeping countryside instead of the noisy old city, she could so easily bring to mind the faces of the regular London bus conductors; the men and women in their flat caps and uniforms, who were nearly always bright and happy as they dinged the bell just before the bus approached the next stop. She missed seeing her favourite smiling ticket collector with his ticket machine held to his body by a leather strap that went from shoulder to waist. She also missed nipping down the underground to catch the tube to her grandparents' house. And sometimes she longed to be able to breeze in and out of the Bethnal Green museum and the Whitechapel art gallery, where she and Nathan had once tormented the life out of the attendants until they agreed to let them in free of charge when they should have been slipping two pence into a slot in the turnstile.

She hungered for the picture palaces, the youth clubs and young people's lively pubs and, of all things, those familiar red double-decker buses. The epitome of old London town. At least she had come to terms with no longer being able to hear the old steam train on the railway track first thing in the mornings while still in her bed, because they were no longer running. But settling into Norfolk hadn't been easy because she hadn't made a best friend. And she still felt detached from the life-style that her parents had taken in their stride.

Rita and Eddie, being social animals, had immediately set about joining a team of card players who came to their house once a week. The only thing that Charlotte had been able to join was the local school. This she left when she was just fifteen and hadn't managed during her time there to bond with anyone. Now that she was earning her own living and could be independent if she wanted, she felt that she was seen by the locals as a mature young woman who should be engaged to be married. Quite a few country born and bred girls of her age were.

Gazing into the river and settling for the fact that there wasn't going to be anyone around to talk to, Charlotte placed her handbag on the ground to use as a makeshift pillow. She then lay on the grass in the warm sunshine. At least she was making the most of the lovely weather, enjoying the sight of swans gliding lazily by, near where water was falling from sluice gates at the Old Water Mill. The mill had once been used for grinding coffee beans, her favourite beverage. According to the talk of the Bridgeford elders, the rich aroma of the roasting beans had once filtered through the air.

She could hear the laughter of boys who were swimming close by and felt a touch isolated from the life going on around her. The lads were splashing about, yelling to each other that they should make their way down to the wider part of the river where youngsters liked to lark around together and adults liked to sunbathe on the grassy banks. During her lunch break, on nice days like this, Charlotte often sat or lay in this spot where occasionally one or other of the girls or women who worked in the council offices would join her. Nowadays it made little difference whether they did or not because she had got used to being by herself.

She and Nathan had kept in touch by letter at first but this had gradually tailed off. She thought that this was probably because she hadn't anything new or interesting to tell him and her letters were dull. He, on the other hand, from the sound of his occasional letters, was now immersed in London life, where things seemed to be changing all over the place. Families were still on the move while the heart of old London was being rebuilt in places that had been wrecked during the war. With her friend in her thoughts, she could hardly remember when their letters to each other had stopped. She had missed his at first, but when four or five months passed by without a word she presumed that he had found himself a new life – perhaps even a sweetheart. She imagined Nathan going off every morning to work in an accountants' office, and smiled at the thought of him rushing to catch the train and dabbing his forehead with his familiar big white handkerchief. She could see him in her mind's eye, anxiously looking out of the window each time the train pulled into a station so as not to miss his stop.

Right up until she had left Bethnal Green her friend had always seemed to be hurrying towards or away from somewhere for no real reason. At other times, when she knocked on his door, she might find him neatly pressing his school trousers in between wiping his steamed-up glasses or adjusting them on his nose. Nathan had always been a good and thoughtful person and someone who shouldn't have been picked on. She recalled one of the worst times, when she had seen him from a distance in the park grounds. He had one hand against a tree and was looking about him when one of the bullyboys had suddenly stepped out, leaned towards him and spat in his face.

Drawing breath as she remembered the ghastly things he had had to put up with, she was warmed by the voice of an old boy drifting towards her. 'Look at that scruffy little old stray, Charlotte,' he said, as he strolled up to her, smiling. 'Course I knew straight away that our little old mongrel was a little too near the side of starving today, so I went up to the butcher's shop. I went in and I say to him, hev you got a few old bones with a little meat on. And do you know what? A new woman who was working at the counter thought thet I was a blooming old tramp. What d'yer say to thet then? Do I look that poor?' He quietly laughed.

'Of course you don't, Eric. And it was a lovely thing to do,' she said.

'Well, you can't jes' let the poor ole thing go hungry. I shouldn't think any one of us would like to be a stray with no home to go to.'

'No, Eric,' she smiled. 'I shouldn't think we would.'

The old boy then tipped his cap at her and continued on his way, and whether he knew it or not he had lifted her spirits. Apart from anything else, she loved the sound of the broad Norfolk accent.

Her thoughts drifted back to Nathan. In a strange way old Eric, who was now shuffling along with his hands in his pockets, reminded her of Nathan – except of course that her friend would have been pretending that his attention had been taken elsewhere. There had been so many times when she had been at boiling point because of the way he had been intimidated. She still sometimes woke in a sweat at night after a bad dream to do with him. A dream of times such as when the leader of the pack would be standing outside the large school gates, arms folded, grinning and sniggering at Nathan. Nathan's only hope of escape at such times, before the boot went in, was that a parent might happen along to pick up their offspring. But seeing an adult nearby didn't always help. There had been one occasion when three goading lads had surrounded Nathan and a tall, well-built sports teacher strolled by. Too deep in a world of his own to grasp the situation, he had simply nodded at the boys and walked on.

Once he was out of sight and roaring away in his car, Nathan, her faint-hearted friend, had been on the end of even worse abuse. As usual, he had removed his wonky National Health glasses to wipe them dry of steam and sweat, and resigned himself to an onslaught of fists and feet. On that occasion she strode forward, determined to help, but the boots had already gone in. Her only option then was to run and get help from inside the school building. By the time she had found a teacher and he had come running to the rescue, the boys had gone and Nathan was bleeding on the floor. Bleeding from the nose and doubled up in pain.

Even though Charlotte had managed to wipe most of this kind of thing from her mind, still she would sometimes wake in the night having had another night-mare to do with horrible scenes centred on her friend. Worse of all was the memory of Kenny the bully. Times when he had stared into Nathan's face, saying, 'Can you see us without the National Health specs, Four Eyes? Can you? Can you see us, Jew boy? Will you be able to see my fucking boot when I kick your face?'

'Of course I can see you,' had been his feeble stock answer. On one of those occasions tears had filled Charlotte's eyes when he had said, 'You're in Mr Spartan's class. He's very strict, isn't he?' Nathan's pathetic attempt at trying to befriend the bastards had never worked but simply fuelled their desire to draw blood. She had seen him humiliated at the end of one vicious attack, when he had been booted in the crutch as a farewell gesture, and all he had said was, 'Please may I have my specs back now?'

Pushing one of the boys out of the way, nervous but angry, Charlotte had squeezed herself between Nathan and the bully. She stared into the bully's face, saying, 'Come on. Punch me in the face! Come on! You pick on boys with glasses when they're alone, so you're capable of beating up a girl. Kick *me* black and blue . . . and then see what everyone at school thinks of you. You lousy rotten cowardly bastard!'

This had taken the heat out of things, but there had been other times he had suffered just as much when the gang had found him wandering around by himself. But at least the flash boy on that occasion had been belittled by having a girl challenge him in front of his pack. His response had been to walk away, calling Charlotte all kinds of names, then turn and stick up two fingers at her. Once they had all drifted away, Nathan had made a fist and told Charlotte that he had just been about to put the boot in when she came along. His noble attempts at bravery still brought tears to her eyes. But all of this was history, and the last time he wrote, he was fine. He was working as a junior in an accountancy firm in Bishopsgate and of course he was involved in the theatre group.

The more Charlotte thought about Nathan, the more she fancied the idea of paying a surprise visit to see how he was faring. She could afford to buy a second-class train ticket to London and knew that she could sleep over at her grandparents' house whenever she wanted. She wondered what Nathan might look like now, five years on. The only thing about her that had changed was that her natural blonde hair was no longer cut in the urchin style but was shoulder-length with a thick straight fringe to her eyebrows. She was a few inches taller of course, and a little curvier, and she wore eye-shadow, mascara and pale apricot lipstick. But deep down, the same old adventurous Charlotte was in there and desperate to spread her wings.

She wanted to write to Nathan, but felt that no matter how she worded her letter he was bound to pick up on her true feelings, realise that she was getting in touch because she was lonely. She didn't want pity, but she did want to see him again. And she wanted to see his wonderful parents, who had invited her into their home from the first week of the family moving into the block of flats when she and Nathan had been playing jacks on his doorstep. Forcing back tears, she drew breath and ordered herself to stop all this. To stop reliving the past just because the present was so lonely and her only contact with like-minded people of her own age seemed to be through the television. Programmes such as *Juke Box Jury* and *Top of the Pops*. On the walls of her bedroom she had posters of the Beatles, the Kinks and the Rolling Stones. She decided there and then that this being a Friday, when her parents would be in their local with friends, enjoying their regular end of the working week night out, she would phone Nathan come what may.

Later, alone in the house again, Charlotte was sipping hot milky Ovaltine from her special mug. She had the television on for a bit of company but with the sound down low. Curled up in an armchair, she was thinking again of her old life and Nathan and was suddenly spurred to take action. She drained her cup, then went to the telephone in the hall and dialled his number, picturing the look on his face when he heard her voice.

She had no idea why her stomach should be churning other than a thought which crossed her mind – that Nathan and his parents, like so many other families, her own included, might have moved out of the East End. And that this was perhaps the reason why his letters had stopped. If this was the case, then she was going to have to face up to the fact that she had lost touch with a close and trusted friend, someone who she had over the years seen as a brother that she loved. The receiver pressed against her ear, she prepared herself for a stranger on the other end of the line. But her fears were groundless because she immediately recognised Nathan's father when he said hello. With laughter in her voice she said, 'Hello, Mr Cohen, I don't know if you'll remember me. It's Charlotte.'

'Charlotte sometimes known as Charlie? Skinny Charlotte with the white hair? Of course I remember. How are you, darling?'

'I'm all right. I miss the East End though.'

'You miss it? Do me a favour! Your parents did right to get out. I wish I had done the same. My sister went to live in Brighton and we should have gone too. It's not the same any more.' His voice dropped a couple of octaves as he said, 'I take it you heard about my wonderful Lilly?'

Lost for words, the silence that hung between them could have been cut with a knife. 'I've not spoken to Nathan in ages, Mr Cohen . . .'

'So then you won't have heard,' he cut in. 'Listen, it

was quick, and you can't wish for more than that other than her still being here, but not bloody well nagging the life out of me. She dropped dead while she was trying on a gown in Mervyn's in Whitechapel, can you believe? Her sister persuaded her that we should go to a posh do, a distant relative's golden wedding anniversary. She was so excited over a gown she'd seen in the shop window she nearly wet herself.'

Charlotte could hardly take this in. Nathan's parents were not that much older than her own. There was an awesome silence between them until she said, 'I don't know what to say to you, Mr Cohen.'

'There's nothing to say, darling. She died happy. The gown I was going to cough up for had a price tag on it to turn both her sisters green with envy. I'm telling you the truth – she died laughing. And even though it's almost six months ago I can still see the look of joy on her face. Standing there, showing off in that frock in that shop one minute and on the floor the next. Thank God it didn't happen at home after I had paid out for the gown.'

Gently laughing at him, Charlotte said, 'I don't believe for one second that you gave a toss whether you'd already bought it for her or not.'

'You see what I mean? I haven't seen you for years and still you know me inside out. And I'll tell you something else. I don't like this bloody flat I'm living in. I shouldn't have let Nathan talk me into it.'

'You've moved?' Charlotte could hardly believe it. 'But the phone number—'

'Nathan arranged it with the GPO,' the old boy cut

in. 'He wanted that I should keep the number. I don't know how they did it but they did, and there we are. I'm in a bloody rabbit hutch of a flat but I've got the same phone number. I'm supposed to be thankful for small mercies.'

'So you didn't move far away then?'

'No. I'm in an old Victorian archaic bloody flat. Ravenscourt Buildings in Columbia Road, by the flower market. Nathan arranged it all. He knows somebody in the right place, by all accounts. They're gonna pull this lot down in a year or so and we'll get a brand new maisonette – according to my clever dick son. So for now I must live like Fagin . . . in a dump.' There was a moment's pause but she knew he hadn't finished talking. 'Why don't you come visit us? Bring a bit of sunshine into my life. You always were a little ray of sunshine. Lilly often said that if you had been born Jewish she would have made Nathan marry you one day.'

'So where is Nathan living?' she asked quickly, before he went into another confabulation.

'Where do you think? With me, of course. It's a poky two-bedroom medieval flat. Give me your number and I'll get him to call.'

'He's already got my number.'

'So when did he last speak with you?'

'About two years ago.'

'What? Two years? The little sod. I didn't know that. We could all have dropped dead for all you knew. It's all this bloody theatre business lot he's mixed up in. And now he tells me that we might move out of the

65

East End altogether, one day, that he would like to buy something small and get on the property ladder in a couple of years' time. God knows where he wants to drag us to. It's got something to do with promotion and new towns. He lugs me around from one place to another as if I'm the bloody suitcase.'

'Listen,' said Charlotte, getting in quick so as to get off the phone. 'I've got to go, but get him to give me a call when he's got time. And I'm really, really sorry about your sad loss.'

'Loss? I shouldn't think so. I couldn't lose that woman if I dropped her off in the middle of a bloody desert. She's still around me. Waiting. Waiting for me to die. Waiting to grab hold of me again. She thought the world of me you know.'

'I know she did, and you loved it. Mind how you go.'

'Mind how I go? Go where? I wouldn't go anywhere in this bloody area if I could avoid it. It's a dump. I should never have left our beautiful council estate. I'll tell Sir that you called. But first things first. Give me your address, darling, and your telephone number – in case he's lost it. Otherwise Nathan will cut, hang and draw me.'

'Okay I will . . . but don't put any pressure on him, will you? He might not want to get in touch. It's been a long time.'

'Sure, sure. Just give it to me. I'm ready with a pen and the notepad that my son insists I must keep by the phone.'

Slowly giving him the details so that he had time to write them down nice and calmly, Charlotte felt a glow filter into her heart and was very pleased that she had taken this first step back to her old life. 'If he doesn't call you I will.' With that the old boy replaced his receiver and all that was left was the sound of the dialling tone.

With mixed emotions Charlotte touched up her make-up and then brushed her hair, determined not to let the sad news of Nathan's mother put her in the gloom. After all, if Nathan's dad could be upbeat about it then she had no right to let it bring her down. She knew which pub her parents would be at with a few of their friends and decided to join them. This was going to be a first, and with a smile on her face she imagined the reaction she would get when she walked into the bar. They had tried to get her to go out with them more often but she had mostly turned them down. It just hadn't felt right that she, an eighteen-year-old, should have to rely on her parents for nights out. But this evening it was different. Not only was she fancying a port and lemon, but she was also thinking about smoking one of her cigarettes in front of her mum and dad so as to get the message across to them that she was an adult. She had been keeping secret packets hidden away in a drawer in her bedroom for quite a while.

Checking herself in the hall mirror before she left the house, for once she was okay about what she saw. She looked all right. More than all right. She was wearing her black and white dog-tooth jacket with matching knee-length pencil skirt, which she had bought off a fashion stall in Petticoat Lane on a weekend flying visit with her parents to visit her gran and granddad. Picking up her handbag, she left the house and made her way through the small town to the pub. It was a pub where there was not only a jukebox, but one that she had been impressed with before when she had on a rare occasion been in there with her parents. There had been a good selection of records to choose from as well as the top ten in the hit parade. This wasn't bad for a quiet little town. It had just turned seven o'clock on a midsummer evening, still light outside so she had no fear about walking along an old and narrow cobbled back street.

Entering the riverside pub, she was pleased to hear a favourite singer and a favourite song drifting out from the open doorway of the public bar: Bob Dylan and 'Mr Tambourine Man'. Lifted by this, she went inside and looked over to a small table in a cosy corner where she could see her parents. It being a Friday night the place was buzzing with happy customers.

Easing her way through the bodies in the crowded bar, Charlotte unwittingly brushed against the last person she would expect to find in there – Kenny, the flash lad from her childhood. He recognised her as someone he knew but wasn't sure from where or when. Narrowing his eyes and giving her sideways glances as she joined a couple who he presumed were her parents and who were clearly pleased that she had arrived, the penny dropped. The man was greeting the girl with open arms. To anyone else it would be just another cosy family scene, but for Kenny it was much more than this. A satisfied smile spread across his face as he inwardly applauded himself for never forgetting a face. He had been so sure that he *had* recognised the man when he had been in this pub drinking with the two flash bastards from London.

And now, standing next to the fellow and looking gorgeous, was the girl that he had always had the hots for back in the East End when he was still at school. Charlie, the girl who used to tease him about his private fantasies, was just yards away. He couldn't help but smile at the irony. He had innocently strolled into the realm of the family who had pulled up their roots and just disappeared.

Giving her the once-over from top to toe, he felt warm around the parts that never got to see the sunshine. He had had the hots for the tart right up until her parents had done a moonlight flit and left him feeling angry and swindled. Charlie had been the star in more than one of his wet dreams. She had been the only girl who he had more than once fantasised fucking. Keeping his head down so as to enjoy a private bit of laughter to do with luck, the short fat Jew boy that the girl used to hang out with came to mind. Now he had to stop himself from laughing out loud. Five years had passed by and right out of the blue a little diamond drops from the sky. He couldn't wait to stalk her.

'I'm glad someone's fucking 'appy,' said his friend Steve, who had come into the pub. 'I lost twenty quid to the bookies today, Kenny boy.'

'Not so much of the boy. I'll go six rounds in the ring wiv you any day.'

'So what's the joke then?' said Steve, looking from

him to the big blowsy blonde serving behind the bar and trying to get her attention.

'That's for me to know and for you not to,' he said. 'Mine's a pint.'

'Well, fucking order it then and get one in for me, you tight bastard.' With that the spiv swaggered over to the jukebox and chose a couple of records: 'You've Lost That Lovin' Feelin'' by the Righteous Brothers and 'I Only Want To Be With You' by Dusty Springfield.

Returning to the bar, he sniffed as he looked around himself. 'Busy in 'ere tonight, innit?'

'Yeah. Bridgeford's bin put on the map. Fuck knows why though. I'm out of 'ere and back to the East End. Nuffing much ever 'appens.' Kenny glanced at his friend's face to see that he was chewing the inside of his cheek. 'It's all right. I've ordered you a Light Ale.'

'Good.'

'Oh dear . . . Been dumped agen 'ave yer?' Kenny grinned and then chuckled. 'State of you. If you're not gutted I'm a fairy queen.' His friend raised an eyebrow. 'Don't worry about it. I won't tell anyone.' Kenny's pint arrived and he downed a quarter of it in one. He then placed his glass on the bar and pulled a packet of Rothmans and a lighter from his jacket pocket.

'Women? Bloody pain in the neck,' said Steve.

'Oh right . . . so the slag did chuck you in then?'

'Chuck me out more like. Fucking women. Most of 'em are not worth the shoes they clip-clop around in.' He took a cigarette out of Kenny's pack and, just as he put it between his lips, the record that he had chosen and was playing seemed to get louder. Kenny tried not to laugh. 'So she's lost that loving feeling 'as she?'

'Shut it, Kenny, I'm not in the mood.' The guy then downed the rest of his drink in one and placed his glass on the counter, saying, 'Stay out of mischief.' He then walked out and left Kenny bent over with laughter.

Regaining his cool composure, he turned his head to a pair of local girls and said, 'That's nice, innit? Leaving me all by myself like that. He's my best mate as well. Gone a bit soft in the head I reckon. Love's lost dream.' He then winked at the one with the long blackish-brown wavy hair who was playing the little girly bit while craftily inching closer along by the bar to be near him.

'Where's your mate gone then?' said the other girl, a bleached blonde who was a bit too confident for her own good and more heavily made up than the tart who was with her.

Kenny drained his glass and licked his lips. 'Dunno where he's fucked off to and I don't much care. He just mumbled somefing about not wanting to catch the clap from tarts that used this pub . . .'

'Fucking cheek,' said the bleached blonde. 'He'll get a slap round the face the next time I see 'im. And I 'ave seen 'im before, so I know that he uses this pub regular. I'll kick 'im in the balls.'

Kenny burst out laughing and then feigned a look of respect. 'Good for you,' he said. 'It's about time decent call girls stood up to 'im. He had no right to call you what he did.'

'Oh? And what was that?'

'Ah nah, no way. I wouldn't offend a lady. Never 'ave, never will.'

'Well, I'll tell you what. I'll spit right in 'is face next time I spot 'im. Talking about us like that. Fucking cheek.' With that the girl with bleached hair mooched off and headed for the Ladies'.

Kenny winked at the other girl, who looked intelligent enough. 'It's about time some of you girls sorted 'im out. See you around, eh?'

'Oh. You're not going are you?' She spoke in a tried and tested mock posh voice.

'Yeah. Gotta go, sexy. Gotta put my old nana to bed. Poor old girl's nearly eighty and going blind. She lives in one of them old people's chalets. I fitted her little front room out wiv a nice bit of cheerful red carpet today.'

'Is that your trade then. Carpet fitting?'

'Yeah. It's a family business that my grandfather started up years back. It keeps the wolf away from the door, the taxman happy and the law off my back. I dabble in a lot of things on the quiet, but my nana don't know. It would break 'er heart to fink that I'm not straight.'

'Ah . . . honest? Ah. And you have to put her to bed as well?' Sympathy and respect was simply oozing from the girl's pores.

'Yeah. Of course I do. Nuffing wrong wiv that though, is there? Any bloke would do the same fing for 'is nana, wouldn't he?' He then sighed with sadness. 'Poor old girl. It is a little bit embarrassing for me as well as it is for her at times. You know . . . times such as when a woman's help is needed so as to give the old lady a bit of self-respect.'

'Ah, you *are* lovely. Would you like me to come and help you? I looked after my gran before she passed away,' said the brunette, lying through her back teeth. She had taken to this good-looking young man and felt as if she wanted to mother him.

'I like old people,' she continued. 'I wanted to work in one of them places for the geriatrics, but my mother didn't fink it would be cheerful enough for a fun-loving girl like me.'

'I think she might 'ave been right, babe. That would be a bit much. My nana's as bright as a new pin. She suffers with rheumatoid arthritis, that's all, but it would be nice if you could come and meet 'er.'

'Ah, what a lovely thing to say. Where do you live then? Nearby?'

'Me? Oh, my pad is just round the corner above a wireless shop.' He glanced at his wristwatch. 'I've gotta go there now as it happens, to pick up a little box of Cadbury's Milk Tray that I bought for 'er.'

'Your own pad, eh? Get you,' said the girl, impressed. 'Bit young to be able to afford your own flat, ain't yer?'

'Course not. Eighteen? That's not young. And anyway none of us is ever too young to make something of ourselves, darling. I do all right. It's not the be-all and end-all but it suits me, for now. I s'pose you could say that it's a state-of-the-art pad. It's a self-contained, one-bedroom apartment wiv a sitting room and a bathroom-en-suite. I make a wicked percolated coffee,' he lied. 'So if you ever fancy a night in listening to my stereo . . .'

'Sounds good to me.' The girl looked into his light green eyes and wasn't quite sure what she saw. This one was a bit of a mystery, but that beat the country yokels by a mile. Some of the other East End boys that had moved up at the same time as her family had were full of shit as to what they were up to. But this one seemed genuine and soft-hearted. Different to anyone she had ever met before, in fact.

'I'm not saying that my pad's a palace mind you, but it's cool.'

'I shouldn't think it would look much like a palace. Not in Bridgeford. Anyway, my name's Rosie, so are you gonna tell me yours?'

'Why not? The name's Kenny. I'm from Bethnal Green. Ronnie and Reggie Kray's patch.' Thinking of his dingy, bare little flat, he couldn't help being proud of his acting ability.

'I work in Woolworths during the week,' Rosie said, and then embroidered her life a little by adding, 'I'm a model for life-drawing classes as well. I'm from Hackney Downs originally.' She smiled at him. 'So what about your family? Did they all move up or are some of them still in the East End?'

Kenny smiled inwardly. He guessed that this one opened her legs to all and sundry but he wasn't all that fussed. And he was up for a laugh tonight for some reason other than being bored. 'Got any paintings of yourself in the nude for me to look at then, 'ave yer?'

'One or two. Course I have. But they're hanging on

the walls in my flat that's part of a mansion 'ouse so you'll 'ave to come round — if you want to view the goods.' She was just as good a liar as he was.

'Mansion house eh?' he smiled broadly. 'Very nice too.' Up for a bit of adventure, he said, 'I wouldn't mind seeing the paintings. I was praised regularly for my drawings when I was at school. Once I've got the new sports car I've ordered I'll cruise round and knock on your door. Where did you say the mansion 'ouse was?'

'I never said. But I will now. It's a fifteen-minute walk out of town in a little village. I share it wiv artists and a couple of writers that live there. The rent's cheap but it's a nice place to live. It's a commune.'

'Yeah?' Kenny smiled. 'Sounds like a place in Aldgate in London. Roughton House. But women are not allowed in.' He laughed.

'Oh yeah? And they're artists and that as well are they? The men who live there?'

'Nah. They're down and outs. Meth drinkers and drug addicts.'

'You saucy fucker.' The girl laughed. 'We're nothing of the kind.'

'Only teasing, darling. Can't you take a joke then?'

'Course I can. I like a fella with a sense of humour. Too many men are too fucking serious if you ask me.'

Each of them knew that the other was full of bollocks but neither of them could see harm in it. The girl was a storyteller and so was Kenny. He had heard about the mansion house that she was referring to and knew that it was mostly filled with drifters. 'My parents are still back in the East End,' he said. 'The old man's got his own carpet fitting business and most of 'is clients are wealthy and live in London. So he'd be mad to walk away and move up 'ere.' He gave her a corny all-knowing wink. 'Dad lives on the edge but Mum don't mind. She likes a diamond ring and a bit of clubbing even though she's getting on a bit. Right flash pair they are,' he said, getting off on his fantasies. From the expression he saw on the girl's face he felt that he might have gone too far. He wanted to impress her, not frighten her off. 'So you're a bit on the arty side then?'

'I suppose you could say that. I do a bit of drawing and that as well as modelling for other artists now and then as well. Where did you say your nana lived?'

'Just over the bridge in the old people's prefabs.' Another lie.

'Ah, bless 'er cotton socks. They're nice though. And they're little council bungalows, not prefabs.'

'Same thing. My nana calls 'em prefabs probably because that's what she lived in back in Stepney. She's living in the past. She gets a bit lonely sometimes. Not a lot though 'cause the other old people pop in and out. But I'm 'er only grandson who's bothered to move near to the old girl for a while. So she's bound to rely on me, aint' she?' In full swing with his fabrications now, he smiled inwardly and then said, 'She's the only reason I moved to Bridgeford to tell the truth. I wanted to be there for 'er. She won't be around for much longer.'

'But why did she come up here in the first place if your family stayed behind?'

This caught him off guard but he was soon on-track.

'Well . . . I wasn't gonna let 'er go into one of them fleapits in London. No way. Filthy rotten dirty fleapits for my nana? Nah. I wrote off to the Bridgeford council and arranged it all. She loves it an' all. Couldn't be 'appier.' So pleased with his spur of the moment fantasy Kenny could not stop himself from grinning.

'You are lovely. You're a bit of a softie on the quiet, aren't you,' said the twenty-two-year-old as she flicked her long straight hair off her face. 'I think that's such a sweet thing to do. But then you're an Easter Ender, the same as me.' She looked into his face with an angelic expression and then said, 'I'll tell you what. When my friend comes back from out of the Ladies' toilets, I'll see if she minds if I go with yer. She's not bothered about being in here by herself. There'll be more of our friends coming in soon so she won't be lonely for long. Not that she would care anyway, she'll be chatted up as soon as I've gone. It is a Friday night after all.'

'Well, if you're sure you don't mind I will take you up on the offer. My nana don't get any visitors so she'd be really pleased. I'll wait outside, shall I?'

'All right then, you do that. I won't be long.'

'We'll 'ave to pop into my pad though before we go. Apart from picking up the chocolates Nana asked me to dig out some old photos of 'er old house in the East End.' Another lie. 'They came in the post today from my mum. I phoned and asked 'er to send 'em.'

'Ah, bless. And I don't mind coming to your flat first. It will be nice to see where you live. All by yerself. All lonely.' She pouted her lips as she squeezed his cheek between her finger and thumb. 'Even if you never 'ad a nana and you was just trying to pull me, I would come to your flat because I think you're lovely.'

Her phoney little girl voice was driving him mad, but she looked as if she couldn't wait to get her hands on his body so what the hell? Arriving back at the bar, the bleached blonde looked from her friend to Kenny and grinned. 'Go on then, you two. I can see you're ready for it.' She winked and then chuckled. 'Lucky cow. If you can't be good be bad.'

'I wouldn't know how to be bad.' Rosie grinned and then mimicked Eliza Doolittle from *My Fair Lady*. 'I'm a good girl I am.' She then slipped her arm into Kenny's and walked out with him as if they had known each other for years. To all and sundry they looked like a young couple who were very fond of each other. With a smirk on her face the second girl now turned to face the good-looking barman who had been giving her the eye. This, it would seem, was going to be a night for a bit of old-fashioned romance all round.

Chapter Five

Walking through the back streets towards his pad, Kenny was a true gentleman when guiding the girl across a narrow road. He was in seventh heaven. No matter what happened tonight with the slut, who was clutching his arm as if they were man and wife, the finger could possibly point at the guy he had been having a drink with. The idiot who, when in the bar, would have been heard to say, in a nasty derogatory fashion, that this girl was a cheap slag. So depending on the way she came across once in his pad it didn't really matter. He was Kenny and could do what he wanted. He had a choice – he could choose to go one way or the other. Keep her as his bedding whore if this was what she wanted or take her more than once if she refused to come across. He felt that she deserved a good shagging for being a teasing scumbag if nothing else. If he chose the latter then he would make the finger of suspicion point to his flash drinking partner. Joking and laughing, they soon arrived at the old small door in the flint wall that would lead up into his pad.

Once inside, the girl was surprised at how perfectly clean and tidy his little place was. It was no palace but neither was it a shit hole. 'This is really cosy,' she said, a little on the worried side. Something didn't seem right but she was unsure as to what it was.

'It'll do for now.' Kenny winked at her and grinned. 'My pad in London's better than this.' He was embellishing the fact a little. The fact being that he didn't have a pad in London but lived with his mum and dad.

'Well, I'm really impressed,' she said, while at the same time feeling just a touch uneasy. Something definitely wasn't right and still she couldn't put her finger on what it was that was causing those little warning bells to go off. She swept any hint of dark thoughts from her mind as she watched Kenny plump up the faded red and gold cushions of a two-seater sofa. He then invited her to sit down and make herself comfortable while he went and put the kettle on so as to make them both a nice cup of tea. A touch easier, the girl slipped off her shoes and pulled her legs under her, making herself comfortable on the old-fashioned sofa. She was beginning to relax more by the minute and when her host returned carrying two glasses and a half bottle of Scotch whisky she sparkled. He was managing to warm her parts before he had even touched her.

'You've got a choice,' he said. 'Scotch and water first or a cup of tea?'

'Scotch,' she said, smiling at him.

Looking at her all cosy and comfortable on the sofa like that he felt chuffed with himself for having drawn her in. And then, as she made herself even more snug on his couch as if she owned it, he felt a seed of anger and knew that this one might have to be added to his shortlist of women who had brought the worst out in him. It wouldn't be the first time that he hadn't been excited enough by a tart to want to screw her. And it wasn't because he didn't fancy her – he did. Now he was wondering if she had been singled out for him by the powers that be. Singled out in the same way that others in the old smoke near Aldgate and Brick Lane had been. Girls with whom to have sex had just not been on the cards. He had needed something far more exciting and dangerous.

The old lust for risk that came and went was back again . . . and he had with him, in his pad, the right girl for the cause. This new-sprung urge that was like a driving force had been coming and going over the past month or so, and it was back. He didn't want her for intercourse – he wanted to kill her. The persuasive voice that had snaked its way back inside his head was telling him over and over to do just this. To kill the prostitute. To kill the slag. To strangle the last putrid breath out of her filthy mouth.

'You all right, sweetheart?' said Rosie, the uneasiness returning. 'You've gone a bit pale and serious.'

'Have I? Well it must be you that's doing it. Seeing you in the orange glow of that table lamp . . .' He smiled.

'You're sweet.' She pulled her knees up and then said, 'Come on. Pour us both a drink and then massage my poor aching feet.' Searching his face and seeing the look in his eyes Rosie felt that his mood had changed. The warmth had gone, as had the cheeky smile. And there was no sign of charm in his eyes any more. 'Smile for me then,' she said, trying to lighten the sudden dark atmosphere. But it was too late. She had not been as canny as she should have been when accepting the invitation into his home.

Kenny was filling with resentment and loathing towards the girl lounging on *his* settee. Lounging as if she *belonged*. And to make matters worse she had slipped her shoes off without asking if she could. He placed one of the empty glasses onto the coffee table and poured himself a measure of whisky straight, which he drank in one. Narrowing his eyes he peered at her and as he did he felt a kind of a smile creep in. She was talking to him but he wasn't really listening.

'Get you,' he heard her say. And then, 'My turn now. I'll give it a try. Whisky, straight please.'

He placed his glass and the bottle onto the coffee table and sat down next to her, slowly shaking his head as if deeply disappointed. He then released a profound sigh as he poured her a drink that she would not be taking. He was a touch disappointed that she had spoken of alcohol and not love or romance since these were going to be her last words. He turned to face her so that he could look into her eyes, into her very soul. She had beautiful hazel eyes. Almond shaped and lovely, but sadly, he felt that they had drunk in too many faces of lusting men who she had given herself to. 'You're very beautiful,' he said as he gently stroked her soft wavy hair. He then ran a finger down the side of her face and touched her full lips, whispering, 'Is it all right if I kiss you?'

The expression of unease as she nervously smiled

filled him with a kind of love and compassion. 'You really are an old-fashioned gentleman on the quiet, ain't yer,' was her answer. 'I've never met anyone like *you* before.' She smiled.

'No, I don't suppose you have.' He grinned and then softly chuckled as he searched her thoughts. Looking more serious and going quiet he whispered gently, 'Sweet dreams and sleep forever peaceful.' He then gently clasped her lily-white neck with one hand to push his thumb into the hollow and brought up his other hand so as to strangle her with his eyes shut tight. He preferred to bring about a quick death rather than an agonising slow end that he felt might possibly lodge in his mind and darken his conscience. He didn't want to see the look of terror in this girl's eyes the way he had needed to with the first of the London whores whom he had delivered from a degrading lifestyle . . .

The flat seemed awesomely silent now that the body of the girl lay limp and lifeless. Kenny had talked to her during the void between her struggle for life and acceptance of death because he didn't want her to think too badly of him. He had said that he had her interest at heart. That she was a slut who was sliding further and further into the depths of the gutter. Then, having brushed long strands of hair off her face, he had carefully lifted her legs so as to lay her comfortably on the sofa before crossing her arms. He knew exactly where he was going to put this sweet young corpse to rest. But he needed a quiet time now and he needed another drink. He also needed it to be as dark as possible outside, with the town sleeping, so that he could carry her unseen to the bottom of the overgrown and somewhat secluded back garden. His plan was to simply drop her down into the ancient disused wishing well that was deeper than deep. When he had first arrived in his little rented flat he had dropped a penny in and made a wish, and had heard no sound of it hitting water or anything else.

Out of interest he had then dropped down a dilapidated watering can that he had seen in the undergrowth and still he had heard nothing. From this he gleaned that the base of this particular old wishing well was way down below ground level and in the pit of hell itself. Now, of course, it would be the perfect private last resting place for the whore – with a few old coins for luck.

Resting back in his armchair and gazing at the girl's peaceful body that looked quite angelic with its arms crossed, Kenny couldn't help thinking that, given different circumstances, she might have made something of herself. Shaking his head and talking under his breath, he berated her for telling him silly lies. A model for an artist? He very much doubted it. No. The only brush that she was ever near as far as he was concerned was the one that she used to tease and torment men so as to earn a living, or at least some cash on the side. The bitch had no self-respect whatsoever. With his breathing and heartbeat more or less back to normal, he decided that he would wrap the corpse in an old grey moth-eaten army blanket, one that he had found in a cupboard when he first came into this furnished pad.

He thought that this was far more humane than simply dropping her down into the depths in only the clothes she had on. He would keep her shoes though, and add them to the others in the battered suitcase that he stored under his bed. Come the day when he would leave this flat, the collection of shoes that were part of his trophies would also be sent tumbling down the well. But not yet. They were, after all, the only mementos that he had to remind him of the girls rescued by himself from the dark side of life and the back alleyways of Wapping.

Sipping his drink, he was overcome by a strong desire to close his eyes and give his brain a rest. He was tired and it was time for a doze in the armchair. Rosie was fine. Rosie was sleeping. Once it was dark enough he would lay her to rest. Entomb her in her final resting place where people in years gone by had dropped spare coppers and made hopeful, desperate wishes. This, of course, was after it had been used as one of the town's watering holes that had become redundant, and was now part of the land that was little more than a sprawling overgrown back garden.

Going into his makeshift kitchen in the passageway, Kenny poured himself a cup of boiled water to help wash away the taste of alcohol and took it into the sitting room and to his armchair. He thought that the girl on the sofa looked like an angel lying there. At peace and no longer worrying about anything. He was pleased. He had done well by her. Saved her from a life of degradation. Prostitutes had been part of his life ever since he could remember. His own mother and her sister used to go out arm in arm in the evenings, dressed up to the nines and sometimes heading for the West End to wealthier clients than could be found locally in the East End. He smiled at the irony. His mother and aunt had been the queens of whores once upon a time, whores who were paid handsomely for their services, and his dad had pretended not to have a clue as to what was going on or where the extra cash came from. So far, Kenny had only ever been able to afford the slags that worked in Brick Lane and Shoreditch. But that had, in its own way, been a light to show him the pathway that he felt he had been born to tread. The way of cleansing a corner of God's earth of women who sold their souls as well as their bodies to dirty old men.

To his mind, now that he thought himself a mature young man, he knew that life was all about the survival of the fittest, about selection. A bit like the chickens at the local farms that were kept for the laying of eggs and were not slaughtered and dished up for Sunday dinner. He thought about his dad, whom he had always believed to be too honest and innocent for his own good until he learned that he had turned a blind eye to what his mother got up to. The money that she had earned as a professional prostitute had, after all, put rump steak on their plates instead of cheap mincemeat. His dad, also hard-working, had never missed a day's work if he could help it. And he had always made sure that Kenny went out in the mornings with two soft-boiled eggs inside him.

He looked at Rosie's white face and wondered if anyone ever did pass away with a smile on their lips the way people said they did. Not that it made any difference. She wouldn't be missed as far as he could tell. This is what pained him more than anything. The poor wretch of a girl would not be missed.

He had put to sleep others of her kind during the past month or so. The first hadn't been premeditated. In fact, it had shocked him to the core once he'd done the deed. But then after a few days he fancied that this was why he had been put on this earth: to cleanse it from the evil that was like a spreading disease. The harmless women who had sold their souls within the East End of London, just so as to have a roof over their heads, had not even been missed. There had been no word of their disappearance in the newspapers or broadcast on the news. The wretched prostitutes working in London's Aldgate and Whitechapel were dead and gone and had not been missed. He had taken them in his dad's van and given each of them a brief but moving service from the bank of the river Thames, in a quiet dark spot close to the Prospect of Whitby in Wapping. Here in Bridgeford, of course, he could not let the river be the last resting place for Rosie because too many people either fished or swam in it. But he had found the girl a nicer place, whether she deserved it or not. She would sleep for ever in peace at the bottom of the long and narrow overgrown wild garden. A little paradise that was often filled with the sound of birdsong and the buzzing of the bees.

Once the trial of laying to rest the girl whose name he had now wiped from his mind was over, Kenny stood in his little bathroom with his shirtsleeves rolled up and the collar of his light blue cotton shirt tucked in. He was ready for a refreshing sluice before he headed for the pub in search of a Dunhill lighter that he hadn't actually lost. This was to be his excuse for going back, to give himself an alibi later on if the tart's friend reported her missing. After all, Kenny was the last one to have been seen with her when they left the pub together.

Ready to go out again, he glanced around the room to make certain there was absolutely no sign of the girl having been there. He then strolled out of his pad as if nothing untoward had happened. As far as he was concerned, the old saying 'no point in crying over spilt milk' was a sound one; he had had it drummed into him since he was a boy. The girl was gone, and to his way of thinking she was better off for it if all she had to look forward to was letting strangers abuse her. He had in a way been her salvation and it felt good. Better in fact than when he had sent the whores back in the East End from the gutter to the depths of the river.

Quietly closing his front door behind him, Kenny whistled a little tune as he strolled out towards the pub, past the old workhouse and prison. He was wondering if it was time for him to return to his roots, and as the vision of the council estate where he had been brought up came to mind so did Charlie, the girl from his childhood whom he'd seen in the pub earlier on. He had heard that she and her parents had moved to Norfolk a few years back but no more than that. Thinking of her and those old days brought the fat Jew boy to mind again, and he wondered if Nathan still lived in the same place. Kenny's own family had moved from their flat three years since to live on the Brine council estate close to Stepney Green underground station. He mused on the fact that the lovely Charlotte and he now lived in the same small Norfolk town. He quietly laughed to himself at the thought of snogging her, the way he had once dreamt of doing when he was a kid. But those fantasies had long since dissipated. He didn't know why nor did he care. He knew that Charlotte had to be all of eighteen by now, so to his mind there must have been a few cornets dipped into her ice-cream and she was probably no more decent than all of the other sluts he came across. It did seem a coincidence, though, that they should be living in the same little orb again. He wondered if fate was having a game with him. Teasing and testing. Given the right circumstances, would he kiss the girl or kill her? Quietly chuckling at the irony, he laughed freely as he pushed open the door into the busy pub as if he had just remembered a joke that someone had told him.

Going up to the bar, which was still fairly busy, he ordered a pint and then casually asked if he had left his make-believe Dunhill lighter there. The barman was too busy to get into conversation at that point so speedily checked under the bar and near the till and then shrugged and shook his head. 'Can't see it any-where, mate.'

'Don't worry about it,' said Kenny. 'It'll turn up. I've got fed up with looking for it now. It was a present from my mum and dad.' More lies. He then grinned and winked and said, 'Any excuse to come back for another pint, eh?'

Taking payment from a customer the barman then pulled a pint for himself and turned back to Kenny, smiling. 'Was she good?'

'Who?'

'The girl.'

'Do me a favour. Not my type, mate. Anyway, we hadn't gone twenty yards or so and someone else caught 'er attention. My own fucking mate who I was drinking wiv earlier nicked 'er from under my nose. I didn't fancy 'er in any case. Too common.'

'You're telling me. If I had my way I would ban that sort of a girl. I've got a reputation to think about.'

Kenny grinned and then chuckled knowingly. 'Me thinks you do protest too much,' he said. 'You've not been giving 'er one on the quiet 'ave yer? While your old woman's not looking?'

'Pigs might fly,' the barman said. 'And not so much of the old woman. We're only in our forties thank you.'

'Are you? Blimey, I had you both down for pensioners.' He laughed and then said, 'Only kidding, mate. And I agree with you as it happens. You don't want slags in a nice family pub like this one.'

'I don't know about family pub, but I s'pose we are getting more married couples coming in and less spivs from London with their swearing and wheeling and dealing.'

'Oh don't mention London,' Kenny said, sporting an actor's pained expression. 'I'm gonna 'ave to pack my bags and go back home before the week's out. The old man's not well. He's had another little heart attack,' he lied. 'The next one will make three and that could be it. He's been warned, but will the stubborn bastard take notice of the heart specialist? Of course not.'

The bartender shook his head gravely. 'It's not wanting to believe it, son. That's what it'll be. Your dad most likely hates the fact that it 'appened to him. What work does he do?'

'Carpet fitter, just like me. He taught me everything I know. We've got our own business. We do all right at it down there in London town.'

'There you go, then. Can you imagine? A hard-working East Ender like myself having to sit in a chair all day long so as not to put strain on the ticker. No way. I'm sorry to hear it, son. You must feel terrible.'

'I do, mate. I do. I'm gutted to be honest. But I've tried not to show it, I prefer to cry alone – if you know what I mean.' Kenny finished his pint, proud of his ability to lie with conviction. 'And we've all got to stand by our parents after all they've done for us, haven't we? Yep. You're right. I think he does hate being ill. I might go back sooner rather than later.'

'Well, don't you just sod off without coming in and saying cheerio, will yer?'

'Course not. You're a mate, even if you do charge over the top for my beer.'

'Well, you can charge a little over the top for that carpet fitting in our bedroom up there that you keep on promising to do.'

'As soon as I'm back. And that's a promise. I'll come in the company van and fetch a bit of good quality thick pile that fell off the back of a lorry.' He gave the barman a wink and left the pub. Once outside he pulled his handkerchief from his pocket and wiped the beads of sweat from his forehead. He had pulled off his bucket of lies, but it hadn't been as easy as he thought it would be. Not only had he started to tremble just before he left but had felt a surge of burning heat sweep through his entire body.

'You're not as hard as you're made out to be, Kenny boy,' he murmured as he leaned against an old flint wall for support. 'But you did well in the pub.' He sighed. 'You did good. Mister barman'd stand up in any court of law and be your alibi if it goes pear-shaped. Which it won't.'

He smiled inwardly as he pushed his handkerchief back into his pocket and then took out his door key. Without a body there couldn't be a murder trial, he told himself. Arriving at his front door, he pushed the key in the lock and realised just how tired he was on this somewhat strange evening. He needed a bit of shut-eye, that was for sure. Getting rid of another whore had taken it out of him. He was in want of his pillow and a decent night's sleep.

With no more thoughts of the girl in the well, Kenny, in his little makeshift kitchen, spread butter onto a piece of sliced bread ready to make himself a corned beef sandwich. His mind was still ticking over. He had all but come to the conclusion that there was nothing in this part of the world for him any more other than some fencing of stolen goods. And besides which, he missed his mum and her lovely homemade steak and kidney pies and apple crumble and custard.

Back in his armchair with his sandwich supper on a cracked plate, he thought about all the good things that he liked about Bethnal Green and Stepney. The list outweighed what Norfolk had to offer, no question. At least he had a choice though. He wondered if he should give it a couple of weeks or so before he made a move, or do a moonlight and leave early in the morning with his bags packed. He decided to sleep on it. Making snap decisions gave him a headache in any case and he had already had to take two painkillers before he had gone back to the pub. None of it really mattered in any case. Home was wherever he laid his hat. And the next day was his most favourite day of the week. Saturday. Saturdays had always felt special ever since he could remember. And all because of the ABC picture palace on the Cambridge Heath Road, which had once opened up especially so as to show films and cartoons for children. He had loved going to the Saturday morning pictures more than anything in the world when he was a little boy. The mere thoughts of those days gone by brought a flow of tears trickling down his face. Then he heard himself sobbing. And it was strangely comforting.

Chapter Six

The next evening Rita and Eddie were keeping company with their small group of friends who had formed a bridge club. Charlotte, once again, was at home watching television alone. This was the Swinging Sixties and yet she had nothing to do and no one to share her time with. She was watching *Top of the Pops*, where Sandy Shaw was singing without shoes while girls danced around her wearing fabulous clothes in the latest style designed by Mary Quant and others of her ilk. She imagined herself wandering along the river in a psychedelic mini-skirt like the dancers on the show were wearing, and with a Vidal Sassoon razor-sharp haircut to show off to people like the old boy Eric or the women at the place where she worked.

And all the while her birthplace and home town of London was smack bang in the middle of a fantastic era and was being heralded as the Swinging City. Beatlemania was going strong and the Rolling Stones were hitting the big time. There was a new revolution pushing forward in the capital on all levels and Charlotte was sad not to be part of it. It didn't seem right since she was a true-blue born and bred Londoner, and the desire to go back home was almost overwhelming. Leaving in 1959 at thirteen going on fourteen was the worst thing that could have happened to a young teenager – and it had happened to her. She switched off the television set, ready to go and have a long soak in the bath with plenty of bubbles. But then, just as she told herself that she had to accept the lonely life that she could do little about, the sound of the doorbell pierced through the silence. She instinctively looked at the clock to see that it had just turned seven, a bit on the late side for a travelling salesman.

Going to the street door she put on the safety chain and then turned the catch to see a tall, good-looking young man around her own age standing on the doorstep. He was wearing a lightweight summer suit and open-necked shirt and didn't have the air of a salesman; possibly a Jehovah's Witness, she thought, and slipped the bolt from the safety chain. She opened the door properly, intrigued by her visitor at first, and then stunned when he spoke in a quiet and familiar voice while smiling at her. 'How long are you going to leave me standing on your doorstep, Charlie?' he said. She could hardly believe her eyes or the way her heart was rapidly beating. Had her old friend really come to her rescue just when she needed him most?

'Nathan? It *can't* be you!' was all she managed to say.

'Charlotte? I *know* it's you.' was his joker response.

'My God, it is you. I can't believe it.' Her face lit up and she started to laugh.

'Why wouldn't it be me? You phoned home and here I am. I don't know if you gave my dad your new address or whether he got it from Directory Enquiries, but it was in my hand the minute I walked in from work on the day that you called him. So? Are you going to let me in?'

Opening the door wide she stood aside and waved a slow but welcoming hand, inviting him into her home. Once he was in the passage she closed the door behind him and as she turned around her childhood friend just stood there, looking at her, until Charlotte finally said, 'I still can't believe it's you.'

'Well it *is*. And you look just as beautiful as I imagined you would be after all this time.'

She looked beautiful? What about him? He had turned into a Prince Charming! 'Well, that's a lovely compliment . . . but my God . . . look at *you*!' She grinned, and shook her head in amazement. He was six feet tall, slim, broad and incredibly handsome. 'Where's my short fat friend gone?' she said.

'Nowhere. He's still right here, inside.' He patted his heart. 'Now are you going to offer me a cup of coffee? Or something stronger?'

'A cup of coffee for now, because I need one. That and a cigarette.' She stood to one side and waved a theatrical hand in the direction of the sitting room, but he was having none of it. He stood looking at her, a gentle smile on his face and a touch tearful. 'Don't I at least deserve a hug?' he said.

'Of course you do. Let's break a habit of a lifetime. We never hugged, Nathan, but perhaps we should have done. We were good friends. We were there for each other but we never hugged – I don't know why.'

'Nor me,' he said, taking her into his arms and kissing her lightly on her soft white neck. His heart was beating faster and he felt the tears coming. Only just managing to subdue his emotions, he said, 'It wasn't that I didn't want to hold you close. I was shy and I didn't think for one minute that you felt the same about me as I felt about you.'

Cupping his face, Charlotte swallowed against the lump in her throat. 'I didn't know what either of us felt. All I know is that I missed you badly when we left. And when you stopped writing to me I felt as if I was in mourning for a lost love. Then I told myself off for being stupid. That helped.'

'Well, I apologise, I really do. I thought that I had to let you lead your life and that I might not be part of it any more. So I threw myself into the world of theatre.' He smiled and then shrugged. 'It helped, but it wasn't a cure.' He then stepped away from her and turned his head so that he could wipe an escaping tear from his eye. He went into the front room, followed by Charlotte.

'I love this house,' he said, attempting to be matter-of-fact. 'I thought you would be living on a council estate up here.'

'We were at first,' said Charlotte, falling in line with his conversational gambit. 'But the work just kept on coming for Dad. Good electricians are not exactly two a penny up here, and what with all the new houses and flats being built . . .'

'Good. He did the right thing then?'

Charlotte slowly nodded. 'For him and Mum, yes . . . I suppose so.'

'But not for you?'

'No. But don't tell them that I said that.'

'How can I if they're not at home?'

Charlotte laughed. 'I'll make the coffee and you make yourself comfortable. Turn the telly on if you want to.'

'No, it's fine. I love the quiet.' Flopping down into a feather-cushioned armchair, Nathan let out a sigh of relief. He was here. He had found the girl that he had missed so badly when she left London. He was under the same roof as his Charlotte at last, content just to relax and not think about anything. He leaned his head back and closed his eyes. It had been a long and arduous journey, one way and another.

Coming back into the room, Charlotte asked if he wanted something to eat. He said he didn't. She asked if he had already eaten on the train. He said he hadn't. 'Well then, after we've had a cup of coffee we'll go for a walk and I'll treat you to the best fish and chips in the world. How does that sound?'

'Heavenly,' he said as he looked into her beautiful face. 'I can't tell you how this feels, Charlie,' he said. 'I just can't find the words.' He let out a long sigh of relief. 'After all this time. And all I had to do was get on a bloody train and then trek from the station to here.'

'Trek? But we're only five minutes' walk from the station, Nathan.'

'I know. But I turned right instead of left and nigh on circled this bloody town. But I've found you now, so that's all right.' He closed his eyes and sighed contentedly.

'You can have a doze if you want to,' she said.

'Don't be mad. I'm just relaxing after the *schlep* up here, for God's sake. Leave me be. Go and fetch our coffee.'

Smiling to herself at the way Nathan had changed and yet at the same time was still his same old self, she felt happy. And happiness was an emotion that hadn't been around for a while. An hour or so later, after they had caught up with each other's lives and talked non-stop, Charlotte then asked if he felt like a short walk to the local pub to say hello to her parents and their friends. He had no problem with this and was up and ready to leave before she had had time to swipe on some fresh lipstick. On the way to the pub they talked more about their lives. All kinds of things to do with all that had happened in the world since they last saw each other, which seemed at least twice as long as it had actually been.

Charlotte had had to use every bit of willpower not to cry when he said, 'At one time I thought that my dad would die of a broken heart once Mum had gone. He took her death very badly. They were so close. From what I can gather she stumbled a little and then keeled over. At least it was quick for my beautiful mother.'

'But when she was alive, she was a really happy person, Nathan. I remember her smiling face.'

'I know. But it was so hard for our parents in the old days. In the early days my mother had to take in dry washing to press. And during the day, on and off, she would look at another pile of clean laundry waiting to be ironed and roll her shoulders back and forth to ease the burning pain before she began again. And that would be after a ten-minute tea break.'

'But she was happy for most of her life.' Charlotte reached out and squeezed his hand. 'You know that she was.'

Smiling warmly at the girl that he was still in love with, Nathan took her hand and kissed it. 'You always were my light in the dark,' he said.

Arriving at the pub, Nathan, feeling as if he was walking on air, opened the door for Charlotte and followed her through the public bar to the room out the back where a game of bridge was in play. Nathan waited while she opened the door marked private and courteously gave her dad a nod to say she wanted to have a quiet word. Turning around, she saw her friend chatting to the guy behind the bar who was pouring another customer a drink. She couldn't believe just how tall, broad and handsome Nathan had turned out. Beyond him and the barman she could see someone staring at her and couldn't think why. She turned her face away, letting him know that she wasn't interested, should this be the reason why he was giving her the evil eye.

Coming out of the back room, the serious expression on Eddie's face melted into a smile as he saw Nathan. He smiled broadly as he joined him and studied the eighteen-year-old's face and then started to laugh. 'Well I never,' he said. 'Look what the wind's blown in. Look at you. You're broader than I am, son!'

He offered his hand and Nathan took it gladly. 'It's good to see you. How you got here I'll never know. But

I'm in the middle of a game so I'll see the pair of you later on. But I'm really pleased. Chuffed. You wait until I tell Rita you've moved up 'ere. She'll be over the moon.'

Nathan didn't have time, nor the inclination, to tell Eddie that he was on a chance visit but Charlotte was in straight away. 'He hasn't moved up, Dad. He's come to visit us.'

Eddie slowly nodded, pleased as punch. 'There's a guest room in our house for you any time you want to use it, son.' He gave him a fatherly wink. 'We'll 'ave a nice chat later on, back at home, before we all go to bed.' With that, Eddie left them to it.

'Well,' said Nathan. 'This really is fantastic. I walk in out of the blue and get invited into the fold.' He was genuinely moved. 'Once we've had a drink here shall we go for a nice stroll along the river?'

'Fine by me. Or we can leave now and have a drink in a different pub a bit further along.'

'I think I would prefer that, actually,' said Nathan. 'I need to be out in the fresh air and walk a bit after travelling all day.' He then took her hand and escorted her out of the pub – a true gentleman.

'Looks like the girl you just had your eye on has got a boyfriend,' said the bartender to Kenny, who had watched them go.

'Does, don't it? Ah, well. You can't win 'em all. Anyway, I've gotta go back to London to take care of Dad.' He shrugged.

'Ne'mind son. You're putting your dad before pleasure and that's no bad thing. You're a good kid.'

'Thanks for that,' said Kenny, a touch on the sentimental side. 'I'll be back though. In a year or so.'

'Course you will, son. Course you will.'

Walking away from the pub with Nathan and through the back streets on the way to the river, Charlotte kicked off the conversation to cover the darker side of their childhood so as to get it over with. She said, 'I wonder what those bullies are doing now. The ones who tormented the life out of the both of us, one way or another? I bet they're mostly married with families and are as dull as ditch water.'

'I don't care where they are, Charlie. I had to force myself to let it go. I had to will myself not to think about those bastards. I focused on my career and made it happen. I didn't want to be a tailor like my dad and I didn't want to run a delicatessen the way my grandpa did for all of his working life.

'Dad keeps himself busy with the list of private customers that he managed to build while working as a tailor which is great, because he works from home now and he prefers that. He makes a respectable living from his trade these days. They say he's a master tailor. He wanted me to follow in his footsteps but tradition or not I wasn't going to have that.

'I didn't want a shop with a cutting and stitching room out the back. My grandpa insists that I should let my dad show me the way to cut a decent suit, though, so that I've got a second string to my bow.' Thinking about his grandpa he chuckled.

'He still smells of Lifebuoy soap – and he still has plans for the kind of house I will buy for my own family one day and where it will be. At the moment he thinks Golders Green is the place to focus on. He drives my dad mad but he also makes him laugh. They're more like brothers with a twenty-year age difference, and the bond between them is really helping now that Mum's gone.' He paused for a moment and then looked into Charlotte's face, saying, 'You know, Mum's funeral was the only one I had ever been to.'

Still holding his hand she guided him through a narrow courtyard with flint stone walls on either side of them. 'It must have been horrible, Nathan. I wish you had let me know.'

'I didn't want to talk about it or tell you, my closest ever friend, because it would have made it real. I just hoped that I might wake up one morning to find that it had all been a horrible dream.'

'I can't imagine what it must have been like. Your mum was so alive and full of spirit. She was too young to die. She can only have been in her late forties.'

'No, she was in her mid-fifties, but she had been taking tablets for high blood pressure for two years before the attack without telling any of us. Dad was angry with our GP at first but then saw that the man was right to respect Mum's wishes. She didn't want anyone to know that something had gone wrong with her heart. She had been advised to take it easy, but can you imagine her not helping out at the delicatessen when they were busy and my grandparents needed her? She left the umbrella factory to work there because it got so busy. She thought of the delicatessen as a second home.'

Touched by the way he was trying to salvage something from his mother's life, Charlotte slipped her arm into his. 'I'm really proud of you, Nathan.'

'What for? What great thing in life have I accomplished? I'm a trainee junior accountant, for God's sake. But I hope to work for myself one day.' He stopped in his tracks and looked into her face. 'I really wanted to see you again but didn't know if you wanted to see me. I swear on my mother's life I've never loved anyone the way I loved you when I was thirteen. I thought you had moved on and forgotten all about me.'

This made her laugh. He hadn't changed at all. 'How could I forget you! And why do you think I made the phone call?'

Blushing, he changed the subject, saying, 'Anyway . . . I'm okay in the two-bedroom flat that I share with my dad. It will do until we get a brand new council maisonette with a garden. Until I can afford to get a mortgage and buy something.'

They continued on their walk. 'So you and your dad will stay together for ever?'

'Of course we will. Until my sister comes back from America, in any case. Her marriage isn't working out, so she's going to move in with my grandparents close by to where Dad and I are living until she decides what she wants to do. My grandparents' Victorian terraced house is in a quiet tree-lined street not too far away from Ravenscourt Buildings where we live. The wily old couple bought it off the landlord years ago for a song – a quarter of what it's worth now.'

'It sounds like there's been a few changes since you last wrote.'

'Yes. And I'm sorry I never let you know about Mum going, but it affected me badly. I didn't want to go out, I didn't want to go to work, I didn't want to wake up in the mornings. I knew I had to think about something horrible and I couldn't bear it. But I'm okay now, I've got used to it. You know, to the fact that life is fragile. I can bring Mum's smiling face to mind, so that's something. I couldn't at first but I can now. I can also see the cross look that she used to give me when I wouldn't hit back.'

'Her being cross with you was only her way of trying to get you to have more confidence in yourself.'

'I know.'

'And now you live with your dad close by to your grandparents. That must be better than living on our estate, surely?'

'Much. But the flat doesn't have an inside lavatory and that's not brilliant if Dad needs to pee in the night. He goes in a bucket. But I like being there. I'm content living with him. He's funny. And he still keeps a paraffin heater in the corner of the room as a back-up in case there's an electricity cut worldwide. And he keeps busy with his sewing machine. He wanted to be closer to my grandparents but not live in and I felt the same. Now that Mum is dead my dad needs me.'

'So things are a lot different for you as well as me, and everyone else I expect,' Charlotte murmured as they paused by a little old wooden bridge that crossed an inlet into the river. 'Hundreds of East End families wanted a better way of living. Hundreds have moved out, from what I can gather from my nan and granddad. We seem to be spread around all over the place. Not them though. They would never leave the East End.'

Taking hold of her hand again, Nathan said, 'Well, I can't blame them. But for you? This is a much better lifestyle, surely? You're surrounded by forests and rivers as well as historic buildings.' He drew her to a wooden bench on the bank of the river and they sat down.

'It is beautiful in this part, Nathan, but the shops and some of the houses of old Bridgeford haven't changed much since time immemorial. We could do with a decent supermarket. It's all very well having fantastic ruins but we do need a bit of twentieth century as well. A bit of modern living.'

'I'm not so sure. I let myself into our flat just after my mother passed away and my dad hadn't heard me come in. He was in the kitchen, sitting at the old walnut table for two wiping his plate with a piece of dried bread. He had fried himself some kippers. I just stood there staring at him and realised that old habits and old ways were helping him through his loneliness.'

'Oh Nathan . . . I'm sorry . . .'

'No, don't be. It happens. We're okay, we're fine. I've got more responsibility than I've ever had in my life but I don't mind. I like being there for him. And he can cook a decent meal any day of the week, so it works both ways.'

Charlotte broke into a comfortable smile. Her child-hood friend hadn't changed one bit, except of course that he was now six feet tall and handsome. He still wore glasses but they were horn-rimmed and up to the minute in their design. So much water had passed under the bridge and five years had been struck off the calendar. She wasn't in the least bit awkward in his company. 'Come on,' she said. 'Let's walk further along by the river. We might see a kingfisher. I've only seen it half a dozen times in all the years I've been here along this part but you never know . . . this could be our lucky evening.'

Without saying a word, Nathan took hold of her hand again and in the most natural way they left the bench together and continued to stroll along, happy and content. When they came to a spot where the bank of the river was far too overgrown to battle with, they paused and looked around themselves. With the sun on his face, Nathan smiled. 'This really is a beautiful place, Charlie. I had no idea.'

They stood watching the water flowing gently and he couldn't resist picking up a smooth pebble and skimming it across the surface of the old river. He had done this many times before when they had mucked about down by the river in Wapping. They quietly laughed, and both of them felt as if they had slipped back in time to when they were messing around on the banks of the old Cut. The boyish look on his face in that moment was exactly as it had been then. Studying his relaxed expression, Charlotte was again taken by the change in him. His shoulders looked so much broader now that muscle had replaced fat.

Tilting his head so as to look at her, Nathan smiled

and then gently sighed, a touch overwhelmed. The dream he had dreamt for all of his childhood and early teens had at last come true. He wanted so much to hold her close and kiss her but didn't know if this was what she wanted. He felt that she still saw him as a brother figure. Looking away and focusing on a swan passing by, he said, 'Do you know something, Charlie? You're even more beautiful now than when we were scruffy kids and I worshipped the ground you walked on.'

'No, you didn't worship me.' She smiled. 'I was your mate. Your tomboy friend.'

'And now you're a beautiful young woman,' he said, in complete awe of her. 'And I'll tell you something else.'

'Go on then,' she said, as she looked around for a clearing where they could sit by the river again.

He turned to face her and reached out for her hand to lead her through to the idyllic spot that he had seen. He took off his jacket and folded it inside out, then laid it on the grassy bank as a cushion for her. Once she was settled he sat next to her and reached for her hand again to hold it the way he did when they were no more than five years old. 'The something else that I want to tell you is that it took me a long time to get over you leaving. I missed you so much, Charlie, that it hurt. But then—'

'Time being the great healer,' she cut in, 'you met someone else to love.'

'Not exactly. I didn't have a girlfriend until two years ago – when I was sixteen and had shot up and lost weight in the process.'

'And are you still with the same girlfriend? Or did you have a string of them once you got going?'

'No.' Still holding her hand he locked fingers and then looked into her lovely face and those beautiful soft blue eyes that he still adored. To be sitting in this spot by the river was almost too good to be true. 'The girl I'm going out with wasn't the first, but there wasn't a string of girlfriends. Only three in fact. The first was from the office block where I work and I only took her out a few times.

'We liked each other but the spark wasn't there for either of us. Then the second one came along right out of the blue. She was a college student doing study work at our library and I met her, of all places if you can believe it, while I was sitting in the park-keeper's hut and sharing a bottle of beer with him. I kept on going to see him once you'd gone and we became really close.'

'Oh Nathan . . . if you go on like this I'll cry, I swear it. Just the thought of you and our park-keeper sitting there . . . he was such a lovely man.'

'He still is. Did I say he was dead?' He smiled at her and then softly chuckled. 'He might be a bit of our past but he's not past it yet. And he still goes on about the old days and when there was no coal to shovel into the grate of the fireplace.'

'Good. He hasn't changed then. I'll go back and see him one day. So what about number three girlfriend then? How long did she last?'

'I think it must be almost a year now. She's from an Orthodox family. I had seen her before at the synagogue when we were kids but I don't think we ever actually said anything to each other.'

She didn't know why, but this news that Nathan was serious with a girl made her heart sink. She quickly brought herself to heel, though. 'We were all too young and busy surviving to think about all that love stuff, I suppose.' Looking across the river again, this time at a man who was sitting on the bank in a world of his own while fishing, she just couldn't leave it there. She had to know. 'And what about now, Nathan? Are you and number three planning to get engaged? Or have you already slipped the diamond ring on her finger? Are congratulations in order?'

'It's number four whose finger I would love to slip a ring onto, actually. Number four who used to be number one.'

Charlotte laughed. 'You bloody flirt! So what's she like then? The new girl who you're head over with.'

He drew breath and looked thoughtful. 'Well . . . she's a Christian and I've loved her for quite a while. Love's lost dream I suppose you could say.'

'So it wasn't mutual then?' Part of her hoped not.

'I don't know. I don't think so.' Shaking himself out of this confessional mood he had talked himself into, he laughed. 'Love's young dream is what it was. On my part that is. I had already made up my mind that I would marry her when I was ten years old, can you believe? From the age of five when I first saw her in class at the infant school I wanted to marry her. I loved the smell of her. I think it was Camay soap. Not perfume, just a nice soap smell that she used to wash with every day.'

'Nathan? Do you have a penchant for soap? You asked me during a geography lesson about my soap, then during history the next week and then when we were walking home from school together . . .'

'Did I?'

'Yes.'

'Well, there we are then. It must have been you that I loved so much I couldn't sleep at night.'

'Oh stop it. You'll have me in tears in a minute . . . let's forget about memory lane and make the most of now.'

'Memory lane,' he whispered. 'Yes, I suppose that's what it is. Just a memory.' He turned his head a little to look at her face. 'But this isn't a memory, is it? This is the here and now.'

'That's true, but it will be by tomorrow once you've gone back to London. It will all be another recollection to bring up in a few more years time when we might just find each other again.'

'Who knows?' He drew a slow breath and then looked sideways at her. At her beautiful face and her beautiful natural blonde hair. 'I like the new hairstyle. You look like Sandy Shaw except that you're prettier and blonde. It suits you. It's very fashionable.'

'And that's surprising, is it? Me having an up-to-date style even though I've turned into a carrot cruncher. A country bumpkin.'

Nathan giggled. 'Country bumpkin? I don't think so. You can take the girl out of the East End but you can't take the East End out of the girl. You're still a Londoner.'

'Good. I'm glad you think so too. I know where my roots are.'

'And I'll tell you something else.'

'If you must, Nathan.' She sighed and then looked into his warm brown eyes. 'Well, go on then. No holds barred.'

'Really? I can really say whatever I want?'

'Well, you always did. Why stop now? Go on, I can take it. Criticise me if you must.'

'Criticise?' Again he laughed, and loved the way she was now blushing pink. 'No. I wasn't going to do that. I was going to say . . . what I am saying . . . is that I would love it if you were to consider moving back to London. I missed you so much when you left that I got a pain in my chest that wouldn't go away. There was nothing medically wrong. I just kept wishing you hadn't gone. I suppose I was suffering from what they call puppy love.' He grinned, more from embarrassment than joy. 'We were too busy surviving and too young to even consider what love meant at that time.'

Not quite sure what lay behind this confession, Charlotte leaned towards him and brushed a kiss across his cheek. 'You're just as lovely a person as you ever were. And I still love you and your funny ways.'

Seizing the moment of a lifetime he placed an arm around her so that she could not escape. 'Am I allowed to kiss an old friend on the lips then?' he said.

'I don't see why not.' Charlie blushed a little and smiled.

His voice was soft and husky now and the sky was a lovely light blue and the sun was just beginning to set. 'Is that a yes, then?'

'It think it must be. I've missed you, Nathan.' She smiled affectionately, and then lowered her eyes, a touch shy all of a sudden. 'This is insane,' she murmured. 'I can't believe this is happening.'

'You sound like my dad now. That's one of his expressions that you must have picked up years ago.'

The silence and warmth between them said it all. Her funny fat childhood friend had gone from an insecure boy to a confident, tall and handsome young man. Placing her hands on his shoulders Charlotte realised just how much she had missed those warm brown eyes. 'I love you in the same way as I always did. Even though you've changed. Even though my fat and funny nervous friend has turned into a bit of a Romeo.'

'I've never been anything else where you were concerned.' He placed his hands around her slim waist and gently pulled her close. 'I loved you so much, Charlie, that it hurt. And I still love you. And I can hardly believe that I'm here and with you again. I've been kidding myself for years that I'd got over you, but I don't want to do that any more.'

Looking into his eyes as if they were the only two people around, Charlotte gently pressed her lips against his. Locked in each other's arms as if they were never going to let go, Nathan whispered in Charlotte's ear – 'I think I've never stopped loving you.'

'Stop it, Nathan, or I'll be in a flood of tears,' she whispered back.

'I don't care if you do cry. I want you to cry . . . on my shoulder. You don't know how I've longed to kiss those lips ever since I was five years old.' His voice was filled with emotion and love. 'I never stopped thinking about you. I *couldn't* stop thinking about you. I was so lonely after you'd gone I thought I would die. I haven't stopped wishing that you would come back home since the day you left.'

Gazing into his solemn handsome face again, Charlotte used the tip of her thumb to wipe away a little smudged lipstick from his face and he used his thumb to wipe away an escaping tear that was trickling down her cheek. 'Who would have thought that you would have grown into Prince Charming,' she said.

A touch embarrassed he eased himself away and drew breath. He then slipped his hand inside his jacket pocket to pull out a packet of cigarettes and the Zippo lighter given to him by his granddad. Once he had lit his cigarette, he slowly shook his head. 'My grandpa gave this to me when I confessed that I had had a few drags of a cigarette from a packet of five Woodbines that I bought two days after you left for Norfolk. I wonder what he would say if he could see me now? Here with you like this? He always said that you were a very special girl.'

'And I always thought that he was a lovely person. What about your dad? Did he know that you had the smoke?'

Nathan chuckled and they walked slowly onwards. 'Probably. He's never mentioned it and he doesn't criticise me now for having taken up the habit. He doesn't smoke. I don't think he ever did. But he doesn't interfere with what I do.' He drew on his cigarette and then blew a smoke ring. 'Thank God we left the old house in the courtyard and moved onto that council estate, else I might never have met you. But it doesn't matter now. Now that we've found each other again.'

'And it doesn't matter that I was dragged out into the back of beyond to Norfolk . . . now that you're here.' Charlotte slipped her hand into his.

'Our estate was lovely though, wasn't it? We had all those grassy areas; a proper football pitch that doubled up for cricket.'

'And there were lovely cottages with front and back gardens as well as the four-storey blocks of flats everywhere. I loved living there.'

Taking a last drag of his cigarette he then flicked it into the river. 'Would you like us to go for a meal this evening? I saw what looked like a very nice Chinese restaurant along by the main bridge on my way into town.'

'I'd prefer fish and chips.'

'Good. So would I.' He smiled and asked, 'Do you think that your parents are really fine with me sleeping over?'

'Of course they are. They wouldn't dream of you going into a bed and breakfast. We've got a spare room. It's small but cosy and Mum and Dad would be hurt if you didn't stay. You're our neighbour from the past, don't forget. They'd love to catch up.'

Nathan looked into her face again. 'Really? Well, I can't ask for more than that, can I. After all this time of not seeing each other and I'm welcomed back into the fold.'

'Of course. Why wouldn't you be? You were my best friend, Nathan. And we hardly see anyone from our old neck of the woods nowadays. They'd welcome your dad and your grandparents if you ever wanted to fetch them up here. They always got on well with your family. You know that.'

'Yes, they did, didn't they. I'll phone Dad later on and tell him I won't be back home tonight.'

'Good.' She brushed a few fallen leaves off the shoulders of his jacket. 'You know . . . just before you turned up out of the blue like this I was feeling miserable and down. I felt like Nora-no-friends.'

'You haven't made friends in all the time you've been here? I can't believe that, Charlie.'

'Well, it's true. I knew I didn't like it here soon after we moved in. The new housing estate we were on at first was great, brand spanking new and we had a lovely back garden. But there was nothing to do. Nowhere to go.'

'And now?'

'Nothing much has changed. It is a lovely old historic town, but people of our age need more. It's great for kids, what with the rivers and new footpaths everywhere, but I've been bored out of my brains and lonely. I can't tell you what it was like. I hated it at first.'

'Nothing for your age group to do then, and now, isn't healthy,' said Nathan, slowly nodding his head and reminding Charlotte of his dad. 'I do see what you mean. What about work for the men? Or have they had to go on the dole?'

'No, of course they haven't. There's plenty of work because of the new firms and factories that keep coming into the town.'

'New firms coming in? Well then, I suppose that's because the rates are low and old factories or pre-pack buildings can be bought on the cheap.'

Charlotte laughed at him. 'A true blue accountant then?' she said.

'Absolutely.' He looked sideways at her. 'I can't believe that we're here together like this by the river and talking. Will I wake up and find it's all a dream, Charlie?'

'No. It's real. This is me and you again – just like old times. Almost.' She smiled. 'All right, we're not sitting in the park-keeper's open shed looking forward, but on the river's edge looking back, with a five-year gap between and a lovely country pub just ahead of us. I think we should drink to that, don't you?'

'Yes,' said Nathan, a little more choked than he would like to be.

Later on, as they strolled back to Charlotte's house, having enjoyed fish and chips and a drink in the quaint old pub by the river, they linked arms and Nathan talked non-stop about what he had been doing with his life. But when it came to Charlotte, she had nothing much to tell him about hers because in truth there was nothing interesting to say. She had filled him in on the little that there was in her world. Nathan was full of enthusiasm.

'So come on,' he said. 'Enough about me. You must have one or two boyfriends?'

'No.' She smiled coyly and shrugged. 'The girls and women at work are really nice but they're mostly older than me with young families. I just don't seem to have been able to make friends up here the way I could down in London. I don't know why.'

'Well, maybe that's because you don't really belong up here. Maybe your roots are calling you back home?'

'I don't know, Nathan. I don't know anything any more. What I want from life, or where I want to live. I just get on with things like everyone else has to. You've been luckier than me.'

'No. Luck's got nothing to do with it. We have to make things happen. You know that. Come on, Charlie! Where's the girl that used to lead the way? What's happened to you?'

Charlotte smiled warmly. Yes, he was the old Nathan that she knew so well. Before she could answer he was off again. 'You like working at the council offices, and you've made a few friends there – even if they're not your age.'

'Nathan! Stop trying to make my little world sound interesting. It's not. Okay?'

'Well, at least you're admitting it, so I suppose that's something.' He shrugged in his lovely old familiar Yiddish way. 'Everyone has to have a passion,' he said, 'especially someone like you.'

'So what do you suggest?'

He stopped in his tracks and turned to face her. 'Come back, Charlotte. Come back to where you belong. Where you were born and grew up. Where your roots are. You said earlier on that you miss your grandparents – well, why not stay with them? Look for an office job and then maybe a bedsit. It's not impossible. Lots of young people are doing that now. You could come with me to the fringe theatre group. It's a great world to be part of, I promise you.'

Charlotte felt her heart sink. 'It's not that easy.'

'Yes it is! You'll shrivel up and die if you stay up here with nothing to do and no one to do it with.'

Charlotte forced herself to laugh so that she wouldn't cry. 'You're still mad.'

'Maybe – but at least I'm happy. Come home, Charlie . . . please?'

'You don't need me. You've been having a great life without me by the sound of it. You don't have to pretend otherwise just to make me feel better about not having done anything to improve mine.'

'Okay. But let me say it just once more. Come home. Stay at your grandparents' house. Be in London and be part of a buzzing world that's going on there right now. You can help me with the theatre group's bookkeeping and backstage management at weekends. You could even fill in as a bit part actor now and then.'

'Talk sense. I can't act.'

'It doesn't matter! None of us can bloody well act. But who gives a shit? We enjoy ourselves and the audience loves it.'

'It does sound like fun,' she murmured. Deep down

she was beginning to feel excited by the possibility of turning her life around.

'You would love it. We hardly make a profit.' Nathan smiled. 'But nobody cares. The entire company is happy to be involved. They love it.'

'And so do you by the sound of it.'

'Me?' He shrugged. 'Of course I do. Haven't I been banging on about it?'

Charlotte could hardly believe how his life had turned around. 'I'm really glad that I made that phone call, Nathan. I'm glad you came. I've missed you.'

'And I've missed you. We might be five years older but we can't have changed that much. I don't ask God that I should marry you one day, it's true, but . . .'

'You silly daft thing.' Charlotte smiled as she looked into his handsome face and those big soft brown eyes. She then took his hand again to walk slowly on.

'Seriously now – aren't we still best friends? Look at us. Strolling along as if the five years hasn't passed. You can't ask for much more than that. And you know what my dad always says? That people, whether they like to believe it or not, even though they change as they grow, they stay the same inside.'

Charlotte considered this and then slowly nodded. She felt just as close to him as she used to when they were kids. She wanted him to put his arms around her and hold her tight. Then just as if he was reading her mind he placed one hand on her shoulder and cupped her chin with the other. 'My mother used to say what goes round comes round. I could have ended up bitter and twisted, you know. From all the bullying and then losing you. But luckily my religion helped me to wave it away and leave it where it belonged – in the past. The little green devils sit on the shoulders of the intimidators. Not on ours.' He then leaned forward and kissed her lightly on those beautiful soft shapely lips that he had loved since the day he had set eyes on her in the infant school.

She looked at him and sighed contentedly. 'And you really think that I would be able to settle in the East End again after living in a world that's surrounded by rivers, forests and fields?'

'You know very well that you would. And you don't need me to tell you that, Charlie. You know you'll slip right back into the way of life and you also know that it's what you want.'

'I'll think about it. Think about whether you're right or wrong.'

'It was only five years ago that you left, and you've got a lifetime in front of you. You don't want to spend your life regretting that you didn't take the chance while you were still young.'

She swallowed against a lump in her throat and tremulously smiled back at him. Feeling a little awkward and needing time to think about both his feelings and hers, she glanced at him to see that he was finding the conversation difficult so changed the subject. Trying to sound casual, she said, 'There used to be a theatre here in Bridgeford. Years ago.'

'You already told me.' Nathan turned his face to look at hers. He knew her so well. She was not only forcing back tears but also trying to find something in common and was using the theatre to do it. And it wasn't necessary. As far as he was concerned nothing had changed between them. 'It's a pity that it's not still going. A small theatre for panto at Christmas would be good. It brings families together for a bit of fun. It could make a big difference to a small town like this.' He looked sideways at her, at his lovely Charlotte. He adored her as much as ever. 'It must have been a lively little town in the old days, Charlie.'

'It was, according to my friend Eric. There used to be an old-fashioned baker, a blacksmith, cobbler, grocer, muffin maker, stay maker and straw hat maker.'

'Your friend Eric?'

Charlotte smiled. 'He's an old boy. But he remembers all the old traders, or so he says.'

Relief swept through Nathan and replaced the fear of someone younger being close to her. But he was soon back on track. 'Most of those old trades are defunct now,' he said. 'More's the pity.'

'There *is* an old-fashioned cinema . . . it reminds me of the one in Bethnal Green but not so run-down. Do you remember that place?'

'How could I forget. It was a bug hole.'

Drawing closer to the street where she lived Charlotte tried not to think about the next day when he would be gone. He was lovely company and the thought of him going away again made her heart sink, but she smiled at the sound of a blackbird's song drifting through the air close by. They reached Charlotte's house. 'Well, here we are then. Back home after a tour of the place where I live.' When she turned the key in the lock she knew in her heart what was going to happen once they were both inside with the door closed behind them.

Putting his arms around her Nathan gently brushed some loose strands of her blonde hair off her face and looked into those lovely blue eyes. His voice low and charged with emotion, he said, 'I can't believe I'm standing here with you like this.'

'Well, you are. This is us and this is real.'

He gently pressed his mouth against hers and then, after all the years of knowing each other, they shared their first real kiss and both wanted more. Much more . . . But they were going to have to wait. Charlotte was young and Charlotte was a virgin. But they kissed lovingly and they held on to each other and this made up for everything.

The following morning before saying goodbye to Nathan, Charlotte was sure of what she wanted. She wanted to see more of her long lost best friend, who she was falling in love with all over again – a different kind of love this time, though. During the years of their living miles away from each other, each of them had grown in their own way, of course they had, but, more importantly, they hadn't grown apart. Now, more than ever, she knew that she had to move back to London. Her first priority, of course, was to look for a position back in London and somewhere to live in the East End. She felt that her parents would be against it, but she was determined to turn her life around. She was going to have to find herself a furnished flat and she was going to have to see if she could transfer from the Thetford office to a branch in London. And in the East End if possible.

Having learned quite a bit while working in the local town hall, as well as going to evening classes locally much earlier on to learn touch typing, she felt quite confident that she could cope in a London office. Her typing speed now was sixty words per minute. Apart from all of this, she knew that her grandparents, Nell and Johnny, would put her up if necessary, and that her parents would help her out financially if she was stuck for cash – once they accepted that she really didn't want to live in a small country town any more. She knew that her gran couldn't wait to have her back in her realm where she could keep an eye on her. And in any case, Charlotte wanted to see more of the funny old couple who had always managed to make her laugh no matter what. It was the banter of her grandparents that she loved – never mind the easy flow of swearing that came naturally to both of them.

Yes, she *was* looking forward to a more cheerful way of life. She could hardly wait.

Chapter Seven

Once Charlotte had said farewell to Nathan and promised to meet him in London to view rooms to let, she felt more positive. And was excited about a few days' break away from home and from her parents and Bridgeford. Getting it past Rita and Eddie that she was going down to London to look for a place of her own was not going to be easy . . . but she had always known that would be the case. She was, after all, their only child, but without realising it they had been overly protective and a little bit self-centred. And now she was ready to sit down with them and talk openly about plans that she had been secretly making for quite a while. In fact, ever since the first year they came to Bridgeford she had, in the quiet of her bedroom, thought about going to live with her grandparents in Bow one day. Nathan's visit out of the blue had been exactly the kick-start she needed to spur her into action, and she silently thanked him for it. And now, taking a leaf out of her gran's book, she was determined not to put off until tomorrow what could be said today.

So, that evening, just as the family of three were settling down and ready to switch on the television, she braced herself for a battle of words. On her favourite armchair and in her pyjamas and dressing gown, her legs curled under her, she looked across to her mum and dad, together on the sofa, and quietly said, 'I need to talk to you.'

Eddie looked sideways at her, a touch amused by her adult tone. He sported a warm smile. 'Can it wait till after *Coronation Street*? You know your mother won't want any interruptions.'

'Nor will you,' said Rita. 'You don't 'ave to pretend to us that you don't like it, watching the goings-on in the Street. We won't tell your mates in the pub.' She looked across to Charlotte and winked at her.

'They wouldn't take any notice of you in any case, Rita. They, just like me, 'ave to give way to the woman of the house.'

'I'll come straight to the point then,' said Charlotte, determined to say what she had to. 'I want to go back to London. To find work in an office and rent a flat.' Eddie smiled and then looked at Rita. 'Over to you, sweetheart.'

'She can do what she likes. She's not a kid any more.' Her eyes were still fixed on her programme. Taken aback by this casual response, Charlotte could think of little else to do other than look at her mother's face and try to read from her expression whether she meant what she said or not. 'I thought that I would take a furnished flat nearby to Gran and Granddad . . .' she murmured.

'Whatever you think best,' was Rita's next easy reply. 'Do what you want. You're only young once.' In truth she didn't think for one minute that her daughter, her only child, would have the gumption to get up and go and find herself somewhere to live as well as somewhere to work. But, as far as Charlotte was concerned, she had just been given the okay and without any arguments. There had been no condescending smirks and no remarks as to how she would not last a week on her own in the capital. And so, while the going was good, she decided there and then to set it in stone.

Her eyes lowered to the floor, she spoke in a quiet voice. 'The thing is . . . I feel as if I missed out on my teens so far by living up here and not being in the East End.'

'Missed out on what?' Rita smiled as she turned to look into Charlotte's face. 'What was there to miss out *on*?'

'Going out on a Friday and Saturday night with my mates. Most of the girls in the third and fourth year of senior school went to our local youth clubs and dance halls when they were fourteen and fifteen. They wore make-up and nail varnish and clothes that were in fashion. That's what I would have done if we had stayed put.'

'What are you talking about? You were only thirteen when we left Bethnal Green. You were still a girl.'

'I know. But thirteen-year-olds who were at my school were beginning to go to local dance halls along with fourteen, fifteen and sixteen-year-olds. They were all jiving and twisting to the latest records, which I would have loved to have done, but you said that I was too young for all of that and then you dragged me up here where there was nothing happening. I missed out on everything. On all of the fun that my mates at senior school were having. I didn't even have a transistor radio to listen to pop records in my bedroom.'

'Well, if you'd 'ave asked we would 'ave given you one for Christmas or your birthday. You never mentioned it. Anyway, you were still wearing socks at that time. I let you have some of those terrible luminous green, yellow or pink ones, if you remember.'

'Course I remember – and I liked them. But eleven-year-olds were wearing them. Thirteen-year-olds were getting used to stockings and pretty suspender belts.'

'Rubbish. And any girl that did wear stockings at that age would 'ave been seen as a Lolita.'

'Charlotte has got a point, Reet,' said Eddie, as ever the pacifier in this small family of three. 'She did spend her early teens up here. And it's true, there wasn't anything for her age group. It never occurred to me at the time.' He glanced at Charlotte and smiled. 'Sorry, babe. I think we might 'ave behaved a little bit on the selfish side without realising it.' He was now thinking about his youth and how he had enjoyed being a spiv in London when swing and jazz was all the rage.

'No. I don't agree,' said Rita. 'Hundreds of girls from the East End would 'ave given an arm and a leg to 'ave been able to live in a house like this with rivers all around us. You couldn't wait to get out of Bethnal Green, Charlotte! You wanted to move up here.'

'Out of Bethnal Green, maybe, but not out of the East End. You always said that one day we would live in one of those lovely Victorian houses overlooking Victoria Park and the boating lake, and then you changed your mind. And in any case, I thought from what you'd said about Bridgeford there was gonna be people of my age around. That's what you said at the time. That couples with young families who were teenagers were moving up here.'

'And . . . some did.'

'Not many. Not in Bridgeford and there wasn't one youth club or dance hall for people of my age to meet up in.'

'What is this?' said Rita. 'I didn't think you meant it when you mentioned it before. You don't think that we're gonna pull up roots and go back to the East End, do you? Is this what it's all about?' Rita was getting redder in the face. 'Because if it is, you're wrong. Me and your dad love it up here. And anyway, being eighteen is a lot different from thirteen. You're old enough now to make up your own mind. Do what you want. Go and rebel against life and have a taste of the youth freedom that the papers keep printing. Take purple hearts. Smoke marijuana. And when you've done all there is to do, you can come back home and appreciate what we've set up for you.'

Charlotte broke into soft laughter and avoided looking at her dad, who was also trapping laughter. 'Forget I even mentioned it,' she said. She knew that there was no point in having a conversation to do with her moving out. But as far as Charlotte was concerned, her mother had, whether in jest or not, given her free rein to leave home and she was going to grab it with both hands and go back to look for somewhere to live and somewhere to work. She would arrange to have time off from work, which would then be deducted from the holiday leave that was due her. She knew that if she were to continue with this conversation now, her parents would take it more seriously and talk her out of it. So she held her tongue.

'It's all this business of the Swinging Sixties that's going to your head,' murmured Rita. 'You wouldn't last six months in London. But go if you must. Have it your way. Find out for yourself. Make your own mistakes. But don't come back here if you get hooked on drugs.'

This was more than Eddie could take. He started to laugh and then got out of the room before Rita gave him an ear-bashing as well. 'I'm glad your father thinks it's funny,' she said, her eyes still focused on the television and Ena Sharples going on and on to Annie Walker about the price of a half-pint of stout.

Pleased that she had started the ball rolling, Charlotte could hardly stop herself from smiling. 'You won't have to worry over me, Mum. I won't take drugs and I'll be safe and sound living close by, if not with, Gran and Granddad. And you like Nathan, don't you? He'll see I'm okay.'

'Whatever you say,' said Rita, fixing on her soap so as not to have to think about it.

Charlotte could hardly believe that it would be so easy. She had managed to get it across that she was going to go ahead with what her mother saw as madcap plans and she wasn't going to try and stop her. And if Rita was right and she found that she had made a mistake and wanted to come back after six months or so, it wouldn't matter. Nothing gained, nothing lost. She was so carried away with the thought of moving on, she hadn't noticed Eddie coming back into the room. He strolled over to the window and gazed out, miles away. The truth of the matter was that he knew how his daughter felt. He remembered when they had first arrived in Bridgeford how he had had the rural blues. He had smiled his way through it for the sake of his wife and daughter, but his romantic vision of a friendly community of rustic villagers turned out to be pie in the sky. He, just like other incomers, had found a touch of resentment from the locals at first because they believed that all of the Londoners would soon buy their own houses and push up property prices beyond the reach of their own born and bred young families. It was different now, of course, because most Londoners still lived in council houses.

Apart from this, Eddie had always kept up with the news about his neck of the woods in London. He knew that from as far back as 1952, East Enders who were moving away were being replaced by a huge influx of people from the West Indies for a start. Hard-working people who would no doubt also want to own their own homes one day. And within the space of just a few years it was being reported in the press that over a hundred thousand people from not only the West Indies but also Pakistan were living in and around the capital. So his fear had been similar to the locals in Norfolk and had turned out to be inconsequential. He had always wondered that, should he and his family want to move back later on, for instance, would he be able to. Would there be any council properties available? And would the cost of private housing rise above what the likes of people like himself could afford? But he was over all of this worry now because he was settled into his new way of life and reasonably happy. But his daughter wasn't, and he couldn't find it in his heart to blame her for wanting to be back in London. She was young and single with her life before her.

Eddie also knew that Rita was more than content with her lot. She had a washing machine and tumble dryer, a refrigerator, a deep-freeze and a new cooker. In London she had always had to use the bagwash or the launderette and had kept butter and cheese in a cool larder cabinet. Now, she had even achieved her dream of having wall-to-wall carpets. Not only were things cheaper to buy in Bridgeford, but there were no charges made for the fitting and fixing of things such as carpets and plumbing. It was all part and parcel of the service. And food was fresher and cheaper. Dairy produce, eggs, poultry, meat and fresh vegetables came into the local market from the local farms on a regular basis. And there was always a homemade cake stall run by the WI and the Red Cross so there was no need for Rita to bend over a hot oven any more. She simply adored her new life. But it wasn't too exciting for a teenager and Eddie was fully aware of this.

A week later, after thinking things through and having made arrangements to go to London, Charlotte was boarding a train from Bridgeford to King's Cross with Eddie seeing her off from the station platform. If truth be known, he felt proud of his daughter for taking this big step. He watched her walk away from him carrying her small suitcase and felt a lump the size of a fist in his throat. Once she was on the train, waving from an open doorway and then giving him the thumbs-up sign to say that all was well, he felt like bursting into tears. His daughter was taking a first big step out into the world of independence and he admired her guts and her confidence for standing up for her rights. Deep down, though, he still didn't quite believe that she would actually give up her position at the council offices, never mind her lovely bedroom in their lovely house. Rented rooms in London, from what he had heard, were seedy and less than desirable. But he knew that his daughter was going to have to find this out for herself. And if he were honest with himself, he would have to admit that he was hoping that this little trip that she was embarking upon would put the lid on her dream because he didn't want to lose her.

He didn't believe for one minute that Charlotte was simply rebelling, but nor did he believe that she truly wanted to be part of the so-called Swinging Capital and youth freedom. She had been wearing mini-skirts for a while so hadn't exactly turned into a country bumpkin. What he couldn't accept was that she was the sort of girl who was cut out for high fashion, boutiques, discos and live concerts. He couldn't imagine her in a crowd, watching the Beatles on stage performing to hysterical girls screaming so loudly en masse that it was impossible to hear the voices of John, Paul, George and Ringo. She just wasn't that kind of a person. At least he didn't think she was.

Walking slowly along the platform towards the exit

and feeling a touch emotional, Eddie spotted Kenny Wood strolling towards the train. The thought of asking him to go and sit next to Charlotte to give her some company flashed into his mind and then flashed out again. The lad who had been known as Ginger had been a little bastard when young, and even though he seemed quiet and placid now, Eddie didn't think that his daughter would appreciate being stuck with him for the duration of the journey. In fact, he knew that she would be furious if he interfered in this newfound independence that she had discovered, and which had at least boosted her morale from what he could tell. So he let go of the idea.

Kenny, having done his homework, now knew that Charlotte's dad was one of the most respected men about town. And since they shared the same local and not being one to miss an opportunity, smiled broadly at Eddie and showed a hand, saying, 'All right, mate? See Charlotte off okay?'

This stopped Eddie in his tracks. How come he knew that Charlotte was on the train? He looked sideways at the teenager and then broke into a warm smile. 'Yeah. She's settled with a window seat, Kenny. I take it that you are that same little fucker with the ginger hair that couldn't be tamed when a kid?'

'Not any more, mate. I've grown up.' Kenny smiled. 'Still, better to be bad when a boy than later on when a man. I know I was a right little bastard. Dad didn't know what to do about me so let it be. He don't think I've turned out too bad. I thought it was you seeing Charlotte onto the train. Anyway, I'm off back home for a bit. Back to my roots and my mum and dad. It's nice up 'ere but I miss all my aunts and uncles and cousins and that.'

'I know what you mean, son. It can be a bit of a wrench moving from your roots. How is your dad? Still in the carpet trade?'

'Yeah. It's a successful little family business now. Keeps me busy and out of mischief. Let me know if you want your place fitted out. I can do you a special price.'

Eddie laughed warmly. 'You're a bit too late, son, we're all fixed up. But if I can put any business your way I will. I'm glad to see that you're following in your dad's footsteps.

'Thanks. I tried to talk Mum and Dad into coming to live up here but they didn't much fancy the idea. I suggested a move to Haverhill as well, where loads of other East Enders are going, but they weren't up for that either.' He shrugged. 'Bridgeford's a lovely old town, don't get me wrong, but my mum and dad and my old gran would feel like fish out of water in this place.'

'And what about you?' said Eddie, hoping he had bought a one-way ticket to London. He felt sure that he had just been told a load of mumbo-jumbo.

'Oh, I reckon it's a lovely little town in the country! But it's not for me on a permanent basis, mate. But there you go. Maybe once I'm married wiv a family and that. Who knows? Anyway . . . it was good to see your familiar face in the pub the other night. Cheered me up that did.'

'Good. And as for your parents not wanting to live

up here, each to their own, boy, each to their own. Take it easy.' With that Eddie winked at him and continued on his way.

He hadn't got far when he found himself wondering if he should have a little chat with Rita and touch on the subject of Charlotte and birth control, and then checked himself for even thinking it. But then he remembered that it hadn't been more than a couple of months of courting Rita back in the old days before they were making love. And now, in the mid-Sixties, from what he had heard, birth control clinics had been set up not only for married couples, but single girls too. He decided to sleep on it, and made a mental note for when he next went into the library to return his books. He thought that he might just pick up a guide to safe sex and leave it around for Charlotte to see when she came back from her London trip. He felt sure that there had to be books on the subject. After all, the contraceptive pill was now available on the National Health, from what he had heard.

Hardly able to believe that he was thinking about his daughter being old enough to be made love to, Eddie blew air as he turned the key in the lock of his car. He blamed the beatnik students of the Fifties, who had proclaimed the right of young people to have sex freely, and with more than one partner, before marriage. He got into his motor and tried not to think about it. It was a fast-changing world and there was nothing that was going to slow it down. He smiled as he recalled when bohemian demonstrators first started to hit the news. They had waved their banners and chanted that nuclear war would soon bring the world to an end so everyone should live for the day. And this was exactly what the young from all walks of life had done and were still doing. Enjoying life to the full regardless of old established standards. They were jiving the nights away at all-night sessions at such places as the Albert Hall, and some had made love on the dance floor with no shame attached. The age of recreational sex for young single women was now seeing a heyday. And his daughter was about to walk smack bang into the centre of it. Nathan had talked quite a bit about his fringe theatre world and the 'arty' friends he mixed with. Whether or not they smoked marijuana he couldn't say. He could only hope not, and this was what he was now doing – hoping his daughter wouldn't be drawn into a set that took drugs and believed in free love.

'Fucking cheek,' murmured Kenny. *'Each to their own? Smart-arse bastard.'* He then climbed aboard the train via the same doorway as Charlotte and as he approached her while choosing somewhere to sit, he winked and smiled all friendly. Pushing his luck he stopped in his tracks and said, 'Look, I hope you don't mind me talking to you like this, Charlie, but . . . I just wanna say I'm sorry for being an evil little sod when I was a kid. And I really do mean that. You might not recognise me now – but I was that little ginger-headed bastard with the crew-cut.'

Taken by surprise, Charlotte was momentarily lost for words. Then, once she found her voice she said, 'I know who you are. I recognise your face. And it's okay, all done and dusted.'

'Can I buy you a drink at the other end? Just to show a bit of good will?'

'No, that's all right, thanks. Say hello to your parents for me.' Charlotte smiled faintly at him. She couldn't believe that he was on the same train as herself but she wasn't going to let it get to her. She could leave all that had happened and been said in the past where it belonged, no problem.

'I will say hello for yer,' he said, 'I will. And may God bless you for being an angel, Charlie.' He nodded farewell and walked through to the end of the carriage with the air of a Jehovah's Witness and only just able to contain his laughter. He could hardly believe what a brilliant actor he could be when the need arose.

Once seated in his chosen place by himself, Kenny had to release a bit of pent-up laughter, albeit quietly. He liked his seat by the window and thought he might sleep on the train until it pulled into King's Cross. As he settled down for the long and boring journey away from what he considered to be a boring town, he wondered what the tart, Charlie, was up to. Maybe she had had enough of Bridgeford too? She had been carrying a small suitcase, so was she staying with her relatives or the tall good-looking dark-haired guy he saw her with in the pub? He thought that it might be fun to discreetly follow her from King's Cross, or even walk boldly beside her along the platform and ask where she was going. He chuckled and then murmured to himself, 'Don't forget what killed the cat, Kenny. Don't forget what curiosity did. Well, fuck the cat and fuck the saying. I'll find out what the slag's up to. For all 'er airs and graces, she's no better than a whore, except that she dresses as if she wasn't born and bred in the same mould as them. Toffee-nosed bitch.'

During her journey, Charlotte had plenty of time to think while she watched the changing scenery from the window as the train made its way to the capital. Most of her time was spent on thoughts of her evening with Nathan, whom she couldn't wait to see again. She smiled at the way his father had talked to her on the phone in the first place – the call that had kick-started Nathan into action. It felt as if it was only yesterday that she was living in the same block of flats as his family on the council estate. And her recollection of those times summed it all up. Country people were kind and obliging but East Enders were this and more. The old-fashioned community spirit that she had been brought up within could not be bottled. And now she couldn't wait to walk on the busy pavements of Whitechapel, Mile End and Bethnal Green again. She was looking forward most of all to being part of the London buzz, living amidst people of mixed religion and race. It wasn't until Nathan had mentioned a Jamaican lad with a great sense of humour who had been in their class at school that she realised she had not seen one black face in Norfolk. Not one. Thinking about this, and other meaningful things about her childhood, she slipped into a lovely sleep and didn't wake up until the train pulled into King's Cross.

Chapter Eight

Once Charlotte had got off the train and was outside the station, she was comforted by the fact that little had changed and everything seemed just as familiar as ever, even though there seemed to be a lot more people about. Five years on, and still it all felt so wonderfully easy to slip back into the hub of things. Instead of feeling like a girl up from the country, which was her worry when she had boarded the train from Bridgeford, she was immediately into the swing of things, as if she had never left in the first place. On the underground train heading for the Angel Islington, with the addresses of two flats that she had acquired from the *Evening Standard* scribbled onto a piece of paper held in her hand, she felt her old confidence flowing back. From the station she made her way towards the High Road as if this was an ordinary everyday occurrence.

When she got to Camden Passage, where the antique market was in full swing with shops and stalls selling furniture, old silver or bric-a-brac, she felt a rush of adrenaline. It was lively and it was colourful and she was ecstatic at being back home, albeit in a different part of the city. Peering at her handwritten directions to the street where she was to meet the landlady of a four-storey house who had advertised a furnished flat to let, she knew that she hadn't far to go.

It had been her granddad who had sent her the property to let page from the *Evening Standard* and she was quietly thanking him for it. The *Standard* was a newspaper that he took regularly and he had lost no time in mailing her that copy. Ever since her grandparents had picked up the tiniest hint that she wanted to try her hand at living by herself in London they had been on the case – they couldn't wait to have her back on home ground. They knew her budget and felt that she could not afford to pay more than three pounds ten shillings, or at the most four pounds a week for lodgings. They had done as she asked and marked any in the paper that they thought suitable, but Charlotte had chosen just one of them. This one in north London she herself had marked with a red pen. The few that her granddad had underlined were, naturally, smack bang in the middle of east London and just a short bus ride away from where they lived. Quite naturally too, her grandparents hoped that she would choose to return to her roots, not too far away from Bromley by Bow – their own little patch of heaven. Deep down, though, Nell and Johnny felt that Charlotte wouldn't last long in furnished digs wherever they were, and certainly not in a part of the capital where she knew no one and would most likely feel like a fish out of water rather than London born and bred. It had been five years since she had lived there, after all. This aside, they had agreed between themselves to hold their tongues when it came to talking too much about her moving in with them. It was what they wanted but they weren't going to push it. So, in their wisdom, they were going to keep shtum, leave things be and wait to see how it all went. And in any case, they didn't know whether she would still love London after all this time or hate it. Only time would tell.

Rita and Eddie were no different. Both of them had eavesdropped on the evening when Charlotte had spoken on the telephone to the owners of each of the two furnished flats that she had fancied of those she had seen advertised. From what they could make out from listening behind the open door, it seemed that both flats were part of large houses that had, at one time or another, been converted. This had made Rita pale and despairing as she whispered to Eddie, 'My God, it sounds like she's going to be living in a commune.' This vision had struck both of them with horror but they managed to allay each other's fears by saying that Charlotte wouldn't last five minutes in that kind of a place and would either move in with her grandparents or soon be home with her tail between her legs.

Now, in the buzzing atmosphere of north London, Charlotte was feeling less and less a girl up from the country. Her stomach was churning a little and her thoughts had been all over the place ever since her parents had tried to brainwash her into believing that she didn't belong in London any more . . . but all her doubts were now draining away. They had been wrong. London was busier than she remembered but then, during the past five years, thousands had come from overseas to live in England, so the numbers of people and the mix of races was to be expected. The sight of the familiar red buses warmed her, as did the black taxis everywhere. Resisting the urge to stroll through Camden Passage and look at the stalls selling everything from old-fashioned kitchen sinks to ornate chandeliers, she pushed on towards her destination, eager to view the first flat.

Before she knew it, she was in the quiet back turning that she had been heading for, having asked directions from a passer-by. She found herself standing outside a large period terraced house, in a street lined with a few trees and with similar houses on both sides. The reality of stepping out on her own like this was suddenly no longer daunting but wonderful. She checked that she was on the right side of the road for uneven numbers and walked slowly along, looking at each of the houses and trying to imagine the kind of people that might live in them.

Arriving outside number forty-one Bethel Place, Charlotte was reassured to see that the small area behind the waist-high brick wall wasn't as pristine as the others in the turning, and neither were the curtains at the windows as posh and expensive-looking. Checking the piece of paper in her hand to be certain that she was where she should be, she went through the small open gateway and up to a dark green painted front door that had an old-fashioned brass knocker and letterbox that was in need of a bit of Brasso and a good rub. Pressing her finger on the old black and white china bell she looked around her and was surprised at how clean the road and the pavements on either side were. There was no litter on the ground, which had been part and parcel of the back and beyond of Stepney and Bethnal Green when she had lived there, and the road sweepers arrived with their huge brooms and push carts.

Standing on the doorstep and listening for a noise from inside the house, she heard the sound of quick footsteps on floorboards and could hardly believe that there would be no wall-to-wall carpet in a house that had been described as splendid. She started to have doubts about the advert, which had painted a very nice picture of the property to let. When the door opened, however, she was immediately at ease because the hallway with its stripped and waxed floorboards and long narrow patterned rug was more than just warm and welcoming – it was lovely. And so too was the gentlewoman who opened the door to her and who looked to be in her mid-thirties.

Looking a touch seriously at Charlotte, she said, 'Are you the girl who telephoned yesterday?'

'Yes, I am.' Charlotte smiled inwardly because she realised that the woman had forgotten her name. 'I'm Charlotte, and I'm sorry if I'm a bit late.' She glanced at her wristwatch to see that she was actually fifteen minutes late. 'I should have kept an eye on my watch. I'm really sorry. I hope I've not inconvenienced you.'

Moving aside, the good-natured woman waved a hand and smiled at her. She then spoke in a whispering kind of voice, saying, 'It doesn't matter. But I am expecting some friends so we might have to be a little quicker than you would like.' She then closed the door behind her, saying, 'Please do call me Petusha.'

'Thank you. I will. And I'm Charlotte,' she said returning the smile and realising that she was repeating herself.

'Yes, of course you are,' said Petusha, who was doing her best to put her at ease. 'I remember now. I was in the garden when you rang, just seeing off the dog from next door who decided to jump over my lovely new low brick wall and pee on the back step for the fun of it.'

'Oh dear,' said Charlotte. 'Was that the first time he's done it?'

'It's a she and no, it isn't the first time. But it's only been happening since we had the builder in and got rid of the old dilapidated fence. It's such a naughty dog and it chases my three cats for the fun of it, knowing that it makes me cross. But her owner is a lovely man, if a bit careless when it comes to the duties of a pet owner. But then he's a journalist and always busy so we must make allowances.'

The woman looked directly at Charlotte and broke into a warm and friendly smile. 'I am so sorry for going on like this. You must think me quite mad. Shall we start at the top where the rooms to let are?'

'Why not?' said Charlotte. 'I like your house. It's got a homely feel to it.'

'Has it? How sweet of you to say so.' Petusha, who had dark hair cut into a kind of scruffy version of the urchin style, said, 'You're a natural blonde, aren't you?'

'Yes,' said Charlotte, wondering why she would ask such a thing. 'I used to hate it when I was small. Mum used to say that the angels forgot to add a bit of colour when they were making me. But I like it now.'

'I should think you do. I've friends who pay a fortune to arrive at what you were born with. How funny that you should have hated it as a child. So many would die to have hair like yours. White blonde is very much in vogue.' Floating up the staircase and leading the way, Petusha gave a running commentary on the area as if time could not be wasted with silences. Following her, Charlotte couldn't help smiling. She had taken an instant liking to this off-the-wall lady, who was wearing a dark red and inky blue striped mini-dress and thick black tights, with slingback shoes that had lavatory-pan heels. Even though she was from a totally different class, Charlotte felt at ease in her house and in her company. She wasn't in the least bit snooty or snobbish.

When they reached the attic flat at the top of the three-storeyed house, they paused for breath then entered a very spacious room with a high ceiling, that was divided by a large framed and beautiful antique silk screen. In the sitting area was an old-fashioned red and gold damask sofa with two matching armchairs either side, set around a coffee table and facing a carved pine fireplace inset with patterned tiles and a small but ornate black grate. Behind the silk screen, which ran the full width of the room, was an old-fashioned double brass bed and a large Victorian pine wardrobe. Off the sitting room there was a short narrow passageway with just enough space to swing a cat. This area led to a small kitchen. The bathroom, Charlotte learned, was off the landing and was to be shared by herself and another tenant, a South African called Mary.

Once they had done the lightning tour the landlady discreetly studied Charlotte's expression and then said, 'What do you think?' She tipped her head to one side and smiled while she waited. 'Is it the sort of place that you were looking for? I've only let it once before and that was to a cousin who was here for several years. He's just bought himself a flat in Battersea close to where he works, which is why you're here of course.' She smiled.

'I think it's lovely,' said Charlotte, pausing to take it all in. Then, just as she was about to ask about house rules and whether or not her parents could stay for a weekend now and then, or whether she was allowed to have a friend stay overnight, the sound of the doorbell could be heard.

'Oh dear . . . I think we are going to be descended upon,' murmured Petusha, looking at her pretty gold wristwatch. 'I'm expecting some friends, but I thought I had at least half an hour to spare. Of course it might not be them.' She waited to see if whomever it was that had rung the bell was going to go away or try again. When the sound rang through the house again she chuckled. 'It *is* my friends, and one of them is clearly enjoying the finger on the bell bit. Please do excuse me while I rush down to let them in.'

'Of course,' said Charlotte. 'I'm fine.'

Turning away gracefully, Petusha was out of the room and on her way down to the ground floor while calling out in a kind of sing-song voice, 'I'm coming! I'm coming!'

Pleased to have the opportunity to be by herself and quietly check out the kitchen, and the bathroom on the landing, Charlotte felt a wave of excitement at the thought of having a place of her own like this. She quite fancied herself living in this private place at the top of the house where she could look out on the world and all of the people that passed by. She glanced out of the window and down at the pavement to see a gaggle of folk in their late twenties or early thirties talking and laughing together. They, similar to the lady who owned the house, were dressed differently from the people that Charlotte mixed with or knew. A completely different set altogether, quite trendy and a touch arty. She had in fact walked into the realm of someone who had fashionable friends.

Having seen as much as she needed of the attic flat, she wandered downstairs and met Petusha halfway. She could see that the woman was a touch flustered. 'I'm awfully sorry to have left you by yourself,' she said. 'You must think me terribly rude, but some of my chums have arrived and—'

'It's all right,' said Charlotte. 'I've seen all I needed to see. And I love the rooms.

'Do you really? Oh well, isn't that marvellous. Do come and meet my chums – we're having a little soirée in the kitchen. They're mostly actors, I fear, so they do tend to be a little flamboyant, which can be taken the wrong way. But they're all very nice beneath the guise.'

'That's okay,' said Charlotte. 'I might be up from the

country but I was born and bred in the East End so I'm used to oddballs.'

'Oh.' Petusha broke in her lovely smile again. 'What a marvellous description. I shall use that myself from now on. Oddballs.' She giggled with delight. 'It sounds quite rude and yet flatteringly eccentric. Depending, of course, on one's wicked mind. I shall tell them what you said.'

'I'd rather you didn't,' said Charlotte. 'At least not while I'm here. Say what you want once I've gone.'

'Oh, darling girl, I was *teasing* you. Of course I wouldn't repeat it. Please do come and say hello.'

'Oh no, thank you, but I won't intrude.' Charlotte was now beginning to feel as if she was being drawn into a cradle of humanity where she didn't belong. She did like the flat though.

Trailing behind Petusha, she said, 'If it's all right with you, I could phone from my grandparents' house later on, once I've talked it over with them. That's where I'll be staying tonight. At their house in Bromley by Bow.'

'Yes, of course you may phone,' said Petusha, waving an elegant hand as she went. 'Whatever you think is right and proper. We don't want to offend your grand-parents.'

Once they reached the ground floor Petusha turned to Charlotte, slipped an arm around her slim waist and, smiling, said, 'Oh, come on – come and meet everyone.'

Having little choice other than to go with the flow, Charlotte drifted into the entrance of the kitchen-cum-dining room, with double doors that opened out to the walled garden. It was clear that this woman, who was

Charlotte's potential landlady, was oblivious to what she had been trying to get across: that she had seen enough and wanted to go, because Petusha was calling her friends in from the back garden to come in and say hello. Feeling embarrassed, her cheeks burning, Charlotte wished that she had stood her ground and left once she had reached the bottom of the stairs.

The guests who were now coming into the kitchen consisted of three very attractive men, dressed expensive-casual, and two women who were looking at her and smiling graciously – no doubt wondering where she was from. Coming towards her with a smile on his lips and a kind of expression of mutual understanding as if she were one of them, a young man in his mid-twenties asked if she would like a cold drink or a cup of tea. This *almost* put Charlotte at ease. She told him that she would prefer a cold drink, which she had spotted on the big old-fashioned pine table. There stood a beautiful large cut-glass jug filled with freshly squeezed orange juice, melting ice cubes and bits of sliced lemon and cut up strawberries.

'I feel as if I might have seen you somewhere before,' said the young, attractive guy, who was wearing a psychedelic cravat, white shirt, grey slacks and navy blazer. 'Or is that too much of a cliché these days?' He held out a limp hand. 'The name's David.'

'I doubt you will have seen my face before,' Charlotte replied, 'but I think I might have seen you on the box?'

'And?'

'And what?'

'Did you enjoy my show?'

'I can't remember.' She shrugged apologetically.

'Oh.' He scratched the back of his neck. 'Fair enough, I suppose. My own fault for being so bloody vain as to ask.'

Before she had a chance to answer him another good-looking young man came up to join them. 'Well, *hello* . . . and *who* have we here?'

'The name's Charlotte,' she said.

'Well *hello*, Charlotte. I'm Bertie the bit-part actor. Not famous like one or two of the others here that I could mention, but who gives a monkey's toss?' He gave her the once-over and showed his approval with a raise of an eyebrow. 'So, sweet child, might I have seen you before today . . . and if not, might I see you tomorrow? I take it that you've come to look at the room with a view?'

'I've come to look at the *apartment*, yes, and no, you won't see me tomorrow. I'll be on the train back to Bridgeford,' said Charlotte, cutting to the chase. 'I'm born and bred East End and my family moved to Norfolk in 1959 when I was thirteen, so I don't think that our paths would have crossed.'

'Really? How interesting. And how long have you been living in the outback of dreary Norfolk?'

'Five years.' Charlotte wanted to tell him to mind his own business but kept her cool.

'Which makes you . . . *eighteen*. So tell me: before you turned into a beautiful swan did you visit Norwich or Bury St Edmunds as a child, to see pantomimes at Christmas?'

'No. I was thirteen when we went to East Anglia. That's a little bit old to be taken to see a panto with the parents.'

'Is it *really*?' he said, shaking his head. 'How times do change.'

'Were you in the pantos in the Theatre Royal then?' Charlotte felt sure that he must have been or he wouldn't have mentioned it.

'Oh, one or two . . .' he said, floating a hand. 'Lovely little theatre. Quaint little towns. I was put on the stage as a boy, you know. It's what Mother wanted, and I have been on it ever since. Well, on and off. How I *longed* to serve in a shop for all of those years and now of course it's too late. I shall be forty next birthday, alas.' He looked slyly at her, inviting her to express surprise at his age.

But Charlotte, not used to actors, didn't take the bite. Really and truly, all that she wanted to do now was to drink her drink and take a look at the garden that she would be sharing – if she decided to live in the house. She also wanted to stroll around the area to see if it suited her before she headed for the next flat in Lavender Square, Stepney Green – her old home ground in the East End.

Finishing her drink, she excused herself and then went out to inspect the garden, politely chatting back to those who chatted to her. They all seemed to want to know when she was going to move in with Petusha. Ready to leave, she told the woman who might end up being her landlady that she had another flat to see before she returned to Bridgeford. She then thanked her for her hospitality and left them to it. She wanted to be out of the place and back in her roots with her own kind. People who didn't tend to go on about Mary Quant clothes, and fashionable boutiques like Biba in posh Kensington. She was an ordinary girl who had no wish to link arms with the famous, even though some shared her working-class roots. Both Twiggy and Jean Shrimpton had been name-dropped by another of her potential landlady's chums who was clearly one of the small group of highly successful photographers. He was also someone who had subtly dropped in that he often worked with rock stars as well as aristocrats. All in all it had been an eye-opener, and one that Charlotte would not forget.

Chapter Nine

Charlotte stepped out of Stepney Green underground station, happy to be back on home ground again. She could almost smell the old days as she went back in her childhood – a time from which she had never quite been able to cut herself free. She was a little early for her second flat viewing, so could afford to take a nice easy stroll with no rush, and this was what she wanted. She soaked up the atmosphere of familiar surroundings, which hadn't changed even though there were far more people about now than when she had lived a stone's throw away. She made her way through the narrow back streets towards Lavender Square and the grand towering terraced house that faced a beautiful arts and crafts building. She felt a surge of nostalgia for the days when she had played in this area, and immediately knew that this was where she wanted to live – where she belonged.

She found the house that could possibly become her home and studied it from the opposite side of the open-gated green. This was a spot where she and Nathan had often gone together as children, and later on when almost into their teens. They had sat there together now and then, discussing the ways of the world, guessing at what might be their future and whether they would be living in this neck of the woods or elsewhere. The old-fashioned square was enclosed on all four sides by ornate black railings, and hedged with established trees. The smoothly worn slate paving stones still had the same wild flowers and weeds growing through the cracks and, to her joy, the four wooden benches were still there. Secured to the old paving stones with heavy bolts, and now weathered and bent with age, they were a sight for sore eyes. Charlotte felt thoroughly at home. She *was* at home. She was back in a world that was familiar to her in every way.

This lovely corner of London also served as an enchanting home for the lady who owned the house with the flat to let. Isabelle Braintree, an agile and elegant woman in her early sixties, lived on the second floor in her large apartment, and on pleasant days such as this would sometimes sit for an hour or so on one of the benches in the garden square. It was an oasis to her, as it was to many others, even though she had her own spacious private gardens to the rear of her property. In the main, Isabelle liked the square because she always seemed to find someone there who was interesting to talk to. This well-bred intelligent woman was in fact writing her diaries to include the recent history of the local people and the area. She intended to self-publish a dozen copies as a record for her family.

The woman had seen many changes taking place over the years and, as far as she was concerned, it wouldn't take a genius to see that by the turn of the next century, the millennium, this little section of old London would look quite different. The East End was close to the City when all was said and done. Charlotte's potential landlady had felt for quite some time that the community would have a different atmosphere by then, even though the historic houses would remain. In her opinion, old London town had for decades been, and still was, spreading outwards to the very edges of suburbia. Small oases such as gardens fenced in by old-fashioned railings might one day be a thing of the past.

Of course, she had no idea that the girl who was coming to view the flat had also once sat in this square, enjoying a bag of piping-hot chips purchased from a nearby fish and chip shop. This little tucked-away place had always been a favourite of the local people, and the sad thing for Charlotte was that the fish and chip shop was now boarded up with a sign informing customers that it would soon be another of a chain of betting shops. This section of the old East End had, a century or so ago, been a mix of the downtrodden and the affluent. A place where the well heeled had private town houses that they came to from their country residences during the fashionable party seasons. Charlotte had not been that interested in local history when she was at school, but now the idea of living in one of the elegant period terraced houses sent a thrill down her spine and brought a smile to her face. It all seemed like a glorious dream. She wondered what the woman whom she had spoken to on the telephone looked like. Her only concern was that she sounded quite posh, posh but friendly. Knowing that she was ten minutes early, she slipped in through the open gate of this little piece of paradise and sat on a bench to soak all of this in before she went to view the flat, unaware that she was being observed by a tenant at the top of the house.

Sitting by her window in the house, her thick black hair highlighted by a few natural silver-grey streaks, the forty-five-year-old woman with lovely dark blue penetrating eyes was indeed observing Charlotte, who, she felt sure, must be the potential new tenant who was due to view. Normally Wendy would have tried to work out what sort of a girl she was by her demeanour, but her mind was filled with the past, recalling times when she had caught the attention of handsome young men who she would have once thoroughly enjoyed having chase her. This was before she had married the man of her dreams who had once loved her deeply, but had left her to run away with his lover and broken her heart. Even now, Wendy believed that he would come in search of her one day. Which was why she would sit by her long sash window and watch out for him every so often. Today, having taken time off work, she was sipping hot lemon juice and waiting for the Aspros that she had swallowed to take effect. She had a bad cold and another of her headaches, but was trying to stay alert because she didn't want to fall asleep for hours on end and possibly miss *Crossroads*, the new television programme that she loved. Comfortable in her self-contained one-bedroom flat up at the top of the house, Wendy was quite content to live alone in what she saw as a serene environment, and had been living this way for almost seven years.

Glancing down at Charlotte, she felt sure this was indeed the girl her landlady was expecting. She hoped so. She liked the look of her and would convey this to her landlady once the viewing was over – should she be correct in guessing who she was, of course.

On the surface, Wendy appeared to be a bit of a loner, and gave little away as to her past life. It amused her to think that her landlady imagined her to be the sort of person who might sleep with a gun under her pillow in case a masked burglar found his way into her flat one dark night. She knew that she was seen as a bit of a recluse, but the truth of the matter was that she had got into the habit of being by herself for most of the time and quite liked it.

Employed at a rather nice book shop in Whitechapel, where she was known as friendly and helpful, this woman wished for little else other than a particular person to re-enter her life. She liked routine, and part of hers was to sit by her window and watch the world go by as well as keeping a lookout for the husband who she hoped would come in search of her. To anyone else, hers would appear a sad and sorry life but Wendy had her memories of happier times – times before her husband had packed all of his clothes into their matching leather suitcases while she had been out shopping for presents one white Christmas. On her return she found that he had gone without a trace. At that point in her life, the handsome couple had been living in Palmers Green, in a lovely, self-contained spacious apartment with a small balcony that overlooked a children's park.

All that her husband had left behind were serious debts. She had hated him with a vengeance at first but then, after a time, began to forgive and forget his bad behaviour. She had let their families know where she was now living, with instructions to give him the address should he ever deign to show his face. Whether she would take him back or not should he come in search of her she couldn't say, but she did want to see him again. She wanted an explanation and an apology. After all, she had now forfeited seven years of her life waiting for him.

From her viewing place Wendy could still see Charlotte, who was now standing on the pavement on the opposite side of the hedged-in green, looking up at this slightly faded grand house. Wendy now felt sure that this was the person who had come to view the vacant flat on the floor below her own – the girl who, the landlady had told her, was coming down from Bridgeford in Norfolk. She thought that the girl looked as if she would fit in. She reminded her of a little lamb wandering around nervously as if a fox was about to pounce. Even from the distance of her window Wendy thought that she could detect apprehension and joy rolled into one. The poor soul also looked a touch on the vulnerable side, which to her mind was no bad thing. She thought that those who appeared vulnerable were actually those who, beneath the surface, were stable; it was the cocksure who were insecure. Whatever the case, she felt that her landlady would like this girl. She had been worried about the medical students from the London hospital that had been coming and going for two or three weeks, all of whom had looked as if they had been smoking marijuana. None of this mattered in any case because none of the students had ticked the boxes that her landlady had set out on a piece of paper, and given a copy to Wendy, which she kept taped to the inside of a kitchen cupboard door. The list was short: *Single person; Full-time employment; If at college then contracts to be signed by parent or guardian*.

She continued to study Charlotte who was now slowly walking around the outside of the fenced green to the wide steps leading up to the entrance of this house. Once she was out of view, the sound of the old-fashioned bell-pull resounded through the building and could be heard by all, except for the tenant in the basement flat, which had a bell of its own. Getting up from her chair by the window, Wendy stole to her front door and opened it just enough to ease herself out and creep onto the landing where she could eaves-drop unnoticed. She had to be mindful of the creaking hinges of her door, hinges that had never been replaced because they weren't broken. This wasn't ideal because, of course, a creaking door goes on for ever . . . but at least the landlady's son, Donald, did oil the hinges now and then.

Wendy was a little hard of hearing, so when her landlady raised her voice to her son when calling from her flat to his, she only heard it as someone speaking normally. The same went for when Donald shouted down to his mother. And the hindrance of her slight deafness was also a help when it came to little annoy-ances that would drive those with excellent hearing quite mad. But the old louvred shutters on her windows that rattled in the draught she could just hear. Apart from such minor irritations, Wendy was quite content and liked to be in touch with all that was going on in the house so as to keep her mind tick-tocking.

The most important thing was for her to know what was happening at the heart of her realm . . . Which was why she tended to eavesdrop now and then. When she first moved in to this house she had little inclination to go out unless she had to. But now, after dinner, she would rest a while and after supper walk almost a mile. She liked to fill her free time as best she could, and listening in the passageway now and then to the mix of people who came and went had become a rather interesting pastime. Her policy was to believe little of what she heard and only half of what she saw – and in her elevated position at the top of the house, she considered herself to be a bit of an eagle. Proud and still, listening to every sound within and watching every move without.

The eagle had always fascinated her ever since she had seen one in a film that her father took her to when she was a child – many decades past. She could remember what her daddy had said when she asked if the bird with the big claws would ever pick up a kitten and fly away with it. His reply had been simple but poignant, and had left her in awe of the feathered friend until she was old enough to know better. He had told her that eagles didn't bother with pint-size, and from this she had understood that he meant they took something more worthwhile to eat – such as a little girl. This fantasy had caused her to have childish wonderland dreams on and off until she grew up.

Now, discreetly hidden on the landing and listening by the stairwell, Wendy felt no guilt at eavesdropping because, since she was going to have to share the common parts with whoever came to live in the house, she felt that she had every right to pass judgement. Or at least be part of the jury, even if she couldn't be the judge as to who should move in to the vacant flat below and who shouldn't. This didn't mean that she didn't trust her landlady's opinion when it came to character – the woman had her own good name and welfare to think of, and had said to her on more than one occasion that she felt it better to live alongside a good kind of a person than a person of good kind. Wendy thought this was very admirable.

Opening the door to Charlotte, Isabelle Braintree was pleased at what she saw. A nice ordinary girl with an intelligent face. 'You must be Charlotte,' she said and smiled. 'Do please come in.'

'Thank you,' said Charlotte. 'You must be Mrs Braintree.'

'Yes, I am.'

Immediately at ease as she stepped into the elegant, generously proportioned entrance hall, Charlotte felt a warm glow inside and knew that her cheeks were going pink. 'This is a lovely house,' she said.

'Yes,' said the gracious Isabelle, 'it is. I've always thought so. I've always loved it. Now then, you've come such a long way . . . would you like to take off your coat and have a nice cup of tea before you view the flat? Or coffee if you would prefer it?'

'No, I'm fine thank you. I stopped in a café and had some lunch soon after I had seen the first flat to let. In Islington.' Charlotte was feeling more comfortable by the minute.

'Goodness, you have been busy.' Isabelle closed the door behind her guest and led the way up the wide staircase to the second floor. 'I trust you're not going back to Norfolk today? That would be quite a lot to fit in.'

'No,' said Charlotte. 'I'm staying with my grandparents overnight. They live in Bromley by Bow.'

'Oh well, that's just a bus stop or two away.' Stopping at a cream-painted panelled door bearing the polished brass number three, Mrs Braintree pushed the key into the lock and then turned the lovely Georgian brass handle. 'I did open the windows an hour or so ago so the rooms should be nicely aired.' She then stood aside and gestured gracefully. 'Please do go in and feel free to look around by yourself. I always think it unnecessary to have everything pointed out.'

Taken aback by this, Charlotte said, 'I'd rather you did show me around. It wouldn't feel right. This is your flat, after all.'

Mrs Braintree smiled warmly. 'What a lovely thing to say. I do hope you're going to like it.' She then led the way, clearly proud of the room they had entered, a spacious sitting room with a high ceiling, pretty cornices, and a lovely pine fireplace set with coal and with a brass poker on a hook next to it.

The room was almost floodlit by the early afternoon sun coming in through the long sash windows and

Charlotte had to pinch her lips together and force herself not to shed a tear of joy. She looked around the room and then at Mrs Braintree. 'I love it,' she said. 'It feels so homely and yet it's so elegant. I really, really love it.'

'Oh I am pleased!' The landlady clasped her hands together, a radiant smile on her face. 'Now then . . . if you would like to open that door you will find the bedroom, and off the bedroom you will find a shower cubicle. And that other door opens to a little kitchen. And if you were to take the flat but prefer to soak in the tub you will find a door into a small bathroom for your sole use is just outside on the landing.'

There really was no more to be said. Charlotte was by the window now and looking down at the square that had been such an important part of her childhood. 'I presume that the rent is a month in advance,' she said. 'And I think that my granddad said that there will be a deposit to pay?'

'One month's rent in advance will be absolutely fine, if you feel that you can run to it. I expect you'll be arranging interviews for a position during your first week here so you won't be having any salary to kick off with so—'

'No, I wouldn't take the flat unless I've already been accepted for the position in the council offices. The interview is lined up for tomorrow morning. I'll fit that in before I catch my train back home.'

'My word, you are organised for someone so young.'

'I'm eighteen,' said Charlotte. 'I thought that was quite adult.'

'Well, of course it is, but to someone of my age it seems young to be setting out on your own and paying your way.'

'My parents are going to let me have the month's rent in advance to give me a clean start. I'm an only child so they do worry about me.'

'I'm sure they must. And luckily we do have a spare room in this house for guests. So if all goes to plan and they wanted to come and visit you now and again I'm sure we could accommodate them.'

'It gets better and better,' said Charlotte, laughing delightedly. 'Although, between you and me, I am really trying to be independent so I won't encourage them. They could stay at my grandparents' house. It's what they usually do when we come down to visit our old home ground.'

'Well . . . am I to take it then that you would like to think seriously about living in this house?' Isabelle smiled.

'Definitely. I don't even have to think about it. I just know I would be very happy here. It's exactly what I could have wished for.'

'Marvellous, I am pleased. Very happy. Now why don't we go into my apartment and have a nice refreshing hot or cold drink. I'm sure you must be ready for one?'

'I am now, thank you. Then I must be on my way to tell my grandparents the good news. I'm really happy about this. I couldn't have wished for a better place to live that's part of my roots.'

The ladies of different generations and walks of life

went down the stairs as if they had known each other for years. Following the warm and graceful lady of the house into her own apartment, Charlotte gasped at what she saw. It was stunning. It was both spacious and homely, jam-packed with antique furniture that was being used and not just for show. Drifting towards the wide-open French doors that led out into the back gardens she could hardly believe her eyes. She felt as if she were in another world, far from the East End.

'On warm sunny days you might enjoy sitting in the back garden,' said Isabelle, waving a graceful hand. 'It's very pretty in all four seasons. Of course neither I nor my tenant Wendy, who lives at top of the house, ever remove any of our top clothing to sunbathe. I've always thought that swimming costumes or two-piece sunsuits are best kept for the beach.' She looked sideways at Charlotte, hoping to get an important message across. 'We have, after all, to consider the two men who live under the same roof as we ladies. There is one gentle-man, a tenant, in the basement, and my son Donald lives on the first floor.'

'It wouldn't be right in any case. Not in this setting.' Charlotte sighed. 'It's so special . . . it's beautiful.'

'Oh, I'm so pleased you agree,' said Isabelle.

Through the French doors, Charlotte saw a raised patio where there was a table with an old-fashioned sun shade over it and four garden chairs. Beyond this was the spacious garden that stretched back to an old and high red-brick wall. 'It must be lovely sitting out there in the quiet and reading,' said Charlotte, totally captivated. 'Especially when the sun's setting. It must be beautiful then.'

'It is, and since it's a shared garden you shall have every right to sit out there whenever you choose. I leave the back door in the hall unlocked during the daytime so that my tenants may go down the steps and into the garden. And I lock it at nine in the evenings unless something special is happening out there. We sometimes have a house barbecue evening when Donald takes over the cooking, which is rather nice. Of course we all chip in to a kitty for the meat and salad and so on.'

Charlotte looked from the grounds to her prospective landlady and smiled. 'It sounds to me as if living in this house is like being in paradise.'

'Well, that's very sweet of you to say so . . . and in a way you're right. We all seem to rub along together quite nicely. Not in and out of each other's lives, but not cool and distant either.'

'It is such a beautiful garden,' said Charlotte, gazing out. 'Perfect for a barbecue. I would love to join in that kind of a thing.'

'Good. And you know you could always come and go if you felt that you wanted to sit by yourself out there to read a book and so on. I should hate to think of you inside the apartment all of the time. So – there we are then. You've seen all there is to see. Can you see yourself living here?'

'I can. It feels right. As if it was meant to be.'

'Good.' The woman beamed. 'I *am* pleased. And you may move in whenever you wish and the sooner the better. I think that rooms left empty for too long tend to get a sad and lonely feel about them.'

Her face now glowing, Charlotte said, 'Thank you again. I've made my decision. And I would love to live here.'

'Oh I *am* pleased,' said Isabelle again. 'Now, would you like to meet Wendy before you go? She'll be your neighbour. She lives at the top of the house, in the flat above the one that's vacant. She's at home today, nursing a dreadful cold, so we would have to keep at arm's length. I can't introduce you to my son who lives on the first floor because he's out at the moment. And the young man in the basement flat, although he is perfectly charming, isn't the sort who would want to meet a potential neighbour. He's quite a loner but does join us for drinks on the terrace very occasionally.'

'To be honest with you? I think I would prefer not to meet anyone yet. It's all been a bit much for me.' Charlotte smiled. 'I think I need to get to my grand-parents' house and tell them about it. Get it off my chest before it bursts.'

'Well, of course you must. But do just let me write down my telephone number.'

'But I've already got it . . .'

'Oh, of course you have. How silly of me.' Isabelle relaxed her shoulders and smiled warmly at Charlotte. 'Do please forgive me. I promise that I shan't mother-hen you once you move in. I really do.'

'Oh, what a shame.' Charlotte giggled. 'I think I'll need every bit of mother-henning once I've made the break from my parents. And you've got your son living under the same roof so you never know, a big brother figure might be here for me as well.'

'Oh, I'm not so sure about that. Donald is a bit of a loner too. A touch of an oddity, in fact. But then that's more interesting in a way than run-of-the-mill.' With that, Isabelle walked with Charlotte to the front door of what was to be her new home and they said their farewells, each of them sensing that they could be close friends even though the difference in their ages would easily place them as mother and daughter.

Five minutes later, with her head in the clouds and feeling as if she was in her seventh heaven, Charlotte boarded a red bus for the first time in ages. Once in a seat by the window she felt more and more at home – almost as if she had never left the East End in the first place. She watched the comings and goings that had once been a major part of her world and couldn't wait to tell her Gran and Granddad about the flat.

Chapter Ten

'Stone the crows, look at the state of your face!' Charlotte's granddad Johnny leaned his skinny body back and roared with laughter. 'It's got success written all over it!'

'Oh, shut up, Granddad, and let me in. I'm dog-tired.'

'I should fink you would be, mutt,' he said, standing to one side. 'What wiv all the travelling. You must feel like a stray that's bin out all of the day and all of the night.'

Passing him, she sniffed discreetly and, as expected, the fumes from his breath matched the redness of his cheeks and the glassy look in his warm hazel eyes. 'Been on the beer already, Granddad?' she said a touch teasingly.

'Beer? At this time of late afternoon? Course not! I've been swigging straight from a bottle of rum.'

'Many a true word spoken in jest,' she said, as she strode through the passage to the kitchen-diner. This was at the back of the house and where her gran was sitting in her tall-backed chair with the *Daily Mirror* open in front of her. She was doing the crossword puzzle. Glancing up over her bifocals that were held together with a sticking plaster on one side, she gave

Charlotte an all-knowing scolding look for mentioning Johnny's drinking habit. It wasn't the first time.

'So what's brought this cockiness about then?' said Nell, doing her best not to smile just yet. 'You look like someone who lost a penny and found a pound. And your granddad 'ad a pint with 'is bubble and squeak. So no more of your sauce.'

'I was only joking, Nan. And as for me being happy . . . I've found a flat.'

'Oh, 'ave you now? And where's your boyfriend? Or are you too ashamed of our humble home to 'ave fetched 'im with yer?'

'Boyfriend, Gran?' said Charlotte as she flopped down into another of the kitchen chairs. 'Now let me see . . . who could you possibly mean? Not Nathan, that's for sure, or you would have spoken his name. You did after all grow up living beside 'is granny in the back and beyond of Whitechapel in slum dwellings once upon a time. Or did I *dream* that you told me all of that?'

'Saucy cow.' Nell then lifted her eyes to her husband who had come into the kitchen, having just nipped into the best room at the front of the house for a spoonful of rum from the bottle. Why he did this in secret was still a mystery to his wife and family because it was as clear as a cucumber to them that he was almost always merrily half-cut. No one minded in the least because he was always so cheerful with it. If asked, he would openly say that he loved his drink and the way it made him feel; that it was a habit he wasn't going to give up while he still earned a wage at the market sweating blood and tears.

'What's she said now then for you to have cause to call 'er saucy?' Johnny winked at his wife and grinned. 'She'd better not 'ave cheeked you, sweetheart. We can't have that.'

Nell raised her eyes and then shook her head slowly. 'Why don't you go out for a nice walk along the Cut? Find one of your mates to talk to.'

'What, and not spend time with my granddaughter who I hardly get to see any more? I don't fink so! I've been looking forward to this day all week.' He looked at Charlotte and smiled. 'I've got a little surprise for you upstairs. I've been busy. I think you are gonna be very pleased. I always said—'

'Oh, for fuck's sake tell 'er what you've done.' Nell raised her eyes to heaven again and shook her head. 'I wouldn't mind it's not yet evening and 'e's tipsy.'

'I am not tipsy, if you don't mind! Not yet I'm not. I've had a celebratory drink that's all. My granddaughter's come *all* the way from *Bridgeford* to see me. Any miserable old sod would drink to that, never mind *me* . . . her flesh and blood.'

'Well, put the kettle on and make your flesh and blood a nice cup of coffee.'

'That would be lovely,' said Charlotte, settled in her chair and easing off her stiletto-heeled shoes.

'Oh. So you're not interested in what your bedroom looks like then? What sort of wallpaper I've put up?'

'Of course I am, but you did send me a square of the

wallpaper with a sample of the paint on the back of it. And I did phone you and say it was lovely.'

Johnny narrowed his eyes, as he looked at her a touch suspiciously. 'No you never.'

'Yes I did.'

'When?'

'The day after it arrived. I can't remember which day it was exactly . . .'

'Ah ha!' Johnny grinned broadly. 'So it's not me who forgets then, is it? It's you, your mother and your gran. I was born with a good memory, me.' He shook his head slowly and then nodded. 'I always came top in class when it was question time.'

Not wishing to get into an argy-bargy over Johnny's terrible memory Charlotte said, 'Well, don't you want to know about the flats I've looked at then, Granddad?'

'Course not!' said Johnny. 'Flats? Who do you think you are? One of them West End girls? You don't wanna live in a flat. Not when you've got that lovely room up there all freshly wallpapered and painted and wiv all mod cons. A lovely little lamp and a gas fire and a two-bar electric fire and all at the flick of a switch or two. And anyway you can't afford to pay rent.'

'Salaries have gone up to match rising prices, Granddad. You should read your Sunday paper more thoroughly. And anyway . . . we've never 'ad it so good is what you've told me more than once.'

'Yeah, but I was talking about the Welfare State and the National Health Service, wasn't I? We all had our doubts in 1948 when it was first established, but now? Now it's *really* kicking in. We're all better off now than what we were. But that's got nuffing to do wiv greedy landlords charging a bomb for flea-pit rooms to live in.'

'Take no notice of him, love,' said Nell. 'What was the flat like, sweetheart?'

'Oh hark at it. All lovey and sweethearts. What are *you* after?'

'Go out for a walk, Johnny, or make a cup of coffee.'

Sighing reluctantly, Johnny set about his chore and switched off from the women's talk and sulked with what he considered to be good reason. It had taken him days, if not weeks, to do that little room up for his granddaughter and she hadn't even wanted to run up there to see it. And his wife had gone on about his drinking in front of her in her own artful way, and now, even though he was making a hot drink for Charlotte, they were acting as if he was invisible. Talk, talk, talking about bloody flats and landladies. And posh landladies at that if all he was hearing was correct. 'I wouldn't mind,' he mumbled, 'but she 'ain't even got a job yet and she's talking about flats. Where's the money gonna come from, that's what I'd like to know. She's got a free room up there and I won't charge a penny for a full breakfast.'

Letting his rambling that he meant them to hear go above their heads, grandmother and grandchild were not only talking about where Charlotte was going to live but also about where her gran had once worked for a couple of months as a scullery maid – in one of the other houses on Lavender Square. Charlotte had not heard this piece of Nell's past before and was fascinated by it. 'So why didn't you stay longer, Gran? It must 'ave

174

been even lovelier when you was young all those years ago.'

'I'm only sixty-four, Charlotte. Same as your grand-dad. That's not old. Anyway . . . I never liked being bossed about and bullied.'

'Bullied? You're not saying that they knocked you about, Nan, are you?'

'With words, Charlotte, not wiv their fists. Had they 'ave done, I would 'ave punched back, make no mis-take. They needed to smell their own backsides that lot. Shit is the same no matter how it's shaped.'

'Oh Nan . . . please.'

'Anyway I did 'ave a bit of a lark there wiv one of the boot boys.' Her eyes now sparkling, a big grin spread across her face. 'We did have some fun in them days. One lad in particular fancied me rotten and he was very popular wiv the other young parlour maids working in the square. Us girls below stairs used to make sand-wiches and homemade lemonade and go fishing wiv the lads down the Cut. I did like that lad – who was in love with me as it happened. I liked him a lot.

'We went to the pictures and then nestled up in the stables that used to be close by. There was always a few bales of fresh hay or straw in there. I'd never enjoyed anything so much in my life. Romance? You younger generation don't know what the word means. I go all tingly just finking about it.' She leaned back in her chair, smiling wistfully as she reminisced, and then murmured to herself, 'It was just as well I wasn't a virgin.'

'See what I mean?' said Johnny. 'See what kind of

talk I 'ave to put up wiv? Now if you were to live wiv us you could set your gran a good example.'

Charlotte laughed. 'Granddad, I am not living here. All right? I'll visit you often but I'm not moving in. Got it?'

'Well . . . you never were one for mincing your words. It suits me, I don't care. Do what you want. I was only trying to 'elp. It took me two weekends non-stop to do that bedroom. Still, there you are. That's life. I did it for a good reason—'

'You did it because I've been nagging you for more than a fucking year to sort out the damp in that spare room and replace the old-fashioned peeling wallpaper. Lazy sod. You should 'ave done it years ago,' said Nell.

Johnny slowly shook his head. 'See what I mean, sweetheart? See how she treats me? It's no wonder I need a little drink now and then.' He went and fetched his bottle of rum from the room and poured a drop out before topping it up with warm water.

'So . . . who's gonna go out and get the fish and chips from the best fish and chip shop in the world then?' Charlotte asked.

'Me, of course,' said Johnny. 'You don't fink that your gran would put 'erself out, do yer? Not while she's got a skivvy like me around. Never mind that I've done a hard morning's work when most people are having fun shopping down the Saturday market.'

'My heart bleeds for you, sweetheart,' said Nell. 'It fucking well pours with blood at times. Sitting on your backside all Saturday afternoon watching the wrestling and boxing on the telly and cheering on your favourites as if you're there in the hall wiv 'em. They'll be calling you Square Eyes Johnny next.'

'See what I mean, Charlotte? She's grown bitter with time. Don't ask me why. I do whatever I can to make 'er 'appy but all I get back is moan, moan, moan.'

'Yeah and pigs fly at night. It's you who do all the groaning when there's nobody around but me to listen to it. It's your fault she don't wanna live with us.'

'Ah . . .' Johnny smiled and his blue eyes lit up. 'That's what this mood's about is it? Why didn't you come out with it in the first place? Tell Charlotte that she should move in wiv us and it's what you've been looking forward to all this time.' He turned to his granddaughter with a pained and worried look. 'It'll break 'er heart you know if you go and move into lodgings instead of—'

'Not lodgings, Granddad. A proper self-contained flat in a fabulous converted period house.'

'I'm sure it's very nice, but how much is it gonna cost you?'

'Four pounds a week plus electricity and gas.'

'Oh. Well, that's not too bad . . . depending on 'ow much you reckon you can pick up a week working in the council offices.'

'Twelve pounds a week if I'm prepared to go in every other Saturday morning, which I am. But I've not even been for the interview yet so let's not get too excited.'

'*How* much?' Johnny could hardly believe it.

'You heard,' said Nell. 'And I think that's very fair money.'

'Fair money? It's a bloody fortune! Stone me blind!

Well, they did say that you post-war children would benefit from our sufferings, and now a girl of your age can earn twelve pounds a week. What we 'ad to get by on don't bear finking about.' He looked across to Charlotte and there was a hint of a tear in his eye as well as pride in his expression. 'Our little granddaughter earning all that money. Well, I might just buy you a bottle of cider to go with your fish and chips to celebrate, Charlotte, love. Well done. And I mean that. Hand on heart.'

'She hasn't got the job yet, you silly old sod. But you can still buy the cider. And once you're in the fish and chip shop ask the fryer straight away to put in a bit of fresh haddock each for the three of us. I don't want any of that drained and dried-up muck.'

'You've never ever had anyfing other than fresh out of the fryer.'

'Exactly. So don't break the habit so that you can be there and back sooner rather than later so as not to miss the wresting on the telly. I saw you looking at the *Radio Times*.'

Clearing his throat and rolling his eyes, Johnny left the room grumbling under his breath.

'You're getting worse, Nan. Always picking on Granddad.'

'He loves it, sweetheart. It's when I give him the silent act that he gets all sorry for 'imself. I know 'ow to play the silly old sod, don't you worry.'

Charlotte chuckled as she tried to imagine herself living with her grandparents, and wondered if it would be more fun than living in the grand house in a flat all by herself. A touch confused, she strolled out of the room telling Nell that she was going to have a look at her granddad's handiwork. Once alone, her nan smiled and then winked to herself. She had deliberately got the banter going between her and her husband because she knew how to amuse her Charlotte. She wasn't certain that she wouldn't try out the flat, but she reckoned that she wouldn't last more than three months coping by herself. And if not, at least she was only a bus ride away. Nell was more than happy.

A little later on that evening, Isabelle was listening to her favourite Johann Strauss record, 'The Blue Danube', while looking through her family photograph album as she often liked to do. On this occasion though, she had Charlotte on her mind and knew instantly that they were going to become good friends. She had immediately warmed to the girl the moment that she had looked into that lovely honest face. She knew that Charlotte, as her tenant, was going to be part of her world. And not only that, but she had been reminded of herself when she had been the same age. When she had also stepped out into the wide world of independence.

She hadn't been quite so brave as to go out looking for a flat in London for herself at Charlotte's age, but she had gone on a trip to Europe – Paris, Rome and Berlin, with her parents just after her eighteenth birthday and, instead of coming back to England after three weeks, had stayed on to study French in Paris for some months. Once back in Britain, Isabelle, young, slim and beautiful, had adored living in this, her family's town house, while they were at home in Suffolk. She loved the house so much that when she married Donald's father, when she was twenty-five, her parents signed it over as a wedding gift. Sadly, her beloved husband, a commanding officer in His Majesty's army, who had been stationed abroad during the war, was killed in action, leaving her to bring up their son alone. Donald had once been her torch in the dark and now she felt that she was his. Her son was not ill or lacking intelligence, but he wasn't an ordinary average young man who wanted to settle down with a family of his own. He had never had a girlfriend, neither had he been attracted to his own sex. He simply didn't seem to need a comforting partner. He had his work as assistant librarian at the local library and he had his hobbies. It was enough. He was content and so was Isabelle.

Both of them loved this part of London, with its interesting mix of people. They were more than happy to stay put for ever, overlooking the lovely square, provided that there weren't too many changes on the horizon, knocking down old characterful buildings and houses to replace them with skyscrapers, as was being predicted in some of the newspapers. Isabelle's old family residence in the heart of the Suffolk countryside, close to the town of Newmarket and the race courses, had provided her with wonderful happy weekends and short holidays in the past with her husband and their son, and that had been enough. Now the house in the country was let out to a wealthy American family who needed a base in England.

Isabella had no idea why Charlotte had had such an impact on her other than, for some strange reason, she reminded her of her younger self. She had come from a wealthier background of course, and she had inherited properties along the way. She was a successful landlady with a handsome income from the house in the country and enough coming in from her tenants here in the square. This suited her very nicely and she felt comfortable with it. But more importantly, she liked this new tenant called Charlotte. She liked her a lot.

Chapter Eleven

That night, having been out with Nathan for a candlelit dinner at the Steak House in Aldgate, which had been wonderfully romantic, Charlotte lay in the single bed in the spare bedroom of her grandparents' two up, two down. Now, realising that the feelings she had for her childhood friend were stronger than she imagined they ever could be, she was worried that she might have let herself get carried away with the romance of it all. Her old friend had been very close to her when they were young it was true, but later on he had led a completely different life in London and had met lots of people of his own age with whom he had things in common. She was now troubled by the possibility that, once he had seen her a few times, he would find her dull compared with the set he now mixed with.

With more and more of these thoughts filling her mind as she tried to imagine the girls he worked with at the theatre, she suddenly smiled as she remembered what Nathan had said to her: '*You'll probably meet and possibly fall in love with more than one man once you're living in London.*' She had been flattered by the remark and, especially, the worried tone in his voice that he had tried to cover. She loved him all the more for it.

And she loved this little terraced house in the quiet

street in Bow, where the fragrance of fresh paint and wallpaper still hung in the air. It was the perfect place and she was in the perfect cosy room to re-live everything, from the time that Nathan turned up on her doorstep in Bridgeford out of the blue, to this very moment. She had seen as much of London as she could take in one day and had loved every minute of it. Now she was more than ready for a good night's sleep, but her thoughts were all over the place and she couldn't wait to see Nathan again. Once back in Bridgeford she was going to have to make do with talking to him over the phone until she returned for good.

She recalled the house and the people in Islington. She would have had Petusha there, but this was not enough. She knew that she didn't belong there and that she would not fit in with the bohemian set of people who were, from what she had gathered, very much part and parcel of that little pocket of the world. A world that she too would have had to be part of should she have taken the flat.

The lovely lady who owned the house that had been converted into four apartments in Stepney, however, she had felt at one with. Even though they were from different backgrounds it hadn't seemed to matter one iota. And to live in a flat that overlooked her favourite square, that held some of her most precious childhood memories, was more than she could have wished for. She had felt a genuine and immediate bond with Isabelle Braintree, and she did love the flat. The woman had a natural mothering persona, and Charlotte knew from gut instinct that Isabelle had taken to her too. She could easily picture herself living in the house, coming and going, and not being drawn into anyone else's world in the way that she might have had to if she'd chosen the flat in north London. So much had happened in such a short space of time that she was already seeing Bridgeford as a retreat rather than a place to live and work. Living in London and having weekend breaks by the river with her parents would be a perfect lifestyle.

Her thoughts flying from one thing to another, the tormentor of old, Kenny, drifted into her mind. She pictured the way he had looked at her when they had been on the train . . . as if they were old buddies. But she was older now and so was he, and the fear that she had once held when it came to him had dissipated. She didn't care if she bumped into him while living in the same area. She was no longer scared of someone who she saw as a coward who picked on those weaker than he was. She no longer loathed him – she simply didn't care.

He had come across as a reformed character on the train and looked like an ordinary guy, but she had wondered if this was partly because his once bright ginger hair had turned into a soft brownish auburn and softened his features. He had seemed capable of all things evil in the early days and had been a bastard when it came to Nathan . . . but that was all in the past. Nathan had turned into someone who could stand up for himself and would throw a good punch if the need were to arise. Snug and warm in her bed, thinking of Nathan, she couldn't believe that her lonely life was turning around almost overnight. As long as she came up to scratch during her interview at the council offices the next day, she would be home and dry.

Feeling hopeful about everything, she turned on her side and curled up ready for a peaceful night's sleep – she was in her grandparents' home and this in itself gave her a warm glow inside. She was happy. And she *was* doing the right thing.

The following morning, after a breakfast of fried eggs, bacon and tomatoes, cooked by her granddad, Charlotte set off, looking very smart in her black and white dogtooth-patterned jacket and skirt. As she made her way to the interview for the post of copy typist and clerk's assistant, she knew that she was going to have to prove that she could live up to the letter she had sent. She had written to say that she had a touch-typing speed of sixty words per minute and a good aptitude for mental arithmetic. As she walked in the warm sunshine towards the bus stop, the butterflies in her tummy began to settle down and she felt less frightened of failure – it was now all in the lap of the gods.

Now that she had had this little taste of being back in her old world, she knew for certain that living in Bridgeford was never going to suit her the way it did her parents. For her that life was over, and Eddie and Rita were going to have to accept it whether they liked it or not. She was not only ready to spread her wings, she was desperate to do so. She couldn't wait to move into the fabulous flat in Lavender Square, or stroll through all of the back turnings that were so familiar and still felt like home. Apart from her own feelings, she knew that her grandparents were overjoyed to have her back in the fold again and living just a bus ride away.

While all of these thoughts were going through Charlotte's mind, Nell and Johnny were sitting around the pale primrose, Formica-topped table in their kitchen. They were enjoying a fresh pot of tea and coming to terms with the disappointment of not having Charlotte under their roof permanently and making a fuss of her.

'We've gotta learn to let 'er go, Nell,' said Johnny, himself not totally convinced that he could stand by and see Charlotte live in a flat by herself. 'She's not a kid any more. And she's got more sense than you 'ad at 'er age.'

'No, she bloody well 'ain't. Going for an interview in that black and white suit and looking like a model! That's not what they wanna see. She should 'ave toned it all down a bit. Wore grey and white with a little bit of red popped in. A neckerchief and a pair of summer gloves.'

'Like in the early nineteen-thirties you mean? When you was a beautiful young woman and working as a secretary at the Houndsditch Warehouse?'

'If you like,' said Nell, a touch sniffy. 'But I don't think I was beautiful so much as very smart with my appearance.' Nell gazed out at nothing as she sank deeper into her memories, smiling and nodding as she remembered one or two of her lovers before she met Charlotte's granddad . . . but she kept these thoughts to herself.

'It will be nice to see a bit more of 'er, though, won't it,' said Johnny. 'She can come round for Sunday dinner and we can take a bus to Stepney Green and visit 'er.' He leaned back in his chair and chuckled. 'Our little Charlotte, all independent and living in 'er own place? I bet she don't last a month before she realises where best her bread is buttered. She loves the way I've done that room up, don't she?'

Nell arched one eyebrow and slowly shook her head. 'Yes, Johnny, she does. But don't keep on going on about it. You'll only take the joy away and bore me to death.'

'I don't know why she can't stop for a few days. What difference would it make? She could take a sick note back to work once she's in Bridgeford.'

'She wouldn't do a thing like that. How many more times must I tell yer? That's three times now that you've said that. Not in so many words but you've repeated it one way or another. And in any case, from what I can make out, she'll be back for good in a couple of weeks' time. Two weeks' notice is what she said she had to give at the council offices, and now that she's found 'erself a flat there'll be no stopping 'er.' Nell gazed at the floor and then smiled. 'She's so much like me, that girl. Makes up 'er mind to do something and not even wild horses will stop 'er.'

Johnny didn't think so. To his mind Charlotte was a chip off the old block all right, but from his block and not Nell's. 'Course she's like you,' he said so as to keep her happy. He liked a nice calm atmosphere. 'I swear on my life that you're like two peas in a pod the pair of you.'

Leaning back in her chair and sipping her tea, Nell was dead chuffed to hear him of all people saying this. She thought that he was mostly too argumentative to agree with anything she came out with. 'I'm really looking forward to 'er stopping overnight now and then – just for a change from 'er rented rooms.'

'So am I.' Johnny slowly nodded. 'I hope she comes straight back here after the interview. I don't wanna be on tenterhooks all day long.'

'Course she will. You promised you'd pop out and get pies and mash didn't you? She won't wanna miss that.'

'Did I? Oh well . . . that'll be a good stomach liner for that train journey to the back and beyond. If she wants pie and mash that is. She might not do, she might want to eat at our table and enjoy a bit of your lovely home cooking.'

'We'll see,' said Nell, fed up with him going on and on. 'Leave it be for now. You've given me a fucking headache.'

The job interview took less time than she had imagined and Charlotte, in a kind of a daze, was making her way through the back streets towards the square where she hoped that she would soon be living. She wanted to make sure that her landlady really would keep the flat vacant for a fortnight until she was able to leave her old life behind her. She was so happy that she could hardly stop herself from smiling. She had got through the interview and the typing test with flying colours and was told that the position was hers if she wanted it. The employment contract was going to be put in the post that same day. Now, she was almost bursting with joy as she realised just how happy she felt being back in this neck of the woods, among people who she had grown up with.

Strolling through the back streets, she imagined herself in the Lavender Square flat, with some of her own special bits and pieces from home around her – things such as the table lamp that she always read by at night, a best-liked bedroom chair, and posters of her favourite pop singers the Beatles, the Kinks and the Rolling Stones. She was longing to get settled into the apartment that she already thought of as her own. Arriving at a red telephone kiosk she felt like phoning her grandparents straight away to tell them her good news but decided against it. They would have appreciated the call but she was eighteen years old, no longer a child that couldn't wait to tell them about the gift – which is how she saw the outcome of the interview. That she had been given a gift.

Deep in thought, she found herself at an Italian café before she realised it. This café, close by Stepney Green underground station, had not been open more than six months and it was the aroma of percolating coffee that had drawn in the East End folk as well the Italians who lived in the area. Going inside, she was pleasantly surprised at how warm and friendly it seemed and didn't feel sorry any more that the old-fashioned shoe menders that it had once been had gone for ever. The place was decorated in warm colours and there were cheerful red, green and orange cloths on each of the tables.

Sitting down by the window so that she could watch people going by, Charlotte remembered a model-motion shoe mender, tapping at the heel of a tiny boot in his wooden hand. She wondered what had become of the little attraction that had once been in the window and was adored by all children. She brushed sentimental thoughts aside. She was ready for a hot drink and one of the cigarettes that she liked to have occasionally when her parents weren't around. Once she had given her order to a young and good-looking Italian waiter, she brought back to mind all that had happened at the Stepney council offices. The woman who had showed her around had been so nice to her and the people who were employed there seemed happy in their work. Their smiling faces had meant more to her than anything else. Content in her little world of recollections, it was a jolt when the last person that she expected to see walked through the door. Kenny the bully.

For a moment she wondered if he was shadowing her, but shook off the thought and told herself not to be stupid. The East End was a small place, after all, and he had come down from Norfolk on the same train as her. Of course he would have been heading for this area where he was born and bred. They were in the same pocket of London at the same time, that was all there was to it. She opened the pages of a *Daily Mirror* that someone had left behind and pretended not to have noticed him as she artfully inched her chair by the window around so as to have her back to him. She didn't think he had spotted her, but he had – way before Charlotte had even stepped over the threshold of the café.

Kenny had seen her walking along the Mile End Road and had followed her. He had wanted to know what she was up to, and now he was settling himself down at a small round table for two in a corner of the café. Once in his chosen seat he gazed out at nothing as if he were deep in thought and behaved as if he hadn't seen Charlotte. He looked every bit the contented harmless young man, not someone who was playing a rather sick game of shadowing her to extract a little revenge for the way she had teased him when they were thirteen-year-olds. And he certainly didn't look as if he would harm a fly, let alone that he could be a serial killer . . .

To his mind, Charlotte still had the air of a snob and behaved as if the likes of him were beneath her . . . never mind that she had been the one to hang out with a Jew years back. And Jews, as far as he was concerned, were still the low understrappers. He hadn't forgotten the time when she had sent him on a wild goose chase. The day when he had been made to look stupid in front of his friends when the bitch had told him lies about the Roman Road gang knocking on his mother's front door. He hadn't found this amusing at the time and he couldn't see a funny side to it now. So, as far as he was concerned, he owed her one for having degraded him in front of the lads in his gang. Lads who had respected him. To Kenny, all of this coming together again, first in Bridgeford and now in his own neck of the woods, meant only one thing: fate was dealing him an interesting card to play in his game of to kill or not to kill.

He hadn't been that surprised to see her walking along the Mile End Road like a stuck-up cow because he knew that she had relatives in the area. He hadn't fully intended to follow her in to the café but neither had he intended to trail her for a short while when he disembarked at King's Cross the day before. It just seemed to have happened, but now that he had, it was as if he was in a scene from an Alfred Hitchcock film. He didn't really know, nor did he care, why he had shadowed the silly bitch all the way to the house that she went to view in Islington. He couldn't say that he hadn't been intrigued to know what she was up to. And he couldn't understand why she would want to come back and live in the East End again when her parents were doing all right living by rivers and forests. It didn't sit right with him. And Kenny wanted to know more. He *had* to know more.

Pretending to study the racing pages in his newspaper, he slyly glanced towards Charlotte every now and then, wondering if he should rattle her cage by going politely to her table to ask if he could join her. She could hardly say no, he thought. But then, as he looked around him, he didn't think it such a good idea for him to be seen with her by those in the café since he didn't know how things were going to turn out with this one. Not that it mattered. He hadn't much on today and he liked the thrill of the stalk. He wondered if Charlotte would lead him to her childhood sweetheart.

Nathan the Jew. He wondered what he looked like now. The same as before but older, and with a bigger nose? He smiled at the thought of it.

Once he had ordered himself a cup of frothy coffee from the young Italian waiter he sat back, every bit the relaxed young man, but kept on peering at Charlotte every so often. He was interested to know where she was going next. It would be an extra bonus if she led him to the Jew, the drip who had lived in the same block before his own family moved from one council estate to another just around the corner from where he now sat. He knew that Charlotte had been thick with Nathan from the first year at the junior school when he had come top in the class at spelling, arithmetic and geometry. Kenny's granddad, who had been a Black-shirt before the Second World War, had told his son more than once to keep an eye on all Jews because they were set on running and owning most of the East End, if not the City itself. He told him that in order to do this, Jews would sit huddled over candlelight through the night just so as to work every God-given hour and save every brass farthing.

Uncomfortable to be in the same place as Kenny, and feeling that she was being slyly watched by him, Charlotte wondered if the bastard who she had once hated was going to be a pain in the neck again. Deciding to take the bull by the horns and face him full on, she took a deep breath, picked up her cup of coffee and went over nice and casual and sat at his table. 'So what brings you back into the East End then, Kenny?' she brazenly asked.

Pulling his head back Kenny pretended surprise. He sniffed as he peered at her, and then broke into a sly smile. 'Are you following me, Charlie?'

'I was just gonna ask you the same thing, Kenny.' She returned his smile.

'Was yer? And why would I want to do that? You're surely not still carrying all that shit from when we was kids are yer? It *was* five years ago.'

'And you've turned over a new leaf, have you?' She raised an eyebrow and then sipped her coffee, waiting to see if he could keep up this chummy stance.

'I don't know about that, Charlie, but neither of us are school kids any more, are we? So where do you live and work now? In Bridgeford or back here? Not that I'm overly interested, but we're adults and making conversation comes with age.' He grinned.

'Oh, right . . . well, as for me, I'm the girl that lives nowhere and works there as well.' She wasn't going to give anything away. 'My parents live in Bridgeford, as you must know because I saw you talking to Dad at the station. But the rest of our family lives here in the East End. I'm always popping down by train to see them.'

'Yeah? And there I was finking you'd turned into a country bumpkin. So what are your plans? Are you gonna go back today or stop a bit longer? We could go for a drink tonight in one of the old local pubs if you've got nuffing planned. I feel like I owe you a drink or two because of all the tormenting I did when I was a little bastard back there in the old days.'

She *was* staying over another night and she was going to meet Nathan that evening but she wasn't going to

194

tell him. 'I'm going to spend time with my grandparents and then go back by train first thing tomorrow,' she said, ending it there.

'Ah, that's a shame. Still, maybe another time, eh?' He pulled a business card from his pocket, one of the original fifty that he had got a mate who worked in a stationery store to print up for him. A mate who was an amateur small-time thief as good as he was.

Taking the card that was offered to her, Charlotte read the print beneath his name: Member of the Charity Trust Society. 'Which charity trust would that be, Kenny?'

'Oh, I cover about ten, but in the main I work for Oxfam, the NSPCC, the Aged and the Jewish poor,' he lied.

Silently laughing at him Charlotte slowly shook her head. 'The Jewish poor? You hated the Jews, Kenny. What kind of a scam is this?'

'It's not a scam. My gran got me into it when my granddad was in the hospice up by Stratford. I spent a lot of time visiting 'im and it went from there, really. I do a lot of charity work as it 'appens. Serve in the Oxfam shops around London that 'ave cropped up 'ere there and everywhere. We 'ave a rota system going.' He looked into her face and showed compassion to cover his lying eyes.

'And what about paid work? What are you doing for a living these days?'

'I can't work, Charlotte. I'm on the panel. I 'ad an accident when I was carrying a heavy roll of carpet on my shoulder.' More lies. 'I ended up flat on my back with two crushed discs for six months. It was murder, but at least it gave me time to reflect. I nearly died, you know.'

'And Bridgeford?' said Charlotte not believing one word of it. 'Have you got relatives there?'

'Nah.' He grinned at her and slowly shook his head again. 'You've gotta be joking. None of my lot would live in that dump. I was there to arrange for one of our charity shops to open up in the town. The Red Cross is interested.'

Now he was beginning to sound as if he just might have turned over a new leaf. 'So you'll be backwards and forwards then?'

'Do me a favour. No. My business there is done and dusted. I did what I could to set things up but the council passed it over to Diss, a quiet little town in—'

'Yeah, I know where it is, I've been there a few times on the local bus.' Charlotte checked her wristwatch. 'I'd best be going soon. Got to fit a lot in before I go back in the morning. I'm staying at my grandparents.'

'I know you are.'

'Do you? How come?'

Kenny looked affectionately at her and then slowly shook his head. 'Because you said so no more than a few minutes ago.'

'Did I?' She couldn't remember whether she had or not and this worried her.

'Listen . . . we all get stressed out now and then. Don't worry about it, Charlie. And look after yerself.' He swallowed the remains of his coffee and stood up to leave. 'Take care of yerself, Charlie, and look after your grandparents. Old people need more loving than most people realise.'

'I'm sure they do,' said Charlotte, fazed by his certainty that she had mentioned staying with Nell and Johnny. Once he had left the table and paid his bill at the till she told herself to slow down a bit and get a grip. She was a bit young to be losing her memory. The truth of it was of course that he had got to her again the same way as he always had done – and she didn't like it. Glancing up, she watched as he left and was puzzled by his smile and the show of a hand once he was outside and had a view in via the window. Could he really have turned over a new leaf? She didn't think so. She checked her wristwatch again, drank the remains of her coffee and once at the till smiled back at the friendly Italian woman as she handed over a two-shilling bit. Giving her the change, the woman said, 'Know him do you, darling?'

'Who? Kenny?'

'Mmm.'

'We used to live in the same block of flats when we were kids. Why do you ask?'

'Why? Because I don't think that he's quite right in the head, if you know what I mean. And if it were up to me I would ban him from coming in here. But who am I? I am only the paid worker.'

'What's he done to rattle your cage?' asked Charlotte, a touch puzzled. He had come across to her as quite tame compared to what he was like when young.

'He always was a little bastard when a kid and I don't think he's changed. Call it a woman's intuition. Call it what you like. But keep an arm's length. I think he's an evil little sod in a false guise.'

'Oh don't worry.' Charlotte smiled. 'I know him from old too. I was surprised to see him come in here though. Where does he live these days?'

'Just up the road on the new council estate. I'm telling you, sweetheart, he's an evil little toe-rag. And it's not just my sixth sense that tells me so. I know his mother. The poor woman has been beside herself at times, wondering what he's been up to when he gets home in the wee hours and then sleeps right through the next day. But don't tell her I said so . . . should you meet up.'

'Of course not,' said Charlotte. 'And thanks for the warning. I appreciate it. See you again.' With that she smiled and left the warm and friendly place with a horrible nagging worry deep down inside her. 'Forget it, Charlotte,' she murmured as she made her way to the place where she hoped she would soon be living. 'He can't harm you. And besides which, gossips are part and parcel of the way of life in this part of the world, you should know that.' Pushing all that the woman had said from her mind, she walked through the back turnings to the square, with the warm glow slowly coming back into her heart. She so wanted to see the beautiful house that had been converted into lovely apartments again. The place that would soon be her new home.

Chapter Twelve

Standing in the shadows of the ground floor of a two-storey block of modern maisonettes with shops below, Kenny had every intention to wait and then follow Charlotte. He knew that she had been holding back the real reason for her being in this little corner of the East End. He didn't know what the reason was but he intended to find out. He had always made it his business to know his patch inside out and she had not been in this particular part for years. So what was she hiding? He wanted to know. And what was he was about to find out? He felt sure that just like most slags she had been lying to him through her back teeth. Yes, she had definitely been holding something back from him, of this he felt certain. And he didn't like it.

He watched her stroll along and commended himself for scrambling her brain a little bit. It was an old trick that he had learned along the way. One of several that he had used when he needed to fuck up someone's thinking the way life had tried to mess up his. He followed in her footsteps once she had turned a corner. Soon he would know what the little bitch was about. He half hoped she was on the game. This would have been the biggest bonus he could have wished for. She would be just another piece of shit that he could rid the world of. Another name that he could add to his list of women that he had now put an end to.

Precisely nine minutes later, according to his wristwatch, he was at the lovely green that was enclosed by the old-fashioned black railings and open gateway. The girl who had tried to intimidate him those years back had returned to the place that she had gone to the day before. Knowing this area like the back of his hand, he slipped in and sat on one of the benches and watched through the gaps in the thick shrubs. The sky was a light blue, the sun was warm, and he was more than content to watch as Charlotte rang the bell of the posh-looking house. To his delight but to Charlotte's obvious disappointment it seemed that there was no one in. After a few minutes of waiting and hoping that someone would appear from inside, Kenny smiled to himself as the girl he once fancied rotten turned to leave but was waylaid by a tall and gaunt guy who had just arrived at the house. Leaning back in his seat, Kenny was quite content to watch as someone who he considered to resemble a weirdo chatted to Charlotte.

Watching them talking all nice and friendly Kenny wondered if his earlier thoughts about her were right – that she had turned into a call girl and that the drip was one of her punters. Smiling, he cupped his chin and observed as the tall and lanky young man pushed the key into the lock of the front door and then stood aside to let Charlotte go in before him. He couldn't believe that someone like this could possibly be a boyfriend that she was shacking up with. Slowly shaking his head, he wondered if she was no better than any other trollop who sold herself for a hot dinner. But then, just as he was about to leave the square and take a slow walk so as to think things through, he saw another woman come along. She too went up the steps to the front door of the very same house.

Recognising her from somewhere, Kenny wracked his brain until the penny dropped. Of course he knew her. She worked in the second-hand bookshop on the Mile End Road where he bought thrillers and dark horror paperbacks for next to nothing because they had been read and thumbed so much. He was intrigued. This was almost like a chapter from one of the books to do with the local serial killer from the nineteenth century that he had read up on. The man who, just like himself, had a loathing for prostitutes. Jack the Ripper. The man who was never caught for his crimes but had been made famous and gone down in the history books. Someone he admired.

He pondered whether he should make friends with the woman when he next went into the bookshop so as to perhaps get inside the front door of the imposing building and see if it was being run as a whorehouse. Thinking back, he felt sure that this woman had given him the come-on more than once when he had been studying the books on the shelves in the bookshop. It would seem that this was his lucky day. He had possibly caught two fucking birds with one stone. He laughed at the thought of it. He liked the idea of kissing one and killing the other. Depending how each of them treated him – with respect or derision. Then, for some reason that he could not put his finger on, he was reminded of something that his dad had said to him that morning. He pushed his hands into his pockets and stayed right where he was on the bench in the tree-lined square, tucked away from people coming and going. His dad, before he had left for work, had popped his head around Kenny's bedroom door where he had been curled up and said, quite sincerely, 'Why haven't you got any mates any more, Kenny boy?'

He had pretended that he hadn't heard, that he had fallen back to sleep after the cup of tea that his mum had brought up to him first thing. It wasn't as if this question hadn't crossed his own mind, it had. But he preferred to be by himself in any case, answering to no one. It was as simple as that. Most people irritated him, and the amusement had gone out of kicking the shit out of someone who got on his nerves. He had never had a girlfriend and nor had he wanted one for that matter. But neither was he a pansy. He quite liked the company of older people who he sometimes sat and had a chat with in one pub or another. He liked hearing about the old days from those who had lived in them rather than reading it from a history book. He didn't know if he was lonely or not because he had nothing to compare his run-of-the-mill life with. But he did have a mission. A mission to continue the good work of Jack.

Given a choice, he thought that his ideal occupation would be to sit on the ship in the North Sea and take the place of Tony Blackburn as DJ on the pirate station Radio Caroline. This kind of work would suit him down to the ground. He could imagine himself tucked away from the world, and away from women who constantly lured him in for the kill. But this was all right. If this was his predestination, then so be it. Who was he to argue?

Having invited Charlotte into the house, Donald, the landlady's son, felt not only obliged to show her around for a second time but also was more than happy to do so. He was delighted to have the opportunity to let her view the flat that she was going to rent so that she could familiarise herself with it once again. Enjoying his sense of importance, the tall and lean twenty-eight-year-old, with dark blond hair cut neatly into a short back and sides, led her into his mother's kitchen first and poured each of them a glass of Lucozade. Doing his best to make conversation so as to have her feeling at ease, he tried to keep a warm smile on his face. She looked very much more at home than he imagined she would and seemed quite comfortable listening to him explain the way of things in the house. It was good to have a bit of company in his mother's big friendly kitchen, with the gentle ticking sound of the old-fashioned wall-mounted clock.

'My own personal apartment was sparsely furnished once upon a time.' He spoke in a quiet voice as he grew more relaxed at the old pine table. Nudging his loose horn-rimmed glasses on to the bridge of his nose, he said, 'My sitting room had an old-fashioned patterned rug over the dark red lino at one time, but I removed it and carried it to a skip that was parked further along the road. I wasn't keen on it. There were all kinds of things in the skip and I think that this was what started me off into being a collector. I think that people living in these houses must be quite rich because they throw away perfectly good pieces of furniture as well as other bits and bobs.'

'Good for you,' said Charlotte, warming to him. She liked this innocent oddball and felt sorry for him without really knowing why. 'I'm sure you won't be the only one who dives into skips for bits and pieces one day and then slips in a bit of your own rubbish the next.' She smiled. 'We all love something for nothing don't we? And we all love to have a clear-out now and then as well.'

'Yes, I think you might be right. I did check that it was fine by my mother for me to get rid of the old mat. And she didn't mind at all and thought that somebody else would be glad of it. This is why I rolled it upside out so that people could see the pile that hadn't flattened and the pattern that hadn't faded. I replaced that one a couple of days later with a rug that I found, which is much brighter. It was in a rag and bone shop in Whitechapel. They let me have it for five shillings in the end. I washed and polished the lino before I put the mat down. It came up a treat. I quite like the idea of polish but I don't think I shall do it again. I couldn't get used to the strong smell of lavender. It woke me in the night and I would sooner sleep when it's dark.'

Charlotte tried not to laugh at him. He was quite funny in his own sweet way and he was also a bit of a conundrum. He seemed a bit on the simple side and yet intelligent. 'I'm sure you *would* rather sleep at night,' she said. 'There's nothing worse, is there, than to be all alone and wide awake when the world is snoring.'

'I suppose not. I don't hear the woman upstairs walking about when I'm asleep in my room of course, but the flat that you'll be taking is directly below hers and she does tend to pace the floor. I did sleep in the flat below hers for a week or so when it was uninhabited, just for a change, and I did hear the floorboards creaking. Hers is not fitted carpet because Mother thinks that kind of a thing encourages dust mites and all sorts of germs. What do you think? I'm not so sure myself.'

Charlotte wasn't quite sure what to say so as not to offend him, or cross his mother should he be the type to report a conversation such as this one. 'I don't know,' she finally said. 'I've never really thought about it.' She then glanced at her wristwatch ready to bring this little chat to an end. 'God . . . I can't believe how quickly the time's gone today. My grandparents will be wondering where I am. I had better scarper.' She smiled.

Seeming as if he hadn't heard what she had said, Donald became thoughtful, rubbing his chin as he spoke. 'I think that you will find that the woman above the flat that you'll be taking really does have a bit of trouble getting to sleep. I think I'll get my mother to have a word with her about the opening and shutting of drawers. This was something else that I heard when I slept below her. It was as if she was always searching for something or other. And then, at other times it sounded as if she was turning out her wardrobe because

I could hear the rattle of the hangers. At least, that is what it sounded like. I could have been wrong, of course.'

'You should try shoving slightly dampened cotton wool in your ears,' said Charlotte light-heartedly. 'That works. That blocks all noises out. I did it when we first moved to Norfolk because of the early morning cockerels and the sound of the birds calling to each other in the woods close by. And I'll do it tonight, because in my grandparents' house the walls are thin and I don't want to hear either of them snoring.'

Thoughtful and serious, Donald slowly nodded. 'Yes, I suppose I could try that. But of course I have my own rooms now. Below yours.'

'I love the flat by the way,' said Charlotte, returning his smile. 'And I can't wait to move in.' There was a small pause, then she said, 'I'm sorry that I missed your mother. Perhaps you could tell her that I came back to say that I definitely want to live here and that I have been offered and have accepted the position at the council offices.'

'Yes, I will tell her. And congratulations on the appointment.' He searched his brain for another conversational angle and said, 'Incidentally . . . do you have use for an ironing board? If so I've got one in the garden shed that you can have.'

'I haven't used one up until now because Mum does all of my ironing back home. But I suppose I'm going to have to do it myself once I move in.'

'Well, I don't want you to waste your shillings. I'll get the one out of the shed for you. This was something else that I found leaning against the skip. It's perfectly all right. Personally, I never press or iron anything. When I take these slacks off, for instance, I lay them flat on the base of my bed and then carefully replace the mattress on top. I do this with most of my clothes so they never need ironing. It's quite a thin mattress but very firm. I mostly wear one of my four Fred Perry shirts during my leisure time, which drip-dry without creases. I'm not certain if this green and white Fred Perry goes with these slacks that I bought yesterday from the Red Cross shop. What do you think?'

'Absolutely fine,' said Charlotte, beginning to feel as if she were talking to a brother. A brother who was a bit simple and somebody that she liked. She did like him, possibly because he wasn't run-of-the-mill. She glanced at her wristwatch again and then raised an eyebrow. 'I could sit here all day and chat to you in this room at this table but needs must. My grandparents will be dying to know whether I got the job so I'd best get going. You don't have to show me my rooms. I just wanted to come into the house again. That's all.'

'Oh, well then, I mustn't keep you.' Her host got up from his chair, and like a true gentleman went round to her chair and gently eased it back for her once she was on her feet. He then walked with her out of the room, into the passage and then the spacious hall that led to the front door. 'I should think that yesterday was probably the best day I've had in a while with regard to my purchases,' he said, crossing his arms as he stood by the rather grand front door. 'I went down to the scrap yard and came back with change from a ten-shilling note, and yet I got quite a lot of useful things. I know I'll be able to make use of every single item. Even the oily bicycle chain once I've soaked it in hot water and suds. I also bought a beautiful pure cut-glass vase. I scrubbed it clean and now I've got it soaking in raw potato water. This will get rid of the old watermark. I've got a very good book on household tips should you ever wish to borrow it.'

'You sound like my granddad,' she smiled. 'The pair of you would really get on. He's always pulling bits and bobs out of skips that he thinks he can make use of and he's got one of the old type of books that you mention.'

'Oh well, then you must let him know about another skip that's just been set down in this road this week.' He stopped talking and cupped his chin thoughtfully and said, 'Look, I don't want you to get the wrong impression. I've no complaints about Wendy . . . the woman who paces the floor. She pays her rent on time and this keeps my mother in good spirits.'

'Well, that's no bad thing and it's one way of looking at it,' she said, opening the main door that led back out to the street and the real world. 'But you don't have to worry about me. I'm a heavy sleeper, and I've always got the homemade earplugs. Thanks for the Lucozade and good luck with the hunting. You seem very good at it.'

'Hunting?' He looked mystified. 'I don't agree with the hunt. I never have done. My cousins in the country have only just accepted that I won't ever join in. What made you think I was one of them?'

'I was talking about the things you find in second-hand shops and in the skips,' said Charlotte.

'Oh . . . yes . . . I see what you mean. How slow of me.' His self-conscious smile touched her, but enough was enough. She bade him farewell, said that she would be seeing him soon and left.

Walking slowly away along the tree-lined pavement and past the enclosed public garden where Kenny still sat, Charlotte felt so happy she almost cried. Not only was she thrilled to be back, but she was also in her favourite place in a quiet spot in Stepney Green that she had always seen as heavenly. She could hardly believe that she was going to be living here. Her thoughts were flying from one thing to another as she walked through the back streets on her way to the bus stop where she would ride to Bow and her grandparents' house. She was ready to have a little rest before Nathan called to see her.

Hidden behind the foliage in the small square, Kenny lit himself another cigarette with a satisfied smirk. If Charlotte was planning to live in the house on the square he couldn't have asked for anything easier. This place was a spitting distance from the council flat where he lived with his mum and dad so he could keep an eye on her. See what she was up to. If she turned out to be someone who simply fancied herself as being independent and living in her own furnished flat that was all right by him. He was just going to have to see how things panned out. He was more taken with having seen the woman who wore too much lipstick and powder going into the house than he had been at seeing Charlotte. The woman who he felt sure he had heard being referred to as Wendy by one of the other assistants in the bookshop.

If she *was* living in that house he felt he could have a bit of fun by playing one woman off against the other. He could pass a little bit of false gossip to Wendy when he was next in the shop – perhaps that Charlotte had been a little whore on the quiet when she had lived in the town of Bridgeford in Norfolk. Then, when he might accidentally on purpose bump into Charlotte, he could tell her that the woman called Wendy, who was like mutton dressed as lamb, was an Aldgate whore after dark.

Laughing to himself, his hands in his pockets and his head lowered, he walked out through the open gateway of the Victorian square to saunter back home. He couldn't believe how his life had livened up during the past four weeks or so. He momentarily thought about the girl who was at the bottom of the wishing well in the overgrown garden in Bridgeford. But then he told himself that even though it was a sad way to end a life of misery, at least she was better off dead than to live the rest of her life soiling her body with randy old men who got off on paid sex. He was more certain than ever that she had been a prostitute on the quiet.

To Kenny's mind he had done that Rosie the biggest favour that anyone could have done, and he felt a rush of self-pride from top to toe. After all, he had given the girl a quick end and a nice resting place in the dark, away from the stinking underbelly world that she had been dragged into.

What he didn't know, and what he hadn't even considered as a possibility, was that back in the small Norfolk town of Bridgeford, questions were being asked about the disappearance of the young woman. The girl's best friend, who she had spent most of her time with, after making several phone calls to the old ramshackle mansion house where Rosie had lived, had called in at the Bridgeford police station and reported her friend missing without a trace. And she hadn't been alone in her worries because other people, with whom the young girl had shared the same roof, had also been concerned about her sudden disappearance. The give-away was that there was no sign of her having packed up any of her personal possessions, and her clothes had been left around her room in an ordinary scattered way. And not only this: her best friend, who had been the last of her friends to have seen her alive in the pub, had seen her go off with a young man – one that she saw as a bit of an outsider who had not been staying in the town for that long, and who had *also* disappeared.

Chapter Thirteen

After spending a nice cosy evening with her grandparents and Nathan and then enjoying a good night's
sleep, Charlotte was back home in Bridgeford after a
tiring journey from London. She was telling Rita and
Eddie how pleased she was that she had not only been
offered the position at the local council offices, but that
she had also found a lovely flat. A flat in the East End
that she loved. Taking her by surprise, there were no
flowing tears from her parents, but a big hug from both
of them. They, having had time to think about it, were
in their own way admitting that it was time for them to
let go. Their little girl was now a young woman after all,
and clearly a young woman with a mind of her own.

Charlotte slept well again that night, but the very
next morning as she was getting ready to go to work,
she picked up on the fact that there was a sombre
mood in the air. Not knowing whether to leave things
be and allow a cooling-off period, she carried on as if
nothing was amiss so as to give her parents a chance to
have their say and get it over and done with. But she
was pleasantly surprised that nothing came in the way
of admonishment, and neither were either of them
causing her to feel guilty for wanting to fly the nest
that they had built for all three of them. In a relaxed

mood, she sipped her tea and looked from her mum to her dad, and said, 'Nan and Granddad were really pleased to see Nathan again. He came to pick me up and we went out for dinner to the Steak House in Aldgate. It was lovely. Really nice. Candles and everything.'

'We know,' said Eddie, as cool as a cucumber. 'Your granddad phoned to tell us.'

'He's a lovely lad,' added Rita, 'and from what I gather he's got a good job.'

'And he's a lifelong friend,' continued Eddie. 'You can't ask for more than that.'

'I'm not saying that we're making plans, other than to go courting, but who knows? His family being Jewish, though . . . I wasn't sure how you'd feel about that.' Now she really was testing the water.

'About what? You're not engaged to be married, for God's sake,' said Rita.

'No . . . but we love each other just as much as we did in the old days—'

'Don't talk daft,' Rita laughed. 'In the old days, as you call them, you were children who were good friends. Love?' She broke into soft laughter again. 'You wouldn't 'ave known the meaning of the word.'

'Whatever,' said Charlotte, shrugging. 'But we do now.'

The room went quiet. Then, shrugging and drawing breath, Eddie said, 'If you're thinking of marriage, Charlotte, you're gonna have to give us time to take this in. We're Church of England and . . .'

Charlotte slowly shook her head. 'So all the old hang-ups of the past are still with us. I might 'ave known.'

'Your dad never said anything about anti-Semitism,' Rita said, a touch coldly.

'Anti-Semitism?' Charlotte smiled. 'Who ate the dictionary for breakfast then?'

'And who was it who once told me that sarcasm was the lowest form of wit?'

'I wasn't being sarcastic, Mum. All I'm saying is that I love Nathan and that he loves me. So try and get used to the idea of it. That's all.'

'But we're not talking about wedding bells, surely?' said Eddie. 'Not yet anyway?'

'No . . . not yet. But who knows? His dad seems overjoyed that we've met up again by all accounts, so I don't think he'll have any problems if we decide to be together for ever.' Charlotte smiled. Then just to change the subject, she asked about the headline in the local paper to do with a missing girl. She focused on Eddie because she knew that Rita was preoccupied with all that she had just told them.

'It's come as a bit of a shock to tell the truth, sweetheart,' said Eddie. 'I know neither me nor your mother knew the girl . . . but it don't make you feel all that easy with something like this on the doorstep. She could be laying strangled somewhere for all we know.'

'Or, she could be lying beside her lover in a bed in a cosy little cottage. Don't forget our local doesn't 'ave much in the way of a headline to report.'

'That's true.' Eddie leaned back in his chair with a faint smile. 'I suppose that me and your mum was getting a bit carried away. The thought of you going missing made our blood run cold. I don't think she was more than a year older than you, sweetheart.'

'Was? Come on, Dad. She's not gonna be murdered, dead and buried. She's probably having a bit of fun somewhere with someone who can afford to give her a lovely time and then drop her back into her own world.'

'If you say so. But from what we heard the boys in blue 'ave been sniffing around a flat above a dingy wireless shop in a side street not far from here. Less than a ten-minute walk in fact.'

'Oh? Well that's a different kettle of fish. And you know for sure that it's to do with her disappearance, do you?'

'According to the talk in our local. They've already taken in a flash lad for questioning who was apparently one of the last ones to have seen 'er alive.'

'Blimey.' Charlotte shrugged. 'Well, that is different. And he's someone from the pub where you and Mum always drink?'

'So they say.'

'And did you know him?'

'Don't think so. It's always packed with lads when I'm in there. It could 'ave been any one of them,' said Eddie.

'Well . . . there you are then. I might be safer in the East End than in this lovely little country town after all.' She looked from her dad to her mum. 'And if this is what's worrying you – I've not only got Nathan, Gran and Granddad to keep a protective eye on me, but the

lovely woman, Mrs Braintree who owns the house —
and her son Donald, who's a sweetheart.'

'Good,' said Eddie. He looked across to Rita. 'Feel
better now, love? Now that we've heard a bit more
about madam living back in her roots?'

'I suppose so.' Rita shrugged. 'But you can't blame us
for worrying, Charlotte, can you? You do hear of
terrible things these days.'

'I'll be all right, Mum. And from what you've just
said, it might not be any more dangerous in London
than anywhere else. Who would have thought that the
police would be crawling over Bridgeford?'

'So,' said Eddie, wishing to change the subject. 'You
love the flat you've seen, you liked the place where you
went for the interview, and you'll be moving out in a
fortnight's time? Is that right?'

'Well . . . it depends.'

'On what?' said Rita.

'I only need to give the council offices here a one-
week notice apparently. They've already got a junior
who works in the post room who will fill my position
and someone further down the line who'll fill hers.
That's the system.'

'So you think you'll be ready to go in a week, do
you?' Eddie sniffed and raised an eyebrow. 'Clothes
washed, pressed and packed in just seven days? Never
mind your bits and pieces that you'll want to take. Such
as your bedding, for example, and your bedside table
lamp that you've had since you was three years old and
won't part with. Your fluffy bedroom rug that you
love . . .'

'I'll be ready if you are, Dad. I'll need a lift down, obviously.'

Rita glanced sadly at her daughter. 'You've got it all worked out then? But we've not seen the place yet. What if we don't think it's good enough for you?'

'It is, Mum, trust me. Please. Just this once trust that I know more than you do.'

Eddie cleared his throat and looked sideways at his wife. This wasn't the kind of a conversation that she appreciated. Far from it. He knew that he had to be a bit of a peacemaker here. 'Let 'er make 'er own mistakes, Rita,' he said, 'and be it on her own head if she comes unstuck. She won't be able to say that you didn't warn 'er.'

'Oh, do what you want, Charlotte. You always have done in any case, in your own quiet way. But if we don't think it's good enough when we take you down next weekend I'm not leaving you there.'

'That's fair enough, Mum. I'll agree to that.'

'Good,' said Rita. 'Now then . . . you'd best write a list of things that we'll need to buy. Kettle, iron, teapot, cutlery, crockery, toaster . . .'

'I won't need all of that! It's furnished!' Charlotte laughed.

'I think you'll find that you will. Phone the woman who owns the property and ask what's included when it comes to the kitchen and the bed linen and bath towels and hand towels and tea towels—'

'Yeah all right, Reet,' Eddie interrupted. 'I think she's got the point.'

'Good,' said Rita, 'because in two minutes' time

Coronation Street's on and I don't want to miss it. Annie Walker's upset Ena Sharples.' Eddie caught Charlotte's eye and winked at her. They had won the battle without too much of a fight. He had previously warned Charlotte that she had to play it just right because if her mother had laid down the law and not agreed to her plans, he would have had to go along with that. It was with a sigh of relief that he leaned back in his chair and tried not to worry if his beautiful daughter would be all right looking after herself. She was going, and that was all there was to it.

Chapter Fourteen

On the morning of her departure for London, once everything had been packed into two large suitcases and furnishings such as her fairly new record player, records and bedside lamp had been loaded into the family car, it was Charlotte who experienced butterflies in her stomach, and not her parents. They had by now got used to the idea of her going and were looking forward to seeing where she would be living.

Settled into the back seat of Eddie's car and on the way, Charlotte broke into a lovely smile and then said to her parents, who were chatting away in the front of the car, 'I can't believe I'm doing this.'

Eddie and Rita glanced sideways at each other, keeping their thoughts to themselves – thoughts that they had discussed more than once about how she would soon miss the home comforts and be back in Bridgeford appreciating the way of life instead of grumbling about the everyday boring existence there. Rita had by now had a change of heart, and instead of worrying about whether her daughter would cope in London after five years spent in a small country backwater, she felt rather proud of her. She wanted her to make a success of it. And having had time for it to sink in, she knew that she was only going to be three or four hours away at the most . . . depending on the traffic. And of course Rita also knew that her own mum and dad would take great care of Charlotte. They loved their granddaughter to bits and they would certainly keep an eye on her. Deep down she realised that she had been a touch over-protective when it came to her only child. Her only child who was now undeniably a lovely young woman.

Hugging her first teddy bear, which was worn and a touch misshapen but that she still loved, Charlotte was tired. All of the excitement and packing had stopped her from being able to drift off to sleep at her usual time the night before, so she rested her head back and, before she knew it, slipped into a welcome doze. She had been relaxed and excited at the same time at the thought of being in the centre of swinging London in the Swinging Sixties. Her mind had gone from one thing to another the night before, even to thinking about Twiggy who hadn't even sat her O-levels when she had been launched into stardom. She wasn't an East End girl it was true, but all three of the celebrated photographers that worked with models of her ilk – David Bailey, Terence Donovan and Brian Duff – were east London born and bred.

Ordinary young working-class men and women, who had made it to the top, were now mixing with the offspring of the old rich. And apart from all of this, with London swinging it was true to say that there was a kind of new religion emerging: the talk was of everyone being able to develop ESP should they set their mind to it. Various stages of consciousness were being discussed in clubs, pubs and coffee bars and LSD was beginning to be passed around. Suddenly there was an abundance of new music and daring lyrics emerging, as well as flamboyant fashion. The culture was changing, and Charlotte wanted to be part of it all, if only in a very small way.

With the roads pretty clear, they were soon crossing the border from Norfolk into Suffolk and then Essex. Driving through to Wanstead and then Leytonstone and Stratford East, they finally arrived into Stepney Green and made for Lavender Square, where Eddie parked outside the grand terraced house that faced the hedged green. Both Rita and Eddie remembered this romantic part of Stepney from their courting days when they had strolled through the old-fashioned back streets – a time when they had sometimes paid homage to the Prospect of Whitby down by the river Thames.

Properly awake after having dozed on and off for most of the journey, Charlotte looked at the front door to which she would soon have a key. A door that she would have every right to enter and leave at any time of the day. She could hardly believe it was happening, and from the expression on her parents' faces neither could they. It was an imposing house, as were those on either side of it in this exclusive terrace overlooking that treasure of a square.

Isabelle Braintree opened the door, smiling sweetly. She then stood aside and waved a graceful hand, beckoning in her new tenant and her parents. 'Please do come in. I have been so looking forward to your coming.'

'I hope we're not too early,' said Rita, a touch at a loss for something to say because she was so bowled over by everything, especially the grand entrance hall. And if the truth be known, she was also a touch intimidated by it all, as was Eddie. But neither of them showed their nervousness as they too smiled and in turn shook the hand of the graceful woman who was so obviously a lady of refinement, born and bred.

'Of course you're not too early,' Isabelle said. 'I expect you must be terribly dry after that long journey. Would you like a cup of tea or a cold drink?'

'No, we're fine,' said Rita, a touch shyly. 'I packed a picnic and we had that on the way. But thank you for offering.'

'Not at all. I expect you'd like to settle your daughter into her new home. I'll show you up to the apartment and then leave you to it, shall I?'

'That would be lovely,' said Rita. 'Thank you.'

As they trooped up the wide staircase, Isabelle told of how quiet the square was, day and night, and how she was sure their daughter would soon feel very much at home. She then briefly spoke of the other tenants before she opened the door into the apartment where Charlotte was to live. 'I'll leave you to show your parents around, Charlotte,' she said, smiling at the girl as she took her leave.

Gently closing the door behind them, Eddie exclaimed, 'I didn't expect it to be this good, Charlotte! Well done, babe. It's lovely.'

Rita went to the window where beautiful, lined William Morris flowery curtains hung and looked out across the square. 'I wouldn't mind living here myself,' she said.

'Nor would I,' said Eddie, joining her. 'Who wouldn't?'

By now Charlotte was inside her small kitchen and grinning like a Cheshire cat. She could see that a kettle, teapot and a tray with four cups and saucers had been set. There was also some instant coffee and a pretty tea caddy. In the small fridge there was a jug of milk and four small fresh cream buns. Seeing all of this she was almost brought to tears. 'She is *so* nice. Look at what she's left out for us.'

Eddie came into the kitchen and slowly nodded. 'You've fallen on your feet here, babe.'

An hour or so later, once they knew that their daughter was well and truly ready to be by herself and unpack at her leisure, the proud parents left to make their way to see Nell and Johnny. Charlotte hugged her parents goodbye, and could tell by the expression on Rita's face that her mum was no longer worrying about whether she would cope in London. After all, her parents knew that Nell and Johnny would keep a close eye on her welfare. And now, with her suitcases unpacked and her other special bits and pieces, such as her old teddy, Charlotte felt like shedding a tear one minute and shouting at the top of her voice for joy the next.

Now that she *was* alone, she slowly walked around the flat that was hers and only hers and looked at every tiny thing, touching almost everything with her finger-tips as if to say hello. As she went back into the kitchen to make her first cup of coffee in her very own apartment, there came a soft tapping on the door. Excited to have a visitor so soon, even though she expected it was only her landlady, she opened the door wide with a smile on her face. But it wasn't Isabelle, it was Wendy from the flat above. The smiling woman was wearing a cheerful red blouse and a flowing white skirt, both of which she had purchased at a charity shop in Whitechapel close to where she worked. In her hand was a small posy of fresh flowers that she had picked from the garden with the permission of Isabelle. Charlotte stood aside and invited her in.

'Darling, I'm not going to intrude,' said Wendy. 'I just wanted to welcome you.' She smiled and then handed her the bunch of flowers.

'Oh . . . that's really nice of you,' said Charlotte, touched by the gesture.

'I won't stay,' said Wendy as she looked around her. 'I do so love this flat, but then I also love mine. You must come up for a cup of tea or coffee in a few days once you've settled in. Do you think that you might like to?'

'Of course I would, that would be lovely. Thank you.'

'Not at all, not at all.' She drew a slow breath and with a contented expression said, 'This is such a pleasant house to live in and the landlady is really very kind. Her son Donald is a bit on the odd side,' she whispered, 'but harmless enough. I think that he's a bit lonely.'

'Oh really?' Charlotte didn't think so. 'He seemed

quite nice and normal when I met him and not in the least bit odd. That was when I came to look at the flat.'

'Well . . . there we are. Time will tell. I have a teeny-weeny inkling that he's rather taken to me as a matter of fact – despite the age gap.' She then laid a theatrical hand on her chest and speaking quietly, said, 'Please don't let on that I said so, Charlotte, will you?'

'I wouldn't dream of it,' said Charlotte, her heart sinking just a little. This woman seemed a touch on the barmy side.

'I don't think that he knows that I've realised this. I expect it's my perfume that draws him to me. It's the very original Evening in Paris. I was introduced to it by my grandmother decades ago.'

'It's a lovely scent.' Charlotte was now wondering if she was meant to offer Wendy a cup of coffee. She didn't want to but wasn't sure what someone else in her situation would do so, more out of politeness than anything else, she did say, 'I'm just going to have a hot drink. Would you like one?'

'That's very lovely of you but I've just had a coffee. Thank you. And don't get me wrong . . . I'm not saying that it wouldn't be nice to have the boy's company now and then but one doesn't want to lead him on. He's one of life's vulnerables I think. I suppose I could ask him in for coffee and biscuits. What do you think?'

'I don't know,' said Charlotte, her mind a blank. All she wanted now was to be by herself and adjust to her new surroundings.

'No, it is rather a tricky one, isn't it. But there, I mustn't keep you. You've got to unpack and all of that.

But remember . . . I'm not far away should you need anything. Any teeny-weeny problem that you might need advice about. I am always happy to help if I can. I'm only just above your head. Isn't that marvellous?' With that the woman almost hugged herself as she smiled. She looked as if she had brought her conversation to an end. But she hadn't. She began again.

'Of course I don't take too much to heart the way that the innocent boy looks at me. I think that he thinks that I don't have a clue as to how he feels. I expect it's my perfume that he can't resist.'

'It's a lovely scent,' said Charlotte again, walking slowly towards the door ready to open it wide as a hint that it was time for the woman to go. She didn't want to know what Wendy was trying to suggest. Donald seemed fine to her.

'Of course, I really don't think that it should be me who makes an invitation. If my landlady's son wants to come in for a chat he should say so. Do you agree?'

'Possibly,' said Charlotte. 'I don't really know. I've not long come down from the country, don't forget. I need time to adjust to London living again.'

'Well, of course you do, poppet. What was I thinking?' Wendy smiled sympathetically at her. 'But you'll soon be in the swing of things, my dear, don't you fret. And as for Donald, well, don't let his strange ways bother you too much. He can be worrying at times, I know. For instance we once had a little disagreement as to which of the two of us best remembered the tenant who rented the basement before the artist. Donald said he could remember a half-caste man. I said that no, it was definitely a young Irish man. And I'm sorry to have to say it, but the look of annoyance in his eyes did set me back a bit. I do believe that he's not a hundred per cent right in the head. I think his poor mother knows this too, but of course she's bound not to let on. If I didn't know him personally, I think that I wouldn't be too keen to come across him in a back turning in the black of the night. But there. I expect I'm just being silly.'

'Oh, I'm sure he wouldn't hurt a fly,' said Charlotte, her patience now running out. 'He's a very genteel type of a person.'

'Well . . . I have to say that there have been reports in the local newspaper recently of local prostitutes going missing. And he does sometimes like to go out very late at night to have a quiet stroll around, as he likes to put it. Let's not forget too easily the old proverb of a sly fox in sheep's clothing.'

With that, Wendy swanned out of the room and Charlotte was left to gaze at the open doorway, shocked by all she had said. She swiftly closed the door and then leaned against it, wondering for a few seconds whether she had done the right thing by moving into this house so quickly before finding out a little more about the tenants. But this thought was immediately wiped away as she looked around again at the lovely room that was now part of her new life. This was her very own pad with its own front door. The old-fashioned floral sofa with its feather cushions and two matching armchairs were homely, and looked absolutely right set around the ornate pine fireplace. A fireplace that was inset with an unlit gas-burning fire and surrounded by beautiful richly coloured patterned tiles. She brought Donald's face to mind again and told herself that perhaps she should keep him at arm's length. He *was* a touch out of the ordinary, but no more than that . . . even so, she thought it best to keep herself to herself for a while.

Back in her own attic apartment, Wendy pulled the chair out from under her writing desk that was in front of her window and sat down to make a few notes in her diary about the new girl. But as she listened to the song of a blackbird, she remembered that she hadn't fed her feathered friends. She went to the kitchen and fetched a brown paper bag in which she kept grated breadcrumbs. She then sprinkled a few on the windowsill for the pigeons, or the sparrows, depending on which of them got there first. It didn't bother her either way . . . she had done her duty and happily so.

Her voice low, she spoke to herself, as was her wont. 'I believe that Donald is someone who wouldn't mind eating baked beans cold straight out of the can.' She then smiled at the image of him when he had once been smoking an old cigar that he found in the silk-patterned smoking jacket purchased from a second-hand clothes stall in Whitechapel market. He really did have a lovely nature and he never minded telling her that some of his clothes were second-hand. In actual fact he seemed quite proud to have found such bargains. She couldn't help but like the boy, even though he was a bit on the odd side.

Slipping into her seat at her writing desk by the

window again, she wanted to see if she could work out for herself what star sign Charlotte might be. But then she glanced out and up at the clear blue skies, and decided there and then that since this was a lovely summer evening she would go out for a stroll. She had always got her best ideas when walking and thinking, and she did want to get on with the novel that she had been slowly writing over the years. Usually at this time of the day she wrote a little piece about each of the people that she had come to know at work and in this house where she lived. Donald, without a shadow of doubt, was the most interesting of everybody she knew because she couldn't quite fathom him. She still didn't know for certain whether he was highly intelligent or mentally disturbed. The word insane floated through her mind, as it had done before, but she brushed it aside as being far too melodramatic. She wrote only a short piece about him since she had other things on her mind such as her walk. She underlined the word barmy with a question mark. She had already begun to write on a clean page a little about the new girl, Charlotte, but kept it brief because she wanted to have a little rest before she got ready for her stroll.

She had been shopping that morning since this was one of her days off and had spent just over three pounds ten shillings in her favourite Oxfam charity shop in Maida Vale to which wealthy women gave almost new clothes. Clothes that had been purchased in such places as Harrods, Selfridges and Liberty's of London. Today she had managed to purchase one complete outfit and several beautiful flowing scarves, which she adored. The outfit that she would wear this evening consisted of a purple and pink three-quarter-length summer coat and dress with one of the chiffon scarves to match.

An only child from a middle-class family, Wendy had been brought up in a privately owned house in Wanstead that had a lovely back garden, and she was quite used to dressing nicely. Sadly, both her parents had been killed in a car crash some years before, and just a few years after this her own husband had gone on that missing list, taking some of her inheritance with him. The adulterer in their marriage, he had left her for a girl called Eileen who cleaned the offices where he was working at the time. She felt sure he wouldn't stay with Eileen for ever and, since neither of them had sought divorce, she took this to mean that one day he would want them to get back together again. Whether she would be able to forgive him for forging her signature on several of her cheques, robbing her of a substantial amount, she wasn't quite sure.

By now she was quite used to living alone and had almost given up the hope of ever seeing him again . . . but not given up entirely. He had been the love of her life and the only man that she had given herself to. To fill her lonely hours when not working at the local bookshop, she had her work as an agony aunt for a quarterly magazine.

To her mind, the people she worked with at the bookshop, as well her fellow lodgers, didn't know that she was an aspiring author. Thus, she would not suffer the embarrassment of failure, should she get rejection slip after rejection slip and never see all that she had written over the years in print. Her pseudonym as an agony aunt, Eartha Fire, was one that she would use once her novel was finished and ready to go off to a publishing house of good repute.

Glancing across the room at the outfit on a padded hanger that she would be wearing that evening, she decided that her stroll would be along the High Road to the rather pleasant hotel nearby across an old-fashioned bridge where the riff-raff hardly ever went. The class of person who drank in the bar of the hotel was mostly from the City, on their way out to such places as Wanstead, Chingford, Chigwell and Buckhurst Hill. Very respectable areas. Whether or not she would meet up with a handsome romantic bachelor who would sweep her off her feet was anyone's guess. She had always felt that she would give her body and her love to a handsome man should one come into her realm, but they hardly ever did. But she wasn't too put out that she hadn't met someone to love and hold since she had been free and single again. To her mind it was all a matter of what might be in her stars. And now the stars, according to her ever faithful astrology ledger, did look strangely interesting . . . so long as she took heed of the teeny-weeny warnings of danger. From what she could fathom her stars were telling her to be cautious when meeting a stranger. She took this to be the new tenant – the girl called Charlotte – so shrugged it off.

Just as Charlotte was about to make herself a second cup of coffee she heard a soft tapping on the door of her flat. When she opened it her heart sank a little to see that Donald was standing there. He looked as though he might have been there for a few minutes plucking up the courage to knock. 'I hope I'm not disturbing you,' he said, going a little pink in the face. 'But I wondered if you would like this vase to put in the flowers from the garden that Wendy picked for you.'

'Oh, Donald . . .' said Charlotte, touched by his thought. 'That's lovely of you.' She thanked him and said, 'But are you really sure you want to part with this? It's beautiful.'

'Oh yes,' he smiled. 'I've brought it back to its former glory. I'm certain that it's genuine cut glass and now I'm wondering whether I should have brought some more cut flowers with me. There are plenty growing in our garden. There's an old plain white vase in the cupboard under the kitchen sink. It would be nice if you could have some blooms in your bedroom as well as in your sitting room. For the fragrance as well as the picture they make.'

'No, I'm happy with those that Wendy brought, but I do appreciate the vase. Thank you very much for thinking of me.'

He broke into a smile. 'That's perfectly all right. In a week's time I'll cut you some more flowers from the garden to put in the vase.'

'Really? Don't you think that you should check with your mother first before you go cutting her blooms?'

'It's my garden too, Charlotte. I do live here. I shall leave you with the vase and come back in a few days' time with some fresh flowers.'

Charlotte thanked him again and closed the door behind him. She was now wondering if the woman who lived above her was right. One minute Donald seemed such a sensitive soul and the next he wore an odd expression. He had told her three times about his clothes-pressing tactic of putting them under the mattress, but she had noticed that he was wearing a brand new white shirt with the cardboard under the collar still intact. Obviously he wanted to keep it perfectly in place, or possibly believed that this was why the cardboard was there in the first place. She had no idea.

A little sorry for him, she now felt a sense of guilt. She hadn't invited him in for a cup of coffee. But then she reminded herself that she had only just arrived in the house a couple of hours ago, and from his demeanour, she felt that Donald wouldn't have accepted the invite in any case. And it was too soon to set any kind of a pattern that might become a habit with anyone living in the house. Because of the style of house, the space on Charlotte's landing was smaller than that outside Donald's door. This didn't bother her in the least but he had said on the day that he had invited her in that he would exchange flats with her if she didn't think it fair. Of course she wouldn't hear of it. It was at this point that she had wondered if he was all the ticket. But he did seem very nice and innocent if not a touch child-like.

Going into her kitchen she heard yet another tap on the door and was reluctant to answer it this time. But then, telling herself that people were only being kind and friendly, she opened it . . . to Donald. 'I've just had an idea,' he said. 'Should I need to speak to you again I'll tap twice on the door and if you don't open it I'll know that you know that it's me and by not opening it I'll be given a message that it's inconvenient. How does this sound?'

'I think that's a clever idea, Donald,' she said, trying not to sound amused. He was certainly different from anybody she had ever come across.

'I think that it's best to be polite but not overly friendly when living under the same roof but in different apartments.' With that he bade her farewell again and was just about to take his leave when he had another idea.

'Oh, and by the way, should you get lonely in the evenings and don't feel like reading a book we could always play a board game. I've got Monopoly now and that can be quite absorbing.'

'That's really thoughtful,' said Charlotte. 'I *am* used to my own company, but should I for one reason or another start to miss the countryside that I'm used to, or my parents, I'll pop down and see you.' She instinctively held off mentioning that she hoped to spend time with her boyfriend.

'That sounds sensible.' Cupping his chin and still in thought, he said, 'In nice weather, incidentally, my mother sits in the garden. I know she won't mind if you join her for afternoon tea or morning coffee. And by the way, my mother feels that I keep far too many things in my room, so apart from this vase I might have some other bits and pieces that you would like for your flat. I'm a bit of a collector, which is all right, but I don't want to end up a hoarder.'

'Thank you for the offer,' said Charlotte. 'I'll let you know if there's anything I'm short of.'

'Good. To have reached this arrangement at the beginning of our relationship suits me down to the ground. So as not to intrude I shall leave things out here on the landing floor should I think them useful or decorative.'

'That sounds fine.' She smiled at him. 'And if I don't have a use for the things I'll leave them where they are.'

'Absolutely,' said Donald, trying his utmost to be correct. 'Much better that we start as we wish to go on.'

Once the door was closed between them Charlotte looked at the vase and felt her stomach churn. Donald seemed sensitive and safe and yet her sixth sense was still warning her to perhaps keep her distance. He was a lovely person but also someone who seemed as if he was a penny short of a shilling, and until she knew what was what in this house, under this roof, she was going to keep herself to herself. Looking around at all of her belongings, bags and boxes on the floor and on the sofa, she decided there and then that what she needed was a bit of music while she unpacked.

Lifting her record player from the sofa to a side table where she could see that there was a socket she selected her favourite LP by the Beatles. While she had the Fab Four in the room with her she knew that she would feel at home. She decided to make herself another cup of coffee and perhaps light a cigarette before she began to unpack properly and settle in. She couldn't wait to sleep in the double divan bed with the big feather pillows. And she couldn't wait to see Nathan again.

A couple of hours later and tired from all of the packing up, travelling and unpacking, Charlotte was resting on the settee. She had phoned Nathan and looked forward to seeing him, but now she was drifting in and out of a light sleep while listening to her music. Feeling peckish, she went into the small adjoining kitchen and found the Tupperware box that Rita had packed for her that morning before they set off. It was only now that she realised she hadn't eaten anything other than snacks since breakfast. While waiting for the kettle to come to the boil for another cup of coffee, she eased the lid off the lunch box to find it jam-packed with sandwiches. There was also a large wedge of Rita's homemade fruitcake, and a chunk of egg and pork pie, everything wrapped neat and separate in greaseproof paper. There was enough to feed two people. She silently thanked her mum for thinking of her and felt the prick of tears as it dawned on her that she had actually left home. That she would not be sitting at the dining table the next day for a meal with her mum and dad. This was it. This was what she had been dreaming of for so long. Drifting back into the sitting room with the evening sun streaming in, she smiled at her ever-changing moods. She loved the room. It was spacious, yet had a cosy feeling about it. There was a mismatch of patterns when it came to the wallpaper, curtains, fabrics and fitted carpet but it all seemed to come together to create a kind of comfortable, almost bohemian, mood.

And now that some of her own bits and pieces were placed on shelves and on the waxed pine mantelshelf above the fireplace, it looked and felt homely.

Going over to the long sash window she glanced down at Lavender Square where it was peaceful and quiet. She then looked along the turning at the trees that were in full leaf. She felt happy in these surroundings. Happy and at home. Across the square she could see an old man who lived opposite. He was sitting at his window with a lamp just behind him to give him a warm light and was gazing out at nothing. He looked quite lonesome. Charlotte waved to him and at first couldn't catch his attention but, determined not to give up, she waved again and this time he saw her. He nodded his greeting at first and then showed a hand. She then turned away to leave him to his own private world and thoughts, wondering if he was as solitary as he seemed to appear.

The old gentleman, who had been pleased with her show of a hand, was a widower in his seventies who lived by himself in what was more of a bedsit than a flat or apartment. In one corner of his sitting room there was a paraffin heater that he used as a back-up for when there was no coal to shovel into the grate of the fireplace. He was a lonely soul, and a friendly wave from someone opposite whose name he didn't even know meant a great deal to him. Rubbing his eyes, he smiled down at his old dog and then prodded him with his slippered foot. 'Somebody nice has moved in across the square,' he said and then softly chuckled. 'Maybe I will get a nice picture of her when she goes out walking.' He looked across the room to his old Box Brownie camera on the shelf. 'I think I might need a new film soon.' He then pulled himself up from the chair and wrote a note on the pad he kept by the door, reminding himself to take his Box Brownie to the chemist so that the young man who worked there could remove the used reel and replace it with a new one. He had caught so much on his camera that would mean little to anyone else but everything to him. His most treasured picture of all was the one that he had taken of his wife just a few days before she passed away three years earlier, when she had had a soft smile on her face that spoke volumes. He knew that she had had enough of hospitals and check-ups, medication and torment, and had been ready to pass on to the next world.

Back in his chair by the window he looked down at his beloved square again and tears filled his eyes as he murmured how he wished that he had died alongside his dear wife. He was fed up with watching too much but never bored with his view. Even though he could see little reason for being alive he felt that there had to be a reason for him having been left to live alone without the love of his life. All he hoped was that that purpose would show itself soon so that he could be left to sleep in peace . . . for ever. And for some unknown reason he felt that the girl who had moved into the house opposite and given him a wave was going to become part of God's bigger picture where he was concerned. It didn't worry him. It didn't excite him. It was simply a matter of fact. He wasn't sure why he felt this but he had given up asking questions of the Lord since his late wife became ill and wracked with pain.

Thinking about the old man, Charlotte felt that it would be okay to pay him a visit one day soon. She then went over to a small cupboard that was set into the wall next to the fireplace. It had a waxed pine door with a lovely old-fashioned brass knob that had been recently polished and shone like gold. Flicking down a small brass bow-shaped catch, she pulled the door open and the musty smell reminded her of her childhood. A time when her nan had been looking after her and let her rummage through her old photograph albums and little knick-knacks in a cupboard by her fireplace similar to this one. Smiling to herself she closed the narrow cupboard door, then turned around to look at her room again and noticed the dust that seemed to be dancing in the rays of the early evening sun. Again she went to the window and looked across at the old man. This time he showed a hand. This made her feel warm inside.

Later on, soaking in the big white old-fashioned bath before getting herself ready to meet up with Nathan outside Stepney Green underground station, Charlotte couldn't stop herself from smiling. Here she was in a strange house and sharing the same roof with people that she hardly knew. If anybody were to have told her just two weeks ago that this would be the case she would have laughed in their face. She could hardly believe the way things had gone or how quickly it had all happened. And apart from the fact that she was now living in her very own apartment, she and her child-hood friend had not only met up again but had fallen in love. And the most wonderful thing of all was that she was back in the heart of the place where she had been born and bred. She had come home.

Closing her eyes and enjoying her soak in the warm suds scented by a Yardley bath cube, she heard the sudden crashing boom of brass band music coming from somewhere in the house and had a feeling that it was coming from the flat below hers. From Donald's room. She remembered that he had said that he was working on an old-fashioned wind-up record player that he had found in a skip, and by the sound of things he had managed to get it working. Sighing at this first sign of trouble she tried to relax again, but the music got louder and the sound of crashing cymbals told her that enough was enough.

'You know what Granddad has always said . . .' she told herself. 'If you've got a complaint don't put it off because it's not likely to right itself. I wouldn't mind if I liked brass band music but I don't. And *that* is very, very loud!'

Deciding to take the bull by the horns she got out of the bath, pulled on her long thick white towelling robe and tied the belt nice and tight. She pushed her wet feet into her bath slippers and made for her flat door, putting the latch on so as not to shut herself out on her very first day. She went downstairs to Donald's door and thumped it with the heel of her hand, but with the noise from within resounding through the hallway she guessed that he wouldn't be able to hear her. Then, as if the Almighty had heard her plea, the noise stopped and she knocked again to try and catch him before another burst of music.

Opening the door to her, Donald was clearly taken aback. It was as if he had no idea that anyone else lived in the house. 'Charlotte. Goodness. There you are in your bathrobe and here I am wearing one of my father's old silk smoking jackets. I don't think anything like this has ever happened before.' He smiled incredulously.

'Donald . . . I'm really sorry to be a spoilsport but that music is very loud.'

'Oh dear.' He sucked on his pipe thoughtfully. 'I didn't realise just how powerful music could be. And if it's upset you enough to have you come down to complain I will certainly lower the sound. This is the very first time that I've managed to get the old wind-up going so I was carried away by my little success. I do apologise. My father always said that had we been born poor I would make a very good electrical engineer. This of course was when I was a lad, a grasshopper as he liked to refer to me. Last week I fixed an electric iron of Mother's that was getting far too hot. Just a small electrical fault but dangerous had I not detected it.'

Charlotte smiled warmly at him. 'No hard feelings then? My asking you to keep the sound down?'

'No, no. No hard feelings. I don't suppose you would like a cup of instant coffee while you're here? I was just going to boil a kettle. Up until last week I always percolated my coffee from ground beans but then I was given a free sample of instant and I found it rather nice. And far quicker to make than percolated.'

'No, thank you, I must go and finish having my bath and then get ready to go out and meet my boyfriend.'

'Ah. Boyfriend. Then indeed I mustn't keep you. And will this boyfriend be taking you somewhere pleasant?'

'For a drink in the Black Boy pub on the Mile End Road and then to my grandparents and then to a Chinese restaurant just five minutes from where they live.'

Donald raised his eyebrows and drew breath. 'Chinese? Oh dear. The Chinese have been known to eat dogs, you know.'

Charlotte laughed. 'Not in our part of the world they don't. Anyway . . . thanks for being so good about keeping the sound down. I do appreciate it.'

'I do have a book on China and its people through the ages and I think you will find that I am right about what they eat and what they don't eat.'

'Well, I'm really not that bothered. As long as I eat what I want, who cares what other people do?'

'I suppose that is one way of looking at it,' he said, all thoughtful. 'But then—'

'I must go, Donald,' she said, before he could get in to another long speech, 'or my bath water will go cold.' With that she smiled, showed a hand and practically ran back up the stairs.

Once back soaking in her bath, she had to ask herself again if her landlady's son was all the ticket. She didn't think he looked much older than herself, maybe a year or two, and yet he spoke as if he was a worldly-wise old man. Clearly he wasn't a normal run-of-the-mill chap and all she could hope was that he was just an oddball and nothing more sinister than that. She felt a chill run down her spine, then berated herself for being mean-minded about the poor soul and allowing Wendy to sow seeds in her mind about his state of mind. He was all right. A bit bonkers but okay.

Chapter Fifteen

Sitting on her favourite padded tall-backed chair by the long sash windows in her sitting room, Wendy, drawing through her gold-rimmed ivory cigarette holder, was enjoying a smoke. Now dressed in her purple and pink three-quarter-length summer coat and dress and with her make-up on, she was recalling a time in her childhood – a time when she would have rather been at home than at a private boarding school. Her parents had wanted her to do well and eventually go on to university, but she hadn't wanted any of that. All that she had ever dreamed of was to one day own her own bookshop in London. Earlier on in life, when just seventeen and before she had married the bastard who had left her for another, she had got a job as junior book buyer at Foyles in the West End of London and taken cheap digs close to the store.

Her parents hadn't been happy about her stubbornness in getting what she wanted and her father had written several times during the early years telling her that unless she returned to the family home she would be left to herself; that neither he nor her mother would visit her. But then her father, who had always ruled with the rod, had simply refused to believe that all she had wanted when it came to a career was to sell books or be a writer. From the age of five, when she had been taken to join the local library, she had simply loved books. The look of them, the feel and the smell, and of course the content.

It was true that she was now sometimes a little on the lonely side, but she had her window and could look down on the square below and the houses opposite. She loved all seasons, but her favourite was when she could see the pink blossom on the trees that lined the narrow road. She loved the square, where she had now lived for a while, especially that lovely green below hedged by cherry trees and waist-high black wrought-iron railings with a pretty gate on a latch.

Her self-contained apartment, as she liked to call it, was probably similar to others in this old-fashioned type of square where most of the period houses had been converted into separate dwellings. Donald had painted her walls and ceiling white just before she had moved in and now it was all looking a touch jaded, but she didn't mind.

She had taken to the new girl Charlotte straight away and felt that she would fit in nicely with the rest of them. She thought that the artist in the basement flat was a touch unsociable and preferred to keep himself to himself, which is what he did for most of the time. But he did show his face now and then when a barbecue had been arranged in the garden. She also liked her landlady, Isabelle, who she got on quite nicely with. Of course, being the landlady she lived in the best and most salubrious apartment of all four and who could blame her? She certainly didn't. Wendy felt that she was in tune with Isabelle even if she couldn't fathom her son Donald. He seemed content enough to maintain a solitary life, with no sign of a girlfriend in the wings. He was pleasant enough but even so, she had decided from the very beginning to keep a friendly distance.

Fortunately, he, just like her, preferred his own company for most of the time. And if he talked to himself, the way she sometimes did at times . . . what did it matter? She preferred to have a one sided-conversation with no one there to hear the private thoughts that she spoke out loud, so why wouldn't he? Once she had lit her second and final cigarette of the day, she poured herself a little more sherry from her beautiful cut-glass decanter, which always stood on a tall side table next to her chair by the window. She so loved this time of the evening.

Her thoughts drifting from one thing to another, Wendy murmured, 'Of course I'm bound to get lonely in my room at times. Anybody would if there's nobody around to talk to. It's not something that I worry over . . . but I do find it offensive when people at work ask if I shouldn't get out a bit more.

'And as for my husband . . . I don't think I do want to see him now. The ball's been in his court for long enough and he's done absolutely nothing about it. He could find me if he wanted to.' She then looked around, saying to herself for the umpteenth time that she really should put back onto the hangers the clothes that she had been trying on.

'I just have to make sure that I look my best and that's all there is to it. I've always been this way. I

246

wouldn't want to be like my landlady. An old wealthy Bohemian? I should say not.' She giggled at the thought of it.

'I wouldn't mind betting that Donald is the only heir, and I'm certain there's got to be a lot of old money floating about. He'll get everything. Lock, stock and barrel, and won't know what to do with it.

'And as for the artist who lives in a basement of all places . . . well, I simply cannot imagine what it must be like to live below ground. I suppose this is why he goes out almost every night. I don't know if he has a hoard of lovers or plenty of lady friends. He's always entertaining but never invites any of us to join in. But never mind . . . Each to their own as my father would always say. Each to their own.

'When I get a chance I shall speak to him again. I shall tell him that the cravats that he wears aren't really in keeping with our surroundings. If he wants to dress flamboyantly like an artist, he should live in Portobello Road. I've been there many times of course, and I know that most of the minglers are actors or writers or painters. I should think that he would suit that area far more than he suits this one . . . in my humble opinion.'

Her sherry glass empty for the second time and her second cigarette smoked, Wendy was now ready to go out into the Saturday evening for her stroll along the High Road. Checking herself in her gilt-framed full-length mirror on curling legs, she thought she looked glamorously sophisticated and younger than her forty-five years. With this thought in mind she left her apartment, double-locked her door, and drifted down the staircase. On reaching the first floor landing she was greeted by Donald, who was turning the key in the lock of his door and was dressed ready to go out himself.

'Goodness me . . . we do look smart in our sports jacket,' said Wendy as she lifted an envelope from her post in-tray and slipped it into her pocket. This was from her optician to remind her that her reading glasses were ready for collection. 'Are we going somewhere special? To meet up with a young lady, perchance?'

'As a matter of fact, Wendy, I am on my way to a very important meeting at the library. A local author whose first book has just been brought out in hardback is giving a talk and I am to conduct a signing session.' They then walked down the stairs together and out of the house.

'How terribly exciting,' she said as they stepped out onto the wide entrance decked with old and worn flagstones. 'You simply must let me know how it goes.'

'Yes I shall,' said Donald, closing the door behind them. 'I'm expecting quite a few people to be there, as well as the local press. It's something that I've been quietly arranging for some time. We need to let the outside world know that not all of the people who live in the East End work in the docks or in the factories.'

Walking down the few steps and onto the pavement, Wendy bade a middle-aged gentleman good evening and he returned the gesture with a smile and the old-fashioned lifting of his trilby hat as he continued on his way. 'Well, indeed, we do need to back our local talent,' she said. 'I would have loved to attend the book signing myself, but I have another engagement so alas I shall have to miss it.' This was a fib but only a tiny one. 'But let's stroll nice and *slowly* along the High Road together until we branch off in different directions.' She hoped that her emphasis on the word slowly would put him off.

Donald raised a concerned eyebrow as he glanced at his wristwatch. 'As much as I would like to escort you, Wendy, I am sorry to say that I'm in a bit of a rush. I have to be there in advance of everyone else so as to make sure that the staff in the library have carried out my instructions to the nth degree. It is a very important evening.'

'Well, of course you must. You hurry along, my dear, and do give me an update tomorrow. It all sounds so terribly exciting.'

'I won't promise, but providing I am not called upon to give an interview to the press or attend a photo shoot, then I shall call in on you and give a full account of how it went. How does this sound?'

'Marvellous. Simply marvellous.'

'Good. And please do have a very enjoyable evening yourself. I must say that you are looking very glamorous.' He then straightened and nodded politely at her before taking his leave.

Watching him walk away, Wendy murmured, 'Mad as a March hare' to herself, then hovered for a few moments so as to give him time to get well ahead of her. The last thing she wanted was to have to walk along with her landlady's peculiar son who sometimes talked non-stop and about nothing of any consequence. She glanced along the wide pavement on this very pleasant evening and decided to take another route for her stroll. A route through the narrow back street. She slipped across the boulevard, as she liked to call the tree-lined square, and was surprised to see a young man on one of the benches. She felt duty bound to bid the lonely-looking soul good evening.

Smiling gently back at her, Kenny felt that this was fate on his side again. He knew exactly who she was, of course – Wendy from the bookshop who lived in the grand house, where he presumed Charlotte was now lodging. He had been toying with the idea of pulling on the old-fashioned doorbell of the house to ask Charlotte if she would like to go out for a drink with him. He wanted to find out why she had been nasty to him when they were kids on the street. And why she had only hung out with the fat Jew called Nathan at that time. He also wanted to know why she had always tried to humiliate him those years back when he had been out and about with the lads to whom he had been leader of the pack.

But an attractive older woman had come into his orbit. A bit of nice old, as his dad would say. The words, *a bit of fun with a bit of old*, drifted through his mind. He couldn't help smiling.

Drawing on his cigarette he pushed away thoughts of Charlie, and focused on this woman. Someone, who to his way of thinking, was mutton dressed as lamb – someone who had the look of a paid whore and someone that he might be able to have a little bit of fun with.

Kenny was bored yet agitated, and when this mood took him he was his own worst enemy. His need for excitement at such times took over, and right now he was in a kind of tormenting frame of mind with nowhere to go and no one around to give vent to his lust for fun. Except for this older woman, this bit of mature cheese, who was now settling herself on another of the benches. She wasn't a bad looker to his way of thinking.

Paying Kenny no attention, Wendy took out of her handbag her packet of cigarettes. She would, after all, have another smoke before she set off to see what the evening had in store. Of course she had noticed that the good-looking lad in the gardens was giving her the eye, but he was far too young and a touch too tall and lean for her taste. She vaguely recognised him as one of her customers from the bookshop and was aware that he was watching her. She turned to glance at him over her shoulder and then leaned back on the bench and drew on her cigarette. Smiling inwardly, she glanced at her delicate hands and manicured nails and the pretty new pale pink varnish purchased that day. She felt quite beautiful and more than ready for a romantic liaison. Soon she would make her way to her favourite pub down by the riverside for a gin and tonic.

She was so carried away with her thoughts that she didn't see Kenny approach, and only just heard him ask her if she would mind giving him a light. Glancing up at him, she was surprised to see that he didn't look quite so gaunt when standing and had quite broad shoulders for a lean young man.

'Be my guest,' she said, offering her rolled-gold slim Dunhill lighter.

'That's very kind of you,' said Kenny. 'Thanks very

much.' He then lit his roll-up and said, 'Haven't I seen you in the second-hand bookshop?'

'Oh . . .' Wendy smiled. 'Well yes, I do work there . . .' She wasn't sure that she wanted to give too much away about her life, especially not to a complete stranger.

'I love second-hand books,' said Kenny. 'I much prefer them to brand spanking new ones. Don't ask me why.'

'I wouldn't dream of it,' said Wendy with a smile. 'I perfectly understand. I too prefer books that have been thumbed just a little.'

'It's not just that though,' said Kenny. 'It's the interesting books that you've got on your shelves. Stacks of books written by famous writers in paperback that are a brilliant read.'

Wendy patted his hand maternally and then squeezed it. 'Young man . . . you have made a woman old enough to be your mother very happy. I love my work in the bookshop. And mostly for the reasons that you mention.'

'Old enough to be my mother? Give me a break.' Kenny laughed. 'You can't be a day older than thirty and even though I'm only eighteen going on nineteen, I think I can tell that you're kidding me.'

'Well, I'm not. But I must say I don't feel my age and in fact I would go as far as to say that I actually feel more like a thirty-year-old. So in a way you are a very perceptive young man.'

'Well, that's really nice of you to say so.' He then cupped his chin and went all thoughtful before saying,

'Would you be offended if I asked you to come for a drink with me?'

'Of course I wouldn't be offended. I was only going for an evening stroll. I chose this purple and pink outfit for this evening because I felt that there might well be a lovely sunset that I could blend into. All dressed up in sunset colours with nowhere in particular to go,' she smiled. 'Everything matches. Even the shoes.'

'I know. I thought you were an actress when you walked in all graceful and natural like. You're a very attractive woman – but then I suppose you know that already.'

'Not really, but thank you for the compliment. And I must say that you're a handsome young man. You could easily find someone of your own age to partner you for a drink, I feel sure of it. A very nice girl at that. One who would enjoy sipping a gin and tonic in your company.'

Kenny offered a cheeky smile. 'So that's your favourite drink, is it?' he said. 'Good. Because when I'm a bit flush, as I am now, that's my drink too.' He lied.

'Really? What a lovely coincidence. And why shouldn't we go for a drink together? Yes, I would very much like to join you for a glass of our favourite. Thank you for asking – if you're really sure you wouldn't rather go to a pub with a girl of your own age.'

'I am sure,' he said, 'and I'll tell you why. Later on, I've to be at my nana's house to read a bit from her favourite novel before she drifts off to sleep. I love my nana and I'm the only one who sits with her. She's lovely but a very lonely soul.'

'Goodness me – what a kind young man you are.' Wendy then gracefully lifted herself from the seat and said, 'Shall we go?'

Smiling at her, Kenny offered his arm and together they strolled away from the square, taking the back route towards the Prospect of Whitby, a romantic kind of a riverside pub down by the docks. This was a place where each of them knew that they could sit on the timber balcony and gaze at the inlet from the Thames flowing by, and once the evening sun went down candles would be lit.

Quietly chatting away about this, that and the other to do with both of their make-believe worlds, they came into a narrow turning with derelict run-down houses on either side. This was a dead-end where bombed-out houses and a small factory showed the result of the war. Stopping in his tracks Kenny said, 'This is where I used to love to play as a kid.'

'Really?' said Wendy. 'How sweet. You would think that by now those buildings would have been razed to the ground, wouldn't you?'

'Well . . .' Kenny sighed. 'In a way I agree with you, but on the other hand it's a bit of history that reminds us of what that war did. Come on. We'll wander down there and we can cut through to the Prospect.'

Loving every minute of this impromptu nostalgic walk, Wendy allowed him to lead the way. 'I'm sure that this back turning should have been reconstructed with new housing by now,' she said. 'But do you know, I quite enjoy the thought of walking through a bit of our local if not our tragic history.'

'I know what you mean,' he said. 'And I'm glad you feel the same as I do. Not everyone goes in for nostalgia, do they?' He then stopped by one of the broken terraced houses without a front door and slowly shook his head. 'You might not believe this but my great-aunt and uncle used to live here.' He was such a convincing liar.

Wendy was all ears and all heart. 'Oh, how sad. Well, look, before this lovely evening turns into the black of night, why don't we go carefully into the house for the sake of auld lang syne? Or would this be too upsetting for you?'

'No, I would like that very much. But I wouldn't dream of asking a lady such as yourself to go into an old place like that,' he said, all convincing.

'But you didn't ask, my darling boy – I am suggesting it. To be able to slip into your ancestor's home before this is all razed to the ground? It's an opportunity and an experience not to be missed, surely?'

'Well,' said Kenny, slowly shaking his head and sighing. 'Put like that . . .'

'We must do it!' she said, all excited.

Taking her hand, Kenny gently led her through the open doorway and into the semi-dark bombed house. 'Be careful,' he said. 'The floorboards could give way and we could end up in my great-aunt and uncle's cellar.'

Once inside the passage and looking into a room that had once been a parlour and was covered in filth and dust, Wendy sighed. 'To think that your relatives once sat in there and ate their supper.'

Turning his head to look into her older but beautiful face, Kenny showed a sad expression and sighed. 'You know, I think you should write books rather than sell them. You have a way with words that gets you here.' He gently patted his chest where his heart was beating like mad. Racing, in fact.

'Well as a matter of fact,' she said, smiling, 'I am a secret writer.' She looked across the room at a small cupboard with its door hanging open on just one hinge that was next to the fireplace.

'Honest to God?' said Kenny, now more than a touch excited by the thought of possibly squeezing the last breath out of this woman. 'You really are a writer?'

'Yes. I write a column for a magazine now and then and I'm also—' She stopped in her tracks as she looked into Kenny's eyes and saw a different expression in them – and on his face. One that she found quite frightening. There was a kind of look of menace about him now. Menace and loathing. 'Are you all right, dear?' she just managed to say as she glanced sideways around this old derelict building.

Of course he was all right. He had clocked her jewellery and could see that she had on a diamond ring to die for. He smiled and then chuckled. 'Am I all right, she asks. Now what's that supposed to mean? You're not gonna start patronising me, are yer? After all, you're nothing but a cheap paid whore. A fucking whore. Who pays for the jewellery, eh? The rich men who like a woman who wears loose silk drawers?'

Stunned, and very frightened by his sudden change of mood, Wendy glanced at the open doorway again and could see that to make an escape one would have to go via the narrow passage. 'I am not a whore, young man,' she said. 'I am nothing of the sort. I thought that we had made friends with each other. Not bosom buddy friends, granted. But then you know this and you're just teasing me for fun.' She forced a smile as she slowly backed away towards the passageway and the opening that led out into the street and fresh air. But Kenny had anticipated this and was casually stepping sideways so as to block her. It was as if he was playing a game and thoroughly enjoying it. A game of scare and dare. His eyes narrowed as if he were in deep thought as he stared into her face. And he was chewing the inside of his cheek.

With her heart pumping faster and her stomach in a knot, Wendy did her utmost to keep calm even though she knew that the young man, who was, of course, no more than a stranger, would be able to see that her fingers were trembling. Cold beads of sweat were now breaking out on her forehead as his cold eyes searched hers. He then spoke in a gentle but intimidating voice, with a smile to match. 'Teasing you?' he said. 'A fucking whore? Why would I want to do that? And do not patronise me.'

'I wouldn't dream of it. Why would I want to?' Wendy's throat was so dry she could hardly get her words out.

Grinning, Kenny stepped closer and cupped her chin. 'Nice jewellery,' he said. 'Nice gold earrings. You've got good taste for a whore.' He then gripped her neck between both hands and pressed his thumbs onto her Adam's apple with every bit of strength he had. He wanted this to be quick.

'You're no fucking better than the rest of 'em. You let men fuck you for a few quid. You and those like you 'ave turned our beautiful country into a place not fit for rats to live in. You fucking whoring bitch.' He tightened his grip and watched her eyes widen as the look of terror on her face fuelled his sense of power. He was getting rid of another whore who lured good men from their families. He squeezed so hard that he could feel himself trembling.

'All things from the soul shines out through the eyes,' he said, and then squeezed the last breath of air out of Wendy, who had never knowingly harmed a soul. He squeezed and she struggled . . . and then she started to choke on her own phlegm as her eyes widened. Then came the familiar sounds of dying that he had come to recognise and love. Trembling with a kind of passion, Kenny held his grip until her head flopped forward and her body was limp.

Exhausted both physically and mentally, he released himself from the corpse to let her drop to the filthy old floorboards in a heap as if she was a bag of dirty old laundry. Standing above her and drawing deep breaths of air he slowly regained composure. All of his energy spent, he dropped to his knees and placed both hands over his face, telling his make-believe master that this was it. This was enough. This would be his last killing. He had done his duty and all that he asked for now was to live a quiet and ordinary life. After a space of time passing, Kenny glanced at his wristwatch and wasn't sure how long he had knelt beside the whore who had coaxed him to kill her. He dragged himself out of the room and into the dark and narrow passage and flopped down onto the staircase, where he sat with his head cupped in his hands in the stinking derelict house not that far away from where he lived.

'You're getting too chancy for your own good, Kenny boy,' he murmured as he tapped his head on the worm-eaten banister of the musty old staircase. A staircase that stank of mildew and rot and was under the shattered roof of a house that he imagined had once been home to some poor bastards, now dead, buried and forgotten. And then, with a sudden change of mood and a rush of self-esteem that seemed to come at times like this, he quietly congratulated himself for having done well. He was exhausted but proud of what he had achieved. He had rid England of another whore. He went back to the corpse and went down on one knee so as to carefully remove all of her jewellery. He took her purse and anything that would identify her so as to slow down the police efforts at uncovering her identity. But he had missed one important thing. In her pocket was the letter from her optician that she had picked up on her way out of the house.

Happy with all that he now had in his pocket, which he saw as payment for his deed of ridding the world of scum, Kenny used one foot and then the other to slowly inch Wendy's body towards a corner of the room. This was where he could see that the floorboards were broken and riddled with woodworm. Once she was in place where he needed her to be, he brought his heel down with an almighty crash onto the boards and then stood back to watch as the body of the woman, in a cloud of musty dank dust, dropped down into the dark cellar below. Pinching his lips together he then staggered to the doorway of the house and drew deep breaths of fresh air. Once composed, he brushed away the filth and did his best to walk innocently into the warm evening, with the swirling leaves rustling along the pavement.

Kenny took the long route back home to his parents' flat on the new council estate where the small family had seemingly settled into a fairly peaceful way of life. He felt okay. He felt that he had done well. He felt satisfied that he and he alone had rid this country of another piece of shite. And now he was hungry and looking forward to whatever his mother had on the stove. She was a good old-fashioned cook, if nothing else.

Chapter Sixteen

Waiting for her son Kenny to come home while her husband was having a drink in his local with a few mates, Liza could not rid herself of the worry that had crept to the forefront of her mind. She knew that her son wasn't like normal lads of his age and she had a horrible nagging sensation in the pit of her stomach that something bad was happening. Her son had been in one of his dark moods again and she sensed that something was wrong, that her only child, now a young man, was very troubled. He had been too quiet since his return from Norfolk and had spent too much time curled up on his bed with the door shut. She knew that it would be useless talking to his father about her fears because he was so stubborn, and adamant that there was nothing wrong with the lad. But then, he hadn't been the one to give birth or breast-feed, and as far as Liza was concerned this was when bonding took place. The expression on her husband's face said it all when she had worried in front of him previously about their boy. He would have none of it. To him, Kenny was just a lazy little bastard who only worked when push came to shove, and that was the root of all his problems, laziness.

And now, as she sat on the edge of the kitchen chair

looking at a pile of clean laundry waiting to be ironed, the distraught woman wondered yet again where her son might have got to. She also wondered what he might be doing or, worse still, what he might have already done. He hadn't been in for his favourite dinner of sausage toad, mashed potatoes and greens that she had put on steam to keep warm for him. Her gaze fell back to the ironing but still she couldn't bring herself to tackle it. Kenny had, and always would, draw her to worry, even though he was now eighteen going on nineteen. He was her son and she loved him.

He had been left so many times when a baby, and then as a child when she had gone out in the evenings with her sister to work the best and most lucrative streets in the West End – and for this she could not forgive herself. Pulling herself up from the chair where she had been sitting for over an hour, she decided to run herself a warm bath and pour in lots of scented bath oil. But just as she went into the bathroom she heard the key turn in the street door and knew that it was her son back from wherever he had been. She waited to see what kind of an expression was on his face. She hoped it wouldn't be the all-telling look of guilt as if he had done wrong. Something bad. Something really bad that would eventually lead to his collapse. This had always been her fear. Going into the sitting room once she knew that he was in there, she stood in the doorway and looked at him. He was pale and drawn and she could see that his hands were shaking. 'What is it, Kenny? What's the matter? What have you done?'

He closed the door of the sitting room and turned to face her, shock and fear showing in his eyes. This time he had gone too far and he knew it. He had killed someone on his own doorstep and felt that this could be his downfall.

The fear in his eyes told Liza that he had been bad again. She watched as he unbuttoned his jacket and when he caught her eye he shrugged apologetically as if to say, 'I've done it again, Mum.' She didn't know what it was that he had been up to when he came home in this kind of a state and neither did she want to. She loved her son so much it hurt. She couldn't bear the thought of him going to prison, and somehow she just knew that whatever it was that he did before coming back like this had to be bad. Very bad. She wasn't going to ask. She never did. 'I'll run you a nice warm bath, sweetheart,' she said. Once in the bathroom she put in the plug and turned on the chrome taps, then dangled her fingers in the water to make sure that the temperature was just right for him. After a long soak he would no doubt fall into his bed and sleep like a baby until the morning. Sleep like a baby and weep in his sleep and sometimes wail quietly. She knew the pattern. She had lain in the dark listening to him enough times now to know. Her son was in the depths of hell and misery.

Charlotte, having been pushed into accepting an invitation over the phone from her granddad to go to his house for supper with Nathan instead of the lad spending his hard-earned money at a restaurant, the young couple were now on the way there. Strolling along a back turning that was lit up by lovely old-fashioned iron lamp-posts and holding hands, she said, 'I feel guilty for caving in on the phone, now. It's not fair on you, never mind me. I should have been more adamant. Told Granddad that I wanted us to go for our romantic candlelit dinner. It's my fault.'

'The older generations are wily, Charlotte. My grandpa is, and so is my dad come to that. They always seem to manage to get their own way. But never mind, I can always book a table for two another time. We've got all the time in the world.'

'That's true,' she smiled. 'And I suppose I can't really blame Gran and Granddad. They hardly ever see me.' She squeezed his hand and then slipped her arm around him. The back street where Nell and Johnny lived was generally quiet at this time of the evening with the glow of indoor lights shining warmly through unlined curtains.

'I won't say that I have any regrets at having been brought up in this part of the world, Charlotte,' murmured Nathan. 'But I would like to live in the suburbs one day. In a similar turning to this one but where it's more open. Wanstead is very nice and so is Woodford Green. Both are almost on the borders of Essex.'

'That sounds like a really good compromise. Living in Norfolk didn't do much for me, but I suppose I would miss the countryside now if we were to move back into this neck of the woods.'

Nathan quietly laughed. 'Now *you* sound like the older generation. *Neck of the woods*. That's your grandparents talking.'

Charlotte smiled back at him. 'My granddad actually. He's always saying it. But we are what we are and we can still learn from the old 'uns. Don't knock it.'

'I wouldn't dare. My dad would have my guts for garters if I pulled him up every time he came out with his old-fashioned clichés. But there are one or two that none of us would want to disappear.'

'Such as?'

'Well . . . how about "I love you more than all the tea in China"?'

Charlotte laughed. 'Is that what he said to your mum?'

'All of the time. And now I'm going to keep up the tradition.' He stopped in his tracks, placed his hands on either side of her face and said, 'But I love you more than all the tea in the world, Charlotte.'

'And I love you more than all the slingback shoes and handbags in the world, Nathan.'

Nathan burst out laughing. 'My God, that takes me back. I remember you saying that you wanted both those things all those years ago.'

Continuing on their way, arms around each other, he then added, 'I really did mean what I said to you when we were kids, Charlotte. That I want to marry you one day.'

'And I really meant it when I said you would have to go down on one knee.' She smiled. 'God, it seems ages ago, back then . . . when we were full of hopes and dreams.'

'When I was short and tubby and scared of my own shadow. When I loved you more than all the sand on the beach at Margate. And here we are, and I may not be the same shy boy but I still love you as much as ever.' Then, after a quiet moment he said, 'I hope you don't break my heart for a second time.'

Melting inside, Charlotte drew breath. 'I won't, and I think you know why.'

'Tell me just in case I don't.'

'I love you as much as you love me.'

Swallowing against the lump in his throat, Nathan could only just get his words out. 'May God let it last. And let's leave it there or I will burst into tears, I swear it. And then what would your grandparents make of me if I walk in with red eyes?'

'I hate to think.' Charlotte smiled. 'You're so sweet and so soft and I love you. I'm sorry we moved away from the East End and I'm sorry that you were so lonely without me.'

'It doesn't matter any more. I've got you back and I'm not letting you go. Ever.'

Gazing at him affectionately, Charlotte stopped in her tracks and turned to face him again. 'I think that in a way we did love each other back then and I don't think that we were too young to know . . . as the song goes.'

'No . . . and we're certainly not too young now. I'm crazy about you, Charlie. I always have been.'

'And you're sure that it wasn't the romantic candlelit dinner and the love songs playing in the background in that little restaurant last weekend that turned your head?'

'Of course not. I booked the table as soon as I knew

you were going to be in London. I was determined to win you over.'

'Well, you have.' Charlotte broke into a lovely smile. 'And now you're gonna have to win my nan and grand-dad over.'

Almost at her grandparents' house now, Nathan said, 'I used to dream about marrying you, Charlotte. But I also used to think that that couldn't ever happen . . . unless your family were okay about mixed-faith wed-dings.'

'They'd get used to it in time. I've got an aunt who married her Jewish boyfriend. Nobody minded a bit, we're not like that. But how about your family?'

'I'm not sure. Dad, and maybe my grandparents, would be okay, but I'm not so sure about all of my aunts and uncles. But then I wouldn't much care what they thought. If two people are in love that's all that matters . . . isn't it?'

'Of course. We might be Church of England but we don't go to Sunday services, or any other come to that, unless it's for a wedding, or a christening or funeral. So we're hardly what you would call religious.'

Nathan quietly laughed. 'Absolutely! But I wonder about the grandparents, yours and mine. Maybe we should test the water this evening. See how they think about their only granddaughter being in love with a Jew. A Jew that she might marry one day.'

'Is that a proposal then?'

'No. I said *might*. Time will tell.' He glanced at her face and smiled. 'We love each other and that's all that matters.' Then, stopping by an old tree, Nathan leaned against it and pulled Charlotte in close to him. 'I'm sorry if it sounds as if I'm rushing things. I'm just so bowled over by all that's happened and I do love you so much.'

Charlotte couldn't help but smile warmly at the expression on his face. He hadn't really changed at all. 'I've not had a boyfriend yet, Nathan, but you've had three steady girlfriends from what I remember you telling me. You're going to have to teach me a thing or two.'

Gazing into her beautiful face, Nathan swallowed again, overwhelmed by her loveliness. He could hardly believe it. He had in his arms the girl that he had so badly missed and had never stopped loving. 'I won't need to. We'll take everything one step at a time. Just don't leave me for a second time. I think I would kill myself if you left me again.'

'No, you wouldn't. Don't talk like that. But I do know what you're saying. Ever since you turned up in Bridgeford I've not been able to get you out of my thoughts. Our time together as kids came flooding back.'

Cupping her face, Nathan sighed. 'I can't believe this is happening. I wasn't expecting to be in love like this, and I would be a liar if I said I wasn't scared. I'm bloody terrified. I don't want to lose you.' He blushed a little and then added. 'Please God . . . be on your toes.'

'Oh Nathan . . . I remember who used to say that.'

'My mother.' A look of sadness filled his eyes. 'May God rest her soul.'

Nathan then placed a gentle hand around her lovely

soft white neck and said, 'I love you, Charlie. I love you so much. I always have and always will. And if I'm honest I would love it more than anything in the world if I could just curl up in that bed in that flat with you.'

'But you wouldn't want to rush me . . .'

'Of course I would, but I won't. I'll wait for as long as it takes.'

Clasping her hand in his they strolled onwards in a warm silence until they arrived at Nell and Johnny's door. Charlotte pressed the bell, wondering if her granddad was going to probe Nathan as to his intentions. She was his only grandchild after all.

When the door opened and Johnny stood looking at them she knew that he was trying to cover the fact that he was thrilled to bits to see them. She couldn't help smiling – he was so predictable.

'Oh, look what the ill wind's blown in,' he said. 'And what's the joke then?'

'There's not one, Granddad. I'm just pleased to see you.' She kissed him on the cheek.

'Come on in, the pair of you.' Johnny stood to one side and waved them into the passage. 'Your gran's been polishing the bloody brass and copper and washing the knick-knacks all day in your honour, Nathan. Go on through.'

Closing the door behind them Johnny followed in their footsteps, talking as he went. 'Gawd only knows how long she's 'ad that chicken and barley soup on the stove. She reckons she knew that famous East End playwright's – what's 'is name – mother who always cooked it for 'im. Your nan reckons that it was his mother who gave her the recipe in the first place. She's fibbing, but it's true that she always got on well wiv our Jewish neighbours.'

They went into the living room with Johnny still rambling. Charlotte knew that his shaggy dog story was her granddad's clumsy way of letting Nathan know that he had no objection to her courting someone of a different faith. 'I know she did, and the playwright you're talking about is Arnold Wesker.'

'Eh?' Johnny, who always smelt of Lifebuoy soap leaned back and stared at her face. 'How'd you know that?'

'The amateur dramatic group that Nathan belongs to put on one of his plays last week and he told me all about it.' She nudged Nathan to give him the cue to get in now. To make something of the fact that her granddad was trying to find something in common that they could talk about.

'What a coincidence,' said Nathan, 'that you should know the playwright who I happen to think is the best that we've got.'

'Go on!' said Johnny. 'Fancy that.'

Once they were in the kitchen, Nell turned away from her stove and wiped her hands on her pinafore and then offered her hand to Nathan. 'How do you do,' she said, too worn out to be anything more than polite right then.

'How does he do?' Johnny laughed. 'Mind your own bloody business.' He then looked at Nathan and slowly shook his head as he looked up to heaven. 'Anyone'd think that you were royalty, wouldn't they. Sit yerself down, son. Our kitchen's not a palace but it's clean and well paid for.'

'You sound just like my grandpa. He says exactly the same thing.'

'Does he? Oh that's good. Our little home is humble, but there's always a welcome mat at the door. That Formica table top's not so humble though – that cost a few bob when it was new. Personally, I would 'ave preferred to 'ave a blue one with little gold stars but the gov'nor wanted pale primrose and so that was that.'

'Take no notice of 'im,' said Nell, smiling. 'He rambles on like this all the time. Now then, do you both want a cup of coffee?'

'That would be very nice.' Nathan smiled and sat down.

'And what about you, Charlotte?'

'I'll have the same, Nan.'

'Right. Put the milk in the little saucepan, Johnny.'

'See what I mean? Do this, do that, skin the cat . . .' Still grumbling jokily, Johnny went to do as he was told.

Nell drew breath and then spoke in a whispering voice, *'Moan, moan, moan.* If only it was still the nineteen-thirties and I was still beautiful and young. I would be off with a secret admirer. I was always tall and slim.'

Johnny lit his Woodbine cigarette with his old chrome Zippo. Then, slipping it back into its worn leather pouch, he said, 'You're too blooming well thin. Pencil thin.'

'And you haven't seen better days?' said his wife. 'I don't know how I put up with him sitting in that chair day in, day out. Don't forget to warm the teapot as well. I don't want coffee.'

'No, I won't forget.' Johnny slowly nodded his head. 'God help you once I do pop my clogs.' He went back to his chores. 'Who'll be at your beck and call then, eh?'

'Here we go again . . .' Charlotte sighed and then laughed. She had heard most of what her granddad came out with many times before.

'I was a secretary once upon a time, Nathan,' said Nell. 'Always smart. Always on time. And I could type forty words per minute on a clanking old typewriter. Admirers? You should 've seen 'em. Queuing up at the door for a kiss and a squeeze they were. Of course, I couldn't afford to be independent the way Charlotte is now. What I wouldn't have given to be able to live in a little flat of my own.' Arching one eyebrow, as was her habit, she sighed. 'But she does remind me of myself when young, I will say that. Independent and rely on no one.'

'You still are independent, Nan. You earn your own little bit of money cleaning at the Moonlight Soap powder factory five mornings a week now, don't yer?' Charlotte smiled.

'That's true. So, are the pair of you gonna stop overnight? Nathan can go on the settee.' She turned to look at him and said, 'It pulls down to a bed again.'

'I hadn't thought of stopping over,' said Nathan, eyeing Charlotte. 'But it would be nice. Or do you want to sleep in your little pad tonight, Charlotte?'

'I don't mind.'

'It's a lovely invitation,' he said, trying to keep his

options open. 'Let's see how we feel later on after we've been out. You might want to get back and Dad will be expecting me in so won't bolt the door before he goes to bed.'

'Well, you can phone 'im and tell 'im to bolt the bloody door, can't yer, so that's settled. And as we said, there's no need to waste good money on a restaurant. We'll 'ave chicken soup with toast and all sit round the table in the morning for a nice fried bacon, egg and tomato breakfast,' said Johnny before going to the sink with his own cup and saucer so as to wash it up before his wife started to nag.

Nell sat down with a sigh and then leaned back in her chair. Smiling to herself, she was dead chuffed that her granddaughter and boyfriend were happy to consider stopping over in their little abode. 'We could 'ave a game of cards. Play for pennies though and not shillings.'

'Play *what* for pennies?' asked Johnny.

'Pontoon.' Nell folded her arms and shot him a look of warning. 'It's what we *all* want to play before we turn in. It's all arranged.'

'No it's not, Nan. Stop telling fibs. We might play cards and we might not. We might stop over and we might not. We were gonna go to a favourite—'

'You're bound to wanna stop over, the way I've done that bedroom up!' Johnny cut in so as to have his way. 'I'm pleased with it. Would you like to 'ave a butcher's at the way I've done the spare bedroom up for madam, Nathan? All my own work that is.'

'Here we go,' said Nell, placing the flat of her hand

on her forehead. Then, leaning forward in her chair she said, 'I don't wanna get a migraine, Johnny, so don't go on and on and on about that bloody wallpaper and paint.'

'I wasn't gonna! But I will say this and I'll say no more. That little cupboard, next to the old-fashioned fireplace up there that I painted in a nice ivory cream, does remind me of when I was boy.' He slowly shook his head, all thoughtful. 'I used to hide in my old gran's little cupboard which was very similar.

'When I was in that cupboard I imagined I was back there in the olden days with Oliver Twist and Charles Dickens and that. Then, later on in life when this place came up for us and I went into that bedroom . . . well, I was taken right back. Back to when my old granny used to look after me. I could smell the must. She used to let me rummage through her old photograph albums and that. Kept me quiet for hours that did.'

'Do you take sugar, Nathan? Only you look as if you've been on a diet. You was a fat little sod when a kid,' said Nell.

'Two please,' said Nathan, ignoring the fond insult.

'Charlotte's got a bed all to 'erself up there – home from home. When I was a kid I 'ad to share with two brothers. Which is why I appreciated it when I stayed at my granddad's. I used to lay on the bed and listen to the song of a blackbird. They were a happy couple, my old grandparents. Warm and affectionate as well as friendly. And they never nagged each other neither.' He looked slyly at Nell. 'My old granddad used to do all the decorating as well, and my nan used to keep the place lovely.

Kept on top of the dust and that without you even seeing the duster in 'er fingers. You never saw dust floating in the ray of the sunshine coming in through the windows in that old house the way you do in this one. You only 'ave to open a door in this place to see it dancing. Ain't that right, sweetheart?' He smiled. He was tormenting Nell and he knew that she knew it.

'I wouldn't know, Johnny . . . my mind's not on dust all fucking day long, as it just so happens.'

Johnny winked at Nathan. 'If you don't keep on top of dust it'll choke you to death in the end.'

'Well, you'd better do the dusting from now on then, Johnny – instead of sitting on your backside and listening to sport on the wireless or the telly hour after hour. He never folds his clothes, Nathan, he just leaves them crumpled in a heap on the bedroom floor. Sometimes I wish he would go to sleep for years and then wake up the man he was when I first met him.'

'God help you once I've gone.' Johnny smiled with a certain look of self-satisfaction. 'You'll 'ave no one to nag and no one to make pies for. And if you don't make pies you can't brag about it down at the laundry doing your washing.' Taking the Woodbine from the corner of his mouth and placing it on the edge of a saucer he was using as an ashtray he chuckled and then said, 'It sounds like a song, don't it?' He hummed a little tune and sang, 'Down at the old laundry rooms . . . da, da, da, and da . . .'

Half an hour later, once they'd drunk their beverages and the old folk had got used to the youngsters being there, Johnny and Nell were at it again, getting digs in at each other whenever they could. The banter was amusing whichever way it was viewed.

'I should 'ave married the first love of my life. His name was Chris. He was such a quiet chap. A real gentleman,' said Nell.

The two men of different generations looked at each other, suppressing their laughter. 'What 'ave I done now? Why are you trying to make me jealous by fetching up old tales of old boyfriends?' Johnny winked at Nathan.

'What 'ave you done? It's what you *don't* fucking well do. You never wash up, you never vacuum the place for me, you don't cook dinner and you don't do the ironing.'

'I keep the back yard looking like a little garden for yer though, don't I?' he said, trying to look as if she had hurt his feelings.

'And you don't clean the windows neither. Apart from that he's not too bad, Nathan. Some men are worse than him, I dare say. Not many. But some might be. A few. One or two.'

Rolling his eyes, Johnny turned to Charlotte. 'You don't wanna be too late in bed, miss. Not tonight or tomorrow night. You wanna get an early night on both nights. You wanna be nice and rested so that you don't go in to your new job looking like somefing the cat's dragged in.'

'I don't start till Wednesday, Granddad. I went through the contract earlier when I was in my flat and saw the date. Then it clicked. I've been so bowled over by everything that's happening that I got confused.'

'We all do that at one time or another, sweetheart,' said her nan. 'Now then, if you get a bit chilly in the night, Nathan, you switch on the paraffin heater in the corner of the sitting room.'

'You can see a lot from the flames of a fire,' murmured Johnny, 'but there's still somefing cosy about a paraffin heater. All right, with a paraffin heater you might find steam inside the window but so what? On the other side of the road are only houses that are just like this one.'

'You find a reason and an answer to everything, Granddad.'

'Do I? Well thank you, darling. It's nice to get a compliment now and then.' He shot a look at his wife.

'It wasn't meant as a compliment, it was said to shut you up,' sniffed Nell.

'And like I was saying, what if there is a bit of steam? If we can't see out the nosy bastards can't see in, can they?' Johnny grinned. 'I only 'ave to wipe a bit away to see what's going on out there though. I don't get much enjoyment other than to take the mickey out of the neighbours now and then.'

'As well as annoying the relatives if and when they deign to show their faces,' said Nell. 'But there we are. I try to get out as much as I can for a bit of company with people who smile. A smile doesn't cost anything does it? It's a good job that I've got the Women's Institute. That gives me a little bit of pleasure now and then.' She turned to Johnny again. 'You should get out a bit more instead of listening to bloody sport on the wireless all day long. I'm sick of strangers coming into my house through that bloody wireless. Talk talk talk. That's all those bloody sportsmen do.'

'Oh, come on. Don't be like that,' said Charlotte, 'he made the coffee and a pot of tea.'

'Take no notice, Charlotte,' said Johnny. 'Your gran's vying for attention. She's always going out. Once, if not twice, a week when she's not at work. To sit with a load of gossiping women.'

Charlotte looked at Nathan and rolled her eyes and then made a snap decision for the pair of them. 'Me and Nathan are gonna go out for a walk and have a few drinks in one or two of your local pubs. Do you still keep a key on a string or have you got a spare one for me to take, Nan?'

'Key on a string. It's the only one we 'ave got, thanks to your granddad not getting another one cut when he lost the spare.'

'Right – we'll be able to let ourselves in then. I know you both like to be in bed by nine so don't wait up for us. We'll help ourselves to some chicken soup then. Keep it simmering.'

'I should fink I'll be well ready to fall into my bed by then. By the time I've fed the pair of us, washed up, made up the sofa bed for Nathan—'

'Oh no!' said Johnny. 'I'm not 'aving you straining your back pulling that sofa into a put-you-up bed. No. I'll do that.'

Charlotte gave Nathan the eye and a message to move himself and try and show that he was expecting to go for a drink. She wanted to get out before they started going on again and he was only too ready. All he really wanted was to be alone with Charlotte. 'Right. So we'll be off then for a nice romantic evening together back in the East End. Don't wait up.' Charlotte smiled.

With that the couple made a quick exit before Johnny had time to suggest going with them. Once outside in the street Charlotte and Nathan burst into laughter. 'If nothing else . . . your grandparents are very funny,' Nathan just managed to say. 'God help you if you hadn't found that flat and had to live under the same roof. One night I can manage. But no more than that.'

'You and me both.' Charlotte giggled as she slipped her arm into his and strolled along feeling happier than she had ever been in her life.

Once she heard the street door close, Nell, in a provocative mood, put her hands together and closed her eyes, saying, 'Do me a favour, Lord . . . make sure that Charlotte takes to this new job and that they take to her. And if it's not too much to ask, could you please do something about this husband of mine when he's lying next to me in bed talking non-stop, snoring or grinding his teeth.'

'I don't talk non-stop and I don't snore,' said Johnny. 'And I 'aven't any back teeth to grind any more.'

'Well then, it must be an old nightmare from when you did that comes back to haunt me.'

'Don't talk daft. Now then . . . do you fancy a drop of sherry left over from last Christmas?'

'Why? What are you after?'

'Well . . . with all the romance in the air between them two . . . it's brought back lovely memories of when we were young. I thought we might go up for a cuddle. What d'yer reckon?'

'Fetch me a glass of sherry and I'll think about it.'

'Oh . . . so I can take that as a yes then, can I?'

'I don't see why not. I quite fancy a bit of the other between them fresh clean sheets I put on today as a matter of fact. And you'll do – I suppose.' She smiled.

'Well, at your age you're not gonna find anyone more handsome. So shall I take the sherry upstairs then?'

'Yes, please. That'll be lovely. A nice little drink before a nice bit of nookie and then another nice little sip of sherry afterwards.' She looked at her husband and recognised a certain smile on his face that she didn't get to see too often. 'You're still a handsome man you know . . . even if you are a torment.' She stood up and swaggered out of the room calling over her shoulder, 'And don't go too heavy on the after-shave!'

'Oh gawd . . . she wants me to 'ave a shave an' all. I wish I hadn't of said anything now. Still, there you are, Johnny boy. She still finds you irresistible even though she pretends otherwise for most of the time. So we'll make the most of the hay while the sun shines, as they say.'

He peered into the small mirror above the kitchen sink to check whether he could get away with the six o'clock shadow without her noticing. 'Waste of bloom-ing energy, shaving at this time of the day, when I'm not even going down the pub for a pint with the blokes.' He gave a pained sigh and turned off the gas under the saucepan, ready to go upstairs to their little bathroom.

'Johnny!' Nell's somewhat sweeter loud voice echoed from above him.

'Hello! What d'yer want now?'

'Fetch up the rest of the sherry. So I can be sipping that while you're 'aving a quick wash-down? I'm resting on top of the bed!'

Slowly shaking his head Johnny puffed air. 'Oh gawd . . . is it bloody well worth it for a bit of the other?'

Chapter Seventeen

Nathan had woken before anyone else in the house the next morning and not because he was uncomfortable in the makeshift bed but because he was happy to be there – to be in the home of the grandparents of the girl he loved. He was remembering the day when Charlotte had told him she and her family were going to move out of London to Norfolk. A time when he had been too gutted to think straight and had to hold firmly onto the only bit of bravery that he could muster then, when he was thirteen. Smiling to himself, he wondered if Charlotte remembered what he had said when she left. Something that he had heard his dad say more than once. 'Everything, with the exception of a ring, comes to an end at some point.' And soon he would be slipping a ring on to her finger. He had loved her just as much then as he did now. He remembered her saying that her mother was going to buy her a pair of slingback shoes soon after they settled into the new house. Whether or not this came about, he didn't know. Five years had passed but the style she had thought to be the best thing since sliced bread was still in fashion, and he knew as he hugged his pillow what he was going to buy her at the end of the week on payday. Shoes *and* a beautiful leather handbag to match. He made a mental note to find out what size shoe she took and then wondered if Charlotte was awake yet. He could hear noises coming from the kitchen and he could smell bacon frying.

Charlotte, just like Nathan, was still in bed, but awake and thinking of him tall and broad and having to sleep on an old-fashioned put-you-up settee that pulled down into a bed. Glancing at her wristwatch she could see that it had just gone nine o'clock and suddenly remembered that Nathan had told her nan that he had to be washed, dressed and fed by ten-thirty. He wanted to be back at home with his dad and go with him to see his grandparents. Of course she knew that Nell wasn't going to let him go out without a Sunday breakfast inside him. A fried breakfast without the bacon, though – Nathan, being Jewish, didn't eat it – would be a challenge for her. Nell was too old-fashioned for her own good at times.

Wearing one of her gran's thin cotton white night-dresses, purchased from Charlie's cheap stall in the Mile End waste market, Charlotte felt a touch chilly even though it was summertime, but she could see that Nell, having crept in at the crack of dawn, had laid an old-fashioned thick candlewick housecoat at the foot of her bed. She pulled herself up into a sitting position, plumped up her big feather pillow and then sank back into it and smiled contentedly. There was a lovely warm glow inside her, partly because she was in a familiar room that held childhood memories but mostly because she was in love. In love with Nathan. All cosy in her grandparents' spare bedroom, she was making the most of the tranquillity before she was called down for breakfast. She thought of her flat, her very own flat that she couldn't wait to get back to. Thinking about the house and the people living there she felt a kind of sisterly warmth when she pictured Donald. Now she was regretting having been a bit short with him when she had gone downstairs to ask him to lower the sound of his music. She made a vow that once she was back in the house she would push a little note through his door thanking him for the welcome and the vase and his offers of help.

'I've not only found a sweetheart in Nathan,' she whispered, 'but I think I might have found a brother figure in Donald.'

Contented and relaxed, she compared all of this with living in Bridgeford. It hadn't been dire by any means but she had been lonely for a long time and now she couldn't be happier. She had missed small things such as the old mix and match streets, courtyards and alleyways and the friendly housing estates. She couldn't wait to go to the Whitechapel Art Gallery again and she was looking forward to strolling through the back streets to the Tower of London, stopping for pie and mash on the way. These were things that had once been ordinary everyday occurrences.

She brought to mind the strong man who escaped from thick chains and all of the tourists who poured into the area at Tower Hill to watch him. People would arrive in their droves in nice weather and sit by the river on the small man-made beach. She couldn't wait to go back whenever she felt like it, and she looked forward to taking the tube to such places as the King's Road for general window shopping and Biba to treat herself to something small and inexpensive.

The best thing about it all was that she could now catch up on everything in London without having to make a day of it as if she was a tourist down from the country. She could go with Nathan to dance halls, pop concerts and coffee bars. And from what he had told her when they had spent time together in Bridgeford, being part of the theatre group and working with them nearly every other weekend meant that he was always being invited to parties. Parties that were going on all over the place. And this is what she so wanted. What she was ready for. What she was in need of.

Pleased to have had a bit of time to herself, she left her cosy warm bed and went downstairs, hungry for one of her gran's great fry-ups. She knew that the newspapers would have arrived by now because her granddad always kept the owner of the corner shop on her toes when it came to the delivery boy. Pulling on the dressing gown left out for her, she tiptoed down the stairs, wondering if Nathan was still asleep on the couch bed. Going into the room that led into the kitchen she wondered no more. There, at the Formica-topped table her granddad and Nathan were reading the newspapers as if they were novels that they could not put down. On seeing her come into the room Johnny looked across to Nathan and raised his eyes to heaven.

'It's very quiet in here,' Charlotte said. 'What's up? The cat got both of your tongues? You all right, Granddad? All well on the home front, is it?'

'Not too bad, sunshine. I slept like a log. Your nan's all right. She's getting on wiv cooking the breakfast and that.'

'I know, I can smell it.' She glanced from Johnny to Nathan, who was looking sadly back at her. 'So what *is* the matter then? It's like a morgue in here. Is there something in the paper that's shocked you both? Has one of the royal family died or something?' She glanced at the paper that Johnny was reading and chuckled. 'You don't still read the *News of the World* and take it seriously do you, Granddad?'

'Show your paper to her, Nathan, son. Let her read the *Mirror* for 'erself. Give her the newspaper,' said Johnny.

Nathan glanced at Charlotte and then said, 'Come and sit down.'

'Why? What's happened?' She looked from one to the other.

'Women – they're all the same. Nosy by nature. Got to know all the ins and outs before they read up on a story.'

Leaning back in his chair, Johnny hunched his shoulders and then released a low sigh before quietly saying, 'A local woman's been murdered, sweetheart. It's all over the front pages.'

Cutting to the quick, Nathan took a deep breath and then spoke quietly to her. 'It's the woman who lived in the house where you're renting a flat. They've taken your landlady's son in for questioning over it . . . according to one neighbour's account of it.'

'What!' Charlotte could hardly take it in, never mind

believe it. 'Donald's been arrested for murder? I was there yesterday and all was normal. You've got it wrong, you must have. It can't be true. Donald's not that common a name in this neck of the woods, but even so—'

'Charlotte, it's true,' said Nathan. 'Come and sit down and read it for yourself.'

'No. I don't wanna read about a murder! I've only just got up!' She backed away and stood in the doorway to the passage. 'You read it out to me, Granddad, and read it properly! That's if it's something that I should know about.' She then called out to Nell who was hovering in the kitchen, too bewildered by the news to know what to say.

'Nan! Did you hear what Granddad said?'

'You don't 'ave to bloody well shout! I'm not a million miles away. And I heard it all. Sit down and listen to what they're trying to tell you. I'll fetch you a cup of coffee.'

Folding the newspaper that he had been reading, Nathan spoke in a quiet and tender voice. 'Charlotte, it's true. The body of a woman has been found. And it's a woman who was lodging in the house according to a neighbour who spoke to the press.'

'But the house where I'm gonna be living is just one in that square. It can't be the only one. Gossips always get something wrong. Always have, always will.'

Nell came in from the kitchen and handed her granddaughter the hot drink. A mug of coffee made the way she liked it best, half milk and half water. She then placed a hand on Charlotte's shoulder and tenderly patted it. 'We'll 'ave to phone your mum and dad, darling. They can come and fetch you. We'll help you pack your things up. You can't go back to that place now. And I know you don't want to live with us two old fogeys. And nor should you want to. You're too young.'

'Nan? Stop it. Stop talking as if you're someone else. What's happened? What's got into the three of you? You're reading the Sunday papers, for Christ's sake. They always go in for shocking stuff whether it's true or not. You know that. Granddad 'as always said that they're jam-packed with gossip and lies.' She turned to Johnny for a bit of support. 'Aint that right, Granddad?'

'You can phone the council offices in the morning,' murmured Nell sadly. 'To explain why you're going back home and why you won't be starting work there.'

'What are you talking about, Nan? Of course I'll be starting work there! And I'll be living in my rented flat! All my things are there. The press have got it wrong. I've paid the rent for my flat and I like it there! You know I do! I'm not going back to fucking Norfolk! I'm going to my flat and staying there!'

A horrible silence then filled the room until Charlotte, close to tears, murmured, 'It's gotta be a mistake. It must be another house in another square. Neither of you 'ave read your papers properly. And anyway . . . Sunday papers are always full of sensational gossip. You should know that! You know what you've always said about the *News of the World*, Granddad. But you still fucking well read it!'

'Don't swear, Charlotte. Not in front of me and your

nan anyway.' He looked at his beloved granddaughter and felt his heart melting. 'It's been on the wireless, as well, sweetheart. On the eight o'clock news. I caught the tail end of a report but I didn't pick up on the area. But it's here in black and white.'

Charlotte stared into Nathan's face. 'Did you hear it on the wireless?'

'Yes.'

'But I was there only yesterday. There was a lovely atmosphere in the house. They've got the wrong area. The wrong address. They must have done!'

Looking from one to the other of them, and seeing no change of expression other than serious and sad, Charlotte felt sick. 'Granddad . . . say something.'

Keeping his voice low, Johnny shook his head. 'And to fink that the landlady's son was in your room giving you a cut-glass vase for the flowers that that woman he murdered had picked for yer. It could 'ave been you lying dead in that old cellar.'

Charlotte glanced from one to other of them. And then in a quieter voice said, 'Did they name the woman?'

'Read it for yourself, Charlotte,' said Nathan. 'And calm down a bit.'

'It don't bear thinking about,' murmured Nell as she stared out at nothing. 'The wicked bastard needs to be hung, strung and quartered. Whoever he is.'

His full attention on his granddaughter, Johnny said, 'Sip your hot coffee, Charlotte. It'll help, I promise you.'

'According to the paper they're linking this murder

with another two women who went missing,' said Nell. 'One of which was—'

'Yeah, all right . . . don't go into the sordid details,' said Johnny. 'Give 'er time, for gawd's sake.'

'I've read it twice over, Charlotte,' murmured Nathan. 'I can fill you in a bit later on . . . if you want.'

'No,' said Charlotte, her voice no more than a whisper now. 'Tell me now. I'll know if it's all bollocks or not.'

Nathan drew breath and then began. 'A woman was found in the cellar of an old house close by the river and not far from the square where your flat is. Some boys who were messing around in the early evening in one of the dilapidated houses. One of them shone a torch through rotting floorboards and saw the body. The newspapers are linking it with two other murders. Two women who had gone missing were dredged out of the river about a week ago. They hadn't connected them as victims of a serial killer but according to the paper, they are now.

'Your landlady has identified the dead woman. There was something in her pocket . . . a letter from an optician. This is what led the police . . . and then the morbid sightseers, to the door of the house. Apparently, the landlady's son was the last one to be seen talking to her, by a man who lives in the house two doors along. He made a statement. He got involved when he heard the lads yelling as they ran past his house about a dead woman that they had found in a cellar.

'The police, according to what this paper says, had

been keeping quiet about the two women they pulled out of the river until they knew more. Up until now they had no lead about either of the two prostitutes reported missing. The paper is saying that it's Jack the Ripper all over again, except that this one goes in for strangling his victims.'

'I can't believe it. I just can't take this in.' Charlotte's face was now paler than pale. 'Yesterday . . . I was there. In the house.'

'You can't go back there now, Charlotte. The place will be swarming with the press and nosy parkers. The boys who found the woman ran through the streets screaming the odds so it couldn't be kept quiet.'

'It's not Donald,' she said. 'I know it's not. He is odd but harmless. He wouldn't hurt a fly. I'm sure of it.'

Then, as tears filled her eyes she whispered Wendy's name. 'That poor woman. She was so lovely. I can't believe this. I can't believe that such a thing could happen. Not on our doorstep. And why would someone lure her away to a derelict house and then strangle her? The landlady's son's not stupid but nor is he that bright. He wouldn't 'ave been able to lure a mature woman like Wendy away. It doesn't add up.'

'Well, maybe the lad isn't all he appears to be, sweetheart. Maybe he's just clever enough to pull the wool over your eyes? It didn't take him long to draw you in, did it? Flowers and a vase and you thinking what a nice gesture it was.'

'Your granddad's right, Charlotte,' said Nathan.

'I can't believe she's dead. Only yesterday she came to see me, and she was up there in the flat above mine.

It can't be real.' Tears filled the back of Charlotte's eyes. 'This wasn't the way it was meant to be,' she just managed to say.

The sudden intrusion of the telephone ringing pulled them all up sharp. In a whispering voice, as if whoever was on the end of the line could hear, Nell said, 'You might be wanted for questioning, Charlie. That might be the police on the end of the line.'

'Silly cow! Of course it won't be the police!' said Johnny. 'How the bloody hell would they know where she is? They don't know she's here! They don't know our address!'

Nell pulled a face to show her dread as she picked up the receiver to the sound of her husband still going on in the background. She cupped the mouthpiece and told him to shut up and then offered the receiver to Charlotte. 'It's Daddy, love. He's in a right state. He's read the bit in the Sunday paper as well.'

'Tell him I'll call back, Nan. I'm only just about able to take this in. I feel sick. I'm going upstairs for a five-minute lie down.'

'Of course, you must do,' said Johnny. 'But it'll all come out right, you'll see.' He only just stopped himself from saying that she could move in with them. He knew that this wasn't the right time.

Taking the phone off his wife while she went and got herself a glass of water from the kitchen, Johnny told his son-in-law over the phone not to worry. That his girl would stay that night at theirs again. 'We'll keep Charlotte with us for as long as you want, son, don't you worry.'

But this wasn't enough for Eddie. 'She was one of the last people to have seen that woman alive, Johnny. The police are bound to want to interview her. Now if she doesn't go back to the house they'll put her on the missing list and the Bridgeford police will be on our doorstep in no time. The landlady's got our address, don't forget. She's got to either go back or at least phone the police and let them know where she is!'

'All right, son, all right. Don't get aerated. She's safe and sound while she's here. But, yeah . . . you're right. All three of us will go for a stroll . . . back to the square and into the house. And then round to the local police station to let them know she's okay.'

'They'll want to interview her, Johnny, you can bet your life on it.'

'Of course they will. But we'll go with 'er, as will Nathan. She ain't done nuffing wrong so stop bloody worrying! It'll all turn out right. They've arrested the weirdo—'

'What do you mean? Weirdo?' said Eddie.

'Well . . . Charlotte said something about 'im not being the same as everybody else, that's all. Harmless enough but a bit loopy.'

'Harmless? He's been taken in for fucking murder for Christ's sake! I'm driving down to fetch 'er home. Tell 'er not to go back to that house. Tell 'er that if the police do want to talk to her then they can come to fucking Bridgeford. I'm not having her approached on all sides by the bloody newspapers! This is your fault, Johnny! You and Nell! Encouraging 'er for months on end to move back to London!'

'All right, all right. Keep your shirt on. And stop worrying. We'll deal with it and keep you in touch until you get 'ere. Okay?' There was a silence. 'And as it happens, I don't fink there's any point in you rushing down here to London. She's got her nan and me and she's got Nathan. He's a sensible young man.'

After a quiet pause, Eddie spoke in a quiet voice. 'How do you know?'

'How do I know? Because he stopped over with us last night and we 'ad a lovely time. We got to know each other.'

'What d'yer mean? He slept over? Where exactly did he sleep over?'

'Oh gawd . . . you and your over-protective—'

'I'm not being over-protective! I just want to know where Nathan slept!'

'He went on the couch that pulls down into a bed! And he thought it was very comfortable too. All right? What kind of a girl do you think my granddaughter is?'

There was a silence and then a long emotional sigh. 'I'm sorry, Johnny, but I'm all on edge. This 'as scared the bloody life out of me. I want her back here where it's safe. Fucking London. I might 'ave known!'

Closing his eyes, Johnny sighed deliberately and then said, 'All right, Eddie. I'll tell her you'll call back later then, shall I? Or will you be out and in one of your posh friends' houses playing bridge?' The soft click and then dialling tone coming down the line made him smile. 'Bloody snobs, the pair of 'em.' He then turned to Nathan who was still in his chair at the table and blew air. 'What a turn-up for the books, eh?'

'I just can't believe it.'

Joining him at the table, Johnny shook his head and then glanced through to the kitchen where Nell was making egg and bacon sandwiches. He knew that she knew that no one was going to sit at the table with knife and fork and eat as if nothing had happened. Sandwiches were portable. And apart from this he knew that this was a sign that his wife wanted to be by herself. 'Who would have thought it?' He sighed again and said, 'Two lads mucking around in a broken house that they'd most likely gone in for a secret smoke and what do they find? A woman's shoe in the rubble close by to a bloody great hole in the floorboards where she fell to 'er death.'

'Pushed more like it. Once she had been strangled.'

'Yeah . . . all right, son. Don't get too detailed about it.'

'If the boys hadn't have gone in for a secret cigarette she could have lain there rotting and never have been found until she was a skeleton.'

'Yeah, well . . . I s'pose your mind would fink like that. You being in the theatre world and all that. It was just as well that they were there, though. I'll give you that. If they 'adn't of run out screaming the odds are the police wouldn't 'ave been called and she would have rotted and turned to dust. Them bloody headlines about another serial killer makes my blood boil, though. Serial killer? Anything to sell their bloody newsapers.'

'It says that he's another Jack the Ripper. What do you think?'

'She was strangled, not slashed, son. As were the

other two London girls who've been dredged up from the Thames. It does sound like an open and shut case and that's why it's probably not. That young man they arrested was the last one to have been seen speaking to the woman by a gentleman who was passing by. That's not evidence.'

'No . . . but another woman from another building in the square saw them from her window. She said that the accused and the woman murdered seemed quite intimate when chatting.'

'People say all kinds of bloody things at a time like this. And you can't believe all you read in the paper.' He was worried but wasn't going to let on. The woman wouldn't have taken much notice at the time, but once the police were milling around everywhere she no doubt was out there lapping it up. Giving evidence as a chief witness. Some people love a bit of drama on their doorstep. 'But we can't let Charlotte stay there now. Not after this. She'll have to either move in with us or . . . sadly, she'll go back to Bridgeford.'

Chapter Eighteen

Kenny, reclining on his single bed at home, was enjoying his time in the sun that was shining through the small picture window in the family council flat. He too had read the headlines and the article and could not believe his luck. The witness, who had seen the whore with the weirdo, had not spotted him in the public gardens in the square because of the thick foliage that surrounded it on all four sides. He had once again got away with murder and it was fuelling his passion. Enjoying a cigarette and a cup of tea he laughed to himself. He really had put the cat among the pigeons this time. The bitch that he had once fancied rotten when a kid and who had chosen a Jew over him was more than likely shaking in her shoes in case she would be next.

He wondered if she would sleep that night knowing that not only had a woman who lived in the same building as her been murdered, but believing that she had been under the same roof as the killer. The weirdo. Grinning, he recalled the way the Jew boy, Nathan, used to be always pushing his old and wonky round National Health glasses up onto the bridge of his fat nose so as to focus. A wide smile crossed his face as he remembered when he and his gang of ruffians humiliated the slob, who was short-arsed for his age and as fat as an ugly pig. He could still picture the way Nathan's lips used to quiver when he was trying to get on the right side of Kenny's gang before the boots went in. They would form a chain across his path, their arms folded, and act as if they were the Gestapo before they gave him a hiding and brought him down onto the old cobblestone ground. Suddenly proud of himself for having kept up the good work of the pre-war Black-shirts and Oswald Mosley, he wondered why he hadn't focused on Jewish prostitutes.

He smiled at the thought of coming across Nathan again . . . in that old unlit cobblestone turning with lock-ups on one side beneath the railway line and a park on the other. He had given him a bloody hiding more than once back in the old days. His mind turned back to the headlines and the pathetic drip called Donald that they had taken in for questioning. He toyed with the idea of striking again before the weirdo had been given bail. He could just see the next headline that would put fear into every woman in London: 'Wrong man arrested!' Or 'Strangler still on the loose!'

He lay down again with his pillow over his face to stifle his chortling. His mum was in the kitchen and he didn't want her in asking what he found so funny. She could be an interfering cow at times and this was when he wished he didn't love her so much. He didn't know why he loved her, because she had been a whore in earlier years and left him at home with his dad, night after night after night. What he really wanted to do was ask her why. Why she had to go out whoring for money and why she had not been there to tuck him up in bed when he was small and needed her. Why he couldn't remember a bedtime hug from her. Why she had never sat him on her lap and told him a story by the fireside . . .

Covering his face with his hands and pressing until it hurt, he managed, as he had done a million times before, to stop himself from crying. Once again, as had also happened many times before, his sense of exuberance was fast turning into gloom, but the face of his dad was filling his thoughts. He had often been tormented by his dad when he was young for weeping like a big soft girl after he had been scolded for being naughty. Controlling his emotions the way he had learned to do over the years, he drew breath and then relaxed a few times over until he was ready for another cigarette. Smiling again, he applauded himself for ridding the world of another streetwalker. This was how he viewed Wendy. As nothing more and nothing less than a streetwalker. Done and dusted.

Not quite sure whether to go and do a bit of wheeling and dealing in Aldgate or not, he closed his eyes to think about it. He knew that a load of stolen cigarettes had been delivered that very morning to a disused shop that stank of rats and mould and was boarded up. He also knew that if he didn't get there before three that afternoon the gear would be sold to other punters like himself and he would miss out, but he wasn't broke so it didn't matter. He would get a fair price for the whore's jewellery straight away from an old boy who had a little shop tucked away in the back and beyond of

Aldgate. He was tired, though. Very tired. So, feeling more relaxed now that he had thought things through, he closed his eyes and pulled his bedclothes over him. There was nothing he liked better than to sleep in late on a Sunday morning, before or after he had read the papers.

Curious as to what might be happening in the house where he had seen Charlotte come and go and where the dead prostitute had lived, he did a few of his usual deep breathing exercises to help clear his mind. Soon he would go out and see what was what in and around that old-fashioned tree-lined square. He felt as if he were a main player in a movie. The star actor, the scriptwriter and the director, all rolled into one. And the best of it was that no one had a clue that *he* was the so-called serial killer. He ran the words *serial killer* through his mind and then laughed at the irony. He was famous but nobody knew it other than himself. And this, he realised, was probably what was causing him to be at odds with himself. If he confessed he would be famous but locked up for the rest of his life. If he carried on being clever and got rid of a few more whores and stayed anonymous, he would always only be seen as Kenny the small-time thief and fence. He made a snap decision there and then to go out and cast an all-seeing eye over his patch and perhaps give a few teasing tips to one of the uniformed men on duty. Tips that would no doubt be taken as nonsense but that would hold vital clues, should there be an officer on duty that was as intelligent as himself.

*

As he arrived into an area not far from the square where he was heading, Kenny was delighted to see so many sightseers milling around the area in small groups. He wondered, as he stood watching them, whether he had been daft to cover one of his previous deeds too cleverly by dropping the corpse down the old and very deep well in Bridgeford. He then quietly praised the local lads who had gone into the old wrecked terraced house and discovered the body of Wendy. Between them and himself, they had caused quite a stir with the local people and the press by the look of things. He casually strolled up to a small group of people and asked what all the fuss was about.

'There's another Jack the Ripper on the loose,' said a small rotund woman in her late fifties, who wore her silvery grey hair pulled up into a bun and tied with a blue ribbon. 'Not that it surprises me,' she went on. 'There are more prostitutes in this area now than there was in the eighteen-eighties – more foreigners an' all. I'm not saying that they deserve to be ripped to bits or strangled but I wish they'd go elsewhere to work the streets. They're a bloody nuisance.'

'Do they know who did it?' said Kenny, a touch boyish.

'Who knows? The old bill won't give nuffing away. Not even to us ratepayers who deserve to know what's going on in the parish that we pay for. Too many foreigners, that's the trouble. In they pour, month after month from all over the bloody globe. I'm sick of it.'

Leaving the rubberneckers to themselves, Kenny let it all go above his head. Clearly he was not going to be able to get anywhere near the tree-lined square or his favourite bench that he had now marked as his own by scoring his initials into one of the slats of wood. The police had cordoned off the entrance, which was via a small brick archway, and were only letting those who lived in the square pass through. Looking around at the small crowds everywhere he could see that the small Italian café where he had sat at a table chatting to Charlotte was full to overflowing. He smiled to himself. At least he had brought business into this little corner of London. Turning away from those who he considered nothing but nosy bastards, he saw Charlotte and a guy who was tall, broad, dark and handsome who he thought he had seen with her before but wasn't certain. The couple were approaching the archway into the square and of course he knew that they would be allowed in because Charlotte had taken the flat in the house where the dead woman had lived. Bored now, Kenny sauntered off, more than happy with the thought that he knew better than anyone else in the world what had happened in that old derelict building. He couldn't help but smile.

Once Charlotte and Nathan had shuffled through the police and reporters and were at the entrance to the house she was quickly up the steps and using her key to the front door. In the hallway she was immediately greeted by the very distraught Isabelle. From the look of her face and her red puffy eyes she had been crying non-stop. Holding out her arms as if she was greeting the only person in the world that was left to her, the distraught woman burst into tears.

Gently patting the woman's back as she held her close, Charlotte was close to tears herself. 'It'll be all right, Isabelle, you'll see,' she only just managed to say. 'Your lovely son could never be responsible for killing Wendy. He'll be home soon. You'll see. He'll be back here with us.'

'Oh darling . . . do you really and truly believe that? Honestly?'

'Of course I do,' said Charlotte, gently pulling away so as to be able to look her in the face. 'Just because he was seen talking to Wendy on the steps before he went off to the library to give his talk at the book signing doesn't mean that he killed her. It's ridiculous.'

'I know it is! It's quite mad!' The woman relaxed her shoulders and let out a sigh of relief. 'I am so happy to see you. When you didn't come back last night I thought the worst. Have you let the police know that you're all right, my dear?'

'Yes. I telephoned from my grandparents' house in Bow. I wasn't going to stop out all night but my granddad insisted that Nathan and I slept over. They don't get to see much of me . . .'

'And of course they would want you to stay. And you wouldn't have wanted to be here in any case. Can you believe that the police arrived and went into Wendy's flat to go through her most personal things? It was quite awful. What if they took away her diaries? I should hate to think that when I pass on complete strangers would read my most private thoughts. It's all too ghastly.'

Ghastly it might have seemed, but what Isabelle couldn't possibly know was that Wendy had written more than one entry into her diary to do with Donald. There was at least one that was incriminating when it came to this lovely woman's only son. Wendy had written a short piece about him, which was not unusual, but in this particular one she had underlined the word barmy and then written 'mentally deranged' with a question mark, in brackets.

'I would hate anyone to read my diary,' said Charlotte. 'I shall have to be very careful not to leave mine around for my gran and granddad to peek into.' She smiled.

'Your grandparents wouldn't dream of such a thing, I'm sure. And of course they will see much more of you now so they won't have to read about what you are up to. They'll know. That is, of course, if you haven't decided to leave us because of all this horrid business?'

'No, of course I won't leave. I've not even stayed overnight yet but I love the flat. It's mine. You can rest assured I'm staying – no matter what.'

'Oh thank goodness!' Isabelle clasped her hands together and broke into a lovely smile. 'I am so relieved. All of a sudden all three of you had gone. The artist in the basement is away on holiday. He popped a note in my door before all of this dreadful business had happened. Poor Wendy. I just cannot believe it. I can't take it in. And of all people to arrest as a suspect? My poor innocent boy? He wouldn't harm a fly, Charlotte.'

'I'm sure he wouldn't. Come on, let's go into your kitchen and I'll make us a pot of tea while you get to know Nathan. He's a very close childhood friend who up until a week or so ago I hadn't seen in years.'

'Really? You do surprise me. I would have said that you hadn't ever been separated, you are so right together.' She then turned to Nathan and offered her hand, saying, 'I do apologise for going on. How do you do? I am most grateful for this visit. I can't tell you what it's been like. The phone hasn't stopped ringing and I've spoken to so many newspapers I can't take any more. So I've taken the phone off the hook.'

'Good for you,' said Nathan. 'That's exactly what I would have suggested.'

'Really? You would have done the self-same thing in my shoes?'

'Yes. Now . . . let's do as we're told by Miss Bossy Boots here and sit down while she makes us a hot drink.'

'Yes, of course we must. But you don't have to baby-sit me.' She sighed. 'I feel so much better now that Charlotte has turned up. Much better. Will you be stopping overnight, Nathan?'

'No. My dad will be worried. He's a widower and we live together in Bethnal Green. He will probably have read the papers by now and recognised the address as where Charlotte is going to live.'

'And do you like it where you're living?' asked Isabelle, doing her best to control herself and not to start crying again. 'I ask you this because the flat at the top that Wendy lived in will soon be available, and I think that the actor in the basement will be moving on quite soon, from what he's told me.' As hard as she tried, whether she even realised it or not, tears were trickling slowly down her cheeks and her neck. The poor woman was in shock but couldn't just sit still and do nothing.

Nathan, filled with compassion, gently squeezed her arm. 'That's very sweet of you, and I think that Dad would love to live in a house in Lavender Square. But try not to get things back to the way they were too quickly. You might make mistakes you'll regret later on. Wait until your son has been released.'

'Goodness me, you *are* wise for your age. And of course you're right. Donald will soon be back home with a public pardon . . . of course he will. He is such an innocent boy and not cut out for this sort of a drama. But if you and your father wanted to rent the flat I wouldn't charge you very much. It would be so nice to have some men around the place.'

Joining them at the polished pine kitchen table while the fresh pot of tea stood for a few minutes, Charlotte reached across and took hold of Isabelle's delicate white hands and squeezed them. 'Your son will be home tomorrow and, knowing Donald, even though it's only been for a short time, I personally think he'll be philosophical while at the police station and when he comes home too. He knows he's innocent. And this is the all-important thing. They can't find him guilty of a murder he didn't commit. He was at the library for the book signing.' Charlotte smiled warmly at the grief-stricken woman who was trying so hard to make sense of it all.

'But there's a problem, Charlotte . . . the signing was cancelled at the last minute and he came back. This is why they've taken him in for questioning. He was the last to be seen talking to Wendy. But he wouldn't harm her. They really liked each other, but only in a very platonic sort of way.'

'Of course he wouldn't harm her. It's ridiculous. He's not a serial killer and that's what they're looking for, don't forget. Two prostitutes have been dredged from the Thames, according to the newspaper.' Charlotte then left the table to pour out the tea. All kinds of things were running through her mind, in particular the time when the poor soul Wendy had turned to her for someone to talk to. When she herself had thought that the woman had been fantasising about Donald. Suddenly it all came floating back. Wendy had said that she had been touched by the way the sweet boy looked at her, and that he sometimes hung around outside of her front door. That he was one of life's vulnerable people.

Murmuring quietly to herself, Charlotte could hardly believe what she was thinking. But Wendy had said that she would ask him in for coffee and biscuits. That it would be nice for her to have some company. That it shouldn't be herself who made the first move. That if her landlady's son wanted to go into her apartment for a chat he should say so.

Caught up in her deep thoughts, Nathan's voice drifted into her consciousness as he said, 'Did either of you see the small piece in the *Evening Standard* about the young woman going missing in Bridgeford?'

'No,' said Isabelle. 'I don't take the *Standard*.'

Shaking herself out of the low mood she was slipping into when wondering if there might be more to Donald than met the eye, Charlotte paid attention to what he was saying. 'Dad did say something about the missing woman last week. I think I'll give him a call later on from Gran and Granddad's.' She looked into Isabelle's face apologetically. 'They won't rest if I don't sleep there until this is all cleared up.' Thoughtful again, she slowly shook her head. 'I'm *sure* I heard that she'd been found and was dead. Nothing about being murdered, though.'

'Oh . . . did you think that she had been murdered, Charlotte? Because if so maybe there is a link. And if so, they mustn't keep Donald in any longer. Do you think you might use my phone and call your father?'

At this point Nathan stepped in and with a firm tone to his voice said, 'I think that you've both had a bit of a shock and enough is enough. I take it there is a telephone in Charlotte's flat, Isabelle?'

'Oh, yes. And it's quite new. I got rid of the clunky old-fashioned one months ago. Why? Do you wish to call someone?'

'Yes. And don't worry about all that I said. It was just thinking aloud really. We'll sleep on it and if I still feel the same in a day or so I'll phone Charlotte's father and ask about the girl. You never know – there could be a link. A mass murderer could live anywhere in the world and pick girls off as and when he thinks fit.' The wicked bastard Kenny who had an evil streak was now on his mind. Charlotte had told him that he had been on the train from Bridgeford and then turned up in the Italian coffee bar close by.

Excusing himself from the table, Nathan took the key from Charlotte that would let him into her flat. 'I need to make a call or two. It shouldn't take long.'

'You're perfectly welcome to use my phone,' said Isabelle.

'That's very kind of you but I've been brought up never to bring work into the home and especially not to the kitchen table. And I would rather speak to my colleague about work in private. I think that you've both had enough for now, one way and another.' With that he took his leave, having no intention to phone work but to dial Eddie's number. He was desperate to talk to him because he felt that he was onto something. He sighed thankfully when he heard his voice.

'Hello, Eddie, it's Nathan. And before you ask, we're at the house and Charlotte's fine. She'll sleep at Johnny and Nell's again tonight. But listen to me. I want to know more about the girl that was reported missing in Bridgeford. Have they found her?'

'Why? What's happened now?'

'Nothing, I promise you. The police are crawling all over this part of the East End but telling us nothing. But I really do want to know if there's been any more about that girl. I've got a theory that is probably rubbish but I need to look into it.'

There was a short silence and then a sigh from Eddie. 'Apparently, and this is confidential information,

Nathan, so keep it to yourself, one of the guys at the Freemasons meeting earlier on told me that the police are crawling all over the flat above the old wireless shop as well. Taking fingerprints and taking things away. I also heard that they lowered a bloke in a wet suit down into the well at the bottom of the garden.'

'So they're searching not only for clues but also for a body? Is that what you're saying?'

'Read it which way you like, but don't you dare breathe a word of it, Nathan. It's more than my life's worth. It's good for my business to keep in with the funny handshake lot.'

'Of course I won't say anything. It's just that . . . well I've heard of someone hanging around here who spent a bit of time in Bridgeford.'

'And you're putting two and two together. Be very careful, son, of what you accuse people of. I know what you're getting at and I can't say that the same thought hasn't crossed my mind. I should leave well alone if I were you.'

'Oh really? And what if it does turn out to be who we are both thinking about? Do we leave well alone until he strikes again? And what if it's your daughter that's found in the river, or in a cellar, or in a well at the bottom of someone's garden?'

There was a silence and then a sigh. 'I think that you're letting your imagination carry you away, son. Don't forget the old saying, don't let your heart rule your head. Kenny's not clever enough to have got away with murdering four women. You're barking up the wrong tree. Tell Charlotte I'm coming down to fetch her home at the weekend and until then she's to stop at her grandparents. Tell her to phone the office where she was gonna work and tell them she's not going to start after all. I want her back here. Understood?'

'I think I've got the gist of it, Eddie, yes.'

'Good. It's now your responsibility and not mine. I'm only the messenger. Rita has been going on and on at me, driving me fucking mad!' He replaced the receiver with a slam and all that Nathan could hear was the dialling tone.

'Well, cheers for that, Eddie. Thanks for the advice.' He decided then and there to see Charlotte home to Johnny and Nell's place and then he was going home to have a good talk with his own dad. Tell him what he thought and ask his advice as to what he should do. For his part, he felt like screaming from the top of his voice that Kenny, the evil little shit from the past, was a very strong candidate for the murders. He would place his life and his possessions on it. The bastard had always been evil and it didn't sit right that he had drifted in and out of Charlotte's world in Bridgeford and now in this little part of East London. It could all be coincidence, but he would rather have egg on his face than blood on his hands should another murdered woman be found. Never mind that it could be Charlotte.

Taking a deep breath and doing his best to maintain a calm and composed manner, he went back downstairs and into Isabelle's flat. 'Sorry about that but I had to make that call.'

'Men and their work,' Isabelle smiled. 'My husband was just the same. I think all men are. Well, those who are not lazy, that is. I couldn't bear to have a man around the house all day long. It would drive me to distraction.'

'I think we should be getting back soon, Charlotte, so if you want to collect anything from the flat you'd best get it now. Your grandparents will be worried. And they'll be waiting to hear the latest hot news.'

Charlotte looked from Nathan to Isabelle and smiled kindly at her. 'Are you sure you're all right in the house by yourself? I could sleep here tonight if not.'

'No, dear. I feel so much better for your visit. And of course my son will be let home soon. They can't possibly keep him in. There's absolutely no evidence to suggest anything other than that he is a quiet young man who likes to keep himself to himself.'

Catching Nathan's eyes, Charlotte felt her cheeks going red. She wanted so much to comfort this lovely lady. Her son had been arrested on suspicion of murder, after all, and history books were full of innocent people having been sent to the gallows. Justice did not always out in the end. 'I'm sure he'll be back home with you in a day or so. And meanwhile don't sit in the quiet. Put the television on, and let actors and presenters keep you company. It's what I would do. And I'll phone you from my grandparents' house later on to see how you are.'

'Oh, thank you so much, Charlotte. And do you really mean to come back to live here with us, after all of this?'

'I'll be back for good tomorrow. And that's a promise.'

'Oh splendid!' Isabelle clasped her hands together, joy and relief on her face. The poor woman needed a bit of sunshine in her life and Charlotte wanted to get back on track and live in the flat that she adored. Once they had said their good-byes and the street door had closed behind the young couple, Isabelle went back into her sitting room and sat by the fireplace where no fire burned, and burst into tears. The second worst thing for her was that the police had said that she wasn't allowed to go into Wendy's flat and they had cordoned it off. And now all that she had for company in this once cheerful house was silence and the ticking of her old-fashioned clock on the mantelshelf.

Chapter Nineteen

By the time Nathan got back to his own home he was shattered. He had gone with Charlotte by bus to Nell and Johnny's and spent a bit of polite time with them, and then left to catch another bus back home. Letting himself in with his key he called out to Jacob to let him know that he was back.

'What'sa matter with you?' his dad yelled from the back room. 'You think I don't know when someone comes into the flat? It's a poky hole, not a bloody mansion with me stuck in the tower. I even heard you turn the bloody key in the door!'

'What's rattled your cage?' asked Nathan, suppressing a wry smile. His dad always managed to make him smile or laugh, even when things were bad.

'The television aerial, that's what. I can't get a decent picture. You promised to get me a new one.'

'I did. It's down there in the corner, in that box under the newspapers. It was you who buried it, not me. Have you had anything to eat?'

'Of course I have. Why do you ask? You're not gonna drag me off to the hospital for an investigation of the bowels again are you?'

'I was going to suggest fresh salmon in beigels. I just

passed by the bakers and by the smell of things there's a new batch just out of the oven.'

'Well, that's different. For fresh beigels straight out of the oven I'm always hungry whether I've eaten or not. I don't know about the salmon, though. I don't trust that man with the salmon. I'm not sure that it's always as fresh as he says it is. I'll have cream cheese and gherkins in mine. So where did you sleep last night?'

'On a put-you-up in her grandparents' sitting room. Okay? Charlotte's a decent girl from a decent family.'

'I never said she was anything other than that. Did I say she was a loose woman? I think the world of that girl – you know I do. All she has to do is convert.' He looked slyly at his son to see what he made of the seed he had just sown.

'Forget it. We'll have a civil wedding if and when she accepts me. And before you say that your ancestors will turn in their grave, remember things are different now. Mixed marriages are all the thing. And anyway, we've only just started courting.'

Jacob tried to hide a smile by glancing out of the window. 'So you're going to marry the girl. Mazel tov. You've been in love for donkey's years so you won't be rushing in. I shouldn't keep her waiting, though. A lovely girl like that would soon find someone more handsome than you. She could have her pick of the lads.'

'You haven't bloody well seen her since she was thirteen. How would you know if she's grown ugly or not?'

'I can tell by the voice. A voice speaks volumes. And if she was ugly you wouldn't have come in at this time of night and you wouldn't have left an old man to sleep in this shit hole by himself. Put-you-up in the living room? Do me a favour. You crept into her bed, and if you tell me you didn't you're no son of mine. God gave you a tool to use so be thankful and make the most of it.'

Slowly shaking his head Nathan sighed with a smile. He was used to his dad and the things he came out with but, sometimes, he pushed the boundaries. 'Did you read the Sunday paper yet?'

'Of course I read the bloody paper. What else is there for me to do? I haven't even got a back yard to muck around in. There's nowhere to plant a bloody flower even. At least we had a back balcony and window boxes when we lived in the council flat. On the balcony I could sit on a kitchen chair and talk to God. You think he'll want to come visit me in this old-fashioned dump? I need a garden. Get married, buy a little house and put me in the attic room. I won't mind.' He gave his son a sly look, and added, 'I've got a bit put by for a decent deposit. You could buy a nice little terraced house with a garden back and front in Stamford Hill or Stoke Newington.'

Nathan filled the kettle to make a pot of tea and, ignoring the suggestion, said, 'What did you make of the headlines then?'

'The woman was a prostitute. What did she expect? You live life on the edge you have to expect consequences. Why did you bother to mention it? Have you been with her? Are you upset over it?'

'It's not something to joke over, Dad. And she wasn't a prostitute as far as I can make out. And what makes you think that I would go with a forty-five-year-old woman?'

'Don't knock age, son. She could have taught you a lot. So why did you mention it then? What's so special about that particular woman? And how do we know that she didn't fall down into the cellar? Did anyone see her being thrown down? Of course not. Bloody newspapers. They'll do anything to sell copies.'

'The landlady's son, in the house where Charlotte's renting a flat, has been arrested on suspicion of murder. Murder . . . of the woman who lived in the flat above Charlotte's. That's why I mentioned it.'

The silence that struck the room could have been cut with a knife. Jacob, for possibly the first time in his life, was lost for words. The seconds ticked by and then he asked, 'And where is Charlotte now, pray?'

'Staying at her grandparents. It's a long story. I'll tell you all about it tomorrow.'

'You'll be at work all day, tell me about it now. I'm an old man. I need to know now. I might be dead by the time you come home from work.'

Ten minutes later, father and son, each on an armchair and looking into the imitation flames of the electric fire, were silent. Nathan was thanking God that Charlotte had gone back to her grandparents' house and Jacob was wondering what the world was coming to. 'How could such a thing happen, Nathan? Didn't anyone realise that the lad was a nutcase?'

'Dad . . . I've told you all I know. Charlotte has met and spoken with him and she doesn't believe he's guilty. He's a bit odd but no more than that.'

'A bit odd is all it takes to find the next step to insanity.'

'So do you want I should go out and get some beigels or not?'

'I want. I told you that already. My God . . . what is the world coming to? A woman is strangled and then dumped in a cellar? What was she doing in that dump in the first place?'

'I don't know, Dad.' Nathan stood up to leave. 'I won't be gone long and I won't be long out of my bed once I've eaten. I've had it. I'm all in.'

Gazing at his father he knew that he was devastated. Jacob had lived in the East End boy and man, and knew every back turning and many people in the area. As a boy of nine he had picked up work delivering groceries from the local shop on an old-fashioned bike with a carrying basket attached. 'Was the woman a foreigner?' he murmured.

'No, Dad. But even though she's been in the area for a while she wasn't born and bred here so you wouldn't have known her, and nor would Mum. It's horrible and I wish to God it hadn't happened, but it has. And Charlotte's smack bang in the middle of it. She'll be questioned as well, no doubt.'

'Of course she will. She had already moved into the flat where the murderer lives.'

'We don't know that he did it, and Charlotte thinks that he couldn't have. That he's too nice and too harmless. So if she phones don't put your opinions forward, just say you're sorry to hear what's happened and that I'll call her back.'

Jacob turned slowly in his chair to look up at his son and sighed. 'This is what it's come to? You telling me what to do instead of me telling you?'

Feeling sympathy for his dad who was genuinely upset by the news, Nathan offered a gentle apologetic smile. 'Of course not. I'm just a bit awry at the moment, that's all. You're my father and I would never disrespect you or not listen to your advice.'

'I should bloody well think not. And tell Maurice the baker not to put any bloody black pepper on the cream cheese . . . and no olives either. All of a sudden he wants to follow the Italians. Beigels are Jewish. They've always been Jewish.'

'Sure they have, Dad.' Nathan smiled. 'I won't be long.'

He left the flat and his dad, who was staring into those imitation flames again. 'My God . . .' the old man murmured, 'what is it coming to? And why all of a sudden does my world feel so small and vulnerable? I don't like it, Lilly. I don't like it one bit. So move over, darling, because I don't think that I'm long for this world either. At least I hope not. I don't want any part of it. It's changed, sweetheart. Everything that can be changed has been altered. God rest your soul, sweetheart, and stay a little bit warm for me.'

*

Charlotte, back in the safety of her grandparents' house, was trying to enjoy her favourite thing at the end of a tiring day, a lovely soak in a hot sudsy bath. Once she was out she was going to put on her pyjamas, and Nell's dressing gown, and go back down for a mug of Horlicks. Of course she hadn't been able to stop thinking about the double tragedy of Wendy having been murdered and poor Donald arrested for the crime. But right now she was nursing her head. Before taking some Dispirin it had been thumping with pain. All in all, everything had been too much for her. And while she was running everything through her mind, Nell and Johnny were down below speaking in whispers as if she would be able to hear them if they used their normal voices – which was quite possible.

'I don't fink she should ever go back to that place, Johnny, never mind living there. Not now. Not after all that's happened.'

'Tell me something that I don't know,' said Johnny as he slowly shook his head, deeply worried. 'But you know what she's like. Stubborn as a mule. And if we try and lay down the law she'll baulk against it – you can bet on that. She still insists that the landlady's son is too wimpish to hurt a fly, never mind strangle a woman.'

'Keep your voice down, Johnny!' she hissed.

'She can't hear us, you silly cow. And we're not just talking about one woman but *three* . . . by the sound of things. The two they pulled out of the river and kept quiet about and now this poor cow who done no harm to no one. What must she 'ave gone through? It beggars belief.'

'Don't go on about it. If Charlotte's chose to put on a brave face and push it to one side then we've got to do the same. It's gonna take years for 'er to get over this. Years. And what about his mother? What kind of hell is she going through? I feel as if I want to go round there and keep the woman company.'

'No . . . you can't do that. She don't know you from Adam and by the sound of what Charlotte's told us, she's a bit on the posh side.'

'So? What are you saying? That I'm not good enough to be in 'er company?'

'That's not what I said and you know it. All I meant is that we've gotta leave the woman to 'erself. She must 'ave some family. Brothers, sisters . . . cousins.' He shrugged.

'No doubt she 'as. But would you in her place phone relatives and tell them that your son's been arrested for murder?'

Johnny released a long, low sigh. 'Dear oh dear oh dear. What a thing to 'appen. You know what I think? I think that all them bloody books about Jack the Ripper and the so-and-so strangler should be shredded or burned. To some people bastards like that become heroes, you know.'

'Don't talk rubbish.' Nell had heard enough. 'I'm gonna phone Rita to see how she is. I bet she's in a right state. I bet she's 'aving kittens.'

'Well, go on then, if you must. You've said it enough times. Pick up the bloody receiver and dial the number before she comes down. We've got to try and keep

Charlotte's pecker up. She won't wanna hear you giving a rundown on it. Enough's enough.'

'All right, Johnny. I'll tell 'er a few sidesplitting jokes, shall I? One or two of yours about the Irishman, the Scottish man and the Welshman. Once she's out of the bath.'

Johnny looked into Nell's face and waited but she just looked back at him wondering what he was waiting for. She finally said, 'Well, shall I then?'

'What d'yer keep asking me for? You always do what you fink you will in any case. Go on. Pick up the bloody phone and dial the number.'

Rita was watching television when the sound of the phone ringing in the passage pierced through the air. This was immediately followed by Eddie's urgent footsteps as he ran down the stairs from the box room where he had been getting up to date on his bookwork and filing so as to keep his mind off what was going on back in London. Within no time at all he had the receiver to his ear. When he heard Nell's voice he breathed a sigh of relief. She sounded okay. So Charlotte would be fine, too, was his take on it.

'What's new?' said Eddie, hoping for some kind of upbeat response.

'We've heard nothing more, sweetheart. But I thought I would just let you know that Charlotte's fine. She's having a lovely soak in the bath and then after a mug of cocoa I wouldn't be surprised if she'll be ready for her pillow early tonight.'

'Oh, that's good, that's taken a load off my mind. She

can't go back to that house, Nell. I'm gonna come down tomorrow and fetch her and her stuff back.'

'Well, I can't stop you from doing what you want, Eddie, but I strongly advise you to leave it be. She's old enough to make up 'er own mind, and she doesn't want to go back to Bridgeford. Nathan's been a brick. He thinks the world of her and it shows.'

'So what then? She'll stop with you and Johnny then?'

'That's right,' said Nell, only half telling the truth. The truth being that Charlotte wanted to go back to the flat the very next day. 'Things will settle down soon enough.'

'If you say so. Can I speak to 'er?'

'She's in the bath!'

'Well, get 'er to ring when she comes out of it!'

'Why?'

'Because I want to be sure she's okay.'

'She *is* okay. Leave it be. Rita's not being a mother hen so don't you be!'

'What d'yer mean? She's just as worried as I am!'

'Of course she is, but her motherly instincts are kicking in. She knows when to let go and leave it be. Charlotte will phone you if she needs to. She's doing bloody well so don't upset the apple cart.'

After a long sigh, Eddie finally gave in. 'Fair enough. I suppose you know what you're talking about, but I wish bloody Nathan hadn't of turned up out of the blue the way he did. She'd still be up here with us and none the wiser to all of this dark stuff – other than what's in the papers.'

'You can't keep 'er wrapped in cotton wool for all of 'er life, son. You've got to learn to let go. We all have to let go at some time or another. And this is *your* time to.'

'I s'pose you're right. You usually are. I'll phone you tomorrow for an update. Give 'er our love.' With that Eddie replaced his receiver and all that Nell could hear was the dialling tone.

'Silly daft sod,' she said. Then, as she replaced the receiver she had to swallow against the lump in her throat and will herself not to cry. Not to let go. Not to scream and kick and punch. Because this is how she felt, and had felt ever since she heard about the woman who lived in the flat above Charlotte getting herself strangled. It was all too close to home for her liking. Murders in England were few and far between and to have one happen on her doorstep was terrifying. She, just like hundreds of other women in the area, would not be sleeping too well for a while. After all, the young man who had been arrested could so easily be an innocent soul and the maniac could be still out there, ready for another kill.

Shaking off this dark mood that had crept in again, she put on a brave face for the sake of Johnny who she knew was worried sick and scared. Both of them knew that there was going to be no stopping Charlotte from going back to that house of horror and nestling down. Whether it was the right thing for her to do or the wrong thing – she was not going to be told what to do. She was a chip off the old block. Nell's block. Stubborn as a mule when she thought that right was right. And usually Nell wasn't wrong, and so all that she could hope was that Charlotte was doing the right thing by staying true to her plans, no matter what.

That night, as Nathan lay in his bed in the small second bedroom of the flat in Bethnal Green, he thought about Charlotte and how much he loved her. He tried to imagine living with her in their own house. A house with a back garden where his dad could plant flowers and some vegetables and have a little shed at the back where he could potter about. Nathan was earning a decent salary now, and his dad had his local customers who still wanted a suit made to measure by a bespoke tailor. Jacob's old treadle sewing machine was still oiled and in good working order, and Nathan knew that between them all they would be able to afford a decent mortgage if he could find a modest house that suited all three of them. He also knew that his dad would insist on using his life savings as a deposit.

In his mind's eye, he could see Charlotte ironing his shirts to wear at the office while she listened to her favourite records, and felt a glow of warmth in his chest. But then, as had been happening all day long, Kenny managed to slip back into his thoughts and the old anger, now mixed with a gut feeling that the nasty piece of work was somehow involved in the murder, filtered through every vein in his body. But it wasn't to last long because the sound of his dad in the next room farting, snoring and moaning in his sleep was enough to wake the dead. He was used to hearing this by now and had his earplugs ready and waiting, but he couldn't sleep. He was exhausted but not sleepy. Something was in the air. Something deep down inside was almost telling him to stay awake and it had something to do with the woman who had been murdered. He felt like phoning Charlotte but knew that this was out of the question because it was late. He closed his eyes and left it all to God to keep a watch over those he loved. He then thanked Him for leading him to Charlotte, and thanked Him too for his dad's good health, sense of humour and determination to live until he was a hundred.

Nathan squeezed a silencer into each ear and then laid his head back onto his plumped-up feather pillow, sighing as he brought his lovely Charlotte to mind. He was going to have to think of a different kind of gift to give her now. Something really special. He knew that it was going to take a long time before the vision of that poor woman, lying in the cellar with her handbag empty and discarded and one of her slingback shoes in the debris, would fade away. He tried not to think about it any more. He so needed to sleep, he was exhausted. Just before he slipped into a well-deserved rest a gentle smile crossed his face. Of course he knew what he would give Charlotte! A ring. A beautiful diamond engagement ring with little earrings to match. It would take all of his savings and a bit of money borrowed from his dad, but he didn't care. In fact, he couldn't wait to go to an old family friend who had a lovely little jewellery shop in Whitechapel who he knew would give him a very good deal. And just so as to keep his dad in the picture, he would tell him of his plan and ask him if he would go with him to help him choose the ring. Blocking the thoughts of all that had happened, he waited for sleep and it wasn't long coming. Soon all was quiet in that little flat in the back and beyond of Bethnal Green.

Lying in bed and reading the book he had purchased a year or so ago, and that had become his Bible, Kenny was in a tranquil mood as he underlined passages with a red ink biro. He had read this book from cover to cover and yet could still find something in there that he felt he hadn't read before. Passages, names, places and characters. This was not the only published journal on the subject of past murders that had taken his attention ever since he was a young teenager, but it was one of the few where he felt that the author was closer to the truth than others had been. This particular account of the serial killings was also rather special in that he had bought it at the second-hand bookshop where Wendy had worked. A book that she had in fact personally sold to him. She had given him a smile that spoke volumes and that he had not forgotten. The typical smile of a teasing whore, he thought.

At that time, which now seemed like an age ago, he had felt that this had been an omen, that he was meant to read this account of what really happened in 1888. Once back at home in his bedroom, after he had taken the book out of the paper bag, it had fallen open at a page where there was an old bookmark, seemingly hidden. A bookmark that looked as if it had been lying within those pages for a very long time. He had noticed a sentence that had been lightly underlined in pencil. This read: *There lay dead the instigator of his first serious dark temper that had showed itself that evening. The gutter prostitute had spread a rumour that his manhood was little more than a pink newborn mouse. Small, soft and sickening.* Next to this Kenny had added his bit by scribbling: 'Jack then went on to rid the world of several East End whores. Paid whores. Prostitutes. Good man!'

Closing the book, Kenny rested back on his pillow with his hands clasped behind his head. He told himself that he had done well. That he would go on to do the work of the man he admired until he was forced to stop.

Content in his own terrestrial sphere of dark make-believe and happy that the half-witted idiot, Donald, had been arrested for crimes he had not committed, Kenny was ready for a nice long restful sleep. He felt not one iota of remorse over this latest murder because, as far as he was concerned, he had not only given fame to the trifling idiot who had been taken in for questioning, but he had also rid the world of another whore. How could he feel anything other than proud of himself? Proud, and content that all was going to plan.

Kenny's only real regret was that, having been born in a different time to that of his hero, he hadn't had the opportunity to meet him. But even this could take nothing away from his sense of triumph. So, with a feeling close to happiness, he drifted off to sleep with a smile of satisfaction on his face. He felt that he had done well. That if he were to be run over by a bus the next day, at least he would have left his mark and made the planet a little better for the elimination of the filthy whores who stalked God's pavements and dark alleyways.

Chapter Twenty

It was ten-fifteen and even though Isabelle was mentally and emotionally exhausted, still she could not sleep. She could think of nothing else other than her dear sweet innocent son being locked in a prison cell in a hostile environment. Of course he was innocent, but he had been arrested on suspicion of murder and there was nothing she could do about it. She had already written page after page of letters to newspapers and then screwed them up as being senseless drivel. She didn't want an apology. She didn't want justice. She just wanted her son back. Her gentle and somewhat naive son who she loved so much.

Now in her long, pale blue soft cashmere dressing gown with nightdress beneath, she was sipping a mug of warm milk spiked with whisky, hoping this would help her to sleep. She had cried herself out and was now in a kind of nowhere land where she imagined that thousands of others had been before her. She was in shock. Drifting towards the sash window that looked out onto the square that was now lit by the old-fashioned iron lamp-posts, she wished for the umpteenth time that the clock could be turned back. That Donald had not gone out on that fateful evening.

Feeling as if she was the only one in the entire square

who was awake and alone, she turned around so that her back was to the window and sat on the deep sill the way she had done as a child when her parents had owned this house. The house was so still and quiet and she could not take in the fact that the lovely Wendy was now a corpse in a coffin. Or that her own son was locked in prison under suspicion for Wendy's murder, and the pretty girl called Charlotte who had taken the vacant flat had fled to the safety of her grandparents' home in Bromley by Bow. Suddenly her beautiful house that had been her safe and happy domain for so long seemed as if it was her prison. Her cage. She glanced at the telephone on the stand in the entrance hall and realised that she had nobody that she could call just so as to hear another human voice. 'God please send someone to be with me,' she whispered, as tears slowly rolled down her cheeks and her neck. 'Please just for a few minutes let me have company in this house. Give me somebody to talk to. Sweet Jesus . . . hear my prayer . . .'

Whether or not it was from divine intervention that the doorbell rang through the silent house mattered not. Isabelle, not really thinking who it might be or how late in the evening it was and whether or not she might be opening the door to a maniac, was soon in the entrance hall and, with trembling fingers, was turning the old-fashioned brass mortise lock. She was so in need of company and the sound of a human voice, danger was far down on her list of priorities. At first, the shape of the tall lean man with bent shoulders under the dim porch lamp told her nothing. She opened her mouth to speak and then closed it again, feeling as if she were in some kind of a slow-moving film or a dark dream.

'I know it's very late, madam,' said the old man. 'But I saw that your lights were still on and I thought that it was important that we speak to each other in the quiet, now that the sightseers have gone. My name's Herbert Jenkins. I live across the square and I have something to show you. May I come in?'

'Of course you may!' His voice was like music to her ears. 'You're my neighbour who I sometimes wave to.' She stood aside and waved him in. 'How very sweet of you to come over. I can't tell you how I was so longing for company. May I offer you a glass of something?'

Closing the door behind him, the old boy nodded, smiled and shrugged. 'A drop of whisky would go down very well, madam.'

'Oh please . . . do call me Isabelle,' she said, showing him the way into the small and comfortable snug where she kept the drinks and glasses.

Once they were seated in the matching padded fire-side chairs, Mr Jenkins said, 'So they took your son away and locked him up for questioning.' He slowly shook his head and said with a sympathetic voice, 'And you have been beside yourself ever since. The woman who worked in the bookshop and who lived in the top flat has been murdered, your son has been carted off on suspicion of murder, and the lovely young girl who waved to me from her window has gone away. And you are alone. They say that God works in mysterious ways, but you know what? Sometimes I think that God isn't always looking in the right direction at the right time.'

'Really? Why do you say this?'

He smiled gently at her and shrugged. 'Of course we wouldn't expect Him to carry a camera around twenty-four hours a day, would we?'

Isabelle smiled at him, totally mystified as to what he was going on about but she didn't care. 'Well no . . . I suppose we wouldn't,' she said.

'But maybe he should bring himself up to date a little because the camera doesn't lie. So, once we've finished our drinks, would you mind phoning for a black cab?'

'A taxi? But I rarely use them. I have a driver that I telephone whenever I need to be taken anywhere and that doesn't happen very often because I quite like a nice walk for one thing and there aren't many places that I go out to in the evenings so . . .'

'And this driver? If you were to call him now at this time of night. Would he come out?'

'Well, yes, I think he would – if it were important. Is it?' Isabelle was mystified, but even so she instinctively trusted this man and felt comfortable in his company.

'I think it's very important. I should like us both to go to the station where they are holding your son . . . or if not, to the nearest one to us.' He then pulled a white envelope out of his pocket. 'I went to the chemist today where a good friend works. He develops my films a little sooner than he might do for a stranger, and no matter if it's a day when the shop is closed.'

'Does he really? How very sweet,' said Isabelle, wondering where all this was leading. 'And you were saying that you would like me to arrange for my driver to take you and me to the police station?'

'Yes. But first of all I would like you to look at these three photos. I think this will tell us who did what to whom and who went which way.'

'Goodness . . . how mysterious.' Isabelle took each photo as he handed them to her, one by one. After a moment or two of staring at the first one, she said, 'But this is my son. This is Donald, walking away from the square.'

'That's right. I took it from my window. I wanted to finish the reel so that I could get the film developed. So I just took a few pictures from my window. I didn't realise, of course, just how important they would turn out to be. Take a look at the next one please.'

'Of course. This is quite fascinating. I *am* pleased that you called.' She then glanced at the next and her smile faded. 'Goodness . . . this is Wendy. Oh my goodness me.' Tears immediately filled her eyes. 'You took a photograph of her, on the evening that she was so brutally killed.' Frightened now as to this old man's state of mind she felt her fingers begin to tremble.

'It's okay. You've nothing to be frightened of. Now take a look at the third snapshot. The third, and the most important where your son is concerned.'

Studying the picture, hardly able to believe her eyes, the genteel woman who thought that she was going to lose her beloved son to the injustice of life and the law, gasped. 'Goodness gracious . . . it's Wendy with a young man.'

'Now . . . I said there were three but I have the ace card up my sleeve. Are you ready for it?'

'Well, yes I am. I don't know quite what to—'

Mr Jenkins held up a hand to stop her. 'Hush, hush. Don't get aerated. Be calm. Be patient.'

'Yes, yes I shall. But give me a moment.' Taking a few deep breaths with her eyes closed she finally said, 'That's much better.' And her smile said it all. 'Please do show me the final picture.'

'With pleasure,' he said and handed it to her. 'I think that you will agree that it's a very good shot. Very clear. You can see quite clearly that your poor departed tenant is talking to and walking away with the young man whose face is very clear and recognisable. That's not bad for an old-fashioned Box Brownie camera is it?'

Isabelle looked from the picture to the old man and then back to the picture and finally gazed into his face as tears rolled down her cheeks once again. 'Is this not evidence?' she said. 'Is this not proof that my son went one way and poor Wendy went the other with a stranger in tow?'

Smiling warmly at her, the old boy who had been the neighbour from across the square for years, said, 'Now will you phone for your driver? I think we have a very important ride to take, don't you?'

'To the police station?'

'Unless of course you want to phone and invite them into your house instead.'

Isabelle flopped back into her chair and gazed at her saviour with the caring expression. 'I can't believe this

335

is happening.' She swallowed, and dabbed the corner of her eyes with her lace-edged white handkerchief. 'I would very much like to go with you and my driver to the station. But will you promise me one thing?' she only just managed to say.

'Only if you promise me that you're not going to ask the impossible.'

'No, I don't think I am. Would you promise to stop me if I lose my temper and tell all of the officers on duty at this time of night that the law is an ass?'

Herbert Jenkins laughed again. 'If I must,' he said. 'If I must.'

'And do you think that I shall be fetching my son home tonight?'

'I would have thought so, but let's not bank on it. The wheels of the law can turn slowly or briskly depending on who might be on duty at the station. It could be an ass or it could be a true blue copper with a good brain between his ears and a bit of common sense thrown in for good luck.'

Isabelle slowly shook her head and looked at him again. 'If this is what I think it is – concrete evidence – then I shall insist on his immediate release. Insist on it!' Again she asked if the pictures were true evidence.

'Yes, Isabelle. You may rely on it. Let's not forget that it was I who took the photos to finish a reel. I who saw it all. And I who shall lay my hand on the Bible in the witness box. I have seen that lad before, hanging around and sometimes sitting on a bench in our lovely Lavender Square. I will say that I was curious once or twice but not enough for it to kill a cat.'

Feeling a weight had been lifted from her shoulders, Isabelle broke into a beautiful smile of relief. 'It isn't that far to Harbour Square police station, is it?'

'Hardly more than the stone's throw of a strong man. Why do you ask?'

'I think you know what I am going to say . . .'

'Well then, get your coat and we'll go. A walk in the late summer evening never did anyone any harm.'

'Except for poor darling Wendy.' Isabelle sighed.

'That's true. So let's go and do our duty to our country where the law is concerned while at the same time paying homage to that lovely woman who always waved to me from her window. May God rest her soul.'

'May God rest her soul,' whispered Isabelle to seal it.

To anyone looking out of their window that evening or to those who were walking through the square, the old man and the woman, who had linked arms and were on their way to see justice done, looked like an ordinary couple out for an easy stroll.

And not so far away Kenny was twisting and turning in his bed. The sense of being pleased and satisfied with his work so far had by now worn off. He had woken from a dark nightmare with what felt like a knot in his stomach that was getting tighter and tighter. He felt that something was in the air and that his old friend the devil was calling him. But he couldn't be bothered to get up, get dressed and go out in search of another disgusting whore. So he snuggled down again and left it to others to cleanse the streets. He had done his bit . . . for the time being. He would now take a sabbatical, he told himself, and then quietly laughed himself back to sleep. But it wasn't for too long that he lay curled up and slumbering. The long ring on the doorbell an hour or so later was enough to wake all three of them up, his mother, his dad and himself.

Just before his mother opened the door she crossed herself and when she saw the two officers standing there, one in uniform and one in plain clothes, she knew why they had come and who they would take away. Her Kenny. She had little idea what they wanted him for but she knew that it was something bad. His dark mood swings had worsened and she had spent too long worrying about his state of mind and bearing. And she wasn't too shocked that Kenny went with the men without fuss, argument or struggle. It was almost as if this is what he had been waiting for. What he had expected – even what he wanted. To go down in history with other maniacs of his ilk. The saving grace for his mother was that he had not been taken away in a strait-jacket but had gone quietly. It was over. And as tears slowly flooded her eyes, her chest felt as if there was a dark hole where her heart once beat. Her only son was going to be locked up in a lunatic asylum or a prison – for the rest of his life.

Epilogue

Being taken from his home in handcuffs and under heavy guard, Kenny had looked strangely passive for someone who most likely was about to be locked up. Instead of keeping his head down, as might be expected under the circumstances, he had smiled and nodded at the assembly of onlookers, almost as if he were the innocent victim rather than the homicidal maniac. In fact his demeanour had been one of a man of worthy exploits. But when the jeers and angry responses began, as the small groups crowding the pavements gave vent to their feelings, Kenny did little other than show two fingers and smile contemptuously back at them. As far as he was concerned, they should not be condemning him, but praising him for the good work he had done by cleansing the streets of whores who lured good men from their wives.

He could hardly believe that the locals were behaving as if they were appalled to discover a killer of prostitutes in the East End. To his mind they should have been grateful. But even more infuriating for him was that he had only just got into the swing of things, of cleansing the streets so that decent men, young and old, could walk in the dark without being approached and lured by women who were the scum of the earth. He just couldn't understand why the people weren't shocked to think that prostitution still was rampant in the area where they lived.

Nor could he believe that their parents, and theirs before them, wouldn't have told them about his hero Jack. The so-called Ripper. In Kenny's opinion, the serial killer had done the community more justice than any court of law could. But from what he had read, instead of praising him they had been out for his blood like fierce hounds. But none of it really mattered now. Kenny was vaguely amused by the gatherings of people that had built into a trailing crowd and stopped the traffic from being able to pass. But he hadn't really expected more from people he saw as morons. He was pleased he had managed to show two fingers to his audience even though his hands were cuffed. And when he was bundled into the back of a Black Maria by the two officers who had been firmly holding each of his arms, he chuckled quietly as the yells and jeers grew louder. The louder it got the better he liked it.

The saddest thing of all was, that once the police vehicle drove Kenny away with droves of angry people running behind it showing their fists, his mother had been watching from her sitting room window in the flat on the second floor. Pale and grief stricken she had watched her son, her only child, being hounded by neighbours who had suddenly turned into a pack of wolves.

Watching as the crowd gradually dispersed, the distraught woman turned to her husband – her bewildered husband – and burst into tears. 'When did it all go so

340

wrong? When did our little Kenny turn into someone who hated women so much to want to kill them?'

Comforting his wife, the man only just managed to say, 'I don't know. But I suppose that he wasn't like other kids. He never was quite the same as everyone else. He never had what I would call close friends . . . never seemed to need any. But he did need to be leader of the pack, though.'

Of course his wife knew that he was right, that Kenny had been different from other lads. 'So . . . we can't be blamed for it all, can we?' she pleaded. 'We are for some of it, and we both know what that is.' Of course her husband had to agree but only with a slow nod of head. He hadn't wanted to drag up a part of the past when he had turned a blind eye to his own wife prostituting herself for money, along with her sister. He didn't want to think about the time when their son had spent too much time at home without her. Sometimes the boy had sat watching the clock for over an hour waiting for her to come in. And now his son would be separated from them for good and they were going to have to learn to live without him.

Watching the Black Maria pull away, Herbert Jenkins, whose photographs had saved Donald, turned away from the assemblage of people and the press and police officers and walked slowly back home. He still couldn't believe that such a thing could have happened on his doorstep and to such a wonderful woman whose wave from the window he would sadly miss. But at least he had made a friend in Isabelle. She had all but pleaded with him to move out of his small rented rooms in the less grand house across the square from hers. She had insisted that if he agreed on the move then she would not take a penny more than the low rent that he had been paying for years. The lovely woman had pleaded with him so much that he could not refuse. Nor did he want to. His lonely life, it would seem, was about to change, and the only reason that tears were rolling down his cheeks was because the woman called Wendy was gone and he would soon be sitting at her window looking over at his. The twists and turns of life were known to be strange, but for this old man they were more than that. Now at least he would have someone to talk to. He would have Isabelle and her son, Donald. He would also be living above the lovely girl called Charlotte.

Eddie was gutted that Charlotte was not going to return to the safety of Bridgeford but he knew that there was nothing he could do about it. She was old enough to know her own mind and stand her ground – which is exactly what she was doing. She not only wanted to be back in her roots, but to be close to where Nathan lived. His little girl had flown the nest for sure. There was no point in trying to persuade her otherwise because it was very clear she was in love with Nathan and he was in love with her.

Eddie knew in his heart that it would not be long before Nathan asked him for Charlotte's hand in marriage. So it was with a saddened heart that he drove Rita back to Norfolk, knowing that his daughter was not just testing the water in London but had made up her mind that this was where her home was. He liked Nathan. He liked him a lot. So if he was going to have to lose his daughter at least she was going to be with someone he respected. He had known the boy's family for years so, even though it was with reluctance, he had to admit that things had turned out well for his only child. His cherished daughter. The one thing that he could take consolation from was the old saying, which he ran through his mind over and over while driving: 'You won't be losing a daughter, Eddie – you'll be gaining a son.'

Sitting in a big old-fashioned feather-cushioned armchair in Charlotte's apartment, as she liked to call it, Nathan knew, as he watched her fetching two coffees in bone china cups, that she was the one he wanted as a wife. He had been reminiscing again about their childhood and the time when she broke the news that her family was going to move to Norfolk. He could hardly believe that she was back and that he was with her in a lovely apartment in the house on the square, the kind of house that they had always dreamed of living in when youngsters. Quietly waiting for her to make herself comfortable on the two-seater sofa that matched the armchair, he sipped his coffee and glanced at her. A warm smile on his face he said, 'Charlie . . . you know that I love you and I know that you love me, but I can't carry on playing a guessing game of whether you were carried away on a romantic notion when I turned up at Bridgeford. I have to ask you . . . I just have to.'

'Well, don't look so gloomy,' she said. 'We've been through a horrible dark time, one way and another, because of you know who. Just say what you have to say.' She smiled at him and waited.

'I love you, Charlie. I always have and I always will. I want to marry you.'

Charlotte replied, with all the sincerity that was within her. 'I love you too, Nathan. And I want you to marry me.'

Nathan placed his cup and saucer on the side table and went over to her and got down one knee. 'Now I'm going to seal everything that I've said.' He took a small gift box from his pocket and flicked it open with the nail of his thumb. The solitaire diamond ring that his dad had helped him to choose looked beautiful, gleaming against the royal blue velvet lining of its box. He cleared his throat and then said in a quiet voice, 'Please will you marry me, Charlie.'

She couldn't help smiling at his way of proposing. So proper. So old-fashioned. 'Of course I'll marry you, Nathan.'

And as he slipped the ring on her finger, tears filled her eyes and she said, 'It's beautiful. I love it and I love you. I think I always have and I know I always will.'

There really was no more to be said. But, since actions speak louder than words, he took Charlotte's hand in his and, gently drawing her up and out of the chair, he led her out of the room into another. Into her bedroom and to the big old-fashioned double bed.